British
Bachelors
Rich & Powerful

British
Bachelors
COLLECTION

January 2017

February 2017

March 2017

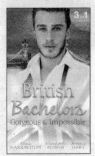

April 2017

May 2017

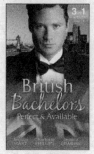

June 2017

British
Bachelors
Rich & Powerful

Maggie   Cathy   Nina
COX   WILLIAMS   HARRINGTON

Published in Great Britain 2017
By Mills & Boon, an imprint of HarperCollins*Publishers*
1 London Bridge Street, London, SE1 9GF

BRITISH BACHELORS: RICH & POWERFUL © 2017 Harlequin Books S.A.

What His Money Can't Hide © 2012 Maggie Cox
His Temporary Mistress © 2014 Cathy Williams
Trouble on Her Doorstep © 2014 Nina Harrington

ISBN: 978-0-263-92778-8

09-0117

Printed and bound in Spain
by CPI , Barcelona

WHAT HIS MONEY CAN'T HIDE

MAGGIE COX

The day **Maggie Cox** saw the film version of *Wuthering Heights*, with a beautiful Merle Oberon and a very handsome Laurence Olivier, was the day she became hooked on romance. From that day onwards she spent a lot of time dreaming up her own romances, secretly hoping that one day she might become published and get paid for doing what she loved most! Now that her dream is being realised, she wakes up every morning and counts her blessings. She is married to a gorgeous man, and is the mother of two wonderful sons. Her two other great passions in life—besides her family and reading/writing—are music and films.

CHAPTER ONE

'Is THE old place just how you remember it, Mr Ashton?'

The innocently asked question from his chauffeur Jimmy, as he drove Drake to his less than agreeable destination cut him open like a knife. *Yes...his home town was just as dreary and dismal as he remembered it. His memory hadn't lied.*

Glancing out through the tinted car windows, noting the rundown buildings and general sense of despair that hung like a gloomy pall in the air, he felt a sensation in the pit of his stomach right then that was very close to nauseous. Was he insane even to *think* of revisiting this place, when it had caused him nothing but heartache and pain? It beggared belief that he had agreed his firm of architects would accept a commission from the government to create affordable, aesthetically pleasing housing to attract new residents to the area.

Drake put it down to a moment of insanity. Why anyone in their right mind would want to live in such a soulless *pit* he couldn't begin to fathom. As his grey eyes stared hard at the drab scenes that flew by the backs of his eyes burned with remembered pain.

Snapping out of his reverie, he realised that Jimmy

was still waiting for an answer. 'Yes, I'm sorry to say it's *exactly* how I remember it.'

'Certainly looks like it could use a facelift.' The broad good-natured face reflected in the driving mirror displayed his sympathy.

'Where did you grow up, Jimmy?' Drake asked him.

'I was born and bred in Essex. The family didn't have a lot of money but we pulled together. Had plenty of laughs along the way, as well as tears.' He grinned.

Drake forced a smile. He wished he could have said the same about his own upbringing, but sadly there had been very few laughs in his home after his mother had walked out. His father had raised him, but he'd done it with an angry and bitter resentment that had made Drake wary of making too many demands. Even the most basic requests had been apt to enrage his father and make him particularly cruel. Very quickly he'd learned to be self-sufficient and resourceful…simply because he'd *had* to.

Enough of this pointless and painful introspection!

Scowling, he leant towards the driver's seat. 'Pull over at the end of the high street, then go and park, Jimmy. I've just spied a coffee place and I'm in need of some caffeine and food. I've also got to look over some papers. Give me at least a couple of hours and I'll ring you to come and pick me up.'

'Sure thing, Mr Ashton. Do you want to take your newspaper with you?'

'Thanks.'

The aroma of rich roast coffee acted like a siren, reeling Drake in as he pushed open the heavy glass door of the café he'd noticed and entered. Years ago, when he was a schoolboy, this old Victorian building had housed the newsagents where his dad had bought his newspaper and tobacco, and later—when it had become a mini-supermarket—his cans of beer too...

The bittersweet memory was apt to sour Drake's anticipated enjoyment of his breakfast, so he jettisoned it to the back of his mind in the same way he ruthlessly eliminated unwanted e-mails from his inbox. Instead he focused on the display of mouth-watering pastries, croissants and muffins in the glass cabinet facing him and his stomach rumbled appreciatively.

To hell with his usual cup of instant black coffee and burnt toast—his typical mismanaged breakfast because he was inevitably in a hurry.

Message to self: *must hire a housekeeper who can cook.* The last one he'd employed had been a dab hand at making beds, cleaning bathrooms and plumping up cushions, but she'd barely been able to boil an egg, let alone cook him breakfast—which was why Drake had fired her. This morning he was definitely in need of more substantial sustenance—especially in view of the task he was about to undertake. But, whatever his feelings about his home town, he would be viewing this visit with his usual detached professional air. At the end of the day he was here to take an unbiased look round. It was a preliminary to starting work with other professionals on the regeneration of an area that had been as tired and broken as an abandoned and rusted lawnmower ever since he could remember.

At first when he had been approached by a government official to become involved he had baulked at the very idea. His memories of the area hardly fostered fond

and sentimental recollections of a happy, carefree childhood that he would be pleased to revisit…anything *but*.
The majority of his work was in the private sector, and
up until now Drake had been happy to keep it that way.
After all, it had made him rich beyond imagining, and
thankfully had taken him far away from the pains of
his childhood and youth. Yet in the end he'd seen accepting the commission as a cathartic exercise and an
opportunity for him to erase a painful part of his past.
For as well as regenerating his home town Drake also
planned to demolish the house he'd grown up in and
build something much more beautiful in its place.

His cruel father was long dead, but this small act
would help Drake feel as if he were mentally freeing
himself from his father's grasp. Drake could imagine
facing his father and saying to the man, *No matter what
you did to me when I was a kid, your despicable treatment is not going to rule the rest of my life. Now I'm the
one who's in control, and I'm going to knock this god-
forsaken house down and erect something in its place
that will be testimony to a member of the family that at
least has some integrity…who cares about making the
environment more beautiful!*

And Drake would do it too. He might have had his
issues whilst living there, but nobody could accuse him
of being a coward in not facing his demons. To help
dissociate the personal from the pragmatic he'd made
the decision to treat this commission just as any other
architectural project he undertook, and he intended to
apply his renowned design skills along with every bit
of dedication and experience he had to help make the
planned improvements an unmitigated success.

Up until now he'd believed the best way to deal with his sorrowful childhood memories was to relegate them to the deepest, darkest corners of his mind and endeavour to forget about them. It didn't always work, but at least his policy of single-mindedly focusing on what was right in front of him had definitely helped bring rewards beyond even his wildest dreams...

'Good morning. What can I get for you?'

Cutting off his distracted perusal of the goodies inside the display case, Drake glanced up into the most arresting pair of glossy brown eyes he had ever seen. If there were any thoughts in his head at all in that moment he couldn't have said what they were. *He was simply mesmerised.* The owner of those eyes was a girl who was breathtakingly beautiful. She was dressed plainly in a maroon T-shirt with the café's logo on it, and a pair of ordinary blue jeans, with a short navy-coloured apron tied round her trim waist. The nondescript clothing merely emphasised her loveliness.

Her thick dark hair was fashioned into a simple ponytail, and her features were nothing less than sublime. The only evidence of make-up that Drake could detect was the dark eye-pencil that underlined her lower lashes. *How refreshing,* he thought. So many women these days dressed for work as if they were going out to a nightclub. The other thing he noticed about the girl was that she bore a passing resemblance to an Italian movie actress he admired...except she was even prettier.

He was totally unprepared for the dizzying pleasure that assailed him. As his avid gaze met and held hers, he felt as if he was drowning in it. He stared helplessly, just like a dumbfounded schoolboy. 'I'd like a large Americano, a couple of plain croissants—and do you have anything savoury, like a panini?' he asked, his voice a little gruff as he answered because the arresting sight of her had so completely thrown him. 'I'm hungry this morning.'

The girl's big dark eyes widened, as if she was amused, but then she quickly lowered her lashes and looked away. 'We don't have any paninis, but you could have a toasted muffin with some bacon, or even bacon and egg?'

As her glance levelled once more with his, Drake saw her polite smile was definitely guarded. *Had she registered his stunned reaction?* A girl with looks like hers must get men hitting on her all the time. She was probably sick of it. No wonder she seemed wary.

'I'll go for the bacon muffin, I think.'

'Okay.' Her hands were already reaching for a large cream mug and a tray, but her brown eyes met his for another fleeting moment before turning towards the gleaming bank of coffee-making equipment behind her. 'Why don't you take a seat at one of the tables and I'll bring your order over to you?'

'Sure…thanks.'

Drake had immediately noted that the medium-sized cosily proportioned café wasn't exactly teeming with customers on this drizzly September morning. He scanned his surroundings with a bit more attention to detail. The décor, with fading artistic prints on the walls, was definitely a little tired, but there were some charming extras—such as comfy sofas scattered with ethnic print cushions and a bookshelf full of well-thumbed books—which helped create a welcoming and friendly atmosphere. Another plus was that everything appeared scrupulously clean and tidy. But for a café that had a prime location on the high street he knew it ought to be a lot busier than it was to make a profit. Also, the prices he'd seen on the menu were far too low. The owner obviously didn't have a business brain.

He frowned, feeling oddly guilty all of a sudden. Clearly the area had not prospered over the years. Drake was struck anew at how fortunate he was to have escaped the poverty that many of the local population were crippled by, and it certainly wasn't going to get any easier for people in the current economic climate, he knew. At any rate, because the place was so quiet it meant he had his pick of the most appealing tables and the inviting sofas. Selecting a corner seat, he pushed his fingers through his light brown hair and found his attention once again drawn to the beautiful young waitress. The graceful way her slender body moved as she went about preparing his order put him in mind of watching a captivating butterfly.

In the midst of the wistful thought, a wave of irritation assailed him. Usually *nothing* tore him away from his work, but right now the compulsion to focus solely on *her* was doing a good job of exactly that. Consequently, the plans of the area that he'd received from the local council didn't immediately get plucked from his briefcase. Instead he scanned the copy of the *Financial Times* that his chauffeur Jimmy had so thoughtfully handed to him as he'd left the car, but every now and again his glance was helplessly lured back to the girl.

Due to his success as one of the most in-demand architects in the country, Drake had never been bereft of interested female attention. But it had been six months now since Kirsty—his party-planner girlfriend of just under a year—had broken up with him, calling him 'spectacularly selfish' and too work-obsessed to fulfil her hoped-for dreams of marriage and children. *He hadn't denied the accusation.* Frankly, he'd been surprised they'd lasted as long as they had. Usually his relationships didn't extend beyond three to four months.

The truth was, Drake wasn't interested in a deeper commitment. He much preferred having his freedom. The only problem with that was the fact he had a very healthy libido, and wasn't keen on soulless encounters purely for sex. His ex and he hadn't been a match made in heaven, but he had definitely missed having a warm and willing woman in his bed for the past six months...

'Here you are.' The brunette stunner who had prepared his breakfast flashed him another wary smile as she placed his coffee and food down on the table. 'Enjoy,' she added, clearly intent on returning to her post as quickly as possible rather than linger and pass the time of day with him.

'What's your name?' The question was out before Drake could check it.

Her slim shoulders tensed visibly. 'Why?'

Her guarded, less than warm response didn't faze him. He shrugged a shoulder. 'Because I'm curious.'

Turning the tables on him, she challenged, 'What's *your* name?'

'Drake.'

'Is that your first name or your last?'

'My full name is Drake Ashton.'

'Of *course*.' Her widened brown eyes reflected dawning realisation. 'You're the celebrated architect who's going to rejuvenate the area by creating attractive and affordable housing for potentially interested residents.'

She could have tagged *supposedly* onto the end of that sentence, because her tone suggested she doubted that he would be able to do any such thing. Drake was suddenly uncomfortably irked. 'Not by myself...there are other people involved.'

'But if the local papers are anything to go by *you're* the one that's excited all the interest.' She frowned, staring back at him with disturbing candour. 'Home town boy made good...that's the story they're running.'

Straightening his back against the red faux leather seat, he met her examining glance with one equally unflinching and frank. 'Is it? Then seeing as I was born here I guess that more than qualifies me to have an interest in the place...wouldn't you agree, Miss...?' He tipped his head, scanning her well-fitting T-shirt for a badge with her name on it, and not immediately tearing his gaze away when he saw that there wasn't one because the lovely shape of her firm, high breasts outlined by her clothing distracted him disturbingly.

'It's hardly any of my business what your motivations for coming back here are. I apologise if you think I was rude.' Colouring slightly, she shrugged. 'I'm sorry but I have to get back to work now.'

'You still haven't told me your name. And, in case you hadn't noticed, including myself there are only three customers in the whole place. You're not exactly rushed off your feet this morning,' Drake observed wryly, glancing round.

Her cheeks reddened again, but whether this was due to embarrassment or irritation with him for being so persistent, he couldn't tell.

'My name's Layla Jerome, and whether it looks busy or not I have to get back to work. I don't just make drinks and serve them,' she retorted, crossing her arms defensively over her chest. 'There's a myriad of jobs that need to be done in a café. You said you were hungry. You'd better drink your coffee and eat your bacon muffin before they go cold.' And without further ado she marched back behind the counter, looking unashamedly relieved when a female customer with a small child in tow came in.

Layla... The beautiful name certainly suited her exotic good-looks, Drake reflected with satisfaction. Smiling to himself, he raised his mug of coffee to his lips, then reached for the temptingly aromatic muffin on his side plate. Before he left the café he fully intended to get her phone number, and when he did it would become a much better day altogether than he'd been anticipating...

The three other customers besides Drake Ashton—including the young woman and her child—had been and gone, and still the man sat there, absorbed in what appeared to be architectural plans. Layla knew this because he'd signalled to her to come over so that he could order another large Americano. She'd breathed more easily when he hadn't tried to engage her in conversation but simply continued perusing the technical drawings he'd spread out on the table, yet the seductive waft of his expensive sandalwood cologne *did* disturb her. Its potent woody notes had hit her straight in the solar plexus when she'd returned to take his order, making her feel ever so slightly light-headed.

The other thing that had unsettled her was the vaguely amused glance from his curiously light grey eyes when she'd delivered his coffee. Why do that? she thought crossly. *Did he think she was some easily impressed featherbrain who would fall at his feet simply because he smiled at her?* It bothered her that she'd wasted even a second mulling it over—especially when she ought to know better. Her experience of men like him—confident, handsome, *rich* men, who took it as their God-given right to say what they wanted to women like her—had not helped Layla feel remotely easy in their company, and neither did she trust them.

Unfortunately she'd reached that conclusion the hard way. It was why she had given up her prestigious job as PA to an ambitious but unscrupulous broker in the City and returned home to work for her brother Marc in his café instead. Her income had plunged dramatically, but it was worth it to live the much more pared-down and uncomplicated life she lived now. No more paying rent on a London studio apartment that was not much bigger than a utility closet, and no more extortionate dry cleaning bills for the suits, skirts and jackets that her ambitious boss had required her to wear to present the efficient corporate image that he insisted best represented him.

Her change of job and income had also meant the end of expensive lunches in fashionable restaurants with colleagues eager to be seen in all the right places and hopefully headhunted by rival prestigious firms so that they could step up a rung or two on the career ladder. But for Layla the best thing of all about leaving her London life behind was that at least now she was working for someone she trusted. And in return her brother Marc respected and valued *her*—unlike her lying boss, who had fleeced her of all her savings with the promise of a money-making opportunity that would set her up for life. *It hadn't.*

Instead the supposedly failsafe deal had cost her every penny of her hard-earned cash. Although she took full responsibility for allowing her desperation to quit a job she'd grown to hate to make her take such a risky gamble with her savings, she didn't intend to allow herself ever to act so desperately again.

Releasing a long, heartfelt sigh, she let her glance settle on the still preoccupied Drake Ashton. His dark head was bent over the drawings and he was chewing the end of a pencil as he studied them. The picture he made called to mind a small boy mulling over his homework. The wave of compassion that swept through Layla at the idea took her by surprise. The polished handsome architect was surely the last man on earth who needed anyone's compassion!

Her thoughts ran on. She wondered if by visiting her brother's simple little café he had some idea of presenting a much more down to earth image than he was usually purported to have?

The local newspaper stated that he had a tough reputation and took no prisoners. It also said that he lived in a house worth millions in Mayfair, as well as owning property in the South of France and Milan, and that he had made his fortune by designing luxurious homes for the rich and famous. No doubt he was used to taking his morning coffee in locations far more affluent and glamorous than here.

Layla swept her hand irritably down over her ponytail. Why should she care where the man usually drank his coffee? What *did* concern her was that he might report back to the council and his other sponsors that their little café was dreary and rundown and, judging by the woeful lack of customers, would it matter if it had to be closed down to make way for a much more viable business?

The idea stirred white-hot fury in her belly, quickly followed by sickening fear. The café meant everything to her brother Marc. If he got wind that Layla had been less than welcoming to the well-known architect, and had potentially sabotaged his chances for investment because she was still smarting from her bad experience with her ex-boss, it was understandable that he would be furious with her.

An uncomfortable flurry of guilt and regret besieged her insides. The government representatives and council members who had headed up the public meetings she and Marc had attended to hear about the intended plans for the town's regeneration had emphasised that everyone should be as helpful as possible to the influx of professionals who would be working hard on their behalf. Well, one thing was for sure… She hadn't exactly got off to an impressive start with the head architect. Was there the remotest chance she could make a better impression without compromising herself? she wondered.

'Layla?'

She almost jumped out of her skin when the man himself called her over again. Her heart thudded hard. Wiping the back of her hand across suddenly dry lips, she presented herself at Drake Ashton's table. 'Would you like some more coffee?' Along with her bright and friendly smile, she ensured her tone was ultra-polite.

His disturbingly frank grey eyes all but pinned her to the spot. 'Two cups at breakfast is my limit, I'm afraid, else I'll be too wired to think straight. So, no…I don't want any more coffee. Could you sit down for a minute? I'd like to talk to you.'

Swallowing hard, Layla panicked a little. Despite her musings about making a better impression, her gaze automatically sought out an escape route…an incoming customer, perhaps, or even her brother Marc returning from his trip to the suppliers? *But no such luck.* 'What if a customer comes in? You know I'm supposed to be working.'

'You can give me a couple of minutes of your time, surely? If you get a customer then of course you must go and serve them, but right now it's quiet. I want to ask your views about something.'

'Oh, yes?'

'Sit down, Layla…*please.* Hovering makes me uneasy. Did you by any chance fill in one of the questionnaires the council sent round to locals?'

Her relief was palpable. He wanted to ask her about the regeneration of the town, that was all… Nothing more threatening or disturbing than that.

Lowering herself into the chair opposite him, she folded her hands neatly in her lap. 'Yes, I did.'

'Good. Would you mind sharing with me what your views are on the question, "What improvements do you think are most needed in the community"?'

The handsome face before her, with its chiselled jaw and high-sculpted cheekbones, suddenly looked very businesslike and serious. Layla wasn't fazed. This was a topic that she took seriously too. 'Aren't you mainly concerned with designing new housing?'

'I am. But my brief is fairly wide. I've been asked to look at not just housing for potential new residents, but also at what other builds might be possible that would benefit the community in general.'

Curling some hair that had come adrift from her ponytail behind her ear, Layla automatically leaned forward. 'That's music to my ears, because in my opinion one of the things that's most needed in this community is more facilities for the young—by that I mean specifically for teenagers. The reason why a lot of teenagers hang around on street corners with their friends and get into trouble is because there's nowhere for them to go and socialise. They're too young to go to the pub and hang out there, and frankly they don't need another excuse to drink when booze is already sold frighteningly cheaply at supermarkets and already causes havoc. No… What they need is a place specifically for *them*.

'The local so-called "community" hall prides itself on keeping them away. The people who run it won't take the time to get to know any of these kids and find out what they're really like, but they're very quick to judge and demonise them. A place where they can go and listen to music together, maybe play snooker or pool, would be fantastic. We could ask for volunteers from the community to help run it. That way it would bring young and older people together and would benefit us all.'

'You sound like quite the crusader.'

'I make no apology about that. It's great that there are so many campaigns to help the elderly, it really is…but the young need help too. Don't you think?'

Remembering his own emotionally impoverished and lonely childhood, when he had often yearned for somewhere to go where he could just be himself and forget about his unhappy home-life, Drake undoubtedly agreed. Layla's impassioned tone as she had voiced her opinions had taken him aback, made him regard her in a whole new light. *It had also strengthened his vow to get her phone number.* In his world he didn't often meet people who cared half as much about the welfare of others, and it certainly didn't hurt that she was beautiful too…

'I agree,' he commented thoughtfully. 'I'm going to look over some plots in the next few days for potential new builds, and I'll definitely bear in mind what you've told me. Of course I can make recommendations, but ultimately the decision to establish a youth club or something similar lies with the council. They're the ones who'll have to allocate the funds.'

'I know that. But an important man like you…' Her eyes shone with renewed zeal. 'A man who grew up in the area himself…perhaps you could bring some of your influence to bear? It would mean such a lot to the kids if you could.'

They both glanced towards the door as it swung

open, heralding the entrance of a frail-looking elderly couple.

'Looks like you've got some customers.' Drake smiled, but his lovely companion was already on her feet and making her way back behind the counter.

Half an hour later Layla noticed that Drake was folding up the plans into a stylish leather briefcase. She chewed down on her lip as he crossed the room to speak to her. It felt as if every sense she had was on high alert as he neared. The man was seriously imposing, she realised. The shoulders beneath his stylish jacket were athletically broad, and his lean, muscular build and long legs meant that he would look good in whatever he wore—whether it was the dark grey chinos and smart blue shirt he was wearing now, or a scruffy pair of jeans and a T-shirt. Suddenly she seemed to be preternaturally aware of everything about him. He moved as if he owned the space and everything in it. And the amused, knowing glint in his silvery grey eyes made her stomach coil with tension.

'The coffee and food were great—particularly the coffee,' he commented, setting his briefcase down on the floor.

'I'm glad you enjoyed it. My brother, who owns the café, buys the very best grade coffee he can get his hands on, and he took great pride in teaching me how to make it. His aim is always to deliver a good product and good service to his customers.'

'In business that's one of the best intentions you can have…that and being dedicated to making a profit. I meant to ask you before who owned the place. So it's your brother? What's his name?'

'Marc Jerome.'

Her questioner tunnelled his long, artistic fingers through his hair, unwittingly drawing her attention to his strong, indomitable-looking brow. There were two deeply ingrained furrows there, she saw.

'Have you always worked for him?' he asked.

'No.' An unconscious sigh left her lips. 'Not always.'

Drake looked bemused. 'You don't care to embellish on that?'

'I worked in London for a few years, but I needed a change so I—I came back home.' Lifting her chin a little, Layla wrestled with her usual reluctance to reveal much more than that.

'What did you do in London?'

'I was a personal assistant to a broker in the City.'

Raising a quizzical eyebrow, Drake looked even more bemused. 'This is quite a career change for you, then?'

'Yes, it is. Is there anything else you want to ask me before I get back to work, Mr Ashton?'

'Yes.' His gaze suddenly became disturbingly intense. 'There *is* something else, Layla. I'd like your telephone number.'

'Why?'

'So that I can ring you and invite you out for a drink. Will you give it to me?'

Shock eddied through her like an ice-cold river. She hadn't missed the gleam of admiration in his eyes when he'd first seen her, but she hadn't expected him to invite her out or to be quite so quick in asking for her phone number.

'If you'd asked for my brother's number, so you could

talk to him about his views on the area's regeneration or about his business, then I would have been more than happy to give it to you. But to be honest I'm not in the habit of giving my number to men I hardly know.'

'But you *do* know who I am. By that I mean I'm not some stranger who's just walked in off the street. And, whilst I would definitely appreciate having your brother's number so that I can ask him a few questions, right now it's *yours* that I'm far more interested in.'

'I'm sorry.' Uncomfortably twisting her hands together, she nonetheless made herself meet his intense silvery gaze unflinchingly. 'My answer is still no. I enjoyed our little chat earlier about what's needed in the community, and I'm very encouraged by your interest, but—well…let's just leave it at that, shall we?' The need to protect herself from another over-confident and arrogant wealthy man like her ex-boss was definitely at the forefront of her mind as she spoke.

With a sigh, Drake stretched his sculpted lips into a slow, knowing smile 'Maybe we will and maybe we *won't*…leave it at that, I mean.'

He didn't sound at all offended. In fact, as he picked up his briefcase, he gave her another enigmatic glance.

'This is hardly the busiest or most populated town in the country. No doubt we'll bump into each other from time to time. In fact I'm certain we will. Have a good day, won't you? Oh—and why don't you give your brother my number? I'd very much like to have a chat with him about his views on the town.'

He slid the business card that he'd taken from his jacket pocket across the counter, not waiting to see if she picked it up to examine it.

Opening the heavy glass door, he stepped outside onto the damp and grey pavement, and as Layla watched him go several seconds passed before she realised she was holding her breath...

CHAPTER TWO

JEROME... The name should have rung a bell as soon as he heard it. Slowing his stride, Drake turned his head to take another look at the faded, worn exterior of the building he'd just vacated. As soon as Layla had given him her surname he ought to have remembered that it was the name of the newsagents that had been in business there before the café. The place had been called Jerome's, for goodness' sake. Had the friendly newsagent who had often discussed the football results with him while he was waiting for his dad to make up his mind about what he wanted been her father? he wondered.

Drake calculated that she must be at least ten years younger than he was. That put her age at about twenty-six. He wondered whether, if he mentioned to Layla that he'd had genuine regard for her father, it might help persuade her to meet him for a drink—better still, dinner. At any rate, unless she had a boyfriend he wasn't going to give up on the idea any time soon. Not when his first sight of her had been akin to falling into a dream he didn't want to wake up from. He'd felt stunned, dazed and disorientated all at once, and it was hard to recall the last time his heart had galloped so hard and so fast.

It struck him that she was the first woman who had ever declined to give him her phone number. *It made him all the more determined to get her to change her mind.*

Shaking his head in a bid to snap out of his reverie about the beautiful waitress, he determinedly walked on further down the street, stopping every now and then to make notes on his observations about the buildings and the retail outlets that occupied them. When he'd travelled about halfway down the road Drake's finely honed instincts alerted him to the fact that he was being followed. Turning, he saw two men that were clearly from the press. It was pointless trying to fathom how they'd known he would be there. Somehow or other they always found out.

One of them was toting a state-of-the-art camera and the other a recording device. He just thanked his lucky stars the pair hadn't invaded the café to try and interview him or he wouldn't have had much conversation with the lovely Layla at all. Because they hadn't, he was predisposed to be a lot less irritated with them than was usually the case when the press unexpectedly cornered him.

'We're from the local newspaper, Mr Ashton. Can we have a picture and maybe a quick interview with you for our readers? As you can imagine, everyone is very excited about your intended rehabilitation of the area and what the social and economic effects might be.' The journalist with the recording equipment planted himself directly in front of Drake with an animated smile.

'Okay. But the interview had better be quick because I've got work to do.'

'Of course, Mr Ashton, but if we could just have a couple of pictures first that would be great.'

He tolerated the photos being taken, and then an interview, with an uncharacteristically amenable attitude—even when a small knot of curious bystanders gathered to see what was going on. The questions had been surprisingly intelligent and insightful, despite the apparent youth of the reporter, but when he had asked, 'Can you tell us a bit about your personal experience of growing up here?' it had been one question too far.

Drake had called an abrupt halt to the exchange, and phoned his chauffeur Jimmy and instructed him to meet him at the top of the high street. His heart was still racing uncomfortably as he turned his back on the journalist, photographer and bystanders and walked briskly away.

He was seriously relieved to see the sleek Aston Martin coming down the road towards him. Now he could focus on his work without impediment. There were a few other areas in the locality he wanted to survey before attending a meeting at the town hall to make a brief report, but after that he would be returning to his offices in London to oversee a couple of prestigious projects that were nearing completion. Projects that, although adding substantially to his bank balance and growing reputation, had been far trickier and more time-consuming than he'd anticipated, consequently causing him more troubled nights of broken sleep than he cared to recall…

'So, what was your impression of Drake Ashton when you met him?'

Her brother had invited Layla downstairs to have

some fish and chips with him that evening. After inheriting the family home in their dad's will, they'd agreed to split the accommodation between them rather than sell it, and had had the two floors converted into self-contained separate flats. Layla had the upper floor and Marc the lower. When she'd moved to London—even though she'd suggested that he rent out her flat while she was gone—Marc had insisted he wouldn't even think of it because it was her home. It would remain unoccupied until she returned, he'd declared, whether that was in one year or ten, and in the meantime she could come home for the odd weekend to see him.

When her career had come to its unexpectedly ignominious and humiliating end because of her crooked boss she'd been very grateful that she had a place to return to where she felt safe again. Being swindled out of her savings had left her feeling vulnerable and unsure of herself, and she hadn't minded admitting to her brother that she needed to retreat from city life for a while to rebuild her confidence. Marc had responded by lovingly welcoming her home without judgement and giving her a job in his café.

Now, as Layla busied herself sorting out condiments and cutlery, Marc unwrapped the fish and chips he'd bought and expertly arranged the food on the plates he'd left warming in the oven. He was looking especially tired tonight, Layla noticed. There were dark rings under his eyes, and with his brown hair clearly not combed and his lean jaw unshaven he was looking a little the worse for wear. *Had he been worrying about money again?* Her heart bumped guiltily beneath her ribs at the mere idea. She knew that the council tax on the business premises had just gone up again, and the café's takings were already substantially below what they would normally expect this month. The recession had hit all the local businesses hard.

'What was my impression?' she hedged, thinking hard about what to say and what *not* to say about her encounter with the charismatic architect. The experience had been on her mind a little *too* much that day, and she wished it hadn't. 'He looks like a man who knows exactly what he wants and how to get it. By that I mean you can tell why he's been so successful. He was very businesslike and focused. I get the impression that very little gets past him.'

'Let's sit down at the table and eat, shall we?' Marc forked a couple of mouthfuls of food into his mouth and swallowed it down before lifting his head to look directly at his sister. 'They say he's an investor as well as an architect. Did you know that?'

'No, I didn't.'

'I'd really like to talk to him about the café.'

'You mean ask his advice on how to help make it more financially viable?'

'Not just that. I want to ask whether he'd be interested in investing in it.' Exhaling a harsh breath, he wiped his napkin irritably across his mouth, then scrunched it into a ball.

Alarmed, Layla laid down her fork beside her plate and stared at him. 'Are we in trouble?'

'We're operating at a serious loss. How could we not be? Trying to attract more customers when everyone around here is so fearful of spending money on anything but the bare necessities is like trying to get blood

out of a stone! I've had two loans so far from the bank
to help keep it going, and I'm in debt to the tune of several thousand pounds. I've invested all the money Dad
left me to start it up and get it going, and now it looks
like I might even lose the premises that he worked so
hard to own. The café needs a serious injection of something, Layla, or else we're just going to have to throw
in the towel.'

Layla would do anything to help her brother feel
more optimistic about the café—his *pride and joy* as
he'd called it when he'd first decided to set it up. It made
her heart feel bruised to see him looking so tired and
worried all the time. But his intention to ask Drake
Ashton to invest in it scared the life out of her. The
man might be admired in his field, and have a glamorous professional profile, but they had no idea what his
character or his values were.

Silently she berated herself again for trusting her
own life savings to a money-making scheme that—
with hindsight—had had so many holes in it. It was a
wonder her boss hadn't handed out life rafts to the gullible fools who had risked their hard-earned cash in it!
If she'd held onto her money she could have given it to
Marc to pay off his bank loan, and straight away ease
his fear and worry about the café's future.

Brushing back her hair with her fingers, she emitted a gentle, resigned sigh. 'He gave me his business
card to give to you,' she told him. 'He said he'd like to
talk to you.'

'Drake Ashton wants to talk to *me*?' Straight away
Marc's dark eyes gleamed with hope.

Layla nibbled anxiously at her lip. 'He's an astute

businessman, Marc, and from what you say the café is losing money hand over fist. I don't get the impression that he'd be in a hurry to invest his money in a concern that doesn't have the potential to make a healthy profit.'

'Thanks for your support.'

At his stricken expression she reached forward and squeezed his hand. 'You know my support and belief in you are unquestionable, and I think the café is wonderful...I just wish more people did too. I don't want you to build your hopes up that Drake Ashton might be the answer to your prayers, that's all. We might have to think of other options other than investment...that's all I'm saying.'

'You're right.' Pulling his hand away from hers, Marc lightly shook his head and smiled. 'Trouble is I let my heart rule my head too much. I realise that's not the best approach to running a business. Wanting a thing to work so much that it makes your ribs ache just thinking about it doesn't necessarily mean it's suddenly going to take flight and make your fortune. But it's worth talking to Ashton anyway...he might give me a few tips at least. Give me his card in the morning and I'll ring him. In the meantime let's eat, shall we? Our supper's going cold.'

Layla smiled, but inside she secretly prayed that when they spoke Drake Ashton wouldn't thoughtlessly crush her brother's dream into the dirt by telling him he should forget about the café and think about doing something else instead...

Turning his head, Drake squinted at the sunlight streaming in through the huge plate-glass windows. The hexagon-shaped chrome and glass building that housed his offices had become quite a landmark amid the sea of sandblasted Victorian buildings where it was situated, and he was justifiably proud of the design. If he'd wanted to shout out his arrival he couldn't have made a bolder or louder statement. His workplace was a professional portfolio all by itself.

When the thought sneaked up on him from time to time that what he'd achieved was nothing less than a miracle, considering his background, he impatiently brushed it away, not caring to dwell on the past for even a second longer than he had to. It had become his motto to concentrate on the now. After all, the present made far more sense to him than the past could ever do.

'Mr Ashton? There's a man called Marc Jerome on the phone. He says you gave your business card to his sister so that he could call you.'

Drake's secretary Monica appeared in the doorway to his office. She was a pencil-slim blonde whose efficiency and dedication to her job belied her delicate appearance. The woman could be a veritable tiger when it came to sifting out and diverting unwanted callers—whether on the phone or if they turned up unannounced. But the knowledge that it was Layla Jerome's brother who was ringing made Drake immediately anxious to take the call. The beautiful woman had been almost constantly on his mind ever since he'd seen her, and if nothing else he wasn't going to miss the opportunity to try and get her phone number again.

'Put him through, Monica. I'll take it.'

At the end of the call Drake pushed to his feet and moved restlessly across to the tall plate-glass panels directly behind his desk. Staring out at the parked cars on the street below, he could barely suppress the gratifying sense of satisfaction that throbbed through him. He had listened to Marc Jerome's views on the needs of his local community, and when the younger man had asked for some business tips he had agreed to meet up with him so that they could discuss it more fully.

When that topic was safely out of the way Drake hadn't been slow to seize the opportunity to ask directly if his sister was currently dating anyone. He had all but held his breath as he'd waited for the answer.

'No, she's not,' Marc had replied carefully, definitely sounding protective. 'As far as I know, she's quite happy being free and single right now.'

Drake had allowed himself the briefest smile. 'I'd really like to ask her about that myself, if you don't mind?' he'd returned immediately. There was a fine line between being bold enough to state your aim clearly and being pushy, but when it came to something he wanted as badly as this, he definitely wasn't a man to let the grass grow under his feet—and neither was he overly concerned if he offended anyone. 'It's probably best if I talk to her outside of work. Maybe even on the day that you and I have our meeting?'

'You'd better ring her first and check and see if that's okay,' had been the distinctly wary-sounding reply.

'Of course.'

And now Layla's mobile phone number was writ large across his notepad.

He made a vow to ring her after lunch, just in case the café was busy, and, breathing out a relieved sigh, stopped gazing out the window and returned to his desk, bringing his focus determinedly back to his work...

'Layla?'

'Yes?'

'This is Drake Ashton. I got your number from your brother Marc.'

In the midst of a leisurely stroll in the park, through the sea of burnished gold leaves that scattered the concrete path, Layla changed direction and strode across the grass to sit down on a nearby bench and take the call, her phone positioned firmly against her ear. Marc had despatched her to eat her packed lunch and get some fresh air after a surprising flurry of lunchtime trade, but any sense of feeling free to enjoy a precious hour in the autumnal sunshine had immediately vanished at the sound of the famed architect's magnetically velvet smoky voice.

'He told me you'd asked him for my number,' she answered, already desperately rehearsing her carefully worded refusal of what she suspected would be another invitation to meet him for a drink.

Inexplicably, and against every impulse to act sensibly, she'd hardly been able to stop thinking about the man since he'd visited the café yesterday, and that was definitely a cause for concern. Just hearing his voice ignited an almost terrifying compulsion to see him again. The ethereal grey eyes that sometimes seemed almost colourless, the high cheekbones and cut-glass jaw seemed to be imprinted on her memory with pin-sharp clarity.

'Then you'll no doubt have guessed that I'm ringing to ask you out?' There was a smile in his extraordinarily hypnotic voice. 'I know you were reluctant to let me have your number, but I'd very much like to see you again. I'd really like the chance to get to know you a little, Layla. What do you say?'

'If I'm honest, I'm not entirely comfortable with the idea, Mr Ashton.'

'Drake,' he inserted smoothly.

The tension in Layla's stomach made her feel as if a band of steel was encircling it and tightening by the second. She drew the canvas bag that contained her sandwiches more closely to her side almost subconsciously, as if for protection. 'I don't mean to offend you, but I'm not interested in seeing anyone at the moment.'

'You don't like dating?'

'I can take it or leave it, to tell you the truth. I'm certainly not a person who needs to have someone special in my life to make me feel whole or worthwhile.'

'Good for you. But is that the *real* reason you're hesitating to meet me, or is it perhaps because your last boyfriend let you down in some way or treated you badly?'

'That's none of your business.'

'Maybe not. I'm just trying to find out why you don't want to have a date with me.'

Layla expelled a heavy, resigned sigh. 'The man who let me down wasn't a boyfriend...at least not at first. But he *was* someone I'd put my trust in—completely wrongly, as it turned out. I was very badly deceived by him. Anyway, I—'

'You'd rather not risk seeing me in case I do the same thing to you?' Drake finished for her.

'No, I'd rather not,' she confessed reluctantly, feeling strangely as though she'd manoeuvred herself into a narrow dead-end she couldn't easily reverse out of.

'Not all men are bastards, Layla.'

'I know that. I'd trust my brother Marc with my life.'

'Speaking of your family—I knew your father, you know?'

Her heartbeat quickened in surprise. 'Really?'

'Jerome's was my local newsagent. That's where I knew him from.'

'It's a small world.'

'I used to go there as a kid. We'd chat about football together. We supported the same team, and he used to tell me about all the matches he'd seen when he was young.'

'He was crazy about football. And he loved having the opportunity to talk to another fan about the game—also about how his team were doing. My dad always had time for the children who visited the shop. He had the kindest heart.' Suddenly besieged by memories of the father she had adored, as well as by a great longing for his physical presence, Layla couldn't help the tears that suddenly surged into her eyes.

'Presumably he's not around any more? What happened, if you don't mind my asking?'

'He died just three months after a diagnosis of cancer of the throat.'

'I'm sorry. That must have been a very hard cross to bear for you and your brother.'

'It was.'

'And your mother? Is she still around?'

'She died when I was nine. Look, Mr Ashton, I—'

'I'd really like it if you called me Drake.'

The invitation sounded so seductively appealing that even though she intuited that he'd used his past association with her father to break down her resistance, Layla found his skilful persuasion hard to ignore. Although her trust in men had been indisputably shattered by the dishonest behaviour of her boss, Drake's regard for her father seemed perfectly genuine, she told herself.

Her lips edged helplessly into a smile. 'You don't give up easily, do you?'

'No, I don't. You don't get far in the world of business if you're not tenacious.'

'I hear that you've agreed to meet with my brother and give him some advice about the café?'

'I'm coming to see him on Thursday. After our meeting at the café I'm visiting the site where the first new builds for residential housing are going to be erected. I expect I'll be there until quite late.'

Not knowing what to say, Layla shivered at the icy blast of wind that suddenly tore through her hair and swept the leaves on the path into a mini-cyclone.

'Look…I really want to see you,' he asserted, 'but I don't want to wait until Thursday. That's far too long.' He made no attempt to disguise his impatience. 'How about throwing any caution you might be harbouring to the wind and going on just one date with me? If you come up to London I'll take you out to dinner.'

'When were you thinking of?'

'Tomorrow… No, wait! *Tonight*…I want to see you tonight.'

'Tonight is a bit short notice.'

Her inner guidance was already sending a loud warning to be careful pounding through her bloodstream.

When her brother had confessed that he'd given Drake her number she hadn't been able to help feeling annoyed at *both* men. She wasn't some desirable commodity to be bartered over, for goodness' sake! Neither had she expected the architect to ring her so soon. She'd like more time to mull his invitation over...*time to come to her senses, more like,* she thought irritably. Her ex-boss had had a way with words too, and had been a master at devising clever strategies to get what he wanted— sometimes underhand ones. She shouldn't forget that. Although when it came to sheer charisma she didn't doubt that Drake Ashton easily had the market cornered.

'Have you other plans for tonight?'

'No, but tomorrow night would suit me better.' Hardly knowing where she'd found the nerve to tell him that, Layla grimaced.

'I might not be able to make it tomorrow night.'

'Never mind.' Holding on to her determination not to be railroaded into flying off to London at the drop of a hat simply because Drake demanded it, she shook her head. 'It will have to be Thursday after all, then.' She deliberately kept her tone matter-of-fact. The other end of the line went ominously quiet. 'Are you still there, Drake?'

His sharp intake of breath was followed by an equally audible sigh of frustration and her insides knotted.

'I'm still here.' Irritation was evident in every sylla- ble. 'Tomorrow night it is, then. Give me your address and I'll send my driver to pick you up and bring you to my office. It's close to the West End, and I'll book us somewhere nice for dinner.'

'You don't have to send your driver. I can easily get the train into London.'

'Are you always this bull-headed?'

Even though Drake was probably still irked with her for trying to thwart him, disconcertingly he chuckled, and the husky sound sent shivers cascading up and down her spine like sparks from a firework.

'Because if you are, Layla, then I think I might have just met my match…'

CHAPTER THREE

She was half an hour late.

Having already been into his secretary's office twice to see if Layla had left a message, Drake now found himself in front of the coffee machine on the landing outside his office, pressing the button for yet another cup of strong black Americano he didn't really want.

Time had moved through the day like silt through reeds—slowly and painfully and laboriously, going nowhere fast. Whenever he thought about seeing Layla his insides were seized by alternate sensations of excitement and disagreeable anxiety. And several times that day a couple of colleagues had enquired if anything was wrong.

He hated the idea that they could see he was unsettled by something. Usually he endeavoured to keep his feelings strictly to himself—sometimes to the point of unsettling *them* because he expressed none of the usual emotional 'ups and downs' as they did. Yet he was quick to sing their praises when they did a good job for him, or worked overtime to help meet a deadline. Having built his reputation not on just designing builds to wow his clients but also by advising on and overseeing a project right up until the finish, Drake had ensured the people he employed were trustworthy and reliable team players. He might have grown up the quintessential 'loner' but he couldn't do what he did without them.

Glancing down at his watch, it jolted him to see the time. *Damn it all to hell!* Why hadn't he insisted that Layla let him send Jimmy to collect her instead of allowing her to make her own way here? He hadn't because he'd got the feeling if he had she would have cancelled their date altogether and told him just to forget it…

'Your visitor has arrived, Mr Ashton.'

The quiet, knowing tone of Monica, his secretary, broke into his unhappy reverie. To his dismay, he knew she'd guessed that the woman he was waiting to see was no run-of-the-mill visitor…that she was in some way special. If he quizzed her she'd call this instinct women's intuition, and Drake couldn't for the life of him understand why women had the gift in abundance and men didn't. At any rate, he intensely disliked people expressing curiosity or interest in his private life— and that included *unspoken* interest.

Monica's announcement that Layla had arrived had him turning towards her so fast that the scalding coffee in his polystyrene cup splashed painfully onto his hand. He uttered a furious expletive.

The secretary's smile was replaced by an immediately concerned frown. 'You'd better get some cold water on that straight away,' she advised urgently, stepping towards him to relieve him of the cup.

'Where have you put her?' Drake barked, the sting of his scald aiding neither his temper nor his impatience.

'In your office.'

'Well, make sure she's comfortable and tell her I'll be there in a couple of minutes. I'm going to the bathroom to run some cold water over my hand.'

Staring at his reflection in the mirror over the sink, and not particularly liking what he saw, Drake scrubbed his hand over the five o'clock stubble that darkened his jaw and ignored the throb of his burn with stoic indifference. Knowing he was going out to dinner, he ought to have shaved—but it was too late now. His date would just have to take him as she found him, even though he more closely resembled a dishevelled croupier who'd been up all night rather than a successful and wealthy architect. At least he was wearing one of his hand-tailored suits, with a silk waistcoat over a white open-necked shirt. That should help him pass muster.

Muttering out loud at the agitation that rendered him nowhere *near* relaxed, he straightened his shirt collar and spun away from the mirror. He refused to put himself through the grinder about anything else tonight. Work was finished for the day and he was going out to dinner with a woman who had rendered him dangerously fascinated the instant his gaze had fallen into hers...

As he made his way back to his office an older colleague attempted to waylay him with a query. Drake was so intent on seeing Layla that he stared at the man as if suddenly confronted by a ghost.

'Ask me about it tomorrow,' he muttered distractedly. 'I'm busy right now.'

'Sorry if I interrupted something important.'

Looking bemused, his fellow architect exited the glass-partitioned landing and Drake continued on into the executive office suite that was his private domain. Standing outside the semi-open door, he sucked in a steadying breath before making his entry. Just before his gaze alighted on the woman he'd been waiting all day to see his senses picked up the sultry trail of her perfume, and the alluring scent made his blood pound with heat. When his eyes finally rested on the slim dark-haired figure standing by his desk, dressed in a classy cream-coloured wool coat over a black cocktail dress, he could barely hear himself think over the dizzying waves of pleasure that submerged him. His little waitress looked like a million dollars.

'You made it,' he said, low-voiced.

'Yes. Though I don't know why I came.'

'What do you mean?'

'I mean that I haven't accepted an invitation to dinner from a man in a very long time, and I'm still not sure why I accepted yours.'

'Well, I'm glad that you did. You look very beautiful tonight, by the way.'

'Thanks.'

His compliment had clearly discomfited her, Drake saw.

'I don't normally dress like this,' she dissembled, 'but I didn't know where we were going so I— Anyway, are you annoyed that I'm late? The tube was delayed in a tunnel for twenty minutes…I don't like to think why. I'm sorry if I kept you waiting.'

'There's no need to apologise. Although I did recommend that my driver pick you up rather than you getting the train, remember?'

'*Recommend?* Is that what you did?' Shaking her

head, Layla forgot her previous awkwardness and emitted a throaty chuckle.

Already entranced by her beauty and presence, Drake was all but undone by the sound.

'As I recall,' she continued with a wry smile, 'it sounded more like a royal command. But then I expect you're used to telling people what to do and having it done?'

He kept quiet, because what she said was perfectly true. Yet he didn't want her to gain the impression he was insufferably overbearing and demanding and not give him a chance to display some of the less 'insufferable' sides to his nature... For the first time ever he was suddenly unsure of his ground with a woman. The percentages that afforded him command of any relationship were usually stacked in his favour—sixty-forty at least...

'Anyway, I still can't believe I'm standing here in your office.' Sighing softly, Layla smoothed her hand down over her hair. 'I guessed it would be impressive, but even my imagination didn't stretch as far as a hexagonal glass building that looks like something out of a futuristic sci-fi film. How on earth do you make something like this?'

'A hexagonal building is definitely harder to construct than a square-cornered one, but apart from its unique exterior it makes for a far more interesting interior to live and work in. I'm all for enhancing domestic and business spaces, and hopefully getting people to enjoy spending time in them. Do you like it?'

'All this glass...' She glanced to her right and then to her left, and then up above her at the ceiling and its breathtaking view of the twilit sky. 'It must be so light in here during the day. I definitely like the idea of that.'

'That's why I had the roof made out of glass. Sometimes I work in here at night, and if the moon is full and the stars are out I switch off the lamps for a while because they're not needed. The illumination from the sky is so bright that it's like a shroud of magical light blanketing everything.'

His companion's big brown eyes were so transfixed by what he said that this time it was Drake who was discomfited. He'd never admitted to anyone that he did such a thing before, and certainly not to any of his colleagues. What on earth had possessed him to be so candid?

In a bid to divert Layla from the too personal confession he smiled and said, 'Want me to give you a tour?'

Her smooth cheeks flushed a little. 'Maybe some other time… Aren't we supposed to be going out to dinner?'

'Are you telling me that you're hungry?'

'I am, actually. But the truth is I don't feel at my best in offices—even one as beautiful as this. My experience of being a personal assistant robbed me of all desire to ever work in one again. The world of "shocks and scares"—as my brother Marc calls it—was like a bear pit, and to work in an atmosphere where there's such a high level of drama and tension every day is apt to make a person permanently on edge. It's a lot more peaceful working in the café.'

Intrigued, Drake walked behind his desk and slipped on the tailored black jacket that he'd hung almost thoughtlessly over the back of his chair. It barely registered these days that the cost of his clothing far exceeded most ordinary people's annual salaries. But then if you wanted the best, you had to pay for the best. *He'd come a long way from the boy whose father had dressed him in charity shop finds.*

Frowning at the bewitching girl who stood in front of his desk, he asked, 'Can you tell me what your boss the broker was like?'

'I'd rather not. At least not right now. Perhaps when I get to know you a bit better?'

His heart slammed against his ribs. 'Can I take it, then, that you're planning on us having more than one date?'

'I'm not planning anything…it's a policy of mine to always try and live in the moment.'

'Mine too.'

'Besides…it's not just up to me, is it? Who knows? By the end of the evening you might be glad to see the back of me.'

'Somehow that's not how I envisage the evening ending.' Quirking a droll eyebrow, Drake gestured that they should move towards the door. 'Let's go to dinner, shall we? I've booked us a table at a nice French restaurant I know.'

They had been escorted by an ultra-polite *maître d'* to what Layla imagined must be the best table in the house. The 'nice' French restaurant Drake had mentioned turned out to be one of the most acclaimed eateries in Europe…let alone London. It had two Michelin stars and was populated tonight by an extremely classy-looking clientele who clearly weren't short of a penny or two. Their table was situated in a discreet far corner of the room, and the candlelit setting was quite simply beautiful. Everything from the polished silverware to the gleaming candelabrum and the white linen table-cloth that was hung with frightening precision was arranged to exemplify the most exquisite good taste, and the genteel ambience was further emphasised by some softly playing classical music.

Drake touched his hand lightly to her back as Layla's seat was pulled out for her by the *maître d'*, and he waited until he saw she was comfortable before seating himself. *Was it normal to have felt his touch as strongly as though a powerful electrical current had penetrated her layers of clothing?* God knew she'd been jumpy enough at his office, but alone with him like this, in an intimate setting far away from any working environment, she feared she would display her unease and self-consciousness by talking far too much. Back at his office she'd already babbled and said more than she'd meant to say. And what on earth had possessed her to suggest she might like to get to know him better? For a woman who had vowed to steer well clear of men of Drake Ashton's elite calibre, she was doing abysmally poorly. Now she was sure that the heat he had ignited in her body with his brief touch must easily be displayed on her burning face.

'I've heard about this place—of course I have—but I never thought I'd be so lucky as to get the chance to eat here. Rumour has it that the waiting list for a table is at least a year long. Is that true, do you think?'

Her restless hands nervously folded and unfolded her

linen napkin. The magnetic silver-grey eyes in front of her glinted with amusement.

'I have no idea. I simply had my secretary ring and book me a table.'

Layla didn't get the chance to comment straight away, because just then a waiter handed them leather-bound menus and a female sommelier appeared to make recommendations for the wine they might like to order. She didn't miss the fact that the attractive and vivacious redhead obviously knew Drake. The woman was completely professional, but she all but lit up when she saw him, and the banter between them sounded as though it was borne of a long-standing association.

When she'd left them alone again Layla sipped at the glass of water another waiter had poured for her and wondered if the sommelier and Drake had ever enjoyed a far closer relationship. *The idea bothered her far more than it had a right to.*

'The reason you have no idea how long the waiting list is for a table,' she announced jerkily, 'is obviously because you're an important man whose name alone gets you an automatic foot in the door.'

'You sound as if that perturbs you.'

Her handsome date narrowed his gaze and she felt as if she'd just voluntarily put herself under a high-powered microscope that would hunt out every flaw and discrepancy in her character and ruthlessly bring it to light.

'Why should it bother you that I can get a table in a good restaurant without having to wait for a similar time as most people do?'

Her skin prickling hotly with embarrassment, Layla frowned, feeling not just guilty and foolish but ex-

tremely gauche. 'I didn't mean to suggest that it bothered me. It was really just an observation. You've
obviously worked hard to have the privileges you enjoy
and I don't even know why I mentioned it. Forgive me.
Put it down to nerves.'

'So I make you nervous, do I?'

'Yes, you do a little.'

'Why is that?'

'Maybe you mistakenly think I'm a lot more confident than I am? The truth is I'm just a girl from an ordinary suburban home, and I'm not that comfortable in
the company of privileged men like yourself.'

She'd hoped her honest admission might alleviate
some of the anxiety she felt around Drake, but it didn't.
Instead she was left feeling even more gauche and un-
sophisticated.

At that very moment the pretty sommelier returned with their wine and proceeded to pour some
into Drake's glass for him to taste and approve. When
he indicated with a nod of his head that he did indeed
approve, she poured some into Layla's. This time her
companion's compelling glance didn't remotely invite
the girl to linger longer than was absolutely necessary.

'Thank you,' he murmured, his businesslike tone
suggesting she should leave. 'Your health and happiness,' he toasted, smiling at Layla.

The gesture was a long way from being businesslike. His captivating eyes crinkled at the corners as he
smiled and his lips curved generously, displaying strong
white teeth. It was a killer combination and her body
tightened helplessly.

'The same to you,' she murmured, lightly touching her goblet-shaped wine glass to his.

'And, by the way, I didn't get the impression that you were especially confident. My general impression is that you're rather defensive, and consequently quite feisty because of it. Like a protective lioness wanting to divert attention away from a predator's interest in her cub.'

'I wasn't trying to protect anyone.'

'Yes, you were.' Drake's rich voice lowered meaningfully. 'You were clearly trying to protect yourself, Layla.'

'Is that so? Then, tell me, exactly what am I protecting myself *from*? I'd be very interested to know.' Inside her chest, Layla's heartbeat mimicked the disturbing cadence of a chugging steam train.

'From *me*.' As he carefully set down his wine glass, still holding onto the fragile stem with his forefinger and thumb, Drake's gleaming intense glance all but devoured her.

'But, saying that, I'm no predator. As far as women are concerned I've never found the need.'

His gaze continued to hold her spellbound, and she was helpless to break free from it.

'I've never had to chase a woman in my life. It's always been the other way round. However...' Again he paused, as if carefully measuring his words. 'I've always guessed that one day there would be an exception to break the rule.'

Feeling as if pure elemental lightning was scorching through her veins, Layla nervously licked her lips, feverishly trying to find coherent words to answer such an incendiary declaration. 'Are you—are you saying that you're pursuing me, Drake?'

His amused, provocative chuckle emanated from deep inside his throat. 'I hope I won't have to, Layla. But I rather think that will be up to you.'

Lifting his glass, he drank deeply from wine that the candlelight on the table seemed to turn into a deeply seductive blood-red river...

'Are you and your guest ready to order, Mr Ashton?'

The waiter's reappearance was well timed. It saved her from having to make a reply to a comment whose repercussions were still imploding shockingly inside her. She wasn't naive as far as men's desires were concerned. Her looks had often invited interested male attention... most of it *unwanted.* But never before had Layla been in a position where a man—a much admired and well-known man—told her so frankly that he would pursue her if she indicated she wasn't interested.

Already she'd discovered that it was near impossible *not* to be interested in Drake. Every moment they spent together she was fighting hard to tamp down the flames of desire his mercurial silver gaze ignited every time his eyes met hers. It was going to be one almighty challenge to resist such an electrifying attraction for long.

At the waiter's polite enquiry Drake opened the menu that had been languishing on the table in front of him, but before scanning it he glanced pointedly at Layla and said, 'I think we need a few more minutes, don't you?'

Not trusting herself to speak right then, she merely nodded her head.

'We need a little more time,' he told the waiter, who

promptly and deferentially blended back into the general hub of the restaurant. 'Shall I pour you some more wine?'

His lovely companion had been silent for the past few minutes as they ate their meal, and whenever Drake found himself helplessly studying her she seemed to be lost in a world of her own. Whilst he didn't particularly mind the lapse in conversation, he was concerned that she might be regretting their date—and that was something he expressly *didn't* want her to do. He should never have admitted so frankly that he would indeed pursue her if she indicated indifference to him. But in that unguarded moment lust and desire had got the better of him and his feelings had been hard to contain.

'No, thanks.' She declined his offer of more wine. 'I can't drink too much tonight. I've got a train to catch, and I've also got to get up early for work in the morning.'

'You don't have to rush to catch a train. My chauffeur will drive you home.'

'How will you get home if your chauffeur drives me?'

Drake shrugged and took another sip of his wine. 'He can drop me off on the way. I only live in Mayfair.'

'I know,' Layla answered, her pretty mouth curving in yet another ironic little smile. 'I read it in the local newspaper. Lucky you.'

He hadn't mentioned that he lived in Mayfair to impress her, but he couldn't deny that he was peeved that she appeared so singularly *unimpressed*...dismissive, almost. It made him feel like the lead character in the story *The Emperor's New Clothes*—a charlatan and a liar hiding behind a façade of wealth and success. In his mind he was still the poor boy living with a father who beat him and despised him and locked him in his bedroom in the dark when he wanted to exact particularly cruel punishment... His mouth tightened grimly as he fought the tide of agonising memory that rolled through him.

'If you find it so disagreeable to accept my offer of a ride home in preference to catching a train then I'm not going to argue with you. As soon as we've finished eating I'll pay the bill and we can go. There's a tube station just round the corner.'

When hot embarrassed colour visibly flooded into her porcelain cheeks Drake firmly schooled himself not to let it remotely disturb him...

CHAPTER FOUR

THEIR date had been an unmitigated disaster.

Layla wasn't quite sure what she had done to make Drake suddenly turn so cold towards her, but the fact was she'd definitely done something. He'd sat beside her in the car in chilling silence as his chauffeur dropped her off at the tube station. Even when she'd thanked him for the lovely meal and said goodbye he'd barely been able to bring himself to reciprocate. He'd merely murmured, 'Goodnight, Layla', and then glanced at her with those glacial grey eyes, as if wondering what on earth had possessed him to invite her out in the first place.

Now, hours after the date, she painfully tried to recall every word they'd spoken at dinner in a bid to discover where she had gone wrong. Several times she found herself revisiting Drake's comment that he lived in Mayfair, and eventually—regretfully—had to own that her tone might well have been a little mocking. In no way had he been showing off to her, yet Layla had responded to the comment as though he *had*.

Because of her sour experience in working for her previous boss, she subconsciously believed that *all* wealthy and powerful men were arrogant and conceited and should be brought down a peg or two. No wonder

Drake had decided to have nothing else to do with her. He probably thought she was an ignorant little fool. Though, to be fair, her remark had been an innocently thoughtless one, born out of her still feeling nervous and not just a little overwhelmed by him. No insult had been intended. But now she couldn't help but believe he would never contact her again.

'I'm taking an hour off at around eleven this morning for a meeting in my office. Can I leave you to hold the fort?'

Her brother's voice broke into her morose musing. As if waking from a deep trance, Layla blinked up at him. She'd been arranging some fresh muffins on a shelf in the glass cabinet on the counter when she'd started reflecting on her date with Drake and wondering if she should risk telephoning him to make an apology.

As Marc patiently waited for her to acknowledge his comment she dusted some icing sugar from her hands and forced a smile. 'Of course you can. We're fairly quiet this morning, as you can see.' She glanced across the café at the two middle-aged women seated on the comfy sofa—regulars of theirs, clearly enjoying their lattes and buttered currant buns and looking enviably content. Apart from them an elderly man and a teenage boy transfixed by his mobile phone were the only other customers.

'The meeting is with Drake Ashton. Did you remember that he was coming today? Only you've hardly said a word about your date last night.'

'Of course.' Layla's lips were suddenly numb. 'It's Thursday, isn't it?'

'Go to the top of the class!' Grinning, Marc wiped

the back of his hand across his brow. As usual his dark hair was slightly awry and uncombed, his black T-shirt crumpled and unironed.

'I ironed you a pile of clean T-shirts yesterday and left them on your bed,' she told him, her gaze raking his clothing. 'How come you're wearing that one? It looks like you slept in it. Don't you think you ought to change if you're having a meeting with Drake?'

'So it's *Drake* now, is it? Clearly you're on much more informal terms with him since your date, then? I had my doubts when I first saw you this morning— you looked like someone had died. That naturally led me to conclude that things hadn't gone well…which is why I haven't quizzed you about it.'

'Never mind about that.' Impatiently Layla glanced round at the clock on the wall behind her. 'He's going to be here in just under half an hour. You need to change out of that scruffy T-shirt and comb your hair and endeavour to look a bit more presentable. That's if you want him to think you're serious about the business?'

'Of course I'm serious about it!' Marc scowled. 'Why do you think I don't sleep at night? Because I *like* going round looking like death warmed up?'

'I don't doubt your commitment. I know how much you care about making the café a success. I'm just saying that having the opportunity to talk to Drake Ashton is a chance that doesn't come along every day, so you need to make the most of it. Look…if you leave now you'll have just about enough time to change. Even if you don't feel confident, it'll help you feel miles better if you put on a clean and ironed shirt and comb your hair.'

'You're right.' Sighing, her brother planted a resounding kiss on her cheek. 'If Ashton arrives before I'm back, make him a nice cup of coffee and give him a bun, will you? Thanks, sis.'

As soon as Marc had left Layla checked her hair and eyeliner in her make-up mirror and tried hard to still the nerves that seized her at the knowledge that Drake was arriving in just a few short minutes for the promised meeting with her brother. *Would he even acknowledge her when he saw her?* she fretted. He'd been like the proverbial 'ice man' when he'd dropped her off at the tube station last night, and he hadn't made any attempt to ring her and clear the air.

Knowing she would be utterly miserable if she succumbed to her feelings of fear and doubt about how he might behave towards her, she swung round to the digital radio on the shelf behind her and turned it on. As a lively pop tune filled the air she determinedly busied herself making the area round the counter even more pristine and inviting than it was already.

Twenty minutes later, after another worrying lull in custom, the glass door at the entrance opened, bringing with it a strong blast of frosted air. A mellow September it was not. Already it felt more like the onset of winter. But right then Layla was hardly concerned about the unseasonal temperature. Not when the reason for the suddenly open door planted his tall, lithe physique in front of the counter and made her heart race with one of his compelling enigmatic smiles. Wearing a stylish chocolate-brown cashmere coat over a fine dark suit, the handsome architect looked good enough to eat. Her blood heated even before he opened his mouth to speak.

'Remember me?'

'Yes, I do. You're the man who cold-shouldered me at the end of our date last night.'

Even as the words left her lips Layla cursed herself for yet again blurting out the wrong thing. How could she have forgotten so soon that she'd intended to apologise for upsetting him—not greet him with a frosty accusation?

Drake's handsome brow creased a little, emphasising the two deep furrows there. 'I'm sorry about what happened…I really am. But I'm beginning to realize, Layla, that you have the propensity to rub me up the wrong way. Anyway, I should have called you straight afterwards and made amends. I wish I had. I certainly didn't want the evening to end the way it did.'

The regret in his voice was accompanied by a glance filled with such intense longing that Layla could hardly believe it was directed at her. It had the effect of making her limbs suddenly feel as though they'd been injected with a powerful muscle relaxant, and she put her hands out onto the counter to support herself.

'I sometimes don't think before I speak,' she murmured, reddening, 'and I wish I did. Whatever I said or did that upset you I'm genuinely sorry for it.'

He nodded. 'Then let's start again, shall we? I'm going to visit a couple of sites after I see your brother, and I'd like you to come with me. I think you'll be interested in hearing what's planned there. I'll drop you back here at the café afterwards. We'll be a couple of hours at most.'

'I'd love to come with you, but I can't take time off just like that.'

Glancing round at the two remaining customers in

the vicinity, Drake's grey eyes glinted with humour. 'Because you're madly busy? Don't worry—I'll clear it with your brother when I see him. Is he around?'

'He'll be here any minute now. He—he had to dash home for something. Can I get you a coffee while you're waiting for him?'

'That would be great. I'll have a strong Americano.'

'What about something to eat?'

The question seemed to put him in a trance. His hypnotised gaze suggested he'd suddenly been plunged into a compelling private world of his own—a dimension that utterly and completely absorbed him. The faraway look in his eyes inexplicably made Layla's heart ache. It was a bit like when his absorption in his technical drawings had put her in mind of a schoolboy concentrating hard on his homework.

She couldn't help frowning. 'Drake?'

'What?' Raking his fingers through his hair, he gave a rueful smile. 'I don't want any food, thanks. I've had some breakfast this morning. A coffee will be just fine.'

As if he was discomfited by his zoning out, he turned away, clearly intending to make for a nearby table. Layla stopped him in his tracks.

'Do you mind if I say something?'

Warily he turned back. 'Go ahead.'

'I'm not for one second telling you how to conduct your business, so please don't take this the wrong way, but Marc is a little fragile at the moment. He needs… well, he needs to hear something good…something that will help give him some hope for the café's future. I'm not asking you to completely sugar-coat your advice, because obviously he needs to hear the truth, but whatever you advise him…would you—could you please bear that in mind when you talk?'

Again he drove his fingers through his hair. Although his expression was thoughtful, he also seemed a little weary, she thought.

'There's no sugar-coating the pill in business, Layla,' he said, 'but whatever advice I give to your brother, you can rest assured it will be fair and considerate…helpful too I hope. Was that all?'

With a self-conscious nod she turned her attention back to the task of making his coffee…

It felt so good to have her near again. As he drove the Range-Rover through the winding roads skirting the town Drake stole several covetous glances at his passenger's arrestingly beautiful profile and now and then couldn't resist lowering his gaze to the long slender legs encased in snugly fitting black cord jeans. He breathed in her perfume. It could have been life-giving oxygen as far as he was concerned, and he felt almost high on it.

After countless hours of hardly being able to concentrate on anything at all but Layla—long hours made even worse by the sleepless night that inevitably followed such pointed introspection—he was walking on air because she'd agreed to accompany him today. It didn't matter that it was ostensibly for work, visiting the sites he'd been commissioned to rejuvenate with attractive affordable housing. How he hadn't caved in and rung her after they'd parted last night he didn't know. Except that he'd maybe had some idea of briefly punishing her with a show of indifference because he'd been so sure she'd been mocking him about living in

Mayfair. He'd convinced himself that her unimpressed attitude suggested that she knew exactly where he came from and wasn't going to let him forget it. But as soon as he'd set eyes on her again in the café, Drake had known it was *himself* that he'd punished. Now he was predisposed to be kinder.

'Warm enough?' he asked. The question earned him a sunny smile that was akin to the pleasure of eating hot buttered toast in front of a roaring fire—preferably with *her*.

'This car has a great heater. The car I share with my brother has a heater that wouldn't warm up a shoebox, let alone anything bigger. By the way, how did your meeting with him go?'

'It was fine.' Drake pursed his lips, amused. He might have known she wouldn't be able to resist asking him about it. 'I think I've given him some food for thought. It's now up to him whether he acts on what I suggested or not. Most of all, he's going to have to learn to be patient. Things take time to change for the better. By the way, we didn't just talk about the café. You came into the conversation a few times too, Layla. The way he lit up at just the mention of your name told me that he adores you.'

It was impossible to suppress the jealousy that churned in the pit of his stomach when he thought about Layla regarding her brother in the same heartfelt way. Never in his life had *he* been on the receiving end of such a devoted sentiment.

Her slim shoulders lifted in a shrug. 'I don't know if it's true that he adores me, but I admit that we've always been quite close. Do you have any brothers or sisters?'

'No.' Drake's hands automatically tightened on the steering wheel. 'I don't. I'm an only child, I'm afraid.'

'That doesn't have to be a negative. Perhaps your parents decided that they only wanted you? Or maybe the reason they only had you was because they couldn't have any more children?'

His companion's innocently voiced assumptions sent a cold, clammy shiver up his spine. 'I've no idea,' he answered tersely. *But he did.* Being intimately acquainted with his family's dysfunctional history, he knew only too well that neither of those scenarios was true. 'I never asked them.'

'And there's no possibility of you asking them now?'

'No. There isn't. My mother walked out years ago, when I was just six, and my dad died when I was a teenager.' It was hard to subdue the bitterness in his tone, and straight away he sensed the embarrassment and discomfort that his comments had inflicted on the woman sitting beside him.

'I'm sorry, Drake…'

The sigh she emitted sounded genuinely heartfelt.

'Forgive me for being so tactless. I had no idea about your background.'

'It all happened a long time ago now, and it's not exactly something I want to broadcast. I'd be grateful if you didn't share the information with anyone else. In any case, as you can see…' Turning his head briefly to observe her, he was instantly perturbed by the concern reflected back at him from her luminous brown eyes. 'I'm a big boy now, and I get on just fine without my parents being around.'

'You're a lot tougher than I am, then.' Her tone was

tinged with sadness and regret. 'I lost my mum when I was very young too. She contracted pneumonia after a bout of severe flu and never recovered. Then, when I was a teenager, I lost my dad. I still miss both of them more than I can say.'

Startled that her losses mirrored his own family scenario—albeit his mother hadn't died but simply walked out—Drake was torn between voicing the usual polite words of commiseration and pulling the car over and impelling Layla firmly into his arms. He was aching with an almost unholy need to do just that. The mere idea of having an opportunity to touch her soft skin and silky hair, to feel her mouth tremble beneath his with what he secretly hoped might be an inflammatory need similar to his own, was almost too powerful to ignore.

But, seeing they were nearing the site he'd proposed they visit together, all he did was say thoughtfully, 'I'm sorry you miss them so badly, but life goes on, doesn't it? We have to try and make the best of things. When bad things happen you can either wallow in the idea that you've been dealt a bad hand or you can be determined to rise above it. Personally speaking, I was never going to stay around here and regard myself as some kind of victim—no matter how difficult or challenging it was to rise above my circumstances.'

He drove into the large denuded area that had already been cleared in preparation for building and pulled up beside one of the several works vans belonging to the contractor he'd hired. A few feet away scaffolding waiting to be erected lay in precisely organised piles on the cold hard ground.

'We're here.' Silencing the engine, he turned to study

his passenger. 'I know the weather's not great, but I'd still like to show you the site and tell you what we've got planned. Are you still up for a look round with me?'

'Of course.' Peering out of the windscreen, she let a fond smile touch her lips. 'There used to be a great playground here when I was a kid. My brother and I sometimes walked all the way from our house to get to it. My dad was inevitably working, so during the school holidays after Mum was gone we were more or less left to our own devices. We used to think it was a bit of an adventure to go to the playground on our own, to tell you the truth. Do you remember it, Drake?'

'I do.'

His own memories of the playground that had once stood on the site were definitely not as fond as Layla's, he mused. He too had visited it on his own, but he hadn't made any friends when he was there. The other kids had probably been warned by their parents to stay away from the boy whose mother had left him and who had a father notorious for being bad-tempered and more often than not *drunk*.

Bringing his focus firmly back to the present, Drake returned his pretty companion's smile. 'By the way, you'll have to wear a hard hat…Health and Safety demands it, I'm afraid. I've got a spare in the boot.'

The word *cold* didn't come anywhere near to describing the effect of the slashing raw wind that cut into Layla's face as soon as she stepped out of the car onto the flattened muddied ground. Shivering hard, and reflecting on the vehemence in Drake's tone when he'd talked about rising above his circumstances after the devastating events of his childhood, she suddenly understood why his success must mean so much to him. From this rundown suburban no-man's land to Mayfair was no small achievement. In fact, thinking about the deprivation in the area—both socially and educationally—his accomplishment was nothing less than remarkable. Wrapping her arms round the insubstantial padded jacket she wore with her jeans, she shivered again, fervently wishing she'd had the foresight to wear something much warmer.

'Let's walk. Some exercise will help warm you up. Here, you'd better put this on first.'

As he came to stand in front of her she saw the glint of concern that mingled with wry amusement in his mercurial grey eyes and her blood started to pump hard even *before* she started to walk round the site. She was so disconcerted by the reaction that as she moved forward to take the spare headgear he was holding out she immediately tripped over a stone and almost fell. The only reason she didn't was because Drake's hands caught hold of her arms just in time to steady her. In the process he grabbed the hard hat she was carrying and threw it to the ground, along with his own, so that he could properly support her.

During those volatile few seconds time slowed to a terrifying immediacy that ripped away all possibility of thought. Instead Layla was aware only of the acutely erotic heat that poured into the air between them. It was a formidable force that was impossible to ignore.

When her shocked gaze fell onto Drake's, only to see the candid hunger that was laid bare in his eyes, she knew with a jolt that they were reflecting the same shocking, raw need that she was experiencing. His steel-like grip on her upper arms didn't lessen as his warm breath hit the icy air with visible little clouds of steam. She yearned to say something…*anything* to restore the situation to some semblance of recognisable normality before it was too late…before she succumbed to something she might live to regret. But the idea abruptly melted away when in that very same instant he took his hands away from her arms to cup them either side of her jaw. The surprising sensation of a couple of rough-edged calluses and warm smooth skin pressed against her cold face was a sensual revelation.

With a harsh breath that was a precursor to the inevitability of his next action, Drake crushed her mouth savagely beneath his.

The combined taste of his lips and tongue was immediately sexy and addictive. Like a heady smooth cognac that she couldn't stop herself craving even when she knew drinking it would likely get her into trouble.

Layla found herself in the midst of a sensually battering storm that threatened to rip her from her moorings for ever, and her ears were filled with the sound of her own breathless gasps as her hands curled possessively into Drake's cashmere coat in a desperate bid to bring his strong hard body even closer to hers. What she wouldn't give to be skin to skin with him right then, instead of wearing restrictive clothing that prevented them from touching each other as passionately as they craved. Even in the teeth of the cutting wind that blew around them the fire they'd lit between them surely blazed hot enough to keep even the most arctic temperatures at bay?

The clawing sexual need that suddenly consumed her rocked her with its force. With an indisputable sense of urgency Drake hurriedly unzipped her jacket and roughly palmed her breast. Even through her clothing his touch was like a lick of raw flame scorching her. With a rough groan he broke off the avaricious kiss that was threatening to get out of control. His mouth's desertion left Layla helplessly pining for more. But she didn't feel abandoned for long, because straight away he pushed her jacket collar aside and pressed his mouth to the juncture between her neck and shoulder.

His heat all but undid her there and then. At the same time as his lips moved seductively over that highly sensitive region he sank his teeth into her skin and bit her. If it hadn't been for the fact that both his hands were holding her fast by her hips she was sure she would have fainted from the sheer scorching pleasure of it. Yet a kernel of common sense somehow engineered its way into the dangerous fog of desire, and with her heart racing she freed herself from the circle of his arms and stepped away. As she moved back her hand gingerly touched the tender place where he'd bitten, feeling the sting that undoubtedly meant he'd left his mark. Her face flooded with violent heat.

'We shouldn't be doing this. We *can't* do this. You were—you were going to show me round the site and tell me about what's planned here. Perhaps we should concentrate on doing that instead of—instead of...'

'Wanting to rip each other's clothes off?'

Drake's throaty intonation and teasing smile came dangerously close to making Layla hungrily return to his arms. To prevent such an occurrence she made herself recall how devastated she'd been when her ex-boss had mercilessly persuaded her to invest her life savings in the financial scheme that had turned out to be totally crooked. The humiliating and hurtful memory reminded her of her vow to steer clear of wealthy charming men for as long as she lived. Better she fell for a factory worker or a postman so long as he was honest and true.

She'd already been burned by someone whose *raison d'être* was money and success, and she was in no hurry to experience a similar scenario.

'I don't know what came over me, but you can be sure it won't happen again. Shall we go and look round the site now? Time's getting on and I need to get back to work.'

She gave Drake the scantest glance she could manage, knowing that if she gazed too long into those magnetically compelling eyes of his her good intentions and warnings to herself would be crushed into oblivion and she would lose all ability to make sensible decisions where he was concerned for good.

'Come on, then.' He bent down to retrieve the hard hats he'd let fall to the ground. After placing one on his own head, he moved across to Layla and handed her hers. 'Put this on. We'll do what we came to do and walk round the site, then I'll take you back to the café. Later on tonight, when you've finished work, I'll ring you so we can talk about when to see each other again. And when we do, I'm going to absolutely insist that you let my driver collect you.'

'Didn't you hear what I said? What if I tell you I've decided I don't want to see you again?'

'I won't believe you. Not after what just happened between us.'

Drake's expression was as serious and formidable as she'd ever seen it. Layla's icily tipped fingers gripped the hard hat tightly, but she wouldn't put it on until she got her feelings off her chest.

'Let me put you straight about something. I'm not interested in having some meaningless sexual fling with you that will burn out in a few days or even a few weeks. I won't deny that I find you physically attractive, but that in itself isn't enough to persuade me that it's a good idea to see you again.'

'No? Then what is?'

'I'll only agree to see you if you let me into your life a little…if you give me the chance to get to know the man behind the successful veneer you present to the world. If you're willing to at least consider the possibility then I'll agree to another date with you. If not, then we may as well forget the whole thing.'

'Setting aside what I do for a living, and my public reputation, I'm a very private man, Layla. I very rarely let anyone get too close to me…especially women.'

He almost didn't need to say the words. Straight away she was aware of the turmoil that raged inside him at the mere notion of allowing her more intimate access into his life. It was as though she was the enemy and he was behind an impenetrable wall of steel keeping her from advancing any further.

Her breathing was suddenly uncomfortably shallow. 'So your previous relationships with women have been based on satisfying sexual desire and nothing more? Is that what you're telling me?'

'This really isn't the time or the place to discuss this.' Drake's troubled gaze turned into a warning glare. 'Right now I need to do my job and look round the site. I'll ring you later on tonight and we can talk then.'

Indignation that she was being palmed off until it was more convenient made Layla bristle. 'Don't bother. I'm not interested in being placated by your no doubt charmingly reasonable explanation as to why you don't want to let me get to know you properly, and neither am I interested in being some convenient bed partner while you're in town.' She unceremoniously shoved the hard hat into his hand. 'Don't worry about giving me a lift back to the café. The walk will do me good. I know the route back into town like the back of my hand.'

'Don't go.'

There was a heartfelt plea in his voice that stopped her in her tracks.

'Why? Why shouldn't I go?' she asked, her heart thudding inside her chest as though she teetered on the edge of a cliff.

'Because I want to show you round the site and explain what we've got planned to improve it.' He expelled a frustrated sigh. 'Aren't you at least interested in that?'

Even though she was mad at him, Layla couldn't deny that she was more than interested in the planned improvements. After all, she knew only too well what it would mean to the town and its downtrodden population. It would feel like a betrayal of everyone she knew who lived there to just walk away and pretend she didn't care.

Pushing her windblown hair out of her eyes, she

slowly nodded. 'Of course I'm interested. All right, then…I'll stay and let you show me around.'

Quirking a wary eyebrow, Drake smiled. 'And what about me ringing you later on tonight so we can talk about another date?'

'If you agree to seriously consider my request about letting me into your life a little…then, yes…you can ring me.'

Shaking his head, as if he knew it was pointless to pursue the matter further, Drake lightly placed his hand at Layla's back and led her onto the site.

CHAPTER FIVE

'So what do you think of the planned improvements?' As he drove them out of the site, Drake stole an interested glance at his passenger and saw that her incandescent brown-eyed gaze was definitely reflective.

'I think it's terrific what you plan to do,' she replied enthusiastically. 'Especially the idea of having a communal garden with lots of lovely planting and an adjoining play area for the kids.'

'You don't think the kids will pull up the plants?'

'No, I don't. Give people a place to be proud to live in, a place that's aesthetically beautiful as well as practical, and in my view they'll do everything they can to take care of it. A lot of the smaller children I know love plants and flowers, and if someone shows them how to plant and water them they'll love them even more.'

'So the plans have your personal seal of approval, Miss Jerome?'

Layla's pale cheeks were suddenly flooded with the most becoming shade of pink. 'You don't need my approval...but I'm glad you asked my opinion just the same.'

'There's one more place I'd like to show you before I take you back—a place that we're planning to improve as well. It's a short, nondescript side-street in one of the more rundown areas.'

'Okay.'

Drake's heart was thundering on the drive to the location where he'd been raised as a boy, but he tried to look beyond the now emptied shabby Victorian houses and envisage instead the more modern and attractive buildings he intended to erect in their place.

'This is the street you were talking about?' his companion asked, her expression puzzled as she peered through the windscreen.

'Yes. It's been empty for a long time now. Do you know someone who used to live here?' Immediately Drake prayed that she didn't. He didn't want her view of him tainted by some gossipmonger's lurid account of his family.

'I don't know anyone that lived here, but I know there are a few locals who are petitioning the council to save the buildings and have them renovated.'

His lips twisted ruefully. 'I heard about that. As well-meaning as those folks are, I'm afraid the petition has already been discarded.'

'Why?'

Taken aback by the look of horror on Layla's face, and a little rattled by it, Drake sighed. 'Because an independent party has purchased the entire street and has plans to demolish the houses and construct more contemporary residences in their place.'

'When did you hear that?' The huge brown eyes that had dazzled him right from the start widened in shocked disbelief.

'About three months ago…when I put in a bid to buy the street.'

Layla's even white teeth clamped down against the soft flesh of her plump lower lip and her slender hand pushed shakily through her hair. 'So *you're* the independent party?'

'Yes…I am.'

'And *you* plan to pull down these historic old buildings and replace them with cheap modern "Identi-Kit" houses with about as much character as cardboard egg-boxes?'

Drake would have grinned in amusement if it weren't for the fact that Layla looked so painfully aggrieved. 'I hope I have a lot more taste than that,' he said dryly. 'And for your information I never build cheap modern houses…no matter where they're situated. First and foremost, it's important to me to build housing that residents will be proud to live in, and I always utilise the most skilled craftsmen I can find to build them— as well as using the very best materials.'

'Be that as it may, the Victorians knew how to build houses that stood the test of time and were elegant too, and I have to tell you that I'm one of the town's residents who petitioned the council. If you're planning on improving the area why can't you just invest your money in renovating what's already here?'

'Because I'd rather rebuild than renovate, that's why.'

'I don't understand. Why won't you consider renovating?'

Even though seeing Layla's obviously distressed glance was akin to being punched hard, and it had shocked him to learn that she had been one of the petitioners who had fought to keep the Victorian terraced houses rather than demolish them, Drake didn't feel up to explaining why he'd rather raze the old buildings to the ground and build new ones. He was feeling somewhat peeved that Layla should take it upon herself to advise him what to do. When he'd last looked, *he* was the architect in charge of helping to regenerate the town.

'I'd better get you back to the café,' he murmured.

'Why won't you answer my question? If you're planning on pulling down the houses you might at least have the courtesy to explain why.'

Turning to face her, Drake bit back his irritation as best as he could. 'I can see that you clearly have some romantic ideas about renovating these properties, but it takes a hell of a lot of money to restore old houses and bring them back to their former glory. Sometimes it's far more economical and easier to build new ones. Don't forget I'm a businessman as well as an architect, Layla.'

Before she had a chance to reply he gunned the engine and reversed the car rapidly down the street, and she glumly averted her gaze to stare out of the window...

Layla had asserted that she wanted him to let her into his life and to get to know the man behind the successful veneer. It was the single most scary thing that a woman had ever said to him.

Drake put down the tumbler with a double shot of whisky in it and morosely folded his arms.

Even scarier was the growing temptation to flirt with the idea of considering her request. But he was worried that after showing her the street where he'd grown up, and telling her he planned to demolish all the houses there and erect new ones, she'd change her mind about wanting to get to know him at all. She'd hardly taken the news of his plans for the street well. Yet it hadn't affected the powerful allure she still had for him. *Damn it all to hell!* Layla Jerome had put a spell on him…either that or he had somehow lost his mind.

The decision to return to the place of his birth to help regenerate the area was seriously backfiring on him. The *very* last thing he'd expected to happen was that he should end up seriously lusting after a beautiful local girl that worked in a café.

He'd come back to Mayfair after finishing work that evening, but he'd neither eaten nor showered. His mind, body and senses had been too caught up in a tornado of longing and lust to accomplish either of those fundamental things so he had headed out to a hotel bar he knew in a bid to hopefully distract himself. Eating held no appeal when there was so much churning going on in the pit of his stomach, and he hadn't showered because he didn't want to wash away the alluring scent of Layla's body. Her seductive smell was all over him, and if he shut his eyes he could recall the wonderful sensation of her soft velvety skin beneath his fingertips and the incredible taste of her sexy mouth…

A bolt of inflammatory need shot straight to his loins and Drake silently cursed the ill-timed inconvenience of it. Even though she'd firmly told him that she wasn't interested in a sexual fling that would last only a few days or weeks he was still hoping to get her into bed soon. She'd asserted that she wanted to get to know him, but he knew if he let her she would probably be extremely uneasy with the taciturn, insecure man behind the glamorous and successful reputation—a man who was still too haunted by his past to be anywhere near comfortable with the idea of making a serious commitment to a woman.

Glancing impatiently down at his watch, and seeing that it was much later than he'd thought, he lifted the glass he'd put beside him on the bar and drank down the remaining contents in one hit. Even though Layla had been less than warm towards him when he'd dropped her off at the café, Drake had insisted he would ring her, and if he left it any later he knew he probably wouldn't get to speak to her at all tonight.

'Had a bad day?'

He glanced round in surprise at the shapely blonde who lowered herself onto the barstool next to him. She wore a fitted silver-grey suit over a dark red shirt with a revealing neckline, displaying enough décolletage to start a small stampede. *Except that the provocative sight left Drake completely cold.* There was only one woman he would head up a small stampede for and that was Layla.

'It wasn't all bad,' he drawled laconically, getting to his feet, 'there were definitely some highlights.'

'You're not leaving?'

The pneumatic blonde didn't try to hide her disappointment. But once on his feet Drake knew emphatically what was next on his personal agenda—and it wasn't whiling away the evening in a bar making small talk with a woman who was clearly on the lookout for a profitable sexual encounter with someone.

'I'm afraid I am. Have a nice evening,' he murmured,

the automatic half-smile that touched his lips quickly fading because all he could think about was getting back home and phoning Layla.

'She's gone to bed?'

On receiving this astounding information from Layla's brother Marc, Drake stopped stirring the mug of strong black coffee he'd made and turned round to lean back against the marble-topped counter in the kitchen.

Feeling stunned and aggrieved at the same time, he couldn't help the irritation that seeped into his reply. 'What do you mean, she's gone to bed? It's barely after ten.'

'She's never been able to hack staying up late. She's a real morning person.'

'And how is it that you're answering her mobile? Is she staying with you at the moment?'

'We share a house. I have the ground floor and Layla the top. Didn't she tell you that?'

'No. She didn't. Anyway, morning person or not, I'd appreciate it if you'd go upstairs and see if she's still awake. I told her to expect my call,' he said, mustering as much authority as he was able—because he was still reeling at the notion of her going to bed and apparently not being the slightest bit perturbed that he hadn't rung earlier. Was it because she was still mad at him for wanting to knock the terraced houses down and build new ones?

'I can't do that, I'm afraid. I've got strict instructions not to. That's why she left her phone with me. She said if you rang I was to tell you that she'll ring you on Monday. I'm really sorry, Mr Ashton, but it's more than my life's worth to disturb her. You may not know this yet, but my sister's got a real temper on her. Trust me—glass can be shattered when she loses it!'

Drake clenched his jaw and curled his palm into an angry fist down by his side. She was going to ring him on *Monday*? Was she playing some kind of game with him that entailed teaching him a lesson for not agreeing to renovate the Victorian terraced houses? he wondered. Could she even *guess* at the depth of frustration she'd left him with earlier today? More to the point, did she believe that her request that he let her get to know him had frightened him off? Clearly if it *had* she certainly wasn't going to lose any sleep over it.

'Okay. Thanks,' he muttered, finding himself completely at a loss to know what else to say.

Crossly replacing the receiver, he dropped down into a nearby chair. *Did she really mean to let an entire weekend go by before she saw him again?* He scowled. If he'd had her address and had been anywhere near the vicinity of her home he would have considered battering down her door to *make* her come and speak to him if he had to…*temper* or no. He wasn't about to let a potential display of volatile emotion put him off his goal. Besides which, the mere idea of Layla losing her temper instigated an immediate fantasy of him subduing it with a long, lazy open-mouthed kiss on that sexy mouth of hers.

Having already sampled her exquisite taste, the fantasy was almost too real to be borne. Releasing a hard to contain groan, Drake pushed impatiently to his feet.

The hot leisurely shower he'd envisaged was going to have to be replaced by one closer to sub-zero temperatures if his frustration was going to be remotely eased tonight…

Layla released a long sigh of relief when Marc told her the next morning that Drake had rung. She'd gone to bed early because she'd been genuinely tired, but she'd also been irritated with him because he wouldn't consider renovating the Victorian terrace. It was clear he was also aggravated with her, because she'd asserted that she wanted to get to know him, that she wasn't just interested in a short-term fling.

The man clearly had issues around allowing a woman to get too close to him and Layla wanted to find out *why*. She also wanted to know why he wouldn't consider renovating the Victorian terrace. Somehow she didn't buy it that it was more profitable to build new residences in its place. Drake might be a businessman as well as an architect, but she didn't believe that financial consideration was the *only* reason he wouldn't look at renovation.

Still, at the end of the day the man was doing far more for the town than anyone had in too many years to mention, and even if she was upset he wouldn't listen to a small local petition to keep the terraced houses she couldn't let that taint her feelings towards him… not when she sensed deep down that he was a genuinely good man.

It was while she was clearing away the debris of her breakfast and stacking the dishwasher that a sudden idea took hold. Maybe it was time she played a more proactive part in their association? Perhaps it was time to turn the tables and this time surprise *him*? She decided that if anything at all was going to come from their association—be it an irresistible and unforgettable fling or a mutual commitment to a much more meaningful relationship—she wanted at least to have joint command of it. Never again would she allow a man's desires to take precedence over her own wants and needs—or, as in the case of her unscrupulous ex-boss, to convince her that *he* knew best.

In particularly good spirits that day, Marc agreed to let her have the afternoon off. He even gave her an affectionate hug when she confessed she was going up to London to see Drake.

'I like him. He's a very astute businessman,' he said, smiling. 'He told me I shouldn't be in a hurry to throw in the towel and sell the café just because the takings are down. At any rate it isn't a good time to sell, and I'd only get peanuts for it. He explained that the whole point of regenerating the area was not just to encourage new residents to move here, but to encourage more successful and appealing retail outlets to inhabit the high street and sell their goods. The influx of new customers would help small businesses like the café become more thriving concerns. "Give it a couple of years at least to see if things work out," he advised. So that's what I'm going to do. I can't tell you how much better I feel at having some direction at last. Say thanks again for me when you see him, won't you?'

The fact that Marc was more than happy at the advice Drake had given him went a long way to firming

Layla's decision to pay him an impromptu visit. In any case, after that smouldering encounter with him yesterday at the building site she knew it was pointless to pretend she wasn't aching to see him again. And she'd dearly love to find out a bit more about his background and childhood if she could. Sometimes he had a near haunted expression in his eyes—a faraway look that suggested he was tormented by some unspoken grief. Did his painful reflections dwell on memories of a troubled past? she wondered.

When the taxi dropped her off outside the stunning hexagonal building Drake had designed, she almost wished she had a stiff drink at hand to give her some Dutch courage. What if he didn't welcome this spontaneous visit of hers and was mad at her for turning up unannounced? Should she at least have rung him to let him know she was coming? *Then it wouldn't have been a surprise.*

Layla softly murmured that thought out loud.

A few minutes later, travelling in the swish modern lift up to Drake's floor, she stole a glance in the mirrored interior to check her appearance. She'd left her shoulder-length dark hair loose today, and it helped cover the small pink abrasion that Drake had so passionately gifted her with. Carefully pushing aside some silken strands, she let her fingers tenderly examine it. Then, feeling somehow guilty, she let her hair fall back into place to hide it.

In a bid to appear a little more relaxed than she had been when Drake had taken her out to dinner, she'd opted to wear light blue denims and a plain white shirt with a lined fawn-coloured trench-coat for her spontaneous visit. But when her gaze honed in on the softly scarlet bloom that highlighted her cheeks, she stopped focusing on her appearance and looked away with a frown.

It had been her hope to present an image of relaxed composure when she saw him, but now there was no chance of that. Why, oh, why could she never seem to prevent her feelings from showing on her face like some people could? Forget composure. Her big-eyed 'caught in the headlamps' expression made her resemble a frightened rabbit rather than a determined young woman intent on taking a potentially volatile situation firmly into her own hands...

'Do you have an appointment with Mr Ashton?'

Drake's efficient, intimidating blonde secretary was like a sentry at the gates of Rome, suddenly alerted to an impending invasion. As she stood behind the desk with her arms folded her diamond chip blue eyes sternly raked over Layla's appearance, as if silently warning her that it was going to take a minor miracle to get past *her* to see Drake.

'No, I don't.' Swallowing hard, Layla knew her smile was uncertain and strained. 'I thought—I thought I'd surprise him.'

The sound of Drake's deep voice suddenly bellowing at someone behind the closed glass door that she knew led into his office made her start. The secretary's coral painted lips stretched briefly in an ironic smile.

'Somehow I don't think my boss is remotely in the mood for surprises, Miss...?'

'Jerome.'

'Yes, of course. You were here the other evening, weren't you? Except he *was* expecting you then.'

'Yes. He was. Look, I've come a long way to see him today. Can you at least tell him that I'm here?'

'I know you must be a friend of his, but I'm afraid I can't. His diary is full for the whole afternoon. Why don't you leave your phone number? Or you can write a message if you'd prefer? I'll make sure that he gets it.'

The other woman perfunctorily pushed a lined pad and a pen across the contemporary glass desk that right then seemed to symbolise an insurmountable barrier Layla couldn't cross. Frozen by indecision, her teeth worrying at her lip, she numbly picked up the pen, then stared down at the writing paper feeling wretched. It had obviously not been one of her better decisions to turn up at Drake's office unannounced. Perhaps she could find a café somewhere nearby and try to reach him on his mobile?

Just as she leant over the pad to write a message his office door opened and he stepped out. Wearing a sky-blue fitted sweater that hugged his hard-muscled lean frame, and dark blue jeans that highlighted his strong long-boned thighs, he too was dressed much more informally today. But she barely had time to realise much else, because he came to an immediate standstill and stared at her as if he couldn't believe his eyes. His piercing silvery gaze made her insides flutter wildly. Behind him, a well-built man dressed in a grey pinstriped suit, carrying what looked like some rolled-up technical drawings, stole the chance to slip away discreetly before his boss noticed that he was gone.

'Layla. To what do I owe the honour?' Drake's almost languorous drawl was tinged with the faintest mockery.

Lying the pen back down on the pad, Layla quelled the flurry of nerves that seized her and straightened up to face him. 'I thought I'd surprise you,' she told him.

'Well, you've certainly accomplished that.'

'I missed your call last night.'

'Yes, you did. Still…you're here now. Do you want some coffee?'

Before Layla had the chance to reply he turned to his secretary and said, 'Monica? Can you get me and my visitor some coffee, please?'

'Have you forgotten that you've got an appointment with Sir Edwin Dodd in twenty minutes, Mr Ashton?'

'Ring him and put him off, will you? Tell him something important has come up.'

The efficient Monica couldn't hide her dismay, or the fact that she was suddenly quite flustered. Layla almost felt sorry for her.

'This is a longstanding appointment…don't you remember? He's probably already on his way, and I don't think he'll take too kindly to being put off at the last minute.'

As he folded his arms her boss's glance was formidably steely. 'Am I labouring under the misconception that *I'm* the one in charge round here?'

'Of course not. I apologise if I was a little too blunt. I'll ring Sir Edwin straight away and make your apologies. Then I'll get your coffee.'

'Thank you.' He directed his gaze back to Layla, and the faintest enigmatic smile touched Drake's lips. 'Why don't you come into my office?'

Following her into the stunning room, with its panoramic view of rooftops and a gloriously cloudless blue sky, he quietly shut the door behind them. 'It's good to see you—if a little unexpected. Let me take your coat and bag.'

As soon as Layla had unbuttoned the fawn trenchcoat she sensed Drake move behind her to help remove it from her shoulders. The potent mix of warm virile man, sexy cologne and the electrifying brush of his hands through the layers of her clothing made her feel quite faint with desire. It was extremely difficult to think straight above such a shockingly imperative need.

In contrast, Drake appeared almost to want to taunt her by moving deliberately slowly, his air definitely preoccupied. But after carefully folding her coat over the arm of a nearby chair, and depositing her shoulder-bag and tote on the seat, he finally returned to stand in front of her. Dropping his hands to his lean masculine hips, he released a long drawn-out sigh. 'Well, well, well… You certainly know how to keep me on my toes, Layla Jerome.'

Fiddling with the ends of her hair, she couldn't prevent the heat that flooded into her face. 'I'm sorry. I should have rung you first.'

'Then your appearance would hardly have been a surprise, would it?'

'No, it wouldn't.'

'Besides…I definitely get the impression that talking on the phone isn't exactly a favourite occupation of yours.'

Moving nearer, Drake curled his hands round her

slim upper arms and slowly but firmly brought her body in closer to his. Layla caught her breath.

'I wanted to wring your brother's neck when he wouldn't go and tell you that I wanted to talk to you,' he confessed huskily.

'It wasn't his fault. I told him not to disturb me.'

'And why did you do that, I wonder? Was it because you were angry that I was going to have those houses demolished in preference to renovating them?'

'I don't deny I was furious about that. I know you left our forgotten little town a long time ago, but there are a lot of things that I still love about it. One of them is the rundown shabby streets with their once beautiful and historic old houses. It makes me terribly sad to think about the hardworking families who once lived in them and experienced all their joys and sorrows there but are now all gone.'

'Do you know for a fact that they were *all* hardworking and happy?' Drake asked, gravel-voiced.

There was something in his tone that made Layla's stomach drop. 'No, I don't. I just—'

'I grew up in that shabby little street, in one of those once "beautiful and historic old houses". As I recall, it wasn't remotely beautiful when I lived in it. Unfortunately I didn't experience much joy there either…plenty of sorrow, yes. And my father *definitely* wasn't hardworking.'

'I'm sorry to hear that. I didn't mean to rub salt into any wounds by expressing my opinions, Drake.'

'Forget about it. Like you said, the ghosts of the past are all gone now. So, tell me, do you usually go to bed so early?'

The humour that replaced the pain in his eyes lifted her heart after the sad confession about his home-life. At least she now knew why he was so determined to demolish those houses.

'During the week when I work I always go to bed early. I know you wanted to speak to me last night, but do you really think talking on the phone is the best way to get to know someone? I personally prefer to talk to my friends face to face…especially when it comes to discussing something personal.'

Drake's answering short laugh made all the hairs stand up on the back of her neck.

'So it's my *friend* you want to be now, is it?'

Brushing her hair out of the way, he laid his hand over her cheek, gently stroking the pad of his thumb down over her flushed skin, eliciting an explosion of goosebumps.

'I'll only agree to be your *friend*, Layla, if I'm afforded certain…shall we say…privileges?' he said, smiling.

As enticing as the idea to afford him those privileges was, Layla determinedly held her ground, even though his touch was seriously making her melt. 'I think that comment sounds very much like an avoidance strategy to me.'

'You think I'm avoiding something, do you? What am I avoiding?' With an incorrigible grin he moved his hand to rest it lightly on her shoulder.

'Answering the question I asked you yesterday— about—about letting me get to know you…giving me the chance to see the real man behind the successful architect.'

Once again she caught her breath as she waited for his reply. His grin faded almost immediately and his grey eyes suddenly acquired a glint of terrifying sadness that made her stomach roll over.

'That question ensured I barely slept a wink last night,' he told her gruffly.

'Why?' she whispered.

'Before I answer that, I have a question for you… Why did you give up a presumably well-paid job in London to move back home? What happened with this boss of yours? You said he wasn't a boyfriend, but I get the feeling something intimate happened between you. Was it an affair that perhaps turned sour?'

Drake's hands were suddenly fastening round her arms again, and his grip noticeably tightened, making her heart thump. 'I didn't have an affair with him. I just—he plied me with drink at an office party and I stupidly succumbed to sleeping with him. It was only the one time, and I hated myself for it straight after.'

Feeling angry that Drake had turned the tables on her, Layla tried to twist free, but he was having none of it and held her fast.

'My boss was like a lot of men who have wealth and power. He thought it was a golden ticket to having anything he wanted, and no doubt after my refusing his requests for a date for so long it helped boost his ego to get me drunk and finally persuade me into his bed.' Her face was suffused with embarrassed heat. 'I despise myself for being so weak, because he was the most unscrupulous and unprincipled man I've ever met.'

'Was that the reason you quit your job?'

Sucking in a steadying breath as the memory of the

shameful betrayal that had finally forced her to leave washed over her, she gazed into Drake's eyes with an unwavering furious stare.

'No. At least, it wasn't the main one. In another stupidly weak moment I let him persuade me to invest all my savings in a deal that was a total scam from start to finish. When I lost every penny, he shrugged as if he couldn't care less and said, "That's the business we're in, Layla. It's all about risk. Sometimes we win and sometimes we lose. You should have known that…silly girl." He wasn't wrong there.' She shook her head bitterly. 'I *was* silly… Let me rephrase that. I was utterly and unforgivably stupid. My common sense deserted me. But at the time I invested in his deal I'd long grown tired of the soulless nature of my job *and* my boss. I was desperate to leave. I wanted to retrain as a youth worker or something along those lines instead…something that could be of use to people. But I knew if I was going to study I'd need money to support myself. That's why I fell for my boss's expert sales pitch. I thought that because he'd reached the heights as a broker, and made a lot of money by speculating and taking risks himself, he must know what he was doing. I never thought for one minute that he might take me to the cleaners because I only slept with him once and refused to do so again. It's amazing what we can convince ourselves of when we're desperate, isn't it?'

'I'm sorry.'

The comment sounded genuinely compassionate, and Drake's firm grip on her arms gentled.

'Not half as sorry as I am. I know one thing for sure. I'll never make a decision out of desperation again.'

'You did nothing wrong, Layla. It's your low-life ex-boss that needs hanging out to dry.'

'Anyway…' She lifted a shoulder in a shrug. 'You live and learn, as my dad always used to say. Are you going to answer *my* question now, Drake?'

Withdrawing his hands, he pressed his fingers deep against his temples. For the first time since he'd appeared in the outer office she noticed the softly bruised shadows beneath his eyes that denoted his previous night's lack of sleep.

'I've been giving it some serious thought.'

Not brave enough to prompt him, Layla neither moved nor spoke.

Lifting his strong cut-glass jaw, Drake gave her one of his searing, compelling glances. 'I want you Layla. I'm sure you know that only too well by now. You're like a fever in my blood that I can't recover from. So I've decided that I will give you more access than I've given to any other woman before and let you get to know me a little. But I want to make it clear that that *doesn't* mean there'll be no holds barred—because it's quite likely there will be.' The glitter in his eyes that followed this statement was almost fierce. 'I don't share my feelings or my thoughts easily. Maybe that's a habit I'll eventually learn to break, but there'll definitely be boundaries if we become more intimate. Think you can handle that?'

With her heart bumping heavily against her ribs, Layla found herself nodding slowly. 'Yes, I do. At least, I'm willing to take the risk.'

CHAPTER SIX

AFTER they had their coffee Drake gave Layla the 'grand tour' of his offices, because he knew if they stayed alone together any longer, cloistered in his private domain, he wouldn't be able to keep his hands off her. As it was he had to contend with the too interested glances of his colleagues...*especially* the men. But how could he blame them when her slim-hipped jeans-clad figure and beautiful face was a magnet for any male with a pulse? No matter how young or old...

From the moment he'd told her that he was willing to let her get to know him—barring one or two no-go areas that he hadn't yet outlined—he'd begun to feel uncharacteristically possessive towards her. It was a new sensation for Drake, and one he'd never experienced before—not even with his ex Kirsty.

As they toured the offices on each floor Layla appeared genuinely fascinated by the different projects his architects and designers were undertaking—taking him and them aback by asking the kind of in-depth questions that he asked his clients himself in a bid to ascertain their construction needs. She was particularly interested in the social and environmental aspects of the various designs, and his younger male architects were only too happy to oblige her with full-length explanations, he saw. The realisation made him proud that he'd hired such good people, but it also made him intensely jealous that they were practically falling over themselves to interact with Layla.

When she stood beside them to examine an architectural model more closely, or leant over their shoulders to view a design or a technical drawing on a computer, did their hearts pound because she was so near as his always did?

He couldn't wait to have her to himself again, and after a couple of hours of this self-inflicted torture Drake was more than ready for them to return to his office.

By the time they reached the executive floor he noted that it was nearing six in the evening and one or two people were packing up for the day, ready to go home. Monica looked decidedly disgruntled as he and Layla arrived back in the outer office, giving him the instant vibe that she wasn't too impressed with his impromptu tour.

'I've rescheduled Sir Edwin Dodd for Monday afternoon at two, but the other appointments you so unfortunately missed all ask if you could call them personally to establish when you'll definitely be available. Other than that...*All Quiet on the Western Front*, as they say—and unless there's anything urgent I'm going home.'

'Thank you, Monica,' he replied, smiling. 'I appreciate your hard work today. I know it can't have been easy cancelling my appointments at the last minute. Are those the phone numbers of the clients that I missed?'

He gestured towards the piece of paper she was holding out to him.

'Yes.' She perfunctorily handed it over, then impatiently hovered as he scanned down the printed list.

'That's fine. Thanks again,' he murmured.

'I'll say goodnight, then.'

Without further ado she slipped on her raincoat, arranged the strap of her bag securely over her shoulder, then exited the office without so much as a backward glance at either him or Layla.

Striding back into his private office, Drake dropped the paper onto his desk and then called out to his guest to come and join him.

'I get the feeling that your secretary's going to view me as enemy number one should I ever dare visit you here again…especially without an appointment.' Stepping into the room and then quietly closing the door behind her, Layla shaped her mouth into a lopsided and rueful smile.

'She runs a tight ship.' Drake grinned. 'She doesn't like it when her captain goes AWOL.'

'I can't say I blame her. You probably missed several important appointments today.'

'Do you really think I care about that right now?'

Planting himself directly in front of her, Drake could no longer resist the impulse to be closer. Watching her talking and smiling with his colleagues had been excruciating torment because he hadn't been free to touch and hold her as he yearned to do. He hadn't even dared catch her eye in case he revealed his longing in front of the people he was ultra-careful to keep his private life a firmly closed book to. At any rate, he fully intended to make up for that self-denial now.

He started by cupping Layla's small, delicately made jaw, and straight away saw her eyes darken and grow even more lustrous beneath the long ebony lashes that swept down over them. His pulse quickened. The sensual silken texture of her skin beneath his fingers made him long to explore all of her without restraint, to drown in her beauty and get drunk on it without the fear of consequences to either his heart or his conscience.

'You mesmerised them out there,' he told her. 'You're going to be the talk of the place for weeks to come.'

'I hardly think so.'

'Then you clearly don't know a lot about the male of the species.'

'That's probably true.'

Her dark eyes were troubled for a moment, and Drake could have kicked himself for reminding her of her dishonest ex-boss.

'Returning to the present, I hope you haven't made any plans for the weekend?' he commented, lowering his voice, holding her gaze with invisible ties that hungrily bound it to his.

'Why's that?'

'Because I'd like you to spend it with me.'

'All of it?'

The wonderment in her voice made Drake chuckle. 'Yes, all of it. And I'll make sure you get home early enough on Sunday that you can get to bed at your usual time.'

'So you're expecting me to stay the night with you? I mean…not just one night but two?'

'Think you could bear it?' He hated the doubt that suddenly surfaced in his mind. He wished he could shoot it dead. 'My house has several guest rooms. If you'd rather we didn't share a room until you get to know me better, then I want you to know I'll respect that.'

'Thanks.'

The gratefully innocent smile she gave him told Drake that he'd said the right thing. He was immensely relieved. He didn't want any more of their days or their evenings together to end in quarrels or disappointment. He'd rather suffer the torment of frustration than that.

'Do I get a kiss for being so thoughtful and considerate?' he teased, smiling.

In answer, Layla reached up on tiptoe and pressed her lips softly against his. Even though his first impulse was to ravish and plunder now that she'd agreed to his request, he summoned some stoic restraint from God only knew where and deliberately kept the kiss on the right side of slow and tender. But even so his hands moved up and down her back, and now and then ventured over the enticing curve of her delectable derrière.

'Time's getting on,' she murmured. 'Shouldn't we go and get something to eat?'

Reluctantly freeing her lips from the sensuous, erotic glide of Drake's gentle and surprisingly tender response to her kiss, Layla found herself staring up at him, noting the tiny bead of sweat glistening in the indentation above his carved top lip and the beginnings of five o'clock shadow already darkening his firm lower jaw. But most of all she registered the carnal hunger his mercurial grey eyes radiated back at her, and wondered how he'd managed to keep it at bay and kiss her with such tender restraint. If the tenor of that lovely kiss had been transformed at any point into a conflagration such as they'd ignited at the building site yesterday, she didn't doubt that her suggestion of getting something to eat wouldn't have been the very first suggestion she made...

Although genuinely relieved when Drake had stipulated he didn't expect them to share a room and that she might like to get to know him a bit better before they became more intimate, she was still breathless at his invitation to stay the night. Not just one night, but two. Funny how things worked out, she mused. When she'd been readying herself to travel up to London to pay him a spontaneous visit she'd somehow found herself packing a toothbrush and a spare pair of undies into her tote...*just in case.* She hadn't been behaving presumptuously, she told herself, just being sensibly prepared for an eventuality such as this. It was surely the practical thing to do when all Layla had to do was glance at the man for her to crave the most lascivious attentions imaginable.

Already it seemed that her vow to be cautious and utilise her common sense around him was seriously coming under fire.

'That sounds like a good idea. How about we go back to my place and I'll cook us something?'

'You can cook?'

His eyes flashed with humour. 'Don't get your hopes up. I'm a million light years away from Cordon Bleu, but I can do basic stuff like a stir fry and spaghetti bolognaise. And if you've got a sweet tooth I have some artisan vanilla ice cream in the fridge.'

'Then lead the way, Chef. My palate is all yours!'

Giving him a teasing grin, Layla moved across to the chair where Drake had left her black leather tote. But before she lifted it, Drake stepped up behind her and reached for her coat.

'Let me help you put this on.'

'Thanks.' She breathed in the heat from his body, along with his arresting cologne, and briefly shut her eyes tight to savour the moment.

'Let's go.' Catching her by her shoulders to spin her round, he dropped a light kiss onto her forehead and smiled.

It was dusk by the time Drake's chauffeur Jimmy pulled up outside the house. Stepping out onto the pavement, Layla registered that the air was surprisingly warm as opposed to the wintry feel of yesterday, when she'd visited the building site with Drake. Her heart leapt with pleasure, because it seemed like a good omen, but her attention was quickly diverted from the balmy temperature to the arresting sight of the impressive Georgian house that loomed up before her.

It was positioned at the end of a precisely mown lawn, with an ornate stone fountain at its centre. The building itself was a perfectly proportioned five-storeyed, elegant townhouse, with large picture windows and a subtly painted green front door that had a carved sunburst pediment above it. The Regency terrace where it was situated was surely one of the best addresses in London, she mused.

Sensing Drake come to stand silently beside her, Layla made sure her tone was perfectly innocuous when she said, 'So this is where you live? It's beautiful.'

'Why don't you come in and see if the inside matches that impression?'

Before she even stepped through the door Layla knew that it would. But what she hadn't expected was that the interior of such a traditional house would be decorated with such an eclectic mix of both traditional *and* modern furnishings and fittings. This was evidenced by the extremely contemporary black metal coatstand that might have been a sculpture standing just inside the door and the beautiful rosewood Regency armchair—both resting against a white marble floor that wouldn't have looked out of place in a luxurious Italian villa.

As Drake led her down the hall to the foot of a staircase with a tasteful green and gold runner, she saw to her surprise that instead of a balustrade it had a sheer glass wall running alongside it. She couldn't help turning towards her companion with a quizzical smile. 'You're a conundrum—you know that?'

His brow furrowed. 'What do you mean?'

'Well…' Sighing thoughtfully, she deliberately chose her words with care. No way did she want to make another inadvertent blunder and offend him. 'You design these incredible state-of-the-art modern buildings, yet you live in a very traditional nineteenth-century house. And when you walk through the door there's another surprise. Instead of traditional furnishings you've plumped for a real mix of old and new. It intrigues me. *You* intrigue me.'

Reaching towards her, Drake all but stopped her breath when he slowly and deliberately tucked some dark strands of her silky hair behind her ear. His silvery eyes glinted with warmth and humour, but Layla detected a surprising hint of vulnerability in the fascinating depths too—a vulnerability that he had to take great pains to keep hidden from the world at large, she was sure.

'I'm very glad that I intrigue you,' he replied. 'Whilst I don't see my wealth and position as some kind of "golden ticket" to get me anything I want, as your ex-boss did, I'll happily accept any advantages that might act in my favour. At least where you're concerned, Layla.'

When he said such seductive things to her he made it very hard for her to gather her thoughts. 'So why do you live in a house like this when you're renowned for designing some of the most contemporary buildings on the planet? That's what I'd like to know.'

'The watchwords for the Regency era were proportion, symmetry and harmony. I rather like that. As well as the desire for aesthetic beauty that the architects used as their guide, there's something very comforting and solid about the houses that were constructed then. But I also like the challenge of modernity…designing buildings that meet more contemporary needs—such as larger spaces to live and work in with plenty of light.' Drake's well-shaped mouth shaped a grin. 'But that's enough talk about design for one day. It feels too much like work. I don't know about you, but my stomach is crying out for some food. Let me show you round the rest of the house, then I'll go and cook our dinner.'

'I admit I'd love something to eat—but I'd also love to see what else you've done here.'

'Then I'll lead the way. But first give me your coat. You can leave your bag on the chair there.' Waiting until Layla had done just that, Drake gestured her to ascend the staircase in front of him. 'It will be my pleasure to show you round.'

After showing Layla three bathrooms with freestanding baths and every conceivable modern convenience that anyone could wish for, several bedrooms with chic French-style beds and original oil paintings on the walls, then a frighteningly elegant living room with exposed brick and French doors that led out onto a charming decked terrace, Drake proposed that they see the rest of the house after they'd eaten. So with that in mind they headed for the kitchen, where he proceeded to extract the ingredients for the stir-fry they'd agreed on from a large stainless steel refrigerator.

The kitchen was another testament to Layla's host's eclectic good taste. Every cabinet, piece of furniture and furnishing had clearly been positioned and designed to complement each other—from the glossed white and grey surfaces of the worktops to the arctic-white marble floor. But in contrast to the highly contemporary look that was one's first impression on entering the room, the evidence of several small antique oils of horses in the park here and there, and a typically high Regency ceiling that hinted at a much more gracious era, reminded visitors that they were in the home of a man who was not wholly mesmerised by designs from the twenty-first century alone.

'I love your home, Drake. I think it's the most inter-esting house I've ever been in,' Layla declared as she watched him reach up to a cabinet for a large stainless steel wok.

Setting the pan down on top of an unlit burner, he turned to face her. 'Can I ask what you mean by "in-teresting"?'

His furrowed brow wore a frown, and she had the distinct feeling that her comment had perturbed him in some way. 'I just mean that it's not the kind of house I expected you to live in, but I really like it...*and* how you've decorated it. That's all.'

'You don't think there's something missing?'

'Like what?'

Dropping his hands to his hips, Drake studied her intently. 'I don't know...warmth, perhaps? Some per-sonal attribute that makes it feel more like a home?'

Intuiting what he was getting at, Layla felt her heart immediately go out to him. 'Do you believe that you lack warmth, Drake?' she asked softly.

Clearing his throat, he tunnelled his fingers rest-lessly through his hair. 'I've lived alone for so long. Sometimes it concerns me that I've become a little too insular. How can I be the best architect I can be if I lose touch with what people really want in a home?'

The statement stunned her. 'You *are* the best archi-tect. Surely your considerable catalogue of work must tell you that? Isn't that why you were commissioned to help regenerate our town?'

The tentative half-smile he gave her was definitely uneasy. 'I don't know why I said what I did. Put it down to me being at work since six this morning. I'm not complaining, but it's been a hell of a long day. Anyway, I ought to crack on with cooking our meal.'

'Is warmth what *you* want in a home?' Layla ventured, her heart bumping beneath her ribs. 'Is it something that you maybe didn't experience as a child?'

The answering warning flash in his eyes was instant and intimidating—like burning embers from a fire that could potentially be dangerous to anyone sitting too close to the flames.

'Remember I told you there were areas in my life where you absolutely don't go? I'm afraid that's one of them.'

Giving his comment her utmost consideration, Layla frowned. 'Do you think if you never talk about those things that they'll somehow just fade away? It's my experience that they don't, Drake. I'm not saying that talking alone makes them easier to deal with, but at least it's a step in the right direction to making your peace with them.'

There was another irritated flash in his eyes, then he swallowed hard. 'The subject is closed. Closed as in you don't bring it up again…at least not until I indicate that you can. Is that clear?'

Mutely Layla nodded. It was definitely clear to her that now wasn't the time to try and delve deeper or prolong the discussion. And she didn't want to spoil their weekend together with a potentially heated argument. She would simply have to accept that she had to tread carefully round Drake until she sensed he was ready for a more intimate discourse about his past. Knowing he might *never* be ready for such a frank discussion, she either had to make her peace with that or walk away.

As he turned back towards the cooker she laid her hand just above his wrist, where a smattering of silken brown hair grazed the otherwise smooth flesh exposed by his rolled-up sweater sleeve. 'Why don't you let me cook the meal? You can pour yourself a nice glass of wine and go and relax in the living room. I'll come and get you when the food is ready.'

'As tempting as that sounds, you're my guest, remember?'

She couldn't help but grin. 'But I'm a very amiable guest, who doesn't mind mucking in when the situation calls for it. The fact that you're so tired definitely warrants my assistance. Go on…pour some wine and go and relax. I'll peer into cupboards and find out where everything is.'

Drake wrestled with her suggestion for just a couple of seconds longer, then relented. The troubled look on his face all but melted away before her eyes.

'You're the kind of guest that I could definitely get used to,' he teased, tipping up her chin and dropping a warm, sexy kiss that was far too fleeting onto her lips.

Layla knew if she slipped her hand behind his head to hold him there a little longer then all further discussion about food and cooking would be put on hold for quite some considerable time…

'Wait until you taste my food and see if you still think that.'

'Will you be okay using the cooker?' he checked.

'Good question.' She sighed, then grimaced as she scanned the large gleaming state-of-the-art hob and oven with its myriad chrome dials and knobs. 'I'm sure I'll be fine. It's an intimidating-looking beast, but surely

I don't need a degree in rocket science to fry a few shrimps and cook some rice…do I?'

Her handsome host chuckled. 'Let me turn on the hob for you.' He flicked a switch, turned a dial, and the hob underneath its black glass shield glowed instantly red. 'It's as easy and as straightforward as that. No degree in rocket science required. Think you'll be okay now?'

'Absolutely.'

'Good. I'll leave you to it, then. Would you like a glass of wine to enjoy while you're cooking?'

'As lovely as that sounds, I'd better not. I might put too much paprika or chilli in the mix, and if I get even the slightest bit intoxicated then our stir-fry will probably be inedible!'

'Warning received.'

Helping himself to a bottle from the sculpted metal rack on the other side of the room, along with a corkscrew and a glass, Drake left Layla with an irresistible lingering smile and a promise in his eyes that—if she let it—could tempt her away from the most sublime culinary feast even if she was starving…

CHAPTER SEVEN

HE KNEW he'd had a lucky escape. But how long could he avoid talking about his past with a woman who made the walls of self-protection he'd carved round himself paper-thin every time she smiled into his eyes, let alone when he kissed her?

His elbows resting on his thighs, Drake stared blankly ahead of him at the glass of ruby-red wine he'd left languishing on the coffee table. He clasped his hands, unclasped them, then clasped them again. In a bid to divert his restlessness he got up and strode across the room to the music centre. When the familiar mournful voice of a male singer-songwriter filled the air he found himself honing in on the lyrics that echoed his own deep-rooted yearning for happiness and peace. Both those longed-for states had been way beyond his grasp ever-since he could remember.

Growing up in an atmosphere of tension and rage had very effectively seen to that. Even at the tender age of six Drake had intuitively understood why his mother had walked out on his father. He'd been a bitter, jealous, angry man who would have kept her under lock and key if he could. She'd had no life with him at all. Yet what Drake didn't understand—and probably never would—

was how she could have walked out on her defenceless son, leaving him with the brute she had married.

His hands reached up to his cheeks to scrub them roughly, as if by doing so he could delete the agonising memory from his mind and heart for ever. He *couldn't,* and his anguished thoughts ran on... How much resolve, faith and sheer grit had it taken for him to overcome his broken and unsupported childhood to reach the position he found himself in now? he asked himself.

Yes, he'd reached the heights of his profession, gained money and a laudable reputation beyond his wildest dreams, yet what good was any of it if at the end of his life he was still alone without someone to share it with? He released a slow harsh breath. With despair in her voice his ex had asked him the same question, and Drake had answered angrily.

'I'm not interested in marriage or having children. That's not for me. If you want that then you should go and find someone else.'

Well, Kirsty had taken him at his word and broken up with him that very night. Drake had heard recently through a mutual acquaintance that she was pregnant and engaged now, and he honestly wished her well. She was a nice woman, but not the soulmate he'd always secretly craved...a soulmate who would accept him for exactly who he was and not try to mould him into some imaginary ideal that she hoped he might become. What he wanted was a woman of infinite understanding with a capacity for unconditional love beyond measuring. It was a tall order.

Was Layla that woman?

Groaning out loud, he shook his head. How could

she be when she was already probing him with uncomfortable questions about his feelings and his past? All he wanted to do was enjoy her body and her company. He wasn't going to speculate much more beyond that. Shutting off the music, he returned to the luxuriously upholstered couch, reaching for his glass of wine and taking a long slug of the rich burgundy before his rear even touched the seat cushions.

Had he done the right thing leaving her to her own devices in the kitchen? he wondered.

His ensuing smile was helplessly wry. Her cooking surely couldn't be any worse than that of the incompetent housekeeper he'd recently let go. Layla worked in a café, for goodness' sake. She was well used to preparing food and making it look presentable. God forgive him, but he very much liked the idea of having her cook for him. In fact—despite his vow that he wouldn't speculate on the future—he very much liked the idea of having her around full-stop...

The shrimp stir-fry had worked out better than Layla had hoped, and she and Drake had finished every scrap. She had to admit that watching him tuck into a meal she'd prepared with such obvious relish had given her a real sense of satisfaction and pleasure—if only because her nervousness round him hadn't caused her to make a complete hash of it.

Immediately after they finished, she automatically stood up to clear the table, her intention to stack the dishwasher.

'Where do you think you're going?'

Although his grey eyes glinted with amusement, Drake's voice had a definitely irritated undertone.

'I was going to rinse the bowls and stack them in the dishwasher.'

'You don't think cooking a meal was more than enough demonstration of domesticity for one evening? Granted I need a housekeeper, but unless I've had a serious lapse of memory I wasn't aware that I'd given the position to you.'

'It's no big deal to clear up.'

'That's not why I invited you home with me.'

His rough-edged tone told her exactly why he'd invited her home, and Layla couldn't deny the same thought had been playing on her mind from the moment she'd set eyes on him back at his office...and even before that, when she'd somehow found herself packing a toothbrush and spare underwear into her tote. But she was still wary about surrendering to her physical desire for him too quickly. It was hard to shake the memory of how she'd been so badly used by her ex-boss.

'You invited me home with you because I presented you with a *fait accompli*, turning up at your office like that.' She stalled, crossing her arms over her chest. 'You probably felt obliged.'

'Obliged? You must be crazy.'

Abruptly getting to his feet, Drake strode round the glass-topped table. He unceremoniously pulled her against him, making her gasp. Suddenly Layla found herself on the most intimate of terms with his hard lean body, and the lust that blazed down at her from his eyes made her heart thump hard.

'I swear to God you've put a spell on me, woman—

because I can't think of anything else but having you in my bed.'

'You told me—you said that you had several guest rooms...that we didn't have to share a room tonight.' Her tongue was so thick she could barely get the words out.

'I must have fooled myself into believing that I had will power, then.'

At the precise moment he stopped talking Layla knew without a doubt that she was fighting a lost cause. Heat was already pouring through her body in a torrent of libidinous need that she could scarce contain, and the idea of spending the night alone in one of Drake's guest rooms instead of in his arms in his bed was akin to attempting to cross a burning hot desert without access to any drinking water. *She simply couldn't do it.*

'And I—I don't want to spend the night alone in one of your spare rooms, Drake.'

'Then come with me,' he husked.

Somehow, her hand held firmly in his, she found herself climbing another glass-lined staircase that led to an upper floor. Barely registering the lush oil paintings that hung here and there on the ivory-coloured walls, or the black velvet sky she glimpsed through the various windows they passed, now *she* was the one who felt as though she was under a spell. When they reached his bedroom she saw that it was an undoubtedly masculine retreat, with clean, uncluttered surfaces and an original restored oakwood floor without so much as a single rug covering even the smallest square of it. The only less than pristine note was the rumpled burgundy silk counterpane on the large king-size bed. It looked as though its owner had attempted to straighten it in a hurry, thought better of it, then irritably decided to just let it be.

Layla refused to entertain the idea that maybe it was rumpled because he'd spent the night in it with a lover. Such a possibility would ruin everything for her.

Briefly letting go of her hand, Drake touched his fingers to a dimmer switch on the wall next to the door and glowing lamps gently filled the room with softly intimate light. Then he closed the door behind them and, turning back, hungrily fastened his hands either side of her hips.

'Let me love you,' he breathed. 'No more talking or making promises we're afraid to keep in case they don't work out. Just let it be you and me alone together in this room…in this bed.'

He touched his lips to hers and the seductive spell already cast became a sensual magical dream that Layla never wanted to wake up from.

The hot thrust of his tongue into her mouth ignited a trail of fire straight to her core, causing her knees to buckle helplessly and making her sag as though drunk against the hard muscular wall of his chest. His arms immediately encircled her waist to hold her upright. Then she was effortlessly lifted up and transported across the room to the rumpled bed.

The moment she was lowered down onto the silken counterpane Layla knew it was imperative to get something off her chest before they went any further. 'I don't know what you've imagined, but I'm not—I'm not very experienced at this. The last occasion when I was intimate with someone was with my boss, and that was the most horrible mistake. Since then…' She screwed up her face. 'Since then I haven't even wanted to get close to a man like this.'

His grey eyes glinting with gentle amusement, Drake touched his palm to her cheek. 'I'm not interested in your past, Layla. The only thing I've imagined is you and me here and now, in this bed, writing a new page to both our histories.'

'I want that too, Drake… But, on the subject of histories, I need to ask has there—has there been anyone that's shared your bed lately?'

The astute grey eyes that seemed to be gifted with the unsettling ability to read her thoughts glinted with ironic disbelief, and perhaps some annoyance too. Layla sensed her cheeks redden helplessly. 'I haven't been intimate with anyone since my ex-girlfriend, and it's been six months since we broke up,' he confided.

'You didn't live together?'

'No. We did not.'

Easing out a relieved sigh, she ventured an apologetic smile. 'I didn't mean to embarrass you, but I had to know.'

'I understand.'

The steady, deeply assessing gaze he returned let her know he did indeed understand.

'Now that we know where we both stand, how about we go back to where we were?'

Feeling suddenly daring, and perhaps a little reckless too, Layla reached up to Drake to cup her hands round his iron jaw and pull his face down to hers. The lower half of his visage was already shaded with bristles, and they inevitably abraded her softer feminine skin as she seductively kissed him, inviting his equally seductive response. Their open-mouthed ravenous kissing quickly and inevitably built into another conflagration, and the passion and fervour that pulsed through Layla's veins secretly frightened her—because whatever came of this hot, wild attraction of theirs she already knew this man had ruined her for anyone else...

Tearing his mouth away from hers and breathing hard, Drake put out a hand and gently pushed her so that she found herself on her back. His silvery gaze searing her like a white-hot laser, he reached down and ripped the two sides of her cotton shirt apart so that the row of tiny buttons that fastened it flew off like confetti.

'I'll buy you a new one,' he murmured.

Before he could apply the same treatment to her front-fastening white lace bra, her heart thundering like a sprinter's as he raced for the finishing line, Layla deftly released the catch herself, so that her bared breasts were suddenly exposed to the silky night air and to her would-be lover's appreciative aroused glance.

'My God...you're even more beautiful than I imagined,' he declared, gravel-voiced.

Hurriedly assisting her to dispose of her torn shirt and bra, seconds later, with his well-developed jeans-clad thighs straddling her, Drake gave her the most intimately seductive smile she'd ever experienced. Then he bent his head to capture one of her tight aching nipples in the scalding cavern of his mouth. She almost hit the roof. The pleasure-pain as his teeth caught the tender flesh and lightly bit was like a lightning strike going straight to her womb. Moving his lips, he gave the same erotic treatment to its twin and, softly whimpering, Layla drove her fingers mindlessly through the silken strands of his hair to hold him to her.

Seconds later he came up for air and sat back on his heels. His hot, slumbrous gaze was filled with unashamed erotic intent, and slowly he unbuckled his leather belt, freed the button at the top of his jeans and unzipped his fly. 'You do the same,' he instructed huskily, at the same time reaching into his back pocket for a foil packet that he expertly ripped open.

Her mouth drying, Layla kicked off her shoes and, with fingers that shook helplessly, unzipped her jeans. Taking hold of both sides, she momentarily lifted her bottom up off the bed so that she could push the heavy denim down over her thighs. In front of her, Drake took the opportunity to discard his own clothing and expertly sheathed his aroused manhood with the latex protection. Her blood pounded with primal need when she saw the sheer magnificence of his strong and proud male body, with toned, well-defined muscles and a flat, lean abdomen. His job might not be physically demanding, but he clearly didn't avoid the necessity to keep himself fit and strong.

Before Layla could rid herself completely of the jeans she had pushed down her legs Drake took over the task with a definitely urgent air, and straight afterwards tugged her silk white panties over her slender hips and jettisoned them carelessly over his shoulder. Bending towards her, he claimed her lips in a crushing hot kiss that not only stole her breath but acted like a seismic eruption in her already overheated blood. He was still kissing her when she felt his hand reach down to firmly press her thighs apart and brush once, twice,

three times over her sensitive feminine core. The pleasure that intimate caress instigated was so intense that,
because he was still kissing her, she had to swallow the
low moan that immediately threatened to surface. But
when he suddenly drove himself deeply inside her in
a possessive motion that bordered on the passionately
rough Layla freed her lips from his to gasp her shock
and pleasure out loud against his shoulder.

She wasn't a virgin, but apart from the unfortunate
encounter with her ex-boss she hadn't had sex for a
long time, and her feminine muscles were tighter than
she'd imagined they would be. Consequently she felt
every exquisite inch of her lover. And now, even though
there was no question that Drake desired and wanted
her, insecurity surfaced. She had so little experience
in knowing how to please a man. What if their lovemaking didn't live up to his expectations? What if she
disappointed him?

Seconds later both those unhelpful thoughts flew
instantly from her mind as he started to move faster
and more rhythmically inside her and she automatically wrapped her arms round his strongly corded neck
to hold on. Making love with Drake was like riding
the most tumultuous exhilarating wave, Layla thought.

As the inflammatory silkily hot sensations building
inside her went way beyond the point where she could
control them she dug her fingernails into his hard-muscled back and cried out as wave after wave of erotic
velvet heat consumed her. With a deep guttural groan,
and the light lustre of perspiration standing out on his
handsome forehead, Drake suddenly stilled, and she

knew that he too had reached the sensual pinnacle of their impassioned union.

Her heart leapt when he didn't immediately move away, as she'd thought he might. Instead he leant forward and, with his face just bare inches from hers—so close that she could almost count every lustrous dark eyelash that swept over his dazzling silver gaze—said, 'You may not have a lot of experience, my angel, but when it comes to satisfying a man's desire, trust me—you have everything that's needed and much more besides.' He finished this comment with a sexy boyish grin that all but stopped her heart.

'You're not so bad yourself.' She smiled.

After dropping a warm and lazy kiss on her surprised mouth, he lay down with his head between her breasts and trailed his fingers gently up and down her bare arm. Revelling in his deliciously erotic male scent, and the weight of his hard, lean body pressing her firmly down into the mattress, Layla resolved to memorise every moment of this ardent union with Drake—knowing that whatever happened to her in the future she would never forget it…

The second time they made love that night it was no less passionate, but the caresses on both sides were infused with tenderness and much more considered. To Layla's delight, Drake paid particular attention to ensuring she received just as much pleasure and satisfaction as he did—if not more—and in turn she loved the fact that her intuition and desire led her to discovering just where and how he liked to be touched. In that discovery all her doubts about knowing how to please him disappeared.

Afterwards, they fell asleep in each other's arms in the softly illuminated lamplit room.

After waking in the middle of the night because she was in need of the bathroom, Layla quickly returned to the sumptuous dishevelled bed she had so briefly vacated and switched off the lamps on the gleaming walnut cabinets that stood either side of it. The room was plunged into a near pitch-black darkness that was punctuated by the sound of Drake's gentle breathing. He appeared to be in the deepest of slumbers.

Pleased at the thought that their lovemaking had helped him to relax, she snuggled down beside him, gently laid her arm across his abdomen and closed her eyes.

What could have been no more than a few minutes later, she found her arm violently pushed aside with an anguished shout.

'Drake, what is it?' Her hand quickly fumbling for the light switch on the lamp next to her, Layla pushed up into a sitting position as once again the room was suffused with a softly diffused glow.

Hearing the laboured breathing of the man lying by her side, she saw with a start that his brow was studded with perspiration, almost as though he was sweating out a fever. When he turned his head to look at her she saw that his wide-eyed gaze was nothing less than terrified. In the depths of his haunted grey eyes she saw the pain and horror of a man who had been shown a devastating glimpse of hell and believed himself to be trapped in that realm, perhaps for ever.

Leaning towards him, she cautiously touched his shoulder, softly murmuring, 'You must have had a nightmare…a bad dream. But it's gone now, Drake. You're safe and here with me. There's nothing to worry about, I promise.'

In response, he shrugged off her hand and roughly drove his fingers through his hair. Then he sat up. After that he simply fell into a kind of stunned trance, remaining mute. His harsh breaths continued for several more seconds before eventually returning to a more regular rhythm.

Still staring straight ahead of him he spoke. And his voice sounded as if it scraped over gravel when he declared suddenly, 'You turned out the lights.'

Tugging the silk counterpane protectively up over her breasts, Layla felt inexplicable fear wash over her like an icy river. The statement had sounded like an accusation. 'I did it automatically…when I returned from the bathroom.'

'I don't sleep with the lights out…*ever.*'

'I'm sorry. I didn't know that. If it makes things more comfortable for you, I can sleep in one of your guest rooms for the rest of the night, if you like?'

The scowl on his handsome face as he turned towards her was forbidding. 'No! I don't want that.'

Layla's blood ran cold for a second time. 'All right, then, I'll—I'll stay here with you.'

'I'm sorry, Layla. I'm sorry if I scared you.' He grimaced.

'It must have been a terrible dream. Do you think that you could tell me about it?'

Although his troubled expression had started to ease

a little, Drake stared at her as if once again cornered by something frighteningly threatening. 'Please don't ask me. It's not something I feel ready to share and I don't know if I ever will.'

'This is one of those places you don't want me to go? Is that what you're telling me?'

He nodded and looked desolate for a moment, and although she desperately wanted to know Layla knew this wasn't the time to enquire more deeply into why he didn't sleep with the lights off. What he needed right now was unquestioning understanding, she decided, and maybe some consolation as well. Nightmares could disturb the strongest of characters.

Pushing aside the silk counterpane, she moved towards him, cupped his jaw, then tenderly kissed him on the mouth. It was like touching flame to dry tinder, and straight away the heat that flared between them made him haul her onto his lap so that her thighs spread over his, and the clash of lips, teeth and tongues became even more urgent and demanding.

When Drake moved his hands to her hips to position her over his already hard member, then pushed up inside her, Layla threw back her head and let loose a deep throated groan. She was still a little tender from their previous energetic coupling, but in a way this raw and elemental coming together was even more inevitable and necessary than both those occasions— because right now Drake really *needed* her. And for the first time in her life she discovered that she finally knew what it was to really need a man too...

As he started to move more deeply inside her his palms hungrily cupped and kneaded her breasts. Every now and then his fingers and thumbs tugged at her rigid nipples, sending fiery heat directly to her womb. With her tousled dark hair falling around her face Layla stared back into his blazing lustful glance, her heart pounding so hard it was difficult to think straight. But most of all she was struck dumb by the sheer intensity of the feelings she saw reflected in his eyes.

'You are one seriously sexy and beautiful woman,' he declared huskily, his breathing ragged with unashamed need and desire.

Leaving her breasts, his hands reached up to pull her face down to his. Just as their lips made contact she sensed him buck beneath her, and even as he kissed her it was with a mixture of shock and pleasure that she registered the hot liquid heat that spurted into her womb. But there was barely time to contemplate the event because in the very next moment her own climax burst upon her. Freeing her lips from his still demanding mouth and oh-so-seductive moist tongue, she let her head fall against Drake's hard-muscled shoulder with a breathless gasp that was quickly followed by several more…

CHAPTER EIGHT

LAYLA was taking a shower and washing her hair. Having left her with one of his finest cotton shirts to replace the pretty blouse he had ripped open last night, Drake had nipped out to a local French *patisserie* to buy warm croissants and a pot of speciality fruit jam for them to enjoy with their morning coffee. Even as his mind teemed with provocative detailed reruns of the events of last night his body throbbed from the passionate lovemaking they had shared. He'd had little sleep, God knew, but this morning he felt on top of the world.

But as he let himself back inside the house, then made his way into the kitchen, it hit him like a steel wave crashing into his gut—how he had awoken in the suffocating dark and for chilling seconds been plunged back into the nightmare of his childhood.

Reaching for the kettle, he witnessed his hand shake slightly and cursed furiously. He still didn't know why Layla hadn't pressed him more for an explanation. Under the circumstances she'd had a perfect right to. What must she have thought when he'd told her that he never slept without the lights on?

He caught his breath when he remembered what she had done instead of probing him for answers. With her beautiful body moving over him, taking him to heaven instead of hell, Drake had quickly forgotten his nightmare of being locked in his bedroom in the dark and then hearing the slamming of the door that told him his father had gone out to the pub.

Even when his father had returned he'd never come up to unlock his son's door or check if he was okay. No, Drake would be forced to stay there until he'd cried himself to sleep.

Needing to shake off the hurt that suffused him at the memory, he filled the kettle from a filtered water jug and pressed the switch for it to boil. Then he measured generous spoonsful of aromatic coffee grounds into a cafetière and arranged the warm croissants he'd bought on two patterned side plates. As he reached into the fridge for some milk, another disturbing realisation stopped him in his tracks. Instead of cursing, this one made him shut the fridge door dazedly and stand there shaking his head in wonder and disbelief.

Caught up in the vortex of uncontrollable need and lust last night, along with the fantasy that maybe Layla was the woman who really *could* help put an end to his nightmares and loneliness for good, if she genuinely grew to care for him, he hadn't given a thought to using protection. And, having not had sex for a long time until her boss had so deviously seduced her by plying her with drink, he doubted very much that Layla was on the pill. In which case it was entirely possible that Drake had made her pregnant. If such an event occurred then it was the most reckless act he'd committed since he'd left his teenage years behind and become a man.

'Hello, again… Are you making coffee, by any chance?'

Standing in the doorway with a shaft of sunlight playing upon her newly washed dark hair, wearing Drake's too-large pristine white shirt over fitted blue jeans, his ravishing lover took his breath away. It struck him that he'd never seen a woman look more beautiful or desirable as Layla did right then.

As he moved towards her his heart skipped a beat. 'Hi. Not only am I making coffee, but I've been out to buy us some croissants and fruit preserve too.'

Walking into his arms as though it was the most natural thing in the world for her to do, she teased, 'You must be trying to win the Most Considerate Man of the Year award, then. Don't worry, as far as I'm concerned you've already won the prize.' Reaching up and kissing him on the mouth, she glanced up at him from beneath her lustrous dark lashes and blushed charmingly.

Drake chuckled. 'Ain't that the truth…? I certainly *have* won the prize.' As his arms tightened a little more round her slender hourglass waist, he smiled. 'By the way, I'm never going to wash that shirt of mine again when you give it back.'

'Why?'

'Because it will have the scent of your very sexy body all over it… From now on it's elevated to being my favourite item of clothing.'

'Well, on that rather provocative little note, I think we should sit down and partake of those delicious-looking croissants you've bought…of course that's as soon as you get your act together and make the coffee, Mr Ashton,' she added mischievously.

As she extricated herself from his arms to move towards the table he caught hold of her hand and, lifting it to his lips, reverently kissed her fingers.

'What was that for?'

'Do I need a reason other than that I simply felt like it?' Feeling his heart swell with the kind of addictive warmth he couldn't ever remember feeling before, Drake kept a hold of Layla's hand, reluctant to let it go. 'That's not strictly true. I just wanted to thank you for last night…for understanding.'

It was a relief to him to know that he didn't have to say any more than that, because staring back into her compassionate brown eyes he knew no other explanation was necessary…at least for now.

'I hated seeing you so distressed. Whatever horrors you were dreaming about, I just wanted to try and help you forget them.'

'Trust me…' He grinned. 'You did.'

As he released her hand so he could return to the counter and make the coffee Layla frowned and briefly touched his arm, indicating that she wanted to extend their little discussion. 'Drake?'

'What is it?'

'Last night when we—when we made love again… we didn't use protection.'

'I was standing here thinking about that just before you came in.' He rubbed his hand round his chiselled jaw and grimaced. 'I'm usually much more careful about such things, but I'm afraid that the power of events rendered my common sense obsolete.' As if subconsciously illustrating the fact, he moved his heated glance helplessly up and down her figure. 'I definitely

wasn't thinking straight, that's for sure. It's understandable that you've been worrying yourself sick.'

'What happened wasn't just down to you, Drake.'
Shrugging a rueful shoulder, Layla nonetheless made
her gaze direct as she levelled it at him. 'You weren't the
only one who wasn't thinking straight. But I'm going to
have to find the nearest chemist when we've finished
our breakfast, so that I can buy an emergency contraceptive pill.'

Drake didn't know why, but a deeply unsettled feeling swept through him. If he had to analyse it he'd
probably describe it as a sense of indignant protest...
as if something he hadn't even known was precious
was being threatened and being taken away from him.

'Anyway, I'll have my breakfast and then head out
and find a chemist. Do you know if there's one nearby?'

Clenching his jaw a little, he answered soberly,
'There is. Don't worry. I'll take you there.'

'Thanks.' Lowering her glance, she wrapped her
arms protectively round her chest, as though perturbed.
Then she silently made her way over to the table and
sat down.

Right then Drake couldn't find the courage to ask
her why she suddenly looked so sad...

The day was surprisingly fair, and they agreed to
kick off their weekend break with a visit to one of the
capital's well-known art galleries. They were running
separate exhibitions by two influential British art-
ists whose work Layla and Drake both admired and
were keen to view. But as they walked slowly through
the lofty wooden-floored galleries with the same rev-

erential sense of visitors to a hushed cathedral, the morning-after pill that Layla had purchased from the chemist all but burned a guilty hole in her coat pocket.

Between them they seemed to have made an unspoken agreement not to discuss the topic again, and certainly Drake hadn't suggested she take the contraceptive straight away. It was probably utter madness, and Layla didn't know why she should be so hesitant in swallowing the pill with the mineral water she'd purchased. Except that if she was really honest with herself she *did* know why. Since last night her heart had been full of a passionate romantic longing she couldn't seem to control, and as she walked round the gallery with her hand firmly encased in her handsome companion's it just grew stronger and stronger.

What would it be like to be the mother of this enigmatic man's child? she wondered. Would he adore his son or daughter as much as Layla undoubtedly knew she would? There was still so much about Drake that she didn't know—places that he'd warned her to stay away from… It had crossed her mind more than once today that the nightmare he'd had last night probably involved some disturbing memories from his past. *What were they?* He'd told her yesterday that he hadn't known much joy in the house where he'd grown up, only sorrow. If only she could persuade him to share some of the experiences that haunted him it might help dispel the hold they had on him.

Stopping in front of a jolting 'warts and all' self-portrait of the artist whose work they were viewing, Layla stared back into bottomless blue eyes that seemed so full of pain and regret and desires left unfulfilled and expelled a helpless sigh of commiseration.

Turning his head to study her, Drake was immediately concerned. 'What's wrong?'

'He looks like such a tormented soul, bless him.'

'By all accounts he was. A latter-day Van Gogh who was plagued by depression and eventually took his own life. But at least while he lived he did what he loved.'

'I suppose we should thank God for small mercies. Do you still love what *you* do, Drake?'

'Of course.'

There was no hesitation in his answer, and Layla was pleased that at least there was one area of his life where unhappiness and a sense of isolation didn't dog him as she was beginning to guess it often did. 'Did you ever do any drawing or painting as a child?' she asked conversationally.

A shadow immediately stole across his face. 'Only when I was at school.'

'And did you enjoy it?'

A corner of his mouth quirked, nudging an engaging dimple in the side of his cheek and dispelling the shadow she'd glimpsed. 'I did. Turns out that I had a bit of a talent for it… I guess it was the precursor of my love of designing houses—which is why I chose architecture as a career. I suppose, as well, I always believed that our homes should be beautiful, and if I designed them I could make them as beautiful as I wanted.'

'That's a lovely intention. You never drew or dabbled with paints at home?'

'No.'

It was a flat no, without any suggestion or possibility of further elucidation, Layla realised.

'Didn't you want to?' she ventured.

Her companion stayed worryingly silent.

'Clearly this must be another one of those places that I'm not supposed to go, then?' She couldn't prevent the note of exasperation that crept into her voice.

He lifted a dark eyebrow and lightly shook his head. 'My home-life was hardly conducive to having the freedom to draw or experiment with paint or colour. That's all I'll tell you for the time being. Perhaps we can talk about this later? Right now I think we should just enjoy the art, don't you? After all, it's what we came for.'

Although Drake's response might not be as warm as she could wish, it did stir a faint hope in her that at last he was coming round to the idea of discussing his past with her.

For some reason all of a sudden she couldn't abide the thought of the all-important pill burning a hole in her pocket. What was she *thinking* of, delaying taking it? She wasn't an immature teenager, for goodness' sake! She was a fully-grown woman and the situation called for her to be sensible and realistic.

What on earth had possessed her to become so entranced by the crazy notion of having Drake's baby? They weren't in a committed relationship. She worked in a low-paid job in a café, and Drake had an important commission to help regenerate their underachieving impoverished town and help set it on its feet again. The last thing he or she needed was to be faced with the prospect of having a baby. Add to this the fact that they'd only known each other for the shortest time, and this sizzling sexual heat they had for each other would likely burn itself out very soon, and it simply confirmed that her decision to take the damn pill was absolutely the right one. Anything else was simply delusional… perhaps *dangerously* so.

Yet it didn't help the ache in Layla's heart whenever she so much as glanced at Drake to become any less intense.

Glancing round, she saw the sign for the ladies' room at the far end of the gallery and, abruptly freeing her hand from his clasp, murmured, 'Excuse me, but I need to go to the Ladies. I won't be long.'

'Layla?' His grey eyes glinted with such concern that it made her insides execute a cartwheel.

'Yes?'

'Are you okay?'

'Yes, I'm fine.'

'When you get back we'll go upstairs to the restaurant and get some coffee. After we've seen everything we want to see here I'd like to take you shopping, to buy a new blouse to replace the one I ripped.'

'There's no need.' Scalding heat poured into her cheeks at the memory of just *how* he had managed to rip her blouse, and as if he'd read her mind Drake's grey eyes twinkled in amusement.

'Yes, there is,' he argued with a husky catch in his voice. 'I want my shirt back.'

She knew he was trying to make amends for his curt tone earlier, and while it warmed her to think that he cared about her feelings, and about replacing the blouse he'd torn in the heat of passion last night, she couldn't deny that she suddenly felt unspeakably desolate at the idea that other than sexually he probably wasn't going to let her get anywhere *near* the wounded man she guessed hid behind the self-contained façade of wealth and success he projected after all. She was feeling less and less sure he really would discuss his past with her.

'Okay. We'll have coffee, see the rest of the exhibition, then go shopping.' Turning away, she headed briskly towards the end of the gallery without checking even once to see if his mercurial haunting gaze followed her progress...

By the time she emerged from the ladies' room Layla had sat in the toilet cubicle breaking her heart for at least ten minutes. Then, when she'd calmed down sufficiently to realise the utter futility of her behaviour, she'd stepped out in front of the bank of unforgiving bathroom mirrors to find her eye make-up tellingly smudged and her face as white as a ghost's. After re-applying her make-up and spritzing the inside of her wrists with the last of her perfume—a precious leftover luxury from her time working in London—she'd finally swallowed the contraception down with at least half a bottle of water, tossed back her hair, lifted her chin and returned to the gallery to find Drake.

She spied him sitting on one of the long wooden benches interspersed here and there in front of the displayed paintings. With his hands loosely linked across his knees and his neck bent because he was staring down at the floor, it wasn't hard to deduce that he wasn't meditating on the stunning art. No, once again he was lost in a compelling world of his own.

'Drake?'

'You're back.'

Layla was dumbfounded by the relief and delight in his eyes. Giving her a smile more precious to her right then than all the world's diamonds, he stood up and gathered her into his arms. Transfixed, she felt as if the priceless art along with every single soul in the gallery simply disappeared. All she could focus on right then were the carved masculine lips that slowly but surely moved towards hers to greet her with an all too brief but hungry kiss. The velvet touch of his mouth and the delicious sensation of his strong arms urging her against him were a powerful antidote to the distressing doubt and fear that had accompanied her to the ladies' room.

As Drake lifted his head to glance down at her she smiled and asked, 'Did you think I wasn't coming back?'

'You were gone a long time. I was getting worried.'

'Well, there was no need.' Seeing by his expression that he wasn't convinced, she felt her heart skip a beat. 'What were you worrying about? Did you think I'd slipped out the back way and abandoned you?' she teased.

'Don't joke about something like that.'

Immediately Layla saw that her unfortunately phrased question had touched a raw nerve and she winced in remorse. 'I meant nothing by it—honestly.'

A searching look crept into his eyes. Lowering his voice he asked, 'Did you take that pill?'

'Yes…I did.'

He stared back at her as if totally at a loss to know what to say.

'It's all right,' she assured him hurriedly. 'It was the right thing to do…the *only* thing.'

'Of course it was.'

'Is there something about what happened between us that you'd like to talk about?'

'What else is there to say?'

'I suppose there's plenty to say if you're willing to be more open about your feelings. You said you'd let me get to know you, remember? I can't help worrying about how I'm going to accomplish that if you keep on blocking every single avenue I try to go down.'

He dropped his arms from round her waist and folded them across his chest instead—across the sky-blue cashmere sweater he wore beneath his stylishly battered black leather jacket. 'I know you're not going to like my answer, but this really isn't the ideal venue for a frank and personal discussion. Why don't we wait until we get back to my place and talk about things then, like I suggested?'

Her heart thudding, once again Layla felt infused with hope. 'You mean it? You'll really talk to me openly and frankly and not refuse to answer any questions you're uncomfortable with? To reassure you—I'm not some unscrupulous reporter who wants to write tittle-tattle about your life, Drake... I—I really care about you.'

'Do you?'

It hurt her heart that there was suspicion amid the flare of hope she detected in his eyes. 'Of course I do. Why do you think I chose to come up to London of my own accord to see you? Also, in spite of the stupid mistake I made with my boss, I'm not in the habit of having one-night stands. I slept with you because it meant something to me...don't you know that?' She stole a quick glance round to check they weren't being overheard.

Drake's broad shoulders lifted in a shrug, and the slight flush beneath his carved cheekbones illustrated his discomfort at the highly personal turn their conversation had taken. 'Okay... I'll agree to be as candid with you as I can,' he relented, 'but only if you respect that talking about my life and my feelings isn't a muscle I flex easily. If any particularly difficult areas come up, I don't want you to be aggrieved or to take it personally if I don't feel I can discuss them.'

In answer, Layla caught and held one of the large smooth hands with its callused forefinger and thumb that were testimony that he didn't shy away from hard physical work as well as more artistic and creative pursuits. 'I'm not the Spanish Inquisition, Drake. If there are things you really don't feel able to discuss then of course I'll respect that. And, just so that we're even, I promise to answer any questions you want to ask about *me*...deal?'

Raising a gently mocking eyebrow, he draped his arm affectionately round her shoulders and pulled her into his side. 'Now I know where the phrase "she who must be obeyed" comes from,' he joked.

CHAPTER NINE

BEFORE they went home Drake took Layla to an exclusive boutique in Mayfair to buy her a new blouse. From the moment he selected the shop to the minute they walked through the door he could sense her growing uneasiness with the project. He couldn't understand why she seemed so reticent. There wasn't one single woman he was acquainted with who didn't like shopping. But then he already knew that Layla was unique. She was constantly surprising him.

The wafer-thin blonde assistant in her short-skirted dogtooth suit lit up like a hundred-watt lightbulb when they entered. Whether or not that was because she scented that Drake had money, he didn't particularly care, so long as Layla was satisfied she'd acquired a blouse she was pleased with and would wear.

When, at his urging, she reluctantly started to examine the exquisite silk blouses on the very selective display rails and picked practically the first item she looked at, as if she couldn't wait to get out of the shop, Drake shook his head with a teasing smile.

'Do you really want that one?' he asked doubtfully, privately thinking how prim and proper the elegant white garment appeared, even if it *was* made from the finest French silk crêpe.

'I don't want you to buy me one at all, if I'm honest.' Layla sighed, self-consciously brushing her hair back with her hand. 'I'm quite happy to wear your shirt until I get home.'

'But you're not going home until tomorrow, remember?'

'Then you can lend me another shirt tomorrow. I'm sure you must own more than one.'

Her caramel-brown eyes sparkled with a mixture of defiance and merriment, and for a long moment Drake was transfixed by the heated longing that gripped him. It struck him like a thunderbolt right then that he was quite simply crazy about her, and almost couldn't bear the thought of having her out of his sight. Excepting the mother who had deserted him, he'd never needed *anyone* that much before. The feeling was terrifying and exhilarating all at the same time…

He levelled his glance. 'As great as my shirt looks on you, I'd really like to buy something exclusively for *you*…something pretty and sexy that will make you think of me every time you wear it next to your skin.'

He was rewarded with the most bewitching and pretty blush.

'You choose something for me then,' she suggested softly.

He didn't miss the slight catch in her voice that told him she'd definitely been aroused by what he'd said. With an undeniable sense of satisfying male pride, and only too happy to oblige, Drake selected a couple of much more delicate specimens, made from what was labelled 'silk Charmeuse' and handed them to her.

'They're far too flimsy,' she protested, dark eyes widening. 'They look more like lingerie.'

'Then they're just what we're looking for,' he taunted gently.

'They are?'

'Trust me—you're going to have the most appreciative audience you can imagine when you wear them.'

The smooth skin between Layla's elegant dark brows creased a little. 'I only need one blouse, Drake, not two.' Leaning towards him, she lowered her voice to a near whisper. 'Have you seen the prices on these?' Turning the labels that were so prettily attached to the garments with slim pink and blue ribbons towards him, she seemed intent on his noting them.

He didn't even trouble to spare them a glance. Instead he chuckled, then tenderly cupped her delicate jaw in the palm of his hand. 'That's the last thing you need to worry about, angel… And I'm not about to apologise for having money just because it makes you uncomfortable either.'

Her lips curved in a conciliatory smile. 'Okay, I'll go and try them on. Seeing as you've picked them out, it would be rude not to. Besides, it's very hard to refuse you anything when you look at me like that,' she breathed.

'How *am* I looking at you? Tell me.'

'Like I'm the gourmet meal you've been anticipating enjoying all day.'

With a provocative grin that sent the blood in Drake's

veins plunging helplessly south, she spun round on her heel and politely asked the assistant to show her to the changing room.

As Drake returned to the living room and placed the two cups of coffee he'd made down on the carved Regency table positioned in front of the sofa, Layla smiled up at him, commenting, 'Mmm…just what the doctor ordered after that great spaghetti you rustled up for dinner.' Curling her hair round her ear, her expression pensive, she added, 'Come and sit down.'

'I was intending on doing exactly that.'

'We've had a wonderful day together, haven't we?'

'We have indeed.'

She fell silent for a few moments, then said, 'Drake?'

'What's on your mind?'

'Do you think we could have that talk of ours now?'

Momentarily distracted by the very feminine ivory-silk blouse she now wore in place of his white shirt, noting as he'd done at dinner that the sheer material meant he could see right through it to the pretty lace bra she had on underneath, Drake didn't immediately register her question. When the words finally sank in his stomach plunged to his boots. Clearly there weren't going to be any preliminaries to this little discussion of theirs, and it was becoming worryingly clear that he wasn't going to be able to hide the truth of his past from her any longer.

His skin prickled hotly, and for one sickeningly uncomfortable moment he felt akin to a cornered animal. Raking his fingers through his hair, he dropped down onto the pinstriped armchair at the other side of the table, resting his forearms on his jeans-clad thighs with a heavy sigh.

'So what do you want to talk about? My favourite music? Or maybe you'd like to hear what my top ten favourite movies are?' He was hedging for time, using humour as a shield to divert any immediately awkward or difficult questions. But when he saw the concerned frown on Layla's beautiful face Drake felt oddly guilty for taking such a cowardly tack.

'Whilst I'd love to know what music you like, also what your favourite movies are, right now I'd like you to tell me a bit more about yourself. Then, as I said before…you can ask me things too.'

Linking his hands, he locked his glance with hers in a deliberately challenging stare. 'Then why don't you ask me a direct question and I'll endeavour to answer it?'

'All right, then.' She nervously licked her lips and curled her hair round her ear again. 'I'd like you to tell me a bit about your childhood.'

'What would you like to know, exactly?'

'Was it hard for you, being an only child?'

'Compared to what? Being one of a large brood? How would I know, since that wasn't my experience?'

'Okay, then, perhaps you'll tell me instead what it was like for you growing up in the area?'

It was the question Drake had feared the most, but he resolved himself to answer it because he didn't want Layla to believe even for a second that he lacked the courage to tell her.

'What was it like? In two words…miserable and lonely.' Moving his head from side to side, he clasped and unclasped his hands. 'I had a mother whose mind was always on leaving, and a father who was a bully and a drunk. After she left his bullying moved up to a whole new level. You can't imagine how creative he could be when it came to devising punishments for me. Consequently I was always dreaming of ways to escape. When my art teacher at school took a serious interest in my ability for drawing and design, and suggested I might try to become an architect, I latched onto the possibility as though it was a lifeline—which indeed it was. From that moment on I didn't care what my father did to me, because I knew that one day I'd get away... I'd carve a whole new life for myself and escape from both him *and* our drab little town for good.'

'So how did you do that? Did you get the grades to go to university?'

'Yes. I worked damned hard and fortunately I did.'

'Did you see your father at all after you went?' As she took a sip of her coffee, then carefully set the blue and white cup back in its elegant saucer, Layla's dark-eyed glance was thoughtful.

'No.' In return, Drake's smile was helplessly bitter. 'I only returned once after I left, and that was to go to his funeral. Needless to say I was the only mourner. Let's put it this way: he wasn't the most popular guy in the world.'

'So how did he die? What happened to him?'

'The silly fool smashed into a central reservation on the motorway whilst driving under the influence of alcohol. He was killed outright.' Drake agitatedly tunnelled his fingers back and forth through his hair. 'It wasn't even his car. He'd borrowed it from some drinking crony who stupidly believed he'd return it in one piece. When I talked to the man he told me that my father was planning on driving up to the university to visit me. That's why he'd borrowed the car. Unless he'd had some profound religious conversion and wanted to atone for his past ill-treatment of me, I very much doubt that it was true.'

'My God, Drake!'

Layla's expression was almost distraught, he saw. Knowing her kind heart, it wouldn't have surprised him to learn that she was feeling compassion for his loser of a father.

'I'm so sorry you had to face such a horrendous and sad ordeal on your own,' she murmured, twisting her hands together in her lap. 'It must have been hard enough for you not to have someone back at home, sending you love and support while you were away studying, but then to hear that your father had died…and possibly on his way to visit you as well…?'

'You think it was *hard* for me, do you?' he challenged, his temper rising. The old, painful wounds that he privately nursed, encrusted with bitterness and resentment, were still apt to make him feel murderous. 'The only thing I felt when I heard the bastard had died was relief like you can't possibly imagine!'

'You said he was cruel. Was his cruelty the reason you don't like sleeping without the light on?'

Sensing all the colour drain from his face, Drake shivered hard at the haunting reminder of his appalling home-life when he was a boy. 'Every night he'd remove the lightbulbs in my bedroom and lock me in for the night in the dark. More often than not he'd go out and leave me on my own until the early hours of the morning, and even when he returned he wouldn't knock on my door to check and see if I was all right.'

'Why? Why did he do that?'

Drake's lips twisted in disgust. 'He told me it would make me a man. Personally, I think he did it simply because he *could*.'

'You should have reported him…told someone at your school what he was doing. That kind of inhuman behaviour is child abuse, Drake.'

'You make it sound so simple—but how does a frightened child tell someone his private horror story when he feels the most sickening shame about it? When he secretly believes he must have done something bad to deserve it?'

'You did nothing wrong. You were only a little boy, for goodness' sake! Your father was the adult in the family. He should have taken proper care of you. You aren't supposed to "deserve" love and care. It's the fundamental right of human children everywhere. I wish someone could have told you that so you wouldn't have carried such shame and fear around with you all these years.'

'Well, they didn't, and I managed. End of story.'

'You may have managed to get by despite your circumstances, but that's not the end of the story, Drake… not if you're still afraid to sleep in the dark and are plagued with nightmares.'

'That's not your concern. I deal with it. Shall we change the subject?'

'I've one more question. Do you mind?'

Before Layla got the chance to ask it, he interjected

quickly, feeling bleak. 'I *do* mind, as I'm sure you know, but ask anyway. Then it's my turn.'

'What about your mother, Drake?'

Her luminous dark eyes were tender and her tone was infinitely gentle, respectful of the now tense atmosphere between them…like an intrepid novice explorer negotiating the walk across a frozen river for the very first time. One false move could make the ice splinter and send her plunging into the freezing waters below.

'Did you ever see her again after she left?'

'No, I didn't. She obviously just wanted to put her seven years with my father behind her—start a new life somewhere else and forget about us both.'

'Why would she want to forget about her little son? I'm sure that can't be true, Drake. Her heart must have been breaking in two to leave you behind with a man like your father. She must have been absolutely desperate for her to carry out such an act.'

He gulped down some of his coffee, then wiped the back of his hand across his mouth. 'Desperate or not, she presumably made a better life for herself somewhere else and decided not to risk ruining it by coming back for me.'

Restlessly he pushed to his feet, absolutely hating the misery and pain that made him feel unbearably exposed and vulnerable in front of a woman he already cared too much about. A woman whose rejection of him, if it ever came, he would probably never recover from. For a few desperate moments he despised Layla for the power she unknowingly held over him. He was also furious with her for goading him into revisiting the tormented past he'd striven so hard to forget.

Before he knew it, Drake had turned on her with a fierce scowl. 'Are you happy now? What else do you want to know about me so that you can sit there smugly making your analysis? An analysis that will no doubt help you feel *so* much better about your own comparatively trivial disappointments.'

Stricken, Layla rose slowly to her feet and folded her arms over the pretty diaphanous blouse Drake had taken such pleasure in seeing her wearing. 'We're not having a competition about who's suffered the most, Drake. All I wanted to do…all I *hoped* to do was get to know you a little, so that you wouldn't feel the need to be anyone other than yourself…your *real* self…around me. Yes, we've all had sadness and disappointment in our lives—and some of us, like you, have experienced dreadfully unhappy childhoods… But that doesn't mean we should be ashamed of our pasts or try to hide them. Sometimes it's our most challenging and difficult experiences that help us evolve into the compassionate and thoughtful people we are.'

'Is that how you felt when your unscrupulous exboss fleeced you of your life savings…*compassionate*?'

Hearing the almost cruel mockery in Drake's tone, Layla hugged her arms over her chest even more, needing to protect herself. *Had she pushed him too far and too soon in getting him to talk about his past?* What if her kindly meant questioning to get him to open up a little about himself so that they might forge a closer bond had done nothing but turn him against her and made him suspicious of her motives? If they didn't have trust then they had nothing worth having at all.

'No,' she replied. 'I didn't feel remotely compassionate towards him. I was too busy blaming him for cheating me and blaming myself for being an idiot for trusting him in the first place…for being so gullible in trusting my savings to his little scheme and for letting him seduce me.'

'He got you drunk.'

Unhappily she nodded her head. 'Yes, but I let him. I could have said no to him, but he was a charmer and I fell under his spell. Anyway, that aside, after some time had gone by I definitely felt as though I'd learned a lesson I'd never forget. For a start, I'd have loved to give the money I had to Marc, to help the business. As for my boss, I know that if he carries on cheating people like he does then inevitably life will teach *him* an invaluable lesson. A lesson that will hopefully make him reflect on his behaviour and stop him seeking to advance himself by exploiting anyone else.' She chewed thoughtfully down on her lip, then smiled uncertainly. 'At least that's my hope.'

Drake started to pace the polished wooden floor, the expression in his fascinating grey eyes suggesting they were reaching internally for some longed-for escape route…perhaps a time warp that could transport them back to the moment when he'd first walked into the room with their coffee, when he might have told Layla he'd changed his mind about having their little discussion.

All her instincts cried out for her to go to him and hold him tight, to tell him how courageous he'd been to reveal the cruelties of his childhood, but sensing he was still tormented by his frank and painful admission she stayed where she was, not wanting to risk upsetting him further.

Coming to a sudden standstill, he swept his still restless gaze up and down her figure. 'What made you decide to take the contraceptive in the end?' he asked.

'Why? Did you think I wouldn't take it and just pretend that I did?'

'No. I never thought you'd try and deceive me. I just...'

'What, Drake? I'm sensing there's something you want to ask me.'

'When you think about the future, do you ever think about having children?'

Breathing out a relieved sigh, Layla couldn't help smiling. 'Of course... One day I'd love to be a mum.'

'One day when the "right man" comes along, presumably?'

Now his voice was rough-edged and cynical and it made her heart bleed.

'If by the right man you mean a man that I love with all my heart and want to be with for the rest of my life, then, yes...that's when I'll be ready to become a mum.'

Drake's eyes bored into her like a laser. 'My ex-girlfriend wanted children.'

'She did?'

'That was one of the reasons we broke up. She wanted them and I didn't. And, more importantly, I didn't want to spend the rest of my life with her, so there was no way I'd make her the mother of my children. When I explained my reasons to her as diplomatically as I could, apart from accusing me of being emotionally crippled and totally insensitive for not understanding her desire for marriage and children, she said I was the most spectacularly selfish man she'd ever met and didn't doubt that I'd end up alone.'

Layla's heart bumped with sorrow and dread as she waited for him to continue.

A corner of his mouth quirked painfully. 'She was right.'

'Sometimes it helps us to have clarity when we know what we *don't* want,' she commented softly, the dread she'd felt inside that he might have stated that he would *never* want marriage or children slowly and thankfully subsiding.

'It does indeed.'

'So how *do* you feel about having children if you— if you meet the right woman?'

'It would definitely be something I'd consider.' He gave her a sheepish look. 'I used to think I'd never want a family. Maybe it's my age, but now I don't think I'd be as closed to the idea as I was before. Shall we leave it at that and get out of here for a while?'

The glimmer of some unspoken urgent idea was evident in Drake's animated gaze, and apart from what he'd just revealed about the possibility of being open to the notion of having children it made Layla's heart race.

'Why? Where do you want to go?'

'I've heard that it's going to be an exceptionally clear night. I'd like to take you to my office and show you that view of the stars through the glass roof.'

Remembering how surprised and moved she'd been when he'd told her that he sometimes turned out the lights if he was working late and the stars were bright, she felt a genuine thrill of anticipation.

'All right,' she agreed, smiling, 'I'll go and get my coat.'

'Layla?'

'Yes?'

'I didn't mean it when I accused you of being smug earlier. I was just… I was just angry that you got me to talk about that stuff. But now—now I'm glad that you did.'

Walking up to him, she gently touched his unshaven cheek with the tips of her fingers and tenderly laid her lips over his mouth. Straight away she sensed the heat they stoked into flame between them—but before she let it consume her, she lifted her head and told him, 'I think you telling me about your childhood was the bravest thing I've ever heard.'

His arms tightened possessively round her waist. 'You're good for my ego, you know that?'

Her eyes were already drifting closed, even before his lips made the fire they'd started to kindle a moment ago burst into uncontrollable flame…

CHAPTER TEN

Drake had laid a blanket and some cushions down on the heated wooden floor in his office, and Layla settled herself down beside him and rested her head in the crook of his arm, staring up in wonder at the cornucopia of dazzling stars that were gloriously twinkling above them through the glass ceiling. He'd been absolutely right when he'd told her that the light they emitted was so bright there was no need to turn on the lamps.

'What a genius idea to do this,' she declared enthusiastically, turning towards him.

'So it's a genius I am now, is it?'

For sheer vivacity and beauty, in Layla's opinion the sparkle in Drake's haunting grey eyes as he glanced back at her was equal to the array of stars that shone down on them. The realisation that she loved him… loved him with all her heart…struck her absolutely dumb. All she could do right then was stare into his carved handsome face and mentally imprint every beloved feature to memory, so that his image might sustain her whenever they were apart.

'What is it?' he asked, frowning, intuiting that something profound had pierced her. 'What's wrong?'

'Nothing's wrong. As a matter of fact, things couldn't be more right.'

Somehow she managed to divert him from learning the stunning realisation that had just rocked her world off its axis. She guessed that now wasn't the right time to share the news—not when he'd already had such a torrid time revisiting his agonisingly painful past. There was also a terrible fear inside her that he might not welcome her revelation—might even reject her if he wasn't ready to explore the possibility of them having a future together. *She decided that she would bide her time.*

'I'm just… I'm really enjoying myself, that's all,' she said lightly.

'Me too.' Reassured, Drake smiled and dropped an affectionate kiss onto her forehead.

For once he looked completely at ease. Even the furrows on his indomitable brow seemed more relaxed.

Layla couldn't help sighing. 'Don't you wish you could capture some of your most magical experiences and keep them for ever? I mean keep them safely locked away in a silk-lined drawer and bring them out whenever you have a bad day or simply need a pick-me-up?'

Hugging her companion's lean trim waist in the chambray shirt he wore loose over his jeans, she pressed closer into his side, breathing in his earthy masculine smell as though it was the most alluring and compelling perfume she'd ever scented.

He chuckled and she felt his fingers ruffle her hair. 'Omit the silk-lined drawer, sweetheart, and I totally concur with what you're saying. This is indeed one of those magical experiences that I'll never forget. But, for me, this whole weekend has been like that.'

'Has it? I was afraid I'd ruined everything by getting you to answer questions about your past.'

'You haven't ruined anything, and you were entitled to question me. Didn't I make a promise that I'd talk to you? I've come round to thinking that perhaps it was about time I opened up to someone about what happened when I was a kid, even though it was probably one of the hardest things I've ever done.' Drake's expression visibly softened. 'I'm glad that it was you I confided in, Layla. I wouldn't have told anyone else and that's the truth…not even a trained counsellor. My deepest darkest secrets would have gone with me to my grave.' His wry smile was reflective.

'Don't say that.' She caught his hand and urgently kissed it. 'I can't bear the thought of you being tormented by the past for the rest of your life and never telling anyone…never having any relief from the pain of it. I'm glad you agreed to talk to me, Drake, even though it was painful and difficult.' Staring deeply into his eyes, she finished, 'I'm also glad that you don't hate me for making you share your secrets with me.'

Bewildered, Drake shook his head. 'I could never hate you…no matter what you did to me. Don't you know that?'

She emitted a relieved sigh and her lips curved warmly. 'We're still friends, then?'

'Is that all you want to be to me…a friend?'

His lowered husky tone was akin to cream liqueur poured into a cup of the finest dark roast coffee…devastatingly warm and rich with a hint of luxurious velvet that was far too enticing to resist. Before Layla could reply, his lips had alighted on hers with an almost savage groan, and in the next instant his hot silken tongue was plundering the satin interior of her mouth as his big hands cupped her face and his hard-muscled body moved on top of hers, his superior weight pressing her spine deep into the luxurious woollen blanket he had lain down on the floor.

As far as Layla was concerned it might as well have been a soft feather bed. There was no sense of discomfort at all. How could there be when every ounce of her attention was intimately focused on the man who was once again taking her to a paradise she never wanted to leave, just so long as she could stay there with him for ever?

When they returned to the house and retired to bed, deliciously sated from their ardent lovemaking, Drake didn't have a single qualm about turning out the light. There was no need to wonder why he suddenly found the normally difficult task easy. The prospect of the black velvet night enveloping him and filling him with dread like it usually did didn't feature even once in his thinking...at least not with Layla lying beside him. Even though he'd fiercely resisted sharing the truth of his past with her, she had somehow broken through his iron defences to show him how sharing his story could actually *help* him banish the ghosts that haunted him— not make them even more cloying.

For the first time in years he'd discovered the true value of confiding in someone he trusted. But the most important thing that he'd learned from their heart-rending conversation was that the belief he'd had about having to deserve love was completely wrong. As a child, it had been his fundamental right to be taken care of, Layla had told him. He hadn't been denied love because he was 'bad'. It was just that his parents had been incapable of taking proper care of him, and how could that be *his* fault?

Talking about what had happened was already alleviating some of the fearful beliefs that had crippled him for too long. Consequently, with his ravishing dark-haired lover warmly enfolded in his arms, for the first time ever Drake slept the deep dreamless sleep of a man whose resentment and fear of the past was blessedly absent.

That night no dark or agonising dreams came to haunt him, and he felt like the most privileged and blessed man in the world when he woke to the joyful sound of birds singing the next morning and witnessed the sun beaming through the windows to herald a bright new day. If he didn't pride himself on being an innately logical man he might have said it was a very good omen. An omen that meant psychologically he'd turned an important corner.

Logical or not, he had the strongest urge to share his reflections with Layla. A jolt of panic knifed through him when he saw she wasn't there. Sitting bolt upright, Drake touched the sheet where her body had lain in sleep. It was still beguilingly warm. Where was she? Taking a shower?

He leapt out of bed and threw open the *en-suite* bathroom door to check. The moist shampoo-scented air in the marbled bathroom told him that she had indeed taken a shower, but had clearly moved on somewhere else. Returning to the bedroom, he pulled on a pair of clean silk boxers and dragged on his jeans. Barefoot and bare-chested, he hurried downstairs to the kitchen, calling out her name as he went.

'I'm in here,' she called back, and when Drake planted himself in the kitchen doorway she turned to him with a smile so beautiful and beguiling that he clean forgot what he'd been going to say to her.

He swallowed hard and cleared his throat, 'You're wearing my shirt again,' he observed, helplessly aroused at the sight of her long bare legs and the provocative outline of her panties, tantalisingly visible through the pristine white cotton.

'Do you mind?' Chewing down on her lip, she smoothed her still damp hair away from her face. 'I just grabbed something to put on after my shower so I could come downstairs and make us some coffee.'

'You can wear whatever you like that belongs to me.' Moving towards her, he grinned. 'Although I'd prefer it if you wore nothing at all.'

'That's not a terribly good idea when I'm boiling water.'

'Are you always so cautious?' Sliding his hands round her waist, Drake let his hungry gaze drink her in as if she was the finest wine he'd ever sampled. But even the most full-bodied Cabernet Sauvignon or French Bordeaux didn't have the power to heat his blood like Layla did.

'Sometimes not cautious enough,' she murmured, flattening her palms against his chest as if to stop him from getting any closer.

'Why? Don't you trust me?'

She lifted an amused dark eyebrow. 'Not when you

come down to the kitchen looking like you've got lascivious intentions in mind rather than wanting to enjoy a cup of my expertly made coffee.'

'Can't I have lascivious intentions *and* enjoy your expertly made coffee as well?'

'I'm sure you can. But my own intentions are to make some toast, because I'm at my hungriest in the morning. By the way, did you sleep all right last night? You certainly looked peaceful when I woke up this morning and saw you. That's why I decided to let you sleep on for a bit.'

His mouth quirked with a wry smile, 'I slept like I'd been pleasantly drugged. I can't recall having even a single dream.'

'So…there were no nightmares?'

'None.' Drake tenderly threaded his fingers through her long damp hair. 'See what a positive effect you have on me, Ms Jerome?'

'I aim to please.'

'Do you indeed?'

A self-conscious tinge of scarlet coloured her cheeks. 'Seriously, though, I'm so glad you slept better. I hope it becomes a regular feature…the start of a much more relaxed and enjoyable phase of your life. You deserve it, Drake. By the way—I've got one more question to ask you.'

'What's that?' A wave of pleasure had rolled through him at her kindness, her genuinely unselfish hopes for his future, but he had a brief moment of trepidation wondering what she might be going to ask him.

'Do you have any marmalade? It's just that it's my favourite thing to have on toast in the morning.'

His relief that her question wasn't more taxing knew no bounds. With a chuckle, he affectionately pinched the end of her nose. 'Baby I've got whatever your heart desires.'

Unable to resist impelling her against his chest, Drake felt the blood in his veins thrum hotly at the delicious sensory pleasure of her soft feminine curves next to his harder masculine body.

The big long-lashed dark eyes that he'd been so mesmerised by when he'd seen Layla for the very first time widened to saucers. 'That's a very beguiling claim, but luckily for you all I want right now is some marmalade.'

'Is that *really* all you want?' He slid his hand all the way down her slim back to rest it on her peach-shaped derrière, then pressed her against him so that she could be in no doubt about how much he wanted her. He was so aroused it was painful.

'You don't play fair,' she chastised, wagging her finger schoolmistress-like at him, her voice completely devoid of sympathy. 'As tempting as you are…as *needy* as you are…I'm afraid I'm going to have to exercise some of that bull-headedness you once accused me of because before I contemplate anything else I *really* need my breakfast.'

Before he could stop her she'd wriggled out of his arms and headed for the bread-bin atop the kitchen counter. He knew it contained the brown seeded loaf that he'd bought at the deli along with their croissants yesterday. Sighing, he realised he would manfully have to subdue his desire—at least until she'd had her breakfast. Clearly there was no stopping the woman when her mind was set on something. His feelings were a provoking mix of frustration and affection.

'I'd be a poor host indeed if I didn't let you eat.' He smiled and, moving across to the large American-style fridge, extracted an unopened pot of marmalade. 'Why don't you make the coffee and let me do the toast?' he suggested. 'After that we'll—'

'Go back to bed?' Layla's chocolate-brown eyes met his with an unwavering amused stare that made Drake's heart miss a beat.

'My thoughts exactly,' he agreed huskily.

It was hard for Layla to accept that their time together was coming to an end. Having already explained that he probably wouldn't be able to see her this week, due to his colossal workload—not least of all their town's pressing and much needed regeneration—Drake had definitely looked unhappy when he'd told her. Telling herself she'd just have to accept his absence and pray that the following week might yield a greater possibility of them seeing each other again, Layla fell silent as he drove them home, not trusting herself in case she broke down and confessed that she loved him.

Why did the prospect of saying goodbye to him this evening feel like a death sentence? she wondered miserably. They'd had such a wonderful day together—laughing and talking and making love till they were breathless and sated, then somehow finding the energy to go down to the kitchen and make themselves something to eat. It didn't seem right that they should be parted for even an hour, let alone a whole week!

'Before I drop you home I'd like to show you something.' Drake's handsome carved profile was disconcertingly serious as he stared out through the windscreen, making the necessary turn that would take them out of the near deserted high street.

The only occupants in evidence were a couple of local teenagers leaning against a galvanised steel grille shop-front, smoking. Compared to the wealthy and elite part of the capital she and Drake had just come from, the shabby provincial town seemed even more rundown and drab than it usually did.

'Show me what?' Layla asked, unable to suppress the feeling of inexplicable apprehension that coiled in the pit of her stomach.

'The house where I grew up.'

He spared her a brief unreadable glance just as she registered that they were approaching the small shabby side-street whose abandoned terraced houses he planned to tear down and replace with modern ones. The house he drew up outside was a dismal grey terrace with all the windows shattered and broken and a large 'Keep Out' sign emblazoned across the dingy charcoal-grey front door. The stone steps that led to the once fashionable arched brick entrance were covered in litter and broken beer bottles, she saw. No doubt some of the population of jobless teenagers and youths hung out there, she thought.

Unsure about what to say, she laid her hand across Drake's, not moving it even when she sensed him flinch uncomfortably.

Now that she knew something of his unhappy past, she hoped visiting the street wouldn't bombard him with tormenting memories. It wasn't hard to imagine what he must be thinking, and no doubt that was why he was so determined to demolish the houses rather than have them renovated. Did he hope that when the houses were smashed to smithereens it would likewise crush the hurtful nightmares of his past? Last night she'd been so encouraged when he'd been able to turn out the light and sleep more easily, and she didn't doubt that trend would continue if only he could realise he wasn't to blame for what had happened to him as a child…that he'd always deserved to be loved just as much as anyone else did.

'It's funny,' he murmured, 'but it looks so much smaller and insignificant than it did when I was a child. If my dad was still alive I bet he'd look smaller and insignificant too.'

'If the thought helps you no longer see him as an ogre, and you can start to put your disturbing memories of him to bed, then I'm glad you think that. But I'm sure that if he could see you now and learn what a successful and wealthy man you've become—through all your own efforts too—he would be proud…even if he couldn't bring himself to show it.'

A muscle flinched in the side of Drake's lean, carved cheekbone, conveying the undoubted tension in his body. 'The old bastard was too mean to be proud of anyone or anything…especially his son. He was totally self-obsessed. But thanks for the thought just the same.'

Grimacing, Layla didn't shy away from the bitterness and sorrow she heard in his tone and lapse into silence. Instead an even stronger determination to stay as positive as possible and not collude with his misery arose inside her. 'You know if it was renovated along with all the others in the street this house could potentially be very nice. Was it in such a sorry state as it is now when you lived here with your dad?' she asked.

Sighing heavily, Drake shook his head. 'It was always rundown, but not as bad as it is now, thank God. As I got older I used to try and keep it free from litter at least. And the windows never got broken because it was my job to clean them. I didn't dare risk kicking a football around outside and potentially ruining all my hard work. Even then I longed for my surroundings to be beautiful.'

Helplessly picturing the small boy who'd taken on the household jobs his father should have assumed, in a bid to maintain some sort of pleasing exterior to what must have been his desperately unhappy interior life, Layla grimaced again. 'Has it helped you coming back here to see it again?' she asked softly.

'Who knows?' The expression in his haunting grey eyes was far away for a moment. 'Only time will tell. The point is I didn't want to hide anything from you— that's why I brought you here. I wanted you to see for yourself the house and the environment I grew up in. I wanted to be truthful and show you exactly where I came from…who I really am.'

'I feel privileged that you trust me enough to show me, Drake. But who you really are isn't defined by your past, you know. You can write a new script every day… every moment, in fact. It didn't happen overnight, but recently I've come to realise that myself. Thinking about how my boss ripped me off just keeps me stuck in the same miserable, unhappy story. It doesn't help me move on and enjoy my life, and just because we've been hurt by someone in the past it doesn't mean that everyone we meet in the future is going to hurt us.'

'I'm sure you're right.' Drake's steady glance was deeply thoughtful for a moment. 'I've got something I want to tell you before I take you home.'

'What's that?'

'I'm not going to have the houses demolished after all. I'm going to have them renovated, as you suggested.'

Layla was speechless. Then, as hope and elation poured through her at the same time, she smiled at Drake and said, 'You *are*? What changed your mind?'

'You did, Layla. You made me see things differently. I've begun to wonder if this regeneration of the town isn't a good opportunity for me to bury the ghosts of the past and start over. I have the means and the know how to help others who live here have a better and more beautiful environment that might inspire them to do something good with their lives instead of feeling hopeless, and that's exactly what I plan to do. I'm also going to turn my old house into that youth club you suggested the town needs.'

'You mean it?'

'Absolutely.'

'I can hardly believe it,' Sighing, Layla slowly shook her head in wonder. 'I'm so proud of you, Drake...so proud. I don't doubt that given time you're going to make a huge difference to people's lives with all you plan to do here.'

'Talking of time—I ought to get you home.'

Lifting her hand in a gentlemanly gesture that might have come straight out of a Regency novel, he brushed his lips against her fingers with almost polite restraint.

Even then Layla realised the heat between them was but a mere breath away, and could be ignited by one unguarded glance, let alone a touch. Breathing out slowly, she somehow found a smile—no easy task when she knew they would soon have to say goodbye to each other. She honestly wondered how she would survive the next few days without seeing him.

As if the same realisation had suddenly occurred to him, Drake clenched his jaw and gunned the engine. But as the car sped along the dark shabby streets Layla believed that he would indeed put the ghosts of his troubled past behind him and truly start afresh. He'd told her she had helped him see things differently. *Did that include her assertion that he could write a new script for his life?* Whether the idea would help him reflect on the possibility of a brighter future with her, she could only hope and pray…

'It's the house on the right-hand side.'

'You mean the large Victorian?'

'That's right.'

Driving through the well-kept streets on the much more affluent side of town, Drake felt the pit of his stomach churn helplessly. From her description of where she lived, he'd already guessed that Layla's upbringing had been a million miles away from his own. Without even hearing her address he only had to remember the kindness of her father who'd run the newsagents to know that she'd been well taken care of. There was also the brother who adored her…the brother who was determined to make a currently unprofitable coffee house a roaring success, and had given her a job when her sleazebag employer had swindled her out of her savings. Who wouldn't be envious of having a sibling like that to rely on?

After spending such an unbelievably joyous weekend with Layla, he hated the insecurity that suddenly seized him. The prospect of not seeing her again for an entire week didn't help. Following her out of the car, Drake struggled hard to win back his equilibrium.

'Will you come in and have a coffee with me before you head back to London?' she asked him, her tone hinting at her uncertainty that he might not.

'That would be great.' Determinedly finding a reassuring smile, he reached for her hand. *Didn't she know that the prospect of spending a little more time with her made him feel as wildly happy as a prisoner on death row who'd been given an unbelievable last minute reprieve?*

As they climbed the steps to the impressive porch of the house the scarlet front door opened from the inside and Marc, Layla's tousle-headed brother, appeared to greet them.

'The wanderer returns.' He immediately stepped forward to envelop his sister in a hard warm hug, and Drake had no choice but to let go of her hand. The cold stab of jealousy that slashed through his insides at being forced to relinquish her even for a moment almost made him feel physically sick it was so strong.

'Are you okay?' The other man wore a frown as he held Layla at arm's length to examine her. 'I tried God only knows how many times over the weekend to reach you, but you'd obviously turned off your phone.' He glanced warily at Drake over her shoulder. 'I tried your mobile as well, but that was turned off too. Anyone would think the two of you had disappeared off the planet!'

Drake's gaze tumbled helplessly into Layla's and their eyes exchanged a very private signal of mutual understanding. 'We stayed on the planet, but I don't deny we shut out the world for a couple of days,' he drawled, low-voiced.

'I was perfectly fine, Marc,' Layla cut in quickly. 'You know I'm quite capable of taking care of myself, so there was absolutely no need for you to worry. Now, I'm going upstairs to my flat to make Drake and me a cup of coffee. Do you want to join us?'

'Thanks all the same, but I won't. The accounts beckon, I'm afraid. By the way—I made a couple of Victoria sponges to take into the café tomorrow. Help yourself if you'd like some with your coffee. It's nice to see you again, Drake…even if you did kidnap my beautiful sister for the weekend!'

'It's good to see you too,' Drake murmured, right then feeling anything *but* friendly towards the other man.

He was glad to be invited upstairs to Layla's flat so that they could have some privacy. Back at the house in Mayfair, he'd asked her if she thought his home lacked warmth. Glancing round the cosy living-room in her flat, with its sandalwood-scented air, homely feminine touches, mismatched furniture, family portraits on the walls and enough candles in the fireplace to light a cathedral, it wasn't a question she would ever have to ask him. Her home was an irresistibly warm expression of the lovely woman who inhabited it, and Drake was suddenly unsure about the hopes he'd subconsciously been nurturing over the weekend.

What could he possibly offer a woman like Layla, apart from what his material wealth could provide? he wondered. Having come into contact with her generous heart and concern for others, he doubted whether that would even be an inducement. Why would she want to leave a home she loved with a brother who adored and looked out for her to move up to London and live with him? he mused. Especially when her experience of living and working there previously had been indelibly soured by an unscrupulous boss who had swindled her out of her life savings and seduced her. Wasn't that why she had retreated from city life in the first place? To lick her wounds in a place of safety?

As sure as night followed day, and despite his plans to regenerate the town and improve it, Drake certainly wouldn't contemplate returning to live with her, no matter how strong his feelings were. And even if they could agree on a mutually acceptable place of residence if they got together permanently, what if one day Layla walked out on him, just as his mother had? What if she made that soul-destroying decision because she'd reached the same conclusion his ex had made about him...that he was 'emotionally crippled' and—despite his wealth and success—a poor bet if he couldn't shake his past? *Could he risk such a devastating possibility and be left to live his life without her?*

'Do you fancy a slice of Victoria sponge with your coffee?' As she returned to the living room from the kitchen Layla's cheerful voice broke into his bleak introspection.

'No, thanks.' He gave an awkward shrug of the shoulders. 'In fact, I don't think I'll stay and have coffee after all. I've had my mobile switched off since Friday night, and I've probably got at least fifty or sixty messages I need to reply to.'

Her lovely face was immediately crestfallen, and Drake felt like the very worst criminal.

'Can't you stay for just half an hour longer? Surely that won't make a lot of difference? In any case, it won't be late by the time you get back to London. You'll have plenty of time to answer your messages then,' she pointed out reasonably.

Her suggestion was more than tempting, but he had already made up his mind to go. They had spent an amazing and intense time together, but now he needed some space and time alone to get his head straight.

Without thinking he moved across the room and took her into his arms. 'I'm sorry, sweetheart, I really am. But I've got a heavy week ahead of me and there are plans and drawings I need to study, as well as replying to my phone messages. We'll see each other again very soon…I promise. I'll ring you just as soon as I know when I can take some time off.'

Her dark eyes looked alternately sad, then resigned. That disappointed and melancholy glance made Drake feel as though someone had punched him hard in the gut.

'If for some reason you can't reach me on my mobile you can leave a message with Marc, either here or at the café,' she told him, her tongue moistening her lips as if they'd suddenly turned dry.

'Great.' His fingers firmed possessively round her

slim upper arms, the warmth of her satin skin provocatively evident in the sheer silk blouse he had bought her. Desolation settled in the pit of his stomach at the thought of sleeping in his bed tonight without her. 'It's been an incredible weekend and I've loved every minute of it being with you, Layla,' he told her honestly, his voice low.

In answer, her pretty lips curved to form the sweetest smile. 'I'll never forget lying on the blanket in your office looking up at the stars through that amazing glass ceiling,' she admitted softly.

'We'll do it again some time soon. That's a promise.'

'I'll hold you to that.' Reaching up on tiptoe, she pressed her lips gently against his. 'You'd better go before I make a complete fool of myself and cry,' she said.

Forcing himself to ignore the instinct to plunder and ravish her mouth, as he longed to do, Drake slowly nodded his head. 'Thanks for everything,' he murmured, reluctantly extricating himself from their embrace and walking to the door.

'It was my pleasure,' Layla murmured, and he turned briefly to give her a smile…

CHAPTER ELEVEN

LAYLA threw herself into a frenzy of activity in a bid to try and keep her anxious thoughts about Drake at bay. When she wasn't working at the café, serving the trickle of customers that came in throughout the day and keeping it spick and span, she was tidying and de-cluttering her flat, and driving the laden boxes of clothes and bric-a-brac she'd collected to a charity shop in support of sick children. After that, she avidly perused her cookery books to come up with new and enticing recipes that she could cook for herself and Marc.

It was only in the unguarded moments that sneaked up on her from time to time that the memory of Drake—how he looked, the sound of his voice, how it felt when he took her in his arms—had the ability to make her catch her breath and her body ache with longing.

As the interminably long week progressed she relived time and time again the frighteningly naked and poignant smile he'd left her with, wishing she'd had the courage to ask him there and then what was really on his mind. Was it that he'd decided he didn't want to commit to a relationship with her after all now that he'd revealed so much about his wounded past? Because it made him feel far too exposed and vulnerable? Didn't he know that she'd rather *die* than betray him by sharing what he'd told her with anyone else?

When the working week drew to a close without any word from him at all, Layla determinedly resisted the overwhelming urge to ring *him*. Instead she drove to the building site where Drake had taken her that day to explain his plans for the area's improvement, in the no doubt unrealistic hope that he might be there. *He wasn't*.

When she arrived she saw straight away that the construction workers had clearly shut up shop for the day. The muddied landscape and recently erected scaffolding looked bleak, cold and abandoned...*the description could well have been applied to her*.

Back in her flat, she nearly jumped out of her skin when the hallway telephone rang. Abandoning the removal of her jacket, she haphazardly shrugged it back onto her shoulders and urgently grabbed the receiver.

It was him...it *had* to be him.

'Hello?'

'Layla? It's me—Colette.'

She'd never been so disappointed to hear the voice of a friend. It was a loyal pal she occasionally enjoyed 'girly' nights in with—drinking wine, putting the world to rights and giggling over the latest rom-com together.

'Hi,' she answered, her hand shaking from the onrush of adrenaline that had poured through her when she'd thought the caller might be Drake. 'How nice to hear from you. It's been a while. How are you?'

'I'm good. How about you?'

'I'm fine, thanks.' It grieved Layla that she wasn't able to sound more convincing. A girl needed her friends—especially at times like these—and Colette was a good one.

'Hmm...' the other girl commented. 'You don't sound fine to me. Want to talk about what's been going on?'

Was she a mind-reader? Flushing guiltily, Layla absently curled some silky dark strands of hair round her ear. 'I've met someone, that's all.'

There was a pause, then Colette asked wondrously, 'You mean you've met a man you're crazy about?'

'How did you know?'

'Because if you weren't crazy about him you wouldn't even tell me you'd met someone. You're not a girl who indulges in casual meaningless encounters... or casual meaningless sex, for that matter. I've always sensed that when you finally met a guy you were genuinely attracted to it would have to be all or nothing. Who is he and where did you meet him?'

Feeling protective of Drake's privacy, and how much or how little she could safely reveal about him, Layla examined the short unvarnished fingernails she'd recently taken to nibbling and sighed. 'I met him here... in the town.'

'Is he local?'

'No. He lives and works in London.'

'What on earth was he doing here, then?'

The incredulity in her friend's voice didn't surprise her. Their town was hardly the jewel of the county...at least not *yet*. 'Working... He's part of the professional team that's working on the regeneration.'

'So he's a town planner or surveyor, perhaps?'

She swallowed hard. 'Something like that.'

'Okaay... I can tell you're being more than a little protective of him... Got any plans for tonight?'

'No...I don't.' Layla wished she was planning on getting ready to see Drake, and it hurt more than she could say that she wasn't.

'That's settled, then. I can tell you're in need of some friendly advice and support. As soon as I get ready, and pop into the off-licence on the way for a cracking bottle of wine, I'll be round to pay you a visit. And don't worry about searching through your collection for a film...we'll have far too much to chat about for that! Bye for now. I'll see you soon.'

As she heard the line disconnect at the other end Layla stared blankly at the wall, wondering miserably if she could summon up the energy to share confidences with a well-meaning friend when in all honesty she'd much rather crawl under the duvet and cry...

He'd sat in the car outside the house for almost ten minutes, mentally rehearsing what he was going to say to her. The first hurdle Drake had to cross was whether Layla was actually in, because he hadn't phoned ahead to let her know he was coming. When he'd seen the lights shining from the windows of the upper floor he had murmured a fervent and relieved, 'Thank God...' and told himself that fate must be on his side after all.

Now that he was here he could hardly believe he'd so foolishly stayed away from her for an entire week. Yes, he had genuinely had a workload that barely gave him time to draw breath, but the real reason he hadn't rung her was because he'd had a nagging story running in his head about her being unwilling to compromise on what she wanted. Consequently he'd allowed the twin gremlins of doubt and fear to prevent him from taking the courageous step he needed to.

This morning, for the first time in days, Drake had woken with the clarity of mind he'd prayed for and his heart filled with absolute certainty about what he should do. But now that he was here, sitting outside the gracious Victorian house that Layla had grown up in, he suddenly felt unsure again. *After all, there was no guarantee that she'd be happy to see him, was there?* Not after he'd so abruptly cut their last evening together short without any real explanation. What if she thought he was a terrible coward…even *worse* an unreliable bastard?

'Damn!' A colourful expletive followed his frustrated exclamation, and hurriedly stepping out onto the pavement from the Aston Martin that he'd told Jimmy he would drive himself that evening, he closed the door shut with a slam.

Straightening the blue silk tie he wore with his tailored suit, he climbed the wide stone steps up to the front door, his heart hammering harder than if he'd received a prestigious commission from the Queen herself. When he rang the bell, and shortly afterwards saw the hallway light come on through the frosted panes in the door, he stood there in dry-mouthed anticipation of seeing Layla again, fervently hoping that nothing would jinx the event.

'Well, well, well—as you said to me when I paid a surprise visit to your office… To what do I owe the honour?'

Dressed in black skinny jeans and a biscuit-coloured

cardigan, with her feet bare, Layla flashed her glossy brown eyes as if Drake was the last person on earth she'd expected or indeed wanted to see. But her less-than-warm welcome made him even more determined to get her to see reason, and his avid gaze roamed her beautiful features with a slow, teasing smile.

'If I tell you that this past week I've missed you more than I've ever missed anyone or anything in my life will that get me an invite in for the cup of coffee I so foolishly declined when I was last here?' he asked, his voice pitched intimately low.

She was still holding onto the doorframe, as if undecided whether to let him over the threshold or not, but there was a glimmer of what he took to be hope in her eyes, and the majority of the tension that had been making his insides ache for days slowly ebbed.

'That's all you want? A cup of coffee?' she quizzed warily.

'A cup of your expertly made coffee would be a start, I suppose.'

'A start to what, exactly?'

'I'm hoping a frank and truthful conversation.'

'That's what I'd like too. Okay. But I'm afraid you're going to have to wait until my friend leaves. She's popped round to give me a little female support.'

Drake frowned. 'Support for what?'

Her cheeks turned engagingly pink. 'There are times when we women need a good friend to turn to. This is one of those times.'

'Are you saying that you needed to discuss you and me?' he asked warily.

'What do you think? Did it even cross your mind that

I might be feeling a little low after you left so abruptly on Sunday? We were getting on so well—you even took me back to the street where you grew up and told me about your plan to renovate the houses instead of pulling them down. But then…then we came back here and you suddenly decided you had to leave. I haven't discussed anything personal with Colette, but I was planning on telling her that I'd met someone that I— Anyway.' She flushed and glanced down at the floor for a second. 'That's when the doorbell rang. You couldn't have timed your arrival more perfectly if you'd tried.'

'And what were you going to tell your friend, I wonder? That I took you back to my house, mercilessly seduced you, then took you home and hurriedly made my exit, never to be seen or heard of again?'

Drake tried and failed to keep the angry hurt from his tone. More than he hated the idea of having Layla discuss him with her friend, he abhorred the idea that she might believe he could indeed be so callous.

Her face fell. 'I would *never* have described what happened between us like that. Did you honestly think that I would?'

'Look…can I come in? Can't you tell Colleen, or whatever her name is, that I've driven down from London especially to see you and I really need us to talk?'

The mere idea of Layla having to entertain her friend when he was near desperate to clear the air between them and tell her his feelings made Drake feel tense and impatient again.

In an aggrieved tone she answered, 'If you're in that much of a hurry to talk to me, why couldn't you have rung me earlier in the week to let me know you were coming this evening? And, by the way, it's Colette— *not* Colleen. She's a good friend, and I don't get to see her that often. I won't risk offending her by asking her to leave just because *you've* suddenly decided you need to talk to me!'

'Okay.' Forcing down his deep disappointment, Drake lifted and dropped his shoulders resignedly. 'I'll just wait until she goes, then…if that's all right with you, I mean?'

'You'd better come in.'

Removing her hand from the doorframe, Layla stood back to allow him entry into the hall. As she went past him to shut the door he had to curl his hand into a fist to stop himself reaching out to touch the shining curtain of dark hair that fell onto her shoulders. *Was it only a few short days ago that he'd had the incredible good fortune to do such a thing with impunity?*

'Let's go upstairs. Colette was about to open the bottle of wine she brought with her. Perhaps you'd like a glass?'

'I think I'll decline. I want to keep a clear head this evening.'

'I'll just make you some coffee, then.'

'That would be great…thanks.'

When his avid gaze fell into hers for a full uninterrupted second, the cascade of heat and hunger that assailed him almost made Drake stumble, and his heart thumped hard when he saw by her darkening pupils that Layla was fighting a similar battle.

'I should have rung you,' he confessed huskily, 'but

I wanted to get my head straight. I had a lot to think over. Can you forgive me?'

'You're here now, and that's all that matters.'

Her gentle smile was like a wisp of ephemeral smoke—there one minute and gone the next. But, having seen it, he couldn't help but feel reassured.

At the top of the stairs a pretty young woman with gently waving blonde hair, wearing a tan-coloured raincoat over a smart blouse and jeans, stood waiting for them.

'You're not leaving, Colette?' Layla asked, startled.

'Sweetheart, you don't need me to hang around now. I didn't mean to eavesdrop, but I guessed when I heard a man's voice that it must be the guy you were going to tell me about.' She glanced up at Drake with a smile, 'I'm Layla's friend Colette.' She reached out and shook his hand, adding, 'And you are…?'

'Drake.' He didn't hesitate to give his real name, because something in the girl's frank blue eyes told him that she was fiercely loyal to Layla. 'Drake Ashton.'

'You're the famous architect that's helping to regenerate the town?'

He grimaced. 'I'm just one of a group of professionals that's been commissioned.'

The blonde's eyes twinkled mischievously. 'And are any of the other professionals as fit as you, Drake?'

'Colette!' Layla shook her head in disbelief at her friend's daring.

'Don't worry, Drake, I'm only teasing. Layla knows I'm very happily married, and right now I'm going to head back home and suggest that my other half and I go out for a nice romantic meal somewhere. Why don't the two of you open that bottle of wine I brought and enjoy it on me?'

Noticing that Layla was frowning, as though concerned that her friend felt under pressure to cut short her visit, Drake caught her hand and gave it a reassuring squeeze. 'I promise that the next time you and Colette arrange a girls' night in I won't break up your evening by demanding you spend time with me instead.'

'That's settled, then. I'm going.' The blonde gave him a satisfied conspiratorial wink.

'And the bottle of wine is on me next time, Colette,' he promised.

'I'll hold you to that. Just make sure the two of you have some fun tonight, won't you? And there's just one more thing, Drake…'

'What's that?'

'Don't break her heart. Trust me, you're a very lucky man that she's interested in you. I was beginning to wonder if she'd ever find someone she really liked.'

His eyes lit on Layla in a penetrating gaze. 'Rest assured I don't take her for granted.'

Tearing her glance from his, Layla stepped round him to give her friend an affectionate hug. 'Thanks for coming over. I'll give you a ring very soon, I promise.'

'I'll look forward to it. Bye, sweetie.'

As soon as she and Drake were alone again, Layla walked in silence back into the flat. It disturbed him that she appeared so ill at ease. *Did she really have no idea how he felt?* Following her into the kitchen, he glanced at the unopened bottle of wine standing on the counter. Standing beside it were two slim-stemmed glasses and a corkscrew.

'I know I said I'd have coffee, but shall we break the ice by having a glass of wine?' he suggested lightly, hunting for a way to help her relax.

'Break the ice?' Layla rounded on him with a disbelieving glare. 'Has our relationship become so brittle since we last saw each other that we need an icebreaker to help us communicate? I for one would rather just get straight to the point.'

'I agree. Why don't we do just that?'

'You agree?'

Resisting the urge to smile, because she looked so damn adorable right then, Drake threw up his hands in a gesture of surrender. 'I do. Why don't you go first and tell me what you've been thinking?'

'All right, then. I will.' Folding her arms, she moved restlessly across the black and white tiled floor and back again. 'Something happened when you dropped me back home on Sunday. You were going to stay for coffee, but then you suddenly changed your mind. Personally, I don't believe your urgent departure had anything to do with work or having to return your phone messages. Something about being in my home made you uncomfortable. What was it, Drake? Did you suddenly fear I'd make some sort of demand on you that you didn't want or perhaps didn't feel ready to meet? Or maybe it was that you wished you hadn't shown me where you'd grown up because it made you feel too vulnerable?'

Wincing, Drake pushed his fingers through his hair and nodded slowly. 'I didn't fear you making demands on me, Layla. But you're right… I *did* have reservations about showing you my old home…at least the first time. The second time we went back I was less tense, because I wanted to tell you that I'd changed my mind about tearing the houses down…that I had decided to renovate instead. But when we came back here and I saw that you'd grown up in a much better part of town than I had…and in such a beautiful home…the home you share with a brother who clearly means the world to you and who clearly adores you too… I wondered what I could possibly offer you that would be an incentive for you to exchange all that simply to be with me?'

Sweeping her fringe back off her face, Layla knew her expression was genuinely stunned. 'You seriously don't *know* what you could offer me that would be an incentive to stay with you?'

His heartbeat accelerated, making it hard for him to articulate his feelings. He drew in a deep breath to steady himself. 'Let's look at the facts, shall we? You have a lovely home here—a home full of warm family memories that you understandably returned to when things turned sour for you in London. You'd probably never consider living in the city again, and even though I came back here to help with the town's regeneration and improve it I'm sure you can understand why it's not a place I would personally ever want to live in again.'

'Going back to what you were saying before. Are you telling me that you *want* me to stay with you, Drake? I mean…as in *living* with you?'

His mouth drying, he moved across the room to stand in front of her. 'Yes…that's exactly what I'm saying, Layla.'

Her soft cheeks flushed rosily. 'Why? *Why* do you want me to live with you?'

The blood in Drake's veins thundered hotly in embarrassment when he realised she didn't know. Instead of telling her how he felt, as he'd planned to do, he'd somehow lulled himself into believing she would intuit everything. Grimacing, he silently made a vow that he would never let fear and doubt stop him from confessing his true feelings to this woman ever again.

He touched his palm to her cheek and held it there, loving the sensation of her warm satin skin. 'I want you to live with me because I'm crazy about you…crazy to the point of feeling like you've put me under some kind of spell. Even when I'm supposed to be working I can't stop thinking about you. What I'm trying to tell you is that I love you, Layla. I love you more than I ever dreamed it was possible to love anyone, and I don't want to blow my one chance at real happiness by letting you go. If you can't live in London, and I can't live here, then we're just going to have to come up with some mutually agreeable compromise.'

Her beautiful dark eyes danced teasingly. 'What makes you think I'd never consider living in London with you?'

Frowning, Drake rested his hands either side of her svelte hips and couldn't resist the compelling urge to bring her closer into his body. 'That low-life of a boss of yours must have hurt you badly with what he did. I perfectly understand why the memory of such a painful experience might put you off the idea of living there. I also understand why it means a lot to you to live *here*. For one thing, apart from the happy memories of your childhood, your brother's here. Not only that, you've got a job working for him. I doubt that you'd agree to resign to come and live with me, would you?'

'You seem to think you know a lot about what I want and don't want, don't you? Will you give me the chance to tell you what I want myself?'

'Of course.'

Emitting a soft breath, Layla smiled. 'First of all, I love you too, Drake... I didn't know it at the time, but maybe it happened when your incredible grey eyes looked back into mine that very first time? I never dreamt I'd fall for someone so hard and so fast, and at first it scared me. It scared me a lot. But the truth is I'd live anywhere you wanted me to just so long as I could be with you. And as for Marc—I'm sure I can persuade him to rent out my flat to help him make some extra money to pay off his debts, and also to give the café some much needed redecoration.'

'What about your job there?'

'I was thinking I'd keep it until the town project comes to an end. I don't mean I'll stay living here, if you want me to move in with you sooner, but when the regeneration is complete I'll get a job somewhere local to wherever we're living.' Pausing, she reached up to gently push some hair back from his forehead. 'There's one more thing I want to tell you. When I lost my life savings I didn't really lose anything of value...at least not in the sense of *true* value. Even though I was upset and demoralised by it at the time, after I moved back here I started to realise I should be grateful for what I *had*...not mourn what I'd lost. And for me it's always been the people I love that I value the most.'

Capturing her hand, Drake brought it up to his lips

and planted a warm lingering kiss in the centre of her palm. 'You are one incredible woman—you know that?'

'No, I'm not. It's you who's incredible. To come back here and help bring hope and new life to the community by improving the town after your sad experiences growing up here…well, it's *beyond* brave in my book. Why *did* you decide to take the commission, by the way? You've never told me.'

He thought hard for a moment, wanting to be absolutely truthful. 'I suppose subconsciously I was looking to reinvent my relationship with the place…to bury my regrets and turn my memories into much more positive ones. When I was first contacted about working on the regeneration my instinct was not to touch it with a bargepole. But I forced myself to think more deeply about it, and in the end I decided to take it on for the very reasons I just explained. Seeing as that decision brought me to you, Layla, I'm guaranteed the good memories I always secretly craved. I never thought for one moment that I'd find the most beautiful girl in the world living here, and that I'd instantly fall in love with her, but I did…I *did*. It really is a dream come true.'

'I'm just ordinary, Drake…hardly the most beautiful girl in the world.'

'Sweetheart, you're going to have to learn to take compliments if you're going to be with me, because I plan to shower you with them every day throughout our long and happy marriage.' He smiled.

This astounding announcement put Layla's mind into a dizzying spin and made her heart clamour wildly. 'You want to *marry* me?' she asked incredulously.

'Just as soon as it can be arranged—and I won't be

slow to pull a few favours from the official powers-that-be to help me achieve that, I promise you.'

'There's one more thing I'd like to ask you.'

'What's that?'

This time when he responded to the notion of her asking what might be another personal question he didn't look remotely wary or defensive, Layla noticed. Instead his glance was infinitely warm and understanding.

'Not jumping the gun or anything…but would you really consider us having children?'

'Would you believe me if I told you that when I realised I might have made you pregnant I honestly considered asking you to go ahead and have the child if there was one? When you told me you'd taken that emergency contraceptive I felt like I'd been robbed of an incredible opportunity that I'd never even realised was important to me.'

Feeling her heart melt, Layla couldn't disguise the wondrous happiness she felt at his words. 'I'd love to have your baby—you know that? Because I know you'll be the most incredibly loving and inspirational father. In which case I'm guessing I should definitely say yes to your proposal, shouldn't I?'

She didn't have a chance to say anything else right then, because Drake lowered his head to hers and kissed her with a hunger that wouldn't be sated until they both capitulated to the desperate need to be even closer—a desperately wild and passionate need that would always be a feature of their marriage until they were old, Layla guessed happily…

* * * * *

HIS TEMPORARY MISTRESS

CATHY WILLIAMS

*To my three daughters,
Charlotte, Olivia and Emma,
and their continuing support
in all my endeavours...*

Cathy Williams can remember reading Mills &
Boon Modern Romance books as a teenager, and
now that she is writing them she remains an avid
fan. For her, there is nothing like creating romantic
stories and engaging plots, and each and every
book is a new adventure. Cathy lives in London,
and her three daughters—Charlotte, Olivia and
Emma—have always been, and continue to be, the
greatest inspirations in her life.

CHAPTER ONE

So IT WAS bad news. The worst possible. Damien swivelled his leather chair so that it was facing the magnificent floor-to-ceiling panes of glass that afforded his office suite such spectacular views of London's skyline.

The truism that money couldn't buy everything had come home to roost. His mother had been given the swift and unforgiving diagnosis of cancer and there was nothing a single penny of his bottomless billions could do to alter that bald fact.

He wasn't a man who ever dealt in *if onlys*. Regret was a wasted emotion. It solved nothing and his motto had always been that for every problem there was a solution. Upwards and onwards was what got a person through life.

However, now, a series of *what ifs* slammed into him with the deadly precision of a heat-guided missile. His mother's health had not been good for over a year and he had taken her word for it when she had vaguely told him that yes, she had been to see her GP, that there was nothing to worry about…that engines in old cars tended to be a little unreliable.

What if, instead of skimming the surface of those assurances, he had chosen to probe deeper? To insist on bringing her to London, where she could have had the best possible medical advice, instead of relying on the uncharted territory of the doctors in deepest Devon?

Would the cancer now attacking her have been halted in its tracks? Would he not have just got off the phone to the consultant having been told that the prognosis was hazy? That they would have to go in to see how far it had spread?

Yes, she was in London now, after complicated arrangements and a great deal of anxiety, but what if she had come to London sooner?

He stood up and paced restlessly through his office, barely glancing at the magnificent piece of art on the wall, which had cost a small fortune. For once in his life, guilt, which had been nibbling at the edges of his conscience for some time, blossomed into a full-scale attack. He strode through to his secretary, told her to hold all his calls and allowed himself the rare and unwelcome inconvenience of giving in to a bout of savage and frustrating introspection.

The only thing his mother had ever wanted for him had been marriage, stability, a good woman.

Yes, she had tolerated the women she had met over the years, on those occasions when she had come up to London to see him, and he had opted to ignore her growing disappointment with the lifestyle he had chosen for himself. His father had died eight years previously, leaving behind a company that had been teetering precariously on the brink of collapse.

Damien had been one hundred per cent committed to running the business he had inherited. Breaking it up, putting it back together in more creative ways. He had integrated his own vastly successful computer firm with his father's outdated transport company and the marriage had been an outstanding success but it had required considerable skill. When had he had the time to be concerned over lifestyle choices? At the age of twenty-three, a thousand years ago or so it seemed, he had attempted to make one serious lifestyle choice with a woman and that had spectacularly crashed and burned. What was the problem if, from then onwards, his choices had not been to his mother's liking? Wasn't time on his side when it came to dealing with that situation?

Now, faced with the possibility that his mother might not have long to live, he was forced to concede that the single-minded ambition and ferocious drive that had taken him to the top, that had safeguarded the essential financial cushion his mother deserved and required, had also placed him in the unpalatable situation of having disappointed her.

And what could he do about it? Nothing.

Damien looked up as his secretary poked her head around the door. With anyone else, he wouldn't have had to voice his displeasure at being interrupted, not when he had specifically issued orders that he was not to be disturbed. With Martha Hall, the usual ground rules didn't work. He had inherited her from his father and, at the age of sixty-odd, she was as good as a family member.

'I realise you told me not to bother you, son…'

Damien stifled a groan. He had long ago given up on telling her that the term of affection was inappropriate. In addition to working for his father, she had spent many a night babysitting him.

'But you promised that you'd let me know what that consultant chap said about your mother…' Her face was creased with concern. She radiated anxiety from every pore of her tall, angular body.

'Not good.' He tried to soften the tone of his voice but found that he couldn't. He raked restless fingers through his dark hair and paused to stand in front of her. She would have easily been five ten, but he towered over her, six foot four of pure muscular strength. The fine fabric of his hand-tailored charcoal trousers and the pristine white of his shirt lovingly sheathed the lean, powerful lines of a man who could turn heads from streets away.

'The cancer might be more widespread than they originally feared. She's going to have a battery of tests and then surgery to consolidate their findings. After that, they'll discuss the appropriate treatment.'

Martha whipped out a handkerchief which she had stored in the sleeve of her blouse and dabbed her eyes. 'Poor Eleanor. She must be scared stiff.'

'She's coping.'

'And what about Dominic?'

The name hung in the air between them, an accusatory reminder of why his mother was so frantic with worry, so upset that she was ill and he, Damien, was still free, single and unattached, still playing the field with a series of beautiful but spectacularly unsuitable airheads, still, in her eyes, ill equipped to handle the responsibility that would one day be his.

'I shall go down and see him.'

Most people would have taken the hint at the abrupt tone of his voice. Most people would have backed away from pursuing a conversation he patently did not want to pursue. Most people were not Martha Hall.

'So have you considered what will happen to him should your mother's condition be worse than expected? I can see from your face that you don't want to talk about this, honey, but you can't hide from it either.'

'I'm not hiding from anything,' Damien enunciated with great forbearance.

'Well, I'll leave you to ponder that, shall I? I'll pop in and see your mother when I leave work.'

Damien attempted a smile.

'Oh, and there's something else.'

'I can't think what,' Damien muttered under his breath as he inclined his head to one side and prayed that there wouldn't be a further attack on his already overwrought conscience.

'There's a Miss Drew downstairs insisting on seeing you. Would you like me to show her up?'

Damien stilled. The little matter of Phillipa Drew was just something else on his plate, but at least this was something he would be able to sort out. Had it not been for the emergency with his mother, it would have been sorted out by now, but...

'Show her up.'

Martha knew nothing of Phillipa Drew. Why would she? Phillipa Drew worked in the bowels of IT, the place where creativity was at its height and the skills of his highly talented programmers were tested to the limit. As a lowly secretary to the head of the department, *he* had not been aware of her existence until, a week previously, a series of company infringements had come to light and the trails had all led back to her.

The department head had had the sternest possible warning, meetings had been called, everyone had had to stand up and be counted. Sensitive material could not be stolen, forwarded to competitors... The process of questioning had been rigorous and, eventually, Damien had concluded that the woman had acted without assistance from any other member of staff.

But he hadn't followed up on the case. The patent on the software had limited the damage but punishment would have to be duly meted out. He had had a preliminary interview with the woman but it had been rushed, just long enough for her to be escorted out of the building with a price on her head. He had more time now.

After a stressful ten days, culminating in the phone

call with his mother's consultant, Damien could think of a no more satisfying way of venting than by doling out just deserts to someone who had stolen from his company and could have cost millions in lost profits.

He returned to his chair and gave his mind over completely to the matter in hand.

Jail, of course. An example would have to be set.

He thought back to his brief interview with the woman, the way she had sobbed, begged and then, when neither appeared to have been working, offered herself to him as a last resort.

His mouth curled in distaste at the recollection. She might have been a five foot ten blonde but he had found the cheap, ugly working of the situation repulsive.

He was in the perfect mood to inform her, in a leisurely and thorough fashion, that the rigours of the British justice system would be waiting for her. He was in the perfect mood to unleash the full force of his frustration and stress on the truly deserving head of a petty criminal who had had the temerity to think that she could steal from him.

He pulled up all the evidence of her ill-conceived attempts at company fraud on his computer and then relaxed back in his chair to wait for her.

Downstairs, in the posh lobby of the most scarily impressive building she had ever entered, Violet waited for Damien Carver's secretary to come and fetch her. She was a little surprised that getting in to see the man in the hallowed halls of his own office had been so easy. For a few misguided seconds she nurtured the improbable fantasy that perhaps Damien Carver wasn't quite the monster Phillipa had made him out to be.

The fantasy didn't last long. No one ever got to the

stratospheric heights of success that this man obviously had by being kind, forgiving and compassionate.

What was she doing here? What was she hoping to achieve? Her sister had stolen information, had been well and truly suckered by a man who had used her to access files he wanted, had been caught and would have to face the long arm of the law.

Violet wasn't entirely sure what exactly the long arm of the law in this instance would be. She was an art teacher. Espionage, theft and nicking information couldn't have been further removed from her world. Surely her sister couldn't have been right when she had wailed that there was the threat of prison?

Violet didn't know what she would do if her sister wasn't around. There were just the two of them. At twenty-six, she was four years older than her sister and, whilst she would have been the first to admit that Phillipa hadn't always been an easy ride, ever since their parents had died in a car crash seven years previously, she loved her to bits and would do anything for her.

She looked around her and tried to stem the mounting tide of panic she felt at all the acres of marble and chrome surrounding her. She felt it was unfair that a simple glass building could fail to announce such terrifyingly opulent surroundings. Why hadn't Phillipa mentioned a word of this when she had first joined the company ten months ago? She pushed aside the insidious temptation to wish herself back at the tiny house she had eventually bought for them to share with the proceeds left to them after their parents' death. She valiantly fought a gut-wrenching instinct to run away and bury herself in all the school preparations she had to do before the new term began.

What on earth was she going to say to Mr Carver?

Could she offer to pay back whatever had been stolen? To make some kind of financial restitution?

Absorbed in scenarios which ranged from awkward to downright terrifying, she was startled when a tall grey-haired woman announced that she had come to usher her to Damien Carver's office.

Violet clutched her bag in front of her like a talisman and dutifully followed.

Everywhere she turned, she was glaringly reminded that this was no ordinary building, despite what it had cruelly promised from the outside.

The paintings on the walls were dramatic abstract splashes that looked mega-expensive...the plants dotting the foyer were all bigger and more lush than normal, as though they had been routinely fed on growth hormones... the frowning, determined people scurrying from lift to door and door to lift were younger and more snappily dressed than they had a right to be...and even the lift, as she stepped into it, was abnormally large. She dodged the repeated reflection of her nervous face and tried to concentrate on the polite conversation being made.

If this was his personal secretary, then it was clear that she had no idea of Phillipa's misdeeds. On the bright side, at least her sister's face hadn't been reprinted on posters for target practice.

She only surfaced when they were standing in front of an imposing oak door, alongside which two vertical sheets of smoked glass protected Damien Carver from the casual stares of anyone who might be waiting in his secretary's outside office.

Idly tabulating the string of idiotic mistakes Phillipa Drew had made in her half-baked attempt to defraud his company, Damien didn't bother to look up when his door was pushed open and Martha announced his unexpected visitor.

'Sit!' He kept his eyes glued to his computer screen. Every detail of his body language suggested the contempt of a man whose mind had already been made up.

With her nerves unravelling at a pace, Violet slunk into the leather chair directly in front of him. She wished she could direct her eyes to some other, less forbidding part of the gigantic room, but she was driven to stare at the man in front of her.

'He's a pig,' Phillipa had said, when Violet had off-handedly asked her what Damien Carver was like. Violet had immediately pictured someone short, fat, aggressive and unpleasant. Someone, literally, porcine in appearance.

Nothing had prepared her for the sight of one of the most beautiful men she had ever seen in her life.

Raven-black hair was swept away from a face, the lines and contours of which were finely chiselled. His unsmiling mouth filled her with cold fear but, in a strangely detached way, she was more than aware of its sensual curve. She couldn't see the details of his physique, but she saw enough to realise that he was muscular and lean. He must have some foreign blood in him, she thought, because his skin was burnished gold. He made her mouth go dry and she attempted to gather her scattered wits before he raised his eyes to look at her.

When he finally *did* turn his attention to her, she was pinned to the chair by navy-blue eyes that could have frozen water.

Damien looked at her for a long time in perfect silence before saying, in a voice that matched his glacial eyes, 'And who the hell are you?'

Certainly not the woman he had been expecting. Phillipa Drew was tall, slim, blonde and wore the air of some of the women he had dated in the past—an expression of smug awareness that she had been gifted with an abundance of pulling power.

This woman, in her unflattering thick black coat and her sensible flat black shoes, was the very antithesis of a fashion icon. Who knew what body was lurking beneath the shapeless attire? Her clothes were stridently background, as was her posture. Frankly, she looked as though she would have given a million dollars to have been anywhere but sitting in his office in front of him.

'I'm Miss Drew… I thought you knew…' Violet stammered, cringing back because, without even having to lean closer, she was still overwhelmed by the force of his personality. She was sitting ramrod-erect and still clutching her handbag to her chest.

'I'm in no mood for games. Believe me, I've had one hell of a fortnight and the last thing I could do with is someone finding their way into my office under false pretences.'

'I'm not here under false pretences, Mr Carver. I'm Violet Drew, Phillipa's sister.' She did her best to inject some natural authority into her voice. She was a teacher. She was accustomed to telling ten- and eleven-year-olds what to do. She could shout *Sit!* as good as the next person. But, for some reason, probably because she was on uncertain ground, all sense of authority appeared to have abandoned her.

'Now why am I finding that hard to believe?' Damien vaulted upright and Violet was treated to the full impact of his tall, athletic body, carelessly graceful as he walked around her in ever diminishing circles. Very much like a predator surveying a curiosity that had landed in his range of vision. He withdrew to perch on the edge of his desk, obliging her to look up at him from a disadvantageous sitting position.

'We don't look much alike,' Violet admitted truthfully. 'I've grown up with people saying the same thing. She inherited the height, the figure and the looks. From my mother's side of the family. I'm much more like my dad was.' The rambling apology was well rehearsed and spoken on autopilot; God knew she had trotted it out often enough, but her mind was almost entirely occupied with the man in front of her.

On closer examination, Damien could see the similarities between them. He guessed that their shade of hair colour would have been the same but for the fact that Phillipa had obviously dyed hers a brighter, whiter blonde and they both had the same bright blue eyes fringed with unusually dark, thick eyelashes.

'So you've come here because…?'

Violet took a deep breath. She had worked out in her head what she intended to say. She hadn't banked on finding herself utterly distracted by someone so sinfully good-looking and the upshot was that her thoughts were all over the place.

'I suppose she sent you on a begging mission on her behalf, did she?' Damien interjected into the lengthening silence. His lip curled. 'Having discovered that her sobbing and pleading and wringing of hands didn't cut it, and having tried and failed to seduce me into leniency, she thought she'd get you to do her dirty work for her…'

Violet's eyes widened with shock. 'She tried *to seduce you*?'

'A short-sighted move on her part.' Damien swung round so that he was back in front of his computer. 'She must have mistaken me for the sort of first-class idiot who could be swayed by a pretty face.'

'I don't believe it…' And yet, didn't she? Phillipa had always had a tendency to use her looks to get her own way. She had always found it easy to manipulate people into doing what she wanted by allowing them into the charmed space around her. Boys had always been putty in her hands, coming and going in a relentless stream, picked up and discarded without a great deal of thought for their feelings. Except, with Craig Edwards, the shoe had been on the other foot and life had ill prepared her to deal with the reversal. Violet was horribly embarrassed on her sister's behalf.

'Believe it.'

'I don't know if she told you, but she was used by a guy she had been dating. He wanted to get access to whatever files he thought you had on…well, I'm not too sure of the technical details…'

'I'll help you out there, shall I?' Damien listed the range of information that had fortunately never found its way into the wrong hands. He sat back, folded his hands behind his head and looked at her coldly. 'Shall I give you a rough idea of how much money my company stood to lose had your sister's theft proved successful?'

'But it *didn't*. Doesn't that count for *something*?'

'What argument are you intending to use to try and save your sister?' Damien drawled without an ounce of compassion. 'The *got-sadly-caught-up-with-the-wrong-guy* one or the *but-it-didn't-work* one? Because I can tell you now that I'm not buying either. She told me all about the smooth-talking banker with an eye to the main chance and a plan to take a shortcut to a career in computer software by nicking my ideas, except your sister, from the brief acquaintance I had with her, didn't exactly strike me as one of life's passive victims. Frankly, I put her down as a co-conspirator who just didn't have the brains to pull it off.'

Violet looked at him with loathing. Underneath the head-turning good looks, he was as cold as a block of ice.

'Phillipa didn't ask me to come,' she persisted. 'I came because I could see how devastated she was, how much she regretted what she had done...'

'Tough. From where I'm sitting, it's all about crime and punishment.'

Violet paled. 'She's being punished already, Mr Carver. Can't you see that? She's been sacked from the first real job she's ever held down...'

'She's twenty-two years old. I know because I've memorised her personnel file. So if this is the first real job she's ever held down, then do you care to tell me what she's been doing for the past...let's see...*six years*...? Ever since she left school at sixteen? If I'm not mistaken, she led my people to believe that a vigorous training course in computers was followed by exemplary service at an IT company in Leeds... A glowing written and verbal reference was provided by one *Mr Phillips*...'

Violet swallowed painfully as a veritable expanse of quicksand opened up at her feet. What could she say to that? Lie? She refused to. She looked at the hatefully confident expression on his face, the look of someone who had neatly led the enemy into a carefully contrived trap. Phillipa had said nothing to her about how she had managed to secure such a highly paid job at a top-rated company. She knew how now. Andrew Phillips had been her sister's boyfriend. She had strung him along with promises of love and marriage as he had taken up his position at an IT company in Leeds. He hadn't been out of the door for two seconds before she had turned her attention briefly to Greg Lambert and then, fatally, to Craig Edwards.

'Well?' Damien prompted. 'I'm all ears.' A part of him was all too aware that he was being a little unfair. So this girl, clearly lacking in guile, clearly well intentioned, had plucked up the courage to approach him on her sister's behalf. Not only was he in the process of shooting her down in flames, but he was also spearheading the arrow with poison for added measure.

The past few weeks of stress, uncertainty and unwelcome self-doubt were seeking a target for their expression and he had conveniently found one.

'Look—' he sighed impatiently and leaned forward '—it's laudable of you to come here and ten out of ten for trying, but you clearly need to wake up to your sister's true worth. She's a con artist.'

'I know Phillipa can be manipulative, Mr Carver, but she's all I have and I can't let her be written off because she's made a mistake.' Tears were gathering at the back of her eyes and thickening her voice.

'My guess is that your sister's made a number of mistakes in her life. She's just always been able to talk her way out of them by flashing a smile and baring her breasts...'

'That's a horrible thing to say.'

Damien gave an elegant little shrug of his shoulders and continued to look at her in a way that made her whole body feel as though it was burning up. 'I find that the truth is something best faced squarely.' Except, he privately conceded, that was something of a half truth. He had nonchalantly refused to face the truth about his mother's concerns over his lifestyle, preferring to stick it all on the back burner and turn a blind eye.

'So what happens now?' Violet slumped, defeated, in the chair. It had been a vain hope that she could appeal to his better nature.

'I'll take advice from my lawyers but this is a serious charge and, as such, has to be dealt with decisively.'

'When you say *decisively*...' She was mesmerised by

the icy, unforgiving lines of his face. It was like staring at someone from another planet. Her friends were all laid-back and easy-going. They cared about humanitarian issues. They joined protest marches and could argue for hours over the state of the world. The majority of them did charity work. She, herself, visited an old people's home once a week where she taught basic art. She had only ever mixed with people who thought like her. Damien Carver not only didn't think like her, she could tell that he was vaguely contemptuous of what she stood for. Those merciless eyes held no sympathy for anything she was saying. She could have been having a conversation with a block of marble.

'Jail.' Why beat about the bush? 'A learning curve for your sister and an example just in case anyone else thinks they can get away with trying to rip me off.'

'Phillipa wouldn't last a day in a prison cell...'

'Something she should have considered before she decided to try and hack into my computers to get hold of sensitive information,' Damien responded drily.

'It's her first offence, Mr Carver... She's not a criminal... I understand that you won't be giving her any references...'

Damien burst out laughing. Was this woman for real? 'Not *giving her references*? Have you heard a single word I've just said to you? Your sister will be put into the hands of the law and she will go to prison. I'm sure it won't be a hardcore unit with serial killers and rapists but that's not my problem. You can go visit her every week and she can productively use the time to reflect on the wisdom of a few personality changes. When she's released in due course back into the big, wide world, she can find herself a menial job somewhere. I'm sure the process of rehabilitation will be an invaluable experience for her. Of course, she'll have a criminal record, but, like I said, what else could she have expected?' He reached into one of the drawers in his massive desk, fetched out a box of tissues and pushed it across to her.

Violet shuffled out of her chair and snatched the box from his desk. Her eyes were beginning to leak. What else was there to say?

'Don't you have *any* sense of compassion?' she whispered in a hoarse undertone. 'I promise I'll make sure that Phillipa doesn't put a foot astray *ever again*...'

'She won't be able to when she's behind bars. But, just out of curiosity, how would you manage to accomplish that feat anyway? Install CCTV cameras in her house? Or flat? Or wherever it is she lives? As long-term solutions go, not a practical one.'

'We share a house,' Violet said dully. She dabbed her eyes. Breaking down was not the way to deal with a man like this. She knew that. Men like him, *people* like him, only understood a language that was similar to the one they used, the harsh and ugly language of cold, merciless cruelty. He wouldn't appreciate a sobbing female and he just wouldn't get the concept of loyalty that had driven her to confront him face to face in his own office.

Unfortunately, being tough and aggressive did not come naturally to Violet. She might have possessed a strength of character her sister lacked, but she had never had the talent Phillipa had for confrontation. 'And I would never dream of spying on anyone. I would keep an eye on her...make sure she toed the line...' Easier said than done. If Phillipa decided to try and defraud another company, then how on earth would she, Violet, ever be able to prevent her? 'I've been doing that ever since our parents died years ago...'

'How old are you?' The connections in his brain were beginning to transmit different messages now. He stared at her carefully. Her eyes were pink and her full mouth was still threatening to wobble. She was the picture perfect portrait of a despairing woman.

'Twenty-six.'

'So you're a scant four years older than your sister and I guess you were forced to grow up quickly if you were left in the role of caretaker... I'm thinking she must have been a handful...' For the first time in weeks, that feeling of being oddly at sea, at the whim of tides and currents over which he had no control, was beginning to evaporate.

Wrong-footed by the sudden change of tempo in the conversation, Violet met those fabulous navy eyes with a puzzled expression. She wondered whether this was a prelude to another rousing sermon on the salutary lessons to be learnt from incarceration. Maybe he was about to come out with another revelation, maybe he was going to inform her in that cold voice of his that Phillipa had done more than just make a pass at him. She was already cringing in mortification at what was to come.

'She went off the rails a bit.' Violet rushed into speech because, as long as she was talking, he wasn't saying stuff she didn't want to hear. 'It was understandable. We were a close family and she was at an impressionable age...'

'And you weren't?'

'I've always been stronger than Phillipa.' He was still staring at her with that speculative, unreadable expression that made her feel horribly uneasy. 'Phillipa was the spoiled one. I got that. She was a beautiful baby and she grew into a beautiful child and then a really stunning teenager. I was sensible and hard working and practical...'

'You must be hot in your coat. Why don't you remove it?'

'I beg your pardon?'

'The central heating here is in perfect working condition. You must be sweltering.'

'Why would I take my coat off, Mr Carver? When I'm going to be leaving in a short while? I mean, I've said everything there is to say and I've tried to appeal to your better nature, but you haven't got a better nature. So there's no point in my being here, is there? It doesn't really matter what I say, you're just going to tell me that Phillipa needs to be punished, that she's going to go to prison and that she'll come out a reformed person.'

'Maybe there's another discussion to be had on the subject…'

Violet hardly dared get her hopes up. She looked at him in disbelief. 'What other discussion, Mr Carver? You've just spent the past forty-five minutes telling me that she's to be held up as an example to your other employees and punished accordingly…'

'Take the coat off.'

Violet hesitated. Eventually she stood up, awkwardly aware of his eyes on her. She harked back to what he had said about her sister trying to seduce him. She had heard the contempt in his voice when he had said that. She wondered what his thoughts would be when he saw *her* without the protective covering of her capacious coat, and then she sternly reminded herself that what she looked like was irrelevant. She had come to plead her sister's case and she would take whatever sliver of compassion he might find in his heart to distribute.

Damien watched the unflattering coat reveal a baggy long-sleeved dress that was equally unflattering. Over it was a loose-fitting cardigan that reached down to below her waist.

'So the question is this…with your sister facing a prison sentence, what would you be prepared to do for her?'

He let that question hang in the air between them. Her eyes, he absently thought as she stared at him in bewilderment, weren't quite the same shade of blue as her sister's. They were more of a violet hue, which seemed appropriate given her name.

'I would do anything,' Violet told him simply. 'Phillipa may have her faults but she's learnt from this. Not just in the matter of trying to do something she shouldn't, but she's had her eyes opened about the sort of men she can trust and the ones she can't. In fact, I've never seen her so devastated. She's practically locked herself away...'

Damien thought that a few days of self-imposed seclusion before rejoining the party scene was a laughable price to pay for a criminal offence. If that was Violet Drew's definition of her sister's *devastation* then her powers of judgement were certainly open to debate.

'So you would do anything...' he drawled, standing to move to the window, briefly looking out at the miserable grey, muted colours of a winter still reluctant to release its grip. He turned around, strolled to his desk where he once again perched on the side. 'That's good to hear because, if that's really the case, then I would say that there's definitely room to negotiate...'

CHAPTER TWO

'NEGOTIATE? How?' VIOLET was at a loss. Would he ask her for some sort of financial compensation for the time his people had spent tracking Phillipa down? If no money had actually been lost, then she could hardly be held accountable for any debt incurred and, even if money had actually been lost, then there was no way that she could ever begin to repay it. Just thinking of all the money his company nearly did lose was enough to make her feel giddy.

This was not a situation that Damien liked. As solutions went, it left a lot to be desired, but where were his choices? He needed to prove to his mother that she could have faith in him, that he could be relied upon, whatever the circumstances. He needed to reassure her. If his mother wasn't stressing, then the chances of her responding well to treatment would be much greater. Who didn't know that stress could prove the tipping point between recovery and collapse in a case such as this? Eleanor Carver wanted him settled or she would fret over the consequences and that was a worst case scenario waiting to happen. He loved his mother and, after years of ships-in-the-night relationships, it was imperative that he now stepped up to the plate and presented her with a picture of stability.

The grim reality, however, was that he had no female friends. The women in his life were the women he dated and the women he dated were unsuitable for the task at hand.

'My mother has recently been diagnosed with cancer…'

'I'm so sorry to hear that…'

'Stomach cancer. She's in London at the moment for tests. As you may know, with cancer, its outcome can never be predicted.'

'No. But…may I ask what that has to do with me?'

'I have a proposal for you. One that may be beneficial to both of us.'

'A proposal? What kind of proposal?'

Damien looked steadily at the woman in front of him. On almost every level, he knew this was, at best, questionable. On the other hand, looking at the bigger picture, didn't the value of the ends more than make up for the means? Sometimes you had to travel down an unexpected road to get to the desired destination.

And now a virtual stranger, a woman he would not have looked at twice under normal circumstances, was about to be ushered into his rarefied world to do him a favour and he was well aware that she would be unable to refuse because her own protective instincts for her sister had penned her into a place in which she was helpless.

'For some time, my mother has had certain…misgivings about my lifestyle…' He realised that he had never actually verbalised any of this to anyone before. He wasn't into the touchy-feely business of sharing confidences. It was reassuring to know that Violet Drew didn't actually count as someone with whom the sharing of confidences was of any significance. He wasn't involved with her. It wasn't as though she would attach herself to anything he said and use it as a way of insinuating herself into a relationship. And yet…he still had to fight a certain hesitancy.

He impatiently swept aside his natural instinct for complete privacy. Hell, it wasn't as though he was in a confessional about to admit to an unforgivable mortal sin!

'Has she?'

'If you're wondering where this is going, then you'll have to hear me out. One thing I'm going to say, though, is that nothing I tell you leaves this room. Got it?'

'What are you going to say?'

'My mother is old-fashioned…traditional. I'm thirty-two years old and, as far as she is concerned, should be in a committed, serious relationship. With a…ah…let's just say a certain type of woman. Frankly, the sort of woman I wouldn't normally look at twice.'

'What sort of women do you look at?' Violet asked, because his remark seemed to beg further elaboration. Looking at him, the answer was self-explanatory.

'Let's just say that I tend to spend my time in the company of beautiful women. They're not the sort of women my mother has ever found suitable.'

'I still don't know what this has to do with me, Mr Carver.'

'Then I'll spell it out. My mother might not have long to live. She wants to see me with someone she thinks is the right sort of woman. Currently, I know no one who fits the bill…'

Enlightenment came in a blinding rush. 'And you think that *I* might be suitable for the role?' Violet shook her head disbelievingly. How on earth would anyone ever buy that she and this man were in any way involved? Romantically? He was aggressively, sinfully beautiful while she…

But of course, she thought, that was the point, wasn't it? Whilst his type would be models with legs up to their armpits and big, long hair, his mother obviously had a different sort of girl in mind for him. Someone more normal. Probably not even someone like *her* but maybe he figured that he didn't have time on his side to hunt down someone more suited to play the part and so he had settled for her. Because he could.

Damien calmly watched as she absorbed what he was saying. 'You're nothing like anyone I've ever dated in my life before, ergo you'll do.'

'I'm sorry, Mr Carver.' Violet wondered how such physical beauty could conceal such cold detachment. She looked at him and couldn't tear her eyes away and yet he chilled her to the bone. 'For starters, I would never lie to anyone. And secondly, if your mother knows you at all, then she'll see right through any charade you have in mind to…to…pull the wool over her eyes.'

'Here's the thing, though, Miss Drew…your sister is facing a prison sentence. Is that what you really want? Do you honestly want to condemn her to the full horrors of a stint courtesy of Her Majesty?'

'That's awful! You can't *blackmail* me…'

'Whoever said anything about blackmail? I'm giving you an option and it's an extremely generous one. In return for a few days of minor inconvenience, you have my word that I'll call the dogs off. Your sister will be able to have her learning curve without having to suffer the full force of the law, which you and I both know is what she richly deserves.' He stood up and strolled towards the impressive window, looking out for a few seconds before returning to face her. 'I wouldn't want you to think for a minute that I won't do my utmost to make sure your sister is punished should you decide to play the moral card. I will.'

'This is crazy,' Violet whispered. But she had a mental snapshot of beautiful Phillipa behind bars. She didn't possess the inner strength to ever survive something like that. She was a woman who was reliant on her beauty to get through life and that had left her vulnerable. Maybe she did indeed need to have a forceful learning curve, but prison? Not only would it destroy her, but if she ever found out that she, Violet, had rejected an opportunity to save her, then would their relationship survive? There was no large extended family on whom to rely, no one to whom either of them could turn for advice. A few second and third cousins up north…and then just old friends of their parents, most of whom they no longer saw.

'No one does stuff like this.' She made a final plea. 'Surely your mother would rather you go out with the sort of women you like rather than pretend to be with someone you don't.'

'It's not quite as simple as that.' Damien raked his fingers through his hair, suddenly restless as the need for yet more confidences was reluctantly dragged from him. 'Of course, if it were a simple case of my mother not approving of my choice of woman, then it would be regrettable, but something we could both live with.'

'But…?'

'But I have a brother. Dominic is six years older than me and he lives at home with my mother in Devon.' Damien hesitated. Nine years ago, before time and experience had done its work, he had been stupid enough to fall for a woman—so stupid that he had proposed to her. It had been an eight-week whirlwind romance that had largely taken place in bed. But she had been intelligent, a career woman, someone with whom he could envisage himself enjoying intellectual conversations. And then she had met Dominic and he had known within seconds that he had made a fatal error of judgement. Annalise had tried to cover her discomfort, and he had briefly and optimistically given her the benefit of the doubt until she had haltingly told him that she wasn't sure that she was ready to commit. He had got the message loud and clear. She could commit to him, but she would not commit to him if he came with the baggage of a disabled sibling, someone he would have to look after when his mother was no longer around. Since then, he had made sure that he kept his relationships with women short and sweet. He had never taken any of them to Devon and only a few had ever met his mother, mostly when he had had no choice.

He had to fight back his natural instinct to keep this slice of his life extremely private. It was a place to which no one was invited. However, these were circumstances he could never have foreseen and, like it or not, he would have to give the woman in front of him some background detail. It wasn't a great position in which to find himself. He restively began to prowl the room while Violet distractedly watched him. There were so many things to process that her brain seemed to have temporarily shut down and, instead, her senses were making up for the shortcoming, had heightened so that she was uncomfortably and keenly aware of the flex of every muscle in his body as he moved with economic grace around her, forcing her to twist in the chair to keep her eyes on him.

'My brother was born with brain damage,' he told her bluntly. 'He's not completely helpless, but he's certainly incapable of leading a normal life in the outside world. He is wheelchair-bound and, whilst he has flashes of true brilliance, he is mentally damaged. My mother says that he was briefly starved of oxygen when he was born. The bottom line is that he is dependent on my mother, despite the fact that he has all the carers money can buy. She believes that he needs the familiarity of a strong family link.'

'I understand. If you're not settled or at least involved with someone your mother approves of…she feels that you won't be able to handle your brother if something happens to her…'

'In a nutshell.'

Looking at him, Violet had no idea how he felt about his brother. Certainly he cared enough to subject himself to a role play he would not enjoy. It pointed to a complexity that was not betrayed by anything on his face, which remained cool, hard, considering.

'It's never right to lie to people,' Violet said and the forbidding lines of his face relaxed into a cynical smile.

'You don't really expect me to believe you, do you? When you spring from the same gene pool as your sister?'

'There must be some other way I can…make amends for what Phillipa's done…'

'We both know that you're going to cave in to what I want because you have no choice. Ironically, your position is very much like my own. We're both going to engage in a pretence neither of us wants for the sake of other people.'

'But when your mother discovers the truth…'

'I will explain to her that we didn't work out. It happens. Before then, however, she will have ample opportunity to reassure herself that I am more than capable of taking on the responsibilities that lie with me.'

Violet's head was swimming. She shakily got to her feet, but then sank back down into the chair. He was right, wasn't he. She *was* going to cave in because she had no choice. They both knew it and she hated the way he had deprived her of at least having the opportunity to come to terms with it for herself.

'But it would never work,' she protested. 'We don't even like each other…'

'Liking me isn't part of the arrangement.' Damien circled her then leant forward to rest both hands on either side of the chair and Violet squirmed back, suffocating in a wave of intense physical awareness of him. Everything about him was so overpowering. There was just *so much* of him. She found it impossible to relax. It was as if she had been plugged into an electrical socket and her normally placid temperament had been galvanised into a state of unbearable, strangulating tension.

'But your mother will see that straight away…she'll *know* that this is just a farce…'

'She'll see what she wants to see because people always do.' He needed her to. He knew he had not been a perfect son. His mother had never complained about the amount of time he spent away. She had always been fully understanding about the way work consumed his life, leaving very little room for much else, certainly very little room for cultivating any relationship of any substance, not that he had ever been inclined to have one. Her unprotesting acceptance had made him lazy. He could see that now but then hindsight was a wonderful thing.

He pushed himself away and glanced at his watch. 'I intend to visit my mother later this evening.' This time when he looked at Violet, it was assessingly. 'I'm taking it that you will agree to what I've suggested…'

'Do I have a choice?' she said bitterly.

'We all have choices. In this instance, neither of us are perhaps making the ones we would want to, but…' he gave an eloquent shrug '…life doesn't always play out the way we'd like it to.'

'Why don't you just hire an actress to play the part?' Violet glared resentfully at him from under her lashes.

'No time. Furthermore, hiring someone would open me up to the complication of them thinking that there might be more on offer than a simple business proposition. They might be tempted to linger after their job's been done. With you, the boundaries are crystal-clear. I'm saving your sister's skin and you owe me. The fact that you don't like me is an added bonus. At least it ensures that you won't become a nuisance.'

'A *nuisance*, Mr Carver?'

'Damien. However gullible my mother might be, calling me *Mr Carver* would give the game away.'

'How can you be so...so...cold-hearted?'

Damien flushed darkly. As far as he was concerned, he was dealing with a situation as efficiently as he could. Drain it of all emotion and nothing was clouded, there were no blurry lines or grey areas. His mother was ill... she was anxious about him...desperate for him to produce someone by his side whom she could see as an anchor... His task was to come up with a way of putting her mind at rest. It was the way he tackled all problems that presented themselves to him. Calmly, coolly and decisively. It was an approach that had always served him well and he wasn't going to change now.

He pushed the ugly tangle of confusion and vulnerability away. He had always felt that he was the one on whom his mother and Dominic needed to rely. After his father's death, he had risen to the challenge of responsibilities far beyond any a boy in his twenties might have faced. He had jettisoned all plans to take a little time out and had instead sacrificed the dream of kicking back so that he could immerse himself in taking over the reins of his father's company. His only mistake had been to fall for a woman who hadn't been able to cope with the complete picture and, in the aftermath, he had wasted time and energy in the fruitless pastime of self-recrimination and self-doubt. He had moved on from that place a long time ago but negative feelings had never again been allowed to cloud his thinking. Indecision was not something that was ever given space and it wasn't about to get any now.

'How I choose to deal with this situation is my concern

and my concern only. Your role isn't to offer your opinion; it's to be by my side in two days' time when I go and visit my mother. And you asked me what I meant by *a nuisance...*' There was no chance that she would become a liability. They were two people who could not have been on more opposing ends of the scale. If she hadn't told him that she didn't like him, then he would have surmised that for himself. It was there in the simmering resentment lurking behind her purple-blue eyes and in her body language as she huddled in the chair in front of him as if one false move might propel her further into his radius. Of course it didn't help that she considered herself there under duress, but even when she had first walked into his office she had failed to demonstrate any of those little signals that heralded interest. No coy looks...no encouraging half smiles...no fluttering eyelashes...

He wasn't accustomed to a reaction like this from a woman and, in any other situation, he might have been amused, but not now. Too much was at stake. So, whatever he thought, he would make his position doubly clear.

'A nuisance would be you imagining that the charade was real...getting ideas...'

Violet's mouth fell open and she went bright red. Not only had he blackmailed her into doing something she knew was wrong, but he was actually suggesting, in that *smug, arrogant* way, that she might start...*what, exactly...*? Thinking that he was seriously interested in her? Or imagining that she was interested in *him*?

He really was, a little voice whispered in her head, quite beautiful but she would never be interested in a man like him. Everything about him, aside from those staggering good looks, repelled her. Her soft mouth tightened and she looked back at him with an equal measure of coolness.

'That wouldn't happen in a million years,' she told him.

'The only reason I'm even consenting to this is because I don't have a choice, whatever you say. And how do I know that you'll keep your side of the deal? How do I know that you won't take proceedings against my sister after I've done what you want…?'

Damien leaned forward. Every line of his body threatened her. 'How do I know that you won't turn around and tell my mother what's actually going on? How do I know that you'll deliver what I need you to? I guess you could say that we're going to be harnessed to one another for a short while and we're just going to have to trust that neither of us decides to try and break free of the constraints… Now, we need to discuss the details…' He strode towards his jacket, which had been tossed over the back of the leather sofa against the wall. 'It's lunchtime. We're going to go and grab something and start filling in the blanks.'

He expected her to follow. Was he like that with *all* women? Why on earth did they put up with it? She had to half run to keep up with him, past the grey-haired secretary who looked at them both with keen interest as she was ordered to cancel all his afternoon appointments, and then back down to the foyer where, it now seemed like a million years ago, she had sat in a state of nervous panic waiting to be shown to his office.

She couldn't fail to notice the way everyone acknowledged his presence as he strode ahead of her. Conversations halted, backs were straightened, small groups dispersed. There was absolutely no doubt that he ran the show and she wondered how her sister could ever have thought that she could get away with trying to steal information from him. Perhaps she had never personally met him, but surely Phillipa would have realised, even if only through hearsay, that the man was one hundred per cent hard line? But then Phillipa had been busy losing her head to a guy who had spotted a way in to making a quick buck via a back door. Her sister, for once, had found herself being the victim of manipulation. Chances were she hadn't been thinking at all.

Her coat was back on because she had expected them to be walking to wherever he was taking her for lunch, but in fact they headed down to a lift that carried them straight to an enormous basement car park and she followed him to a gleaming black Aston Martin which he beeped open with his key.

'Tell me the sort of food you like to eat,' he said without looking at her.

'Is that the first step to pretending we know one another?'

'You're going to have to change your attitude.' Damien was entirely focused on the traffic as he emerged from the underground car park into the busy street outside. 'Two people in a relationship try to avoid sniping and sarcasm. What sort of restaurants do you go to?'

He slid his eyes across to her and Violet felt a quiver of something sharp and unidentifiable, something that slithered through her like quicksilver, making her skin burn and prickling it with a strange sensation of *awareness*.

This was a business deal. They were sitting here in this flash car, awkwardly joined together in a scheme in which neither wanted to participate but both were forced to, and she could do without her nervous system going into semi-permanent free fall.

She needed to hang on to her composure, however much she disliked the man and however much she scorned his ethics.

'I don't,' she told him evenly. 'At least not often. Sometimes after work on a Friday night. I'm an art teacher. I haven't got enough money to eat out in fancy restaurants.'

She wanted to burst out laughing because not only did they dislike each other, but they were from opposite sides of the spectrum. He was rich and powerful, she was… almost constantly counting her pennies or else saving and the only power she had was over her kids.

Damien didn't say anything. He had never gone out with a teacher. He leaned towards models, who moaned about not being paid enough…but usually it meant for the purchase of top end sports cars or cottages in the Cotswolds rather than fancy meals out. Most of them wouldn't have been caught dead in cheap clothes or cheap restaurants. They earned big bucks for strutting their stuff on catwalks. In their heads, there was always a photographer lurking round the corner so getting snapped looking anything but gorgeous and being anywhere but cool was unacceptable.

'When you say *fancy*…' he encouraged.

'What do *you* call fancy?' she asked him, because why should she be the one under the spotlight all the time?

He named a handful of Michelin-starred restaurants which she had heard of and she laughed with genuine amusement. 'I've read about those places. I don't think I'd make it to any of them, even for a special occasion.'

'Really,' Damien murmured. He altered the direction of his car.

'Really. Your mother will be very curious to discover what we see in one another. How would we have met in the first place?' For a few seconds she forgot how much she disliked him and focused on the incongruity of the two of them ever hitting it off. 'I mean, did you just see me emerging from the school where I work and decide that you wanted to come over for a chat?'

'Stranger things have been known to happen.'

But not much, Violet thought. 'Where are we going, anyway?'

'Heard of Le Gavroche?'

'We can't!'

'Why not? You said you've never eaten out at a fancy restaurant. Now's your big opportunity.'

'I'm not dressed for somewhere like that!'

'Too late.' He made a quick phone call and an attendant emerged from the restaurant to take the keys to his car. 'I eat here a lot,' Damien explained in an undertone. 'I have an arrangement that someone parks my car and brings it back for me if I come without my driver. You can't wear the coat for the duration of the meal. I'm sure what you're wearing is perfectly adequate.'

'No, it's not!' Violet was appalled. The surroundings weren't intimidating. Indeed, there was a charm and old-fashioned elegance about the place that was comforting. Damien was greeted like an old friend. No one stared at her. And yet Violet couldn't help but feel that she was out of her depth, that she just didn't look the part. She had dressed for what she had thought was going to be a difficult interview. The clothes she wore to work were casual, cheap and comfortable. She wasn't used to what she was now wearing—a stiff dress that had been chosen specifically because it was the comforting background colour of dark grey and because it was shapeless and therefore concealed what she fancied was a body that was plump and unfashionable.

'Are you always so self-conscious about your appearance?' was the first thing he asked as soon as they were seated at one of the tables in a quiet corner. He eyed her critically. He had never seen such an unflattering dress in his life. 'In addition to allowing your sister to walk free, you'll be pleased to hear that you'll benefit from our deal as well. I'm going to open an account for you at Harrods. I have someone there who deals with me. I'll give you her name, tell her to expect you. Choose whatever clothes you want. I would say a selection of outfits appropriate for visiting my mother while she's in hospital.' He looked at her horrified, outraged expression and raised his eyebrows. 'I'm being realistic,' he said. 'I may be able to pull off the *opposites attract* explanation for our relationship, but there's no way I can pull off a sudden attraction for someone who is completely disinterested in fashion.'

'How *dare* you? How *dare* you be so rude?'

'We haven't got time to beat around the bush, Violet. My mother won't care what you wear but she *will* smell a rat if I show up with someone who doesn't seem to care about her appearance.'

'I do care about my appearance!' Violet was calm by nature but she could feel herself on the verge of snapping.

'You have a sister who's spent her life turning heads and you've reacted by blending into the background. I don't have to have a degree in psychology to work that one out, but you're going to have to step into the limelight for a little while and you'll need the right wardrobe to pull it off.'

'I don't need this!'

'Are you going to leave?'

Violet hesitated.

'Thought not. So relax.' He pushed the menu towards her. 'You teach art at a school…where?' He sat back, inclined his head to one side and listened while she told him about her job. He was taking everything in. Every small detail. The more she talked, the more she relaxed. He listened to her anecdotes about some of her pupils. He made encouraging noises when she described her colleagues. She seemed to do a great deal of work for precious little financial reward. The picture painted was of a hard-working, diligent girl who had put the time and effort in while her pretty, flighty sister had taken the shortcuts.

Violet realised that she had been talking for what seemed like hours when their starters were placed in front of them. Having anticipated a meal comprised of pregnant pauses, hostile undertones and simmering, thinly veiled accusations and counter accusations, she could only think that he must be a very good listener. She had forgotten his offensive observation that she didn't take care of herself, that she had no sense of style, that she needed a new wardrobe to meet his requirements. She wanted to defensively point out that wearing designer clothes was no compensation for having personality. She was tempted to pour scorn on women who defined themselves according to what they wore or what jewellery they possessed. It took a lot of effort to rein back the impulses and tell herself that none of that mattered because none of this was real. They weren't embarking on a process of discovery about each other. They were skimming the surface, gleaning a few facts, just enough to pull off a charade for the sake of his mother. That being the case, she didn't need to defend herself to him, nor should she take offence at anything he said. His request that she buy herself a new wardrobe was no different from being told, on applying for a job working for an airline, that there would be a uniform involved.

'What sort of clothes would your mother expect me to show up in?' Once more in charge of her wits, Violet paid some attention to the food that had been placed in front of her. Ornate, as beautifully arranged as a piece of artwork, and yet mouth-wateringly delicious. 'I don't own many dresses. I have lots of jeans and jumpers and trousers.'

'Simple but classy might be good...'

'And how long would I be obliged to play this part?'

Damien pushed aside his plate to lean forward and look at her thoughtfully. Down to business. Although he had to admit that hearing about her school days had been entertaining. It made a change to sit in a restaurant with a woman who wasn't interested in playing footsie with him under the table or casting lingering looks designed to indicate what game would be played when the footsie was over. He wondered whether she had ever played footsie with a man, which made him speculate on what body was hidden under her charmless dress. It was impossible to tell.

'There will be a series of tests spanning a week. Maybe a bit longer until treatment can be transferred to Devon.'

'I expect your mother will be anxious to get back to her home... Can I ask who is looking after your brother at the moment?'

'We have a team of carers in place. But that's not your concern. You will be around while she is in London. As soon as she leaves for Devon, your part will be done. I will return with her and, during that time, I will eventually break the news that we are no longer a going concern. At that point, I intend to demonstrate that she has nothing to be worried about...' He looked at her flushed heart-shaped face and his eyes involuntarily wandered down to the swell of full breasts straining against the unforgiving lines of the severe dress she had chosen to wear.

Violet sensed the shift of his attention from his unemotional checklist of facts to her body. She didn't know how she was aware of that because his face was so unreadable, the depth of his deep blue eyes revealing nothing at all, and yet she just *knew* and she was appalled when her body reacted with a surge of intense excitement that shocked and bewildered her.

Unlike her sister, Violet's history with men could have been condensed to fit on the back of a postage stamp. One fairly serious relationship three years previously, which had ended amicably after a year and a half. They had started as friends and no one could accuse them of not having tried to take it a step further, but, despite the fact that, on paper at least, it made sense, it had fizzled out. Back into the friendship from whence it had sprung. They kept in touch and since then he had married and was living the fairy tale in Yorkshire. Violet was happy for him. She harboured the dream that she too would discover her fairy tale life with someone. She was certain that she would know that special someone the second he stepped into her life. In the meantime she kept her head down, went out with her friends and enjoyed the company of the guys she met in a group. She didn't expect to be thrown unwillingly into the company of a man of whom she didn't approve and feel anything for him bar dislike. Certainly not the dark, forbidden excitement that suddenly coursed through her body. It was a reaction she angrily rejected.

'You will agree that you'll be profiting immensely from your side of this deal…' More food was brought for them although his eyes never left her face. She had amazing skin. Clear and satiny-smooth and bare of make-up, aside from some remnants of lipgloss which he suspected she had applied in a hurry.

'You still haven't told me where we're supposed to have met.' Violet looked down and focused on yet more artfully arranged food on her plate, although her normally robust appetite appeared to have deserted her. She was too conscious of his eyes on her. Having given house room to the unwelcome realisation that there was something exciting about being in his presence, that that excitement swirled inside her with a dark persuasive force that she didn't want, not at all, she now found that she had to claw her way back to the level of composure she needed and wanted.

'At your school. It seems the least convoluted of solutions.'

'Why would you be in a school in Earl's Court, Mr Carver? Sorry, *Damien*...'

'I know a lot of people, Violet. Including a certain celebrity chef who is currently working on a programme of food in schools. Since I've set up a small unit to oversee the opening of three restaurants, all of which will be staffed by school leavers who have studied Home Economics or whatever it happens to be called these days, then it makes perfect sense that I might be in your building.'

'You haven't really, have you?' Violet was unwillingly impressed that he might be more than an electronics guru. 'I mean become involved in a set-up like that...'

'Why do you find that so hard to believe?' He shrugged. Did he want to tell her how satisfying he found this slice of semi charity work? Because certainly he didn't expect to see much by way of profit from the exercise. Did he want to explain that he knew what it felt like to have someone close who would never hold down a job? He was almost tempted to tell her about his long-reaching plan to source IT projects within his company for a department that would be fitted out to accommodate the disabled because he knew from experience how many of them were capable and enthusiastic but betrayed by bodies that refused to cooperate.

'Don't bother to answer that—' he brushed aside any inclination to deviate from the point '—this isn't a soul-searching exercise. Nor do we have the time to get into too much background detail. Like I said. You smile and leave the rest to me. Before you know it, you'll be on your merry way and everyone will be happy.'

CHAPTER THREE

'BUT *HOW*? *How* did you manage to do it? I know I keep going on about it, but it's just so…incredible!'

Phillipa was sitting across the kitchen table from Violet. In front of her inroads had already been made into a bottle of white wine. She had greeted the news of Damien Carver's unexpected leniency yesterday with stunned disbelief, incredulity, anger that Violet might be stringing her along and, finally, she had taken it on board, although Violet could tell that her vague explanations hadn't quite passed muster.

'I begged and pleaded,' Violet said for the umpteenth time. 'When did you start drinking? It's only five-thirty!'

'*You'd* be drinking too if you were in my position,' Phillipa said sulkily, unwinding her long legs, which had been tucked under her, and standing up to stretch in a lazy, languorous movement like a cat. Stress had not affected Phillipa the way it would other people. She still managed to look amazing. Although it wasn't hot inside the house because the thermostat was rigidly controlled to save money, she was wearing a thin silky vest and a matching pair of silky culottes. Violet assumed that they had been one of the many presents she had received from Craig as he had manoeuvred to get her on board with his plan.

From what Violet had gathered, he had disassociated

himself from Phillipa and denied all knowledge of what she had done. Nevertheless, he was, she had been told only an hour before by her clearly gleeful sister, who had recovered well from her devastation, out of a job and planning on leaving the country. He hadn't deleted her fast enough from his Facebook account to prevent her from maliciously charting his progress but he had as soon as she had posted a message informing the world that he was a crook and a bastard and that if anyone bought that phoney crap about better opportunities abroad then they were idiots.

'I don't suppose you managed to persuade him to let them give me a reference, did you?' Phillipa asked hopefully and Violet stifled a groan of pure despair. 'Okay, okay, okay. I get the picture. But…thanks, sis…'

'You don't have to keep thanking me every two seconds.'

'I know I can be a nightmare.' She hesitated, thought about pouring herself another glass of wine and instead reached for a bottle of water from the case on the ground next to her. 'But I've really had time to think about… everything…and I've been in touch with Andy… So I may have used him just a teeny bit in getting me that job, but he's a good guy…'

A good guy who hadn't been thinking with the right part of his body when he fudged you a dodgy reference, Violet thought.

'And he's been given the sack,' Phillipa continued glumly.

'Was he very angry with you?' She shook her head, reluctantly amused at the half smile tugging the corners of her sister's mouth.

'He adores me.'

'Even after the whole Craig Edwards fiasco?'

'I explained that I just hadn't been thinking straight at

the time… Well, we all make mistakes, don't we? Anyway, seeing that we're both out of a job…we've decided to pool our resources…'

'And do what, Pip?'

'Don't be cross, but he has a good friend out in Ibiza and we're going to take our chances there. Bar work. Some DJing…loads of opportunities… I hocked all that stuff that creep gave me; well, why should I return any of it? When he nearly got me behind bars?'

Violet sat down heavily and looked at her sister. Like a married couple, they had been hitched together for better or for worse ever since their parents had died. She was twenty-six years old and had never known what it might be like to live on her own, without having to accommodate anyone else, without having to compromise, without having to tailor her needs around her sister's. Phillipa had always done her thing and Violet had picked up whatever pieces had needed picking up. She had been the shoulder to cry on, the stern voice of discipline, the nagging quasi parent, the worried other half.

'When would you go?'

'I'm heading up to Leeds in the morning and then we'll take it from there. Andy's got to sort out the lease on his flat…get his act together… You don't mind, do you?'

'I think it's a brilliant idea.' Already her mind was leaping ahead to the following afternoon, when she would be meeting Damien's mother in hospital for the first time. She realised that she had been holding a deep breath, worrying about the possibility of Phillipa asking questions, demanding to know where she was going… Stuck at home, still smarting from losing her job under ignominious circumstances, Phillipa was bored and restless…a lethal combination given the fact that she, Violet, would be trying hard to keep a secret. If Violet was clued up to her sister's foibles, then her sister was no less talented at spotting hers, and an inability to keep a secret was high on the list of her weaknesses. Now, at least, there would be one less thing to stress about.

And perhaps this was a rut... Wasn't there always a point in time when apron strings needed to be cut?

She thought of Damien's casually dismissive remarks about her relationship with her sister and gritted her teeth to block out the mental images of him that seemed to proliferate at speed and without warning. She couldn't think of anyone else, ever, who had managed to infiltrate her head the way he had. From the minute they had parted company, half her waking time had been occupied with thoughts of him and it infuriated her that not all of them were as virulently negative as she would have liked. She harked back to the cold, arrogant words leaving his mouth and then she recalled what a sexy mouth it was...she thought of that hard slashing gesture he had made with his hand when he had condemned Phillipa to jail and then, in a heartbeat, she couldn't help but recall what strong forearms he had and how the dark hair had curled around the dull silver matt of his watch...

Enthused by a positive response, Phillipa was off. Ibiza would be great! She was sick of the English weather anyway! The club scene was brilliant! She'd always wanted to work in one! Or in a bar! Or anywhere, it would seem, where computers were not much in evidence.

She left early the following morning, with promises that she would be in touch and saying she would have to return anyway to pack some things, although she could just always buy out there because they wouldn't need much more than some T-shirts and shorts and bikinis...

Deprived of her sister's ceaseless chatter, which had veered from the high of realising that she wasn't going to be prosecuted to the bitterness of acknowledging that she'd been thoroughly used by someone she had thought to be really interested in her, Violet was reduced to worrying about her forthcoming meeting with Damien.

He had informed her, via text, that he would meet her in the hospital foyer.

'Visiting hours start at five,' he had texted. *'Meet me at ten to and don't be a second late.'*

If the brevity of the text was designed to remind her of her indebtedness to him and to escalate the level of her already shredded nerves, then it worked. By the time she was ready to leave for the hospital, she was a wreck. She had spent far too long choosing what to wear. Damien's offer of a complete new wardrobe from Harrods to replace the one he obviously thought was dull, boring and inadequate, had been rejected out of hand and she was left with only casual clothes, one of her three dresses having already been used up on her interview with him. Having sneakily checked him out on the Internet, she had had a chance to see first-hand the sort of women he went for. Tall, leggy beauties. The captions informed her that they were all models. She actually recognised a couple of them from magazines. Was it any real surprise that he had suggested funding a new wardrobe for her? His mother would have to seriously be into the concept of opposites attracting if there was any chance that they would be able to pull off the charade he had signed her up for. She was short, with anything but a stick-like figure, long, unruly hair that resisted all attempts to be tamed and, as she had quickly discovered after five seconds in his presence, was never destined to be the sort of subservient yes girl he favoured.

She wore jeans. Jeans, a cream jumper and her furry boots, which were comfortable.

He was waiting for her in the designated place at the

hospital. Violet spotted him immediately. He had his back to her and was perusing the limited supply of magazines in the small gift shop near the entrance.

For a few seconds, she had the oddest sensation of paralysis. She could barely take a step forward. Her heart began to beat faster and harder, her mouth went dry and she could feel the prickly tingle of perspiration break out over her body. She wondered how she could have forgotten just how tall he was, just how broad his shoulders were. He had removed his trench coat and held it hooked by a finger over one shoulder. His other hand was in his trouser pocket. Even in the environment of a hospital, where people were too ensconced in their own private worlds of anxiety and worry to notice anything or anyone around them, he was still managing to garner interested stares.

He turned around and Violet was pinned to the spot as he narrowed his eyes on her hovering figure. She was still wearing the shapeless, voluminous coat she had worn when she had come to the office to see him on her begging mission, but now her fair hair was loose and it spilled over her shoulders in waves of gold and vanilla. Against the black coat, it was a dramatic contrast. He doubted she ever went to the hairdresser for anything more than a basic cut, and yet he knew that there were women who would have given an arm and a leg to achieve the vibrant, casually tousled effect she effortlessly had.

'You're on time,' he said, striding towards her, and Violet instinctively fell back. 'My mother is looking forward to meeting you. I see you didn't take advantage of the offer of a shopping spree.'

'I think that either someone will like me or not like me, but hopefully it won't be because of what I happen to be wearing.' She fell into step beside him. Although she tried her best to maintain a healthy distance, there was a magnetism about him that seemed to want to draw her closer, a powerful pull on her senses that defied reason. She had to resist the strangest urge to look across at him and to just keep looking.

He was explaining that his mother had wanted to find out everything about her, that he had been sketchy on detail but had fabricated nothing at all. She had been intrigued to find out that he was dating a teacher, he said.

'And did we meet in the canteen at school?' Violet asked politely as she walked briskly to keep up with him.

'I thought I'd leave it to you to come good with the romantic touches,' Damien told her drily.

'Doesn't it upset you at all that you're lying to your own mother?'

'It would upset me more to think that her health might be compromised because she was worried about my stability.' He glanced down at her fair head. She barely reached his shoulder. He could feel her reluctance pouring through every fibre of her being and he marvelled that she could be so morally outraged at a simple deception that was being done in the best possible faith and yet forgiving of her sister, who had committed a far greater fraud. He wondered whether that was the outcome of family dynamics. Just as quickly as his curiosity reared its head, he dismissed it. He wasn't in the habit of delving too deeply into female motivations. He enjoyed women and was happy to move on before simple enjoyment could become too fraught with complications. And yet this wasn't just another female to be enjoyed, was she? In fact, enjoyment didn't actually feature on his list when it came to Violet Drew.

They had taken the lift up to the floor on which Eleanor Carver had a private room. It was a large teaching hospital with a confusing number of lifts, all of which seemed to have different, exclusive destinations to specialised departments.

'I don't know anything about *you*,' Violet said in a sudden rush of panic. She tugged him to a stop before they could enter the room where his mother was awaiting her arrival. 'I mean, I know about your brother...but where did you grow up? Where did you go to school? What are your friends like? Do you even *have* any friends?'

She had pulled him to the side, where they were huddled by the wall as the business of the hospital rushed around them.

'Now that's just the sort of thing that's guaranteed to make my mother suspicious,' Damien murmured, looking down at her into those remarkable violet eyes. 'A girlfriend who thinks that her guy is such a loser that he can't possibly have any friends. You're supposed to be crazy about me...' He reached out and trailed his finger along her cheek and for a few heart-stopping seconds Violet froze. She literally found that she couldn't breathe. The noise and clatter around her faded into a dull background blur. She was held captive by deep blue eyes that bored into her and set up a series of involuntary reactions that terrified and thrilled her at the same time. She could still feel the blazing path his finger had forged against her skin and belatedly she pulled away and glared at him.

'What are you doing?'

'I know. Crazy, isn't it? Actually touching the woman who is supposed to be head over heels in love with me. You didn't think the charade would just involve you sitting across the bed from me and making small talk for half an hour, did you?'

'I... I...'

'The occasional gesture of affection might be necessary. It'll certainly make up for the fact that we're practically strangers.' Damien pushed himself away from the wall against which he had been indolently leaning. He thought of Annalise, the wife who never was. He had fully deluded himself into thinking that he had known her. In fact, it turned out that he hadn't known her at all. He had seen the perfect picture which had been presented to him and he had taken it at face value. He had committed himself to the highly intelligent, beautiful career woman and had failed to probe deeper to the shallow upwardly mobile social climber. So the fact that he and his so-called girlfriend were strangers hardly made the union less believable as far as he was concerned.

Violet hadn't banked on gestures of affection. In fact, she had naively assumed that she *would* just be sitting across a hospital bed from him and making small talk with his mother.

'There's no need to look so uncomfortable,' he drawled lazily.

'I'm not uncomfortable,' Violet hurriedly asserted. 'I just hadn't thought about that side of things.'

'There *is* no that side of things. There's the pretence of affection.'

'Oh yes. I forgot. You only like women who are decked out in designer gear and have the bodies of giraffes!'

Damien threw back his head and laughed and a few heads turned to stare for a couple of seconds. 'Are you offended because you're not my type?' He thought of Phillipa. How on earth could two sisters be so completely different? One brash and narcissistic, the other hesitant and self-conscious? Yet, curiously, so much more genuine? Intriguing.

Violet blushed furiously. 'I think we've already established that *you're* not *my* type either!' she bristled. 'And shall we just go in now?'

'Is your moment of panic over?'

'I really dislike you, do you know that?'

'You bristle like a furious little bull terrier…'

'Thank you very much for that!'

'And entering the room with that angry expression isn't going to work…'

Violet's mouth was parted as she prepared to respond appropriately to that smug little smile on his face. His mouth covered hers with an erotic gentleness that took her breath away. He delicately prised a way past her startled speechlessness and his tongue against hers was an invasion that slammed into her with the force of a hurricane. It was the most sensational kiss she had ever experienced and all she wanted to do was pull him closer so that she could continue it. Her skin burned and she felt a pool of honeyed dampness spread between her legs. She wanted the ground to open up and swallow her treacherous body whole as he gently eased himself away to push open the door to his mother's room.

He was smiling broadly as he entered and she could not have looked more like a woman in love. He had kissed her at the right time and the right place and her flushed cheeks and uneven breathing and dilated pupils were telling a story that had no foundation in fact.

He wanted his mother to believe that they were all loved up and Violet smarted from the realisation that one clever kiss had done the job. Eleanor Carver was smiling at them both, her arms outstretched in a warm gesture of welcome.

She was smaller than Violet had imagined. Whilst her son was well over six feet tall, Eleanor Carver was diminutive in stature. She looked impossibly frail against the bed sheets but her eyes were razor sharp as she rushed into inquisitive chatter.

'Don't excite yourself, Mother. You know what the consultant said.'

'He didn't say anything about not exciting myself! Besides, how can I fail to be excited when you've brought me this delightful girl of yours to meet?'

Violet stood back and watched as Damien fussed around his mother. He was so big and so powerful and yet there was a gentleness about him as he bent down to kiss her on the cheek and make sure that she was propped up just right against the pillows. It was as though he had slowed his pace to accommodate her and it brought an unwelcome lump to Violet's throat.

'He's like a mother hen now that I'm cooped up here.' Eleanor smiled and patted him on the hand.

Violet smiled back and thought that he was more fox in the coop than innocent hen and, as if he could read her mind, Damien grinned at her with raised eyebrows.

'Violet would be the first to agree that I'm the soul of sensitivity...' He moved so that he was standing next to her and she tried not to stiffen in alarm as he slipped his arm around her.

'I'm not *entirely* sure that's the description that springs to mind...' Violet unbuttoned her coat and slipped it off. In the process, she managed to edge skilfully past him to the chair next to the bed.

Still grinning as he imagined some of the descriptions she might have had in mind for him, he wasn't prepared for the hourglass figure that took his breath away for a few shocking seconds. This was not what he had expected. He had expected frumpy, slightly overweight...someone who could perhaps do with shedding a few pounds. Was it because his expectations had been so wildly at variance with the voluptuous curves on offer now that he felt the sudden thrust of painful response? Or had his diet of thin, leggy models left him vulnerable to the sort of curvy, full-breasted figure that had once haunted his testosterone-fuelled teenage dreams?

Out of the corner of his eye, he caught his mother watching him and he stopped staring to move and stand behind Violet so that he could rest both his hands on her shoulders.

From this position, he felt no guilt in appreciating the bounty of her generous breasts. She was small in stature and a positive innocent compared to the hardened, worldly, sophisticated women he dated. She didn't have a clue how to play the games that eventually led to the bedroom. He thought that if she *did* know them, then she would refuse to play them. So the lush sexiness of her body was all the more of a turn-on. Standing behind her, he could barely drag his eyes away from her gorgeous figure.

It wasn't going to do. This wasn't about attraction or sex. This was an arrangement and he didn't need it to be complicated because his testosterone levels had decided to act up.

He pulled over the other spare chair and sat next to her because staring down at her was proving to be too much of an unwelcome distraction.

His mother had launched into fond reminiscing about his childhood. Halting her in mid-stream would have been as impossible as trying to climb Everest in flip flops, so he allowed her to chatter away for as long as she wanted. He hadn't seen her so animated since she had been diagnosed and, besides, as long as she was chatting, she wasn't asking too many detailed questions. Eventually he looked at his watch and gave a little cough to indicate departure time. He would have to admit that Violet had done well. She had certainly shown keen interest in every anecdote his mother had told and had been suitably encouraging in her remarks, whilst managing to keep them brief. Watching her out of the corner of his eye, he could appreciate what he had failed to previously when he had been too busy putting his plan into action and laying down the rules and boundary lines. She was a naturally warm, empathetic person. It was what had driven her to come and see him in defence of her sister when she must have been scared witless. It was what made her smile with genuine warmth at his mother as she triumphantly reached the punchline of her story involving him, two friends and a bag of frogs.

'We really should be going, Mother. You mustn't over tire yourself.'

'Life will be very limited for me if I can't get excited and I can't get too tired, darling. Besides, there are so many questions I want to ask you both...'

Violet sneaked a surreptitious glance at Damien's hard, chiselled profile and the memory of that kiss snaked through her, bringing vibrant colour to her cheeks. Of course he hadn't been *turned on*. As he had made abundantly clear on more than one occasion, he dated supermodels. She had been chosen to play a part because she was at his mercy and because she *wasn't* a supermodel. He had kissed her like that in order to achieve something and it had worked.

It filled her with shame that *she* had been turned on. She cringed in horror at the realisation that she had wanted the kiss to go on...and on...and on... She wondered where her pride had gone when she could be held to ransom by a man she loathed to do something of which she heartily disapproved and yet, with a single touch, find her willpower reduced to rubble.

'Damien's barely told me anything about how you two met... He said that it was a couple of months ago...but

that he didn't want to say anything for fear of jeopardis-
ing the relationship…'

'Did he?' Violet glanced across, eyebrows raised. 'I
didn't realise that you felt so…vulnerable…' Her voice
was sugary-sweet.

Damien rested his hand over hers and idly stroked her
thumb, which sent her pulses racing all over again, but,
with his mother's eyes on them, what could she do but to
carry on smiling?

'It's a lovable trait, isn't it? Darling?' he murmured,
looking her straight in the eyes and reaching to cup the
nape of her neck with his hand, where he proceeded to sift
his fingers through her hair.

'So how did you meet?' Eleanor asked with avid curiosity.

'Darling—' Damien continued to caress her until every
part of her body was tingling in hateful response '—why
don't you tell my mother all about our…romantic first
meeting…?'

'It really wasn't that romantic.' Violet tried to shift away
from the attentions of his hand, which was something of a
mistake as he promptly decided to switch focus from her
hair to her thigh. 'Actually, when I first met your son, I
thought he was rude, arrogant and overbearing…'

Damien responded by squeezing her thigh gently with
his big hand in subtle warning.

'He…er…came to the school for a…er…meeting with
our head of Home Economics…' The pressure on her thigh
was ever more insistent but, instead of turning her off, it
was having the opposite effect. How on earth could her
body be so wilful? When had that ever happened? She felt
faint with a dark, forbidden excitement that went against
every grain of common sense and reason. She wanted to
squeeze her thighs tightly shut to stifle her liquid response

but was scared that if she did he would duly take note and know exactly what was going on with her rebellious body. He was, after all, nothing like the guys she knew. He was a man of the world and, even on short acquaintance, she suspected that he was as knowledgeable and intimate with the workings of the female mind as it was possible for any man to be. The thought of him second-guessing that she found him sexually attractive was mortifying.

'Do you remember how bossy you were with poor Miss Taylor?' she asked, scoring points wherever she could find them and trying hard to ignore what his hand was doing to her. Out of sight of his mother's eyes because of the positioning of the chairs, his roaming hand came to rest on her thigh just below the apex where her legs met. When she thought of how that hand would feel just there, were it against bare skin, were he able to brush the downy hair with his fingers, her brain went into instant meltdown.

'We all got the impression that you were terribly important—too important to be time wasting at a school because the CEO couldn't make it... I'll admit, Mrs Carver, that my first impressions of your son were that he was a tad on the arrogant, conceited, bossy side...thoroughly unbearable, if you want the truth...'

'And yet you couldn't tear your eyes away from me,' Damien murmured in quick retaliation. He smiled and leaned across to feather a kiss on the corner of her mouth, making sure to keep his hand just where it was. 'Don't think I didn't notice when you thought I wasn't looking...'

'Ditto,' Violet muttered in feeble response because what else could she do, short of launching into a scathing attack on everything she had decided was awful about him?

'So true.' Damien allowed himself the luxury of looking at her with lazy, speculative eyes. 'And how could I ever have guessed that underneath your shapeless clothes was the figure of a sex goddess…?'

Violet went bright red. Was he joking? Continuing with their subtle duel of words which carried an undertone that his mother would not have clocked? Was he *laughing at her*? What else? she wondered, hot and flustered under the scrutiny of his deep blue eyes. She kept her gaze pointedly averted, looking at his mother with a smile that was beginning to make her jaws ache, but every inch of her was tuned in to Damien's attention, which was focused all on her. One hundred per cent of it. She could feel it as powerfully as if a branding iron had been held to her bare skin.

'Hardly a sex goddess… There's no need to tell lies…' she mumbled with an embarrassed laugh, while trying to play half of the loving couple by awkwardly leaning towards him and at the same time taking the opportunity to snap her legs firmly shut on a hand that was getting a little too inquisitive for her liking.

'You're just what my son needs, Violet,' Eleanor confided with satisfaction. 'All those girls he's spent years going out with… I expect you have a potted history of Damien's past…?'

'Mother, please. There's no need to go down that road. Violet is very much in the loop when it comes to knowing exactly the sort of women I've dated in the past…aren't you, darling…?'

'And I find it as strange as you do, Mrs Carver, that someone as intelligent as your son could have been attracted to girls with nothing between their ears. Because that's what you've said, haven't you, dearest? I'm sure they were very pretty but I've never understood how you could ever have found it a challenge to go out with a mannequin…?'

Damien smiled slowly and appreciatively at her. Touché,

he thought. She had been gauche and awkward when she had come to him with her begging bowl on her desperate mission to save her sister's skin but he was realising that this was not the woman she was at all. Warm and empathetic, yes—that much was evident from the way she interacted with his mother. She had also been prepared for him to walk all over her if she thought it would help her sister's cause. However, freed from the constraints of having to yield to him in the presence of his mother, her true colours were emerging. She was quick-tongued, intelligent and not above taking pot shots at him under cover of a smiling façade and the occasional glance that tried to pass itself off as loving.

He found that he liked that. It made a change from vacuous supermodels. Certainly, a charade he had been quietly dreading now at least offered the prospect of not being as bad as he had originally imagined and, ever creative when it came to dealing with the unexpected, he had no misgivings about making the most of a bad deal. So she thought that she'd get a little of her own back by having fun with double entendres and thinly cloaked pointed remarks? Well, two could play at that game and it would certainly add a little spice to the proceedings.

'You're so right, my dear…' Eleanor's shrewd eyes swung between the pair of them. Their body language… their interaction…her son was set in his ways…so where did Violet Drew fit in…? How had the inveterate womaniser become domesticated by the delightful schoolteacher who seemed willing to trade punches…? And where were the airheads who simpered around him and clung like leeches? Sudden changes in appetite were always a cause for concern, as her consultant had unhelpfully pointed out. So what was behind her son's sudden change in appetite? For the first time Eleanor Carver was distracted from her anxiety about her cancer. She enjoyed cross-words and sudoku. She would certainly enjoy unravelling this little enigma.

'Of course…' she glanced down at the wedding ring she still wore on her finger and thoughtfully twisted it '…there *was* Annalise…but I expect you know all about her…?' She yawned delicately and offered them an apologetic exhausted smile. 'Perhaps you could come back to-morrow? My dear…it's been such a pleasure meeting you.' She warmly patted Violet's outstretched hand. 'I very much look forward to getting to know you much, much better… I want to find out every little thing about the wonderful girl my son has fallen in love with.'

CHAPTER FOUR

SO WHO WAS ANNALISE?

Violet was pleased that she had not been tempted to ask the second they had left his mother's room. She didn't know, didn't care and was only going to be in his company for a short while longer in any case.

Infuriatingly, however, the name bounced around in her head over the next week and a half, as their visits to the hospital settled into a routine. They met at a predetermined time in the same place, exchanged a few meaningless pleasantries on the way up in the lift and then played a game for the next hour and a half. It was a game she found a lot less strenuous than she had feared. Eleanor Carver made conversation very easy. Little by little, Violet pieced together the life of a girl who had grown up in Devon, daughter of minor aristocratic parents. Childhood had been horses and acres of land as a back garden. There had been no boarding school as her parents had doted on their only child and refused to send her away and so she had remained in Devon until, at the age of seventeen and on the threshold of university, she had met, fallen head over heels in love with and married Damien's father, an impossibly dashing half Italian immigrant who had wandered down from London with very little to offer except ambition, excitement and love. Eleanor had decided in seconds that all three were a better bet than a degree in History. She had battled through her parents' alarm, refused to cave in and moved out of the family mansion to set up house in a little cottage not a million miles away. In due course, her parents had come round. Rodrigo Carver might not have been their first choice but he had quickly grown on them. He offered business advice on the family estate when fortunes started turning sour and his advice had come good. He had a street smart head for investment and passed on tips to Matthew Carrington that saw profits swell. In return, Matthew Carrington took a punt on his rough-diamond son-in-law and loaned him a sum of money to start up a haulage business. From that point, there had been no turning back and the half Italian immigrant had eventually become as close to his parents-in-law as their own daughter.

Violet thought that Eleanor Carver probably believed in fairy tale endings because of her own personal experience. Whirlwind romance with someone from a different place and a different background…a battle against the odds… Was that why she had accepted her son's sudden love affair with a woman who could have been from a different planet?

She had posed that question to Damien only the day before and he had shrugged and said that he had never considered it but it made sense; then he had swiftly punctured that brief bubble of unexpected pleasure by adding that it was probably mingled with intense relief that she had been introduced to a woman who wouldn't run screaming in horror at the thought of wellies, mud and the great outdoors.

For once, Violet arrived at the hospital shop ahead of schedule and was glancing through the rack of magazines when she heard him say behind her shoulder, 'I didn't get the impression that you were all that interested in the life-styles of the rich and famous...'

She spun round, heart beating fast, and in that split second, realised that the hostility and resentment she had had for him had turned into something else somewhere along the line. She wasn't sure what, but the sudden flare of excitement brought a tinge of high colour to her cheeks. When had she started *looking forward* to these hospital visits? What had been the thin dividing line between not caring what she wore because why did it matter anyway, and taking time out to choose something with him in mind? She had always felt the sparrow next to her sister's radiant plumage. She couldn't compete and so she had never tried. She had chosen baggy over tight and buttoned up over revealing because to be caught up in trying to dress to impress was superficial and counter-productive. So when had that changed?

Everything they said in that room and every fleeting show of affection was purely engineered for the sake of his mother and yet she found that she could recall each time he had touched her. She no longer started when his hand slid to the back of her neck. A couple of days ago he had casually tucked some of her hair behind her ear and she had caught herself staring at him, mouth half open, transfixed by a rush of violent confusing awareness, as if they had suddenly been locked inside a bubble while the rest of the world faded away. His mother had snapped her out of the momentary spell but it was dawning on her that lines were being crossed. She just didn't know what to do about it. She would have to find out just how long the charade was destined to continue. Yes, she had made a deal but that didn't mean that she could be kept in ignorance of when the deal would come to an end. Her life was on hold while she pretended to be his girlfriend. She needed to find out when she would be able to step back to reality.

'Aren't we all?' she snapped, taking a step back and bumping into someone behind her. Flustered, she muttered apologies and then looked straight into Damien's amused blue eyes. Usually he came straight to the hospital from work. Today was an exception. He wasn't in his suit but in a pair of black jeans and a thick cream jumper. She couldn't peel her eyes away from him.

'My apologies. Shall I buy the magazine for you?'

Violet discovered that she was still clutching the magazine and she wondered why because she had had no intention of getting it. 'Thank you, but there's no need. I was just about to buy it myself.'

'Please. Allow me.' He made an elaborate show of studying the cover of the magazine. 'I dated her,' he mused, but his interest stopped short of flicking through the magazine to look further.

If that passing remark was intended to bring her back down to earth, it certainly succeeded and Violet was infuriated with herself for the time she had taken choosing which pair of jeans to wear and which jumper. Ever since he had made that revealing remark about her body, and even if it had been meant for the benefit of his mother, she had chosen her snuggest jumpers to wear, the ones that did the most for a figure like hers. Now she was reminded of just the sort of body he looked at and it wasn't one like hers.

'What's her name?' Violet wondered if it was the mysterious Annalise his mother had dropped into the conversation on that first evening.

'Jessica. At the time, she was on the brink of making it to the catwalk. Seems she got there.' He paid for the magazine and handed it over to her.

'I'm not surprised. She's very beautiful.'

And once upon a time, Damien thought, she would have encompassed pretty much everything he sought in a woman. Compliant, ornamental and inevitably disposable.

He looked down at the argumentative blonde staring up at him with flushed cheeks and a defiantly cool expression and felt that familiar kick in his loins. The complication which he had been determined to sideline was proving difficult to master. He wondered whether it was because denial was not something he had ever had the need to practice when it came to the opposite sex. When he had concocted this plan, he had had no idea that he might find himself at the mercy of a wayward libido. He had looked at the earnest, pleading woman slumped despairingly in the chair in his office and had seen her as a possible solution to the problem that had been nagging away at him. Nothing about her could possibly have been construed as challenging. There had not been a single iota of doubt in his mind that she might prove to be less amenable than her exterior had suggested.

While it was hardly his fault that his initial judgement had a few holes, he still knew that the boundaries to what they were doing had to be kept in place, although it was proving more challenging than expected. Every time he touched her, with one of those passing gestures designed to mimic love and affection, he could feel a sizzle race up his arm like an electric current. Those brief lapses of self-control were unsettling. Now, as they began moving out of the hospital shop, he stopped her before they could head for the lift.

'We need to have a chat before we go up.'

'Okay.' This would be an update on how long their little game would continue. Perhaps he had had word back from the consultant on the line of treatment they intended to pursue. When she thought of this routine coming to an end, her mind went blank and she had to remind herself that it couldn't stop soon enough.

'We could go the cafeteria but I suggest somewhere away from the hospital compound. Walking distance. There's a café on the next street. I've told my mother that we might be a bit later than usual today.'

'There haven't been any setbacks, have there?' Violet asked worriedly, falling into step beside him. 'A couple of days ago your mother said that they were all pleased with how things were coming along, that it seems as though the cancer was caught in time, despite concerns that she might have left it too late...'

'No setbacks, although my mother would be thrilled if she knew that you were concerned...are you really? Because there's just the two of us here. No need for you to say anything you don't want to. No false impressions to make.'

'Of course I'm concerned!' She stopped him in his tracks with a hand on his arm. 'I may have agreed to go through this charade because my sister's future was at stake, but your mother's a wonderful woman and of course I would never fake concern!'

Damien recognised the shine of one hundred per cent pure sincerity in her eyes. For a second, something very much like guilt flared through him. He had ripped her out of her comfort zone and compelled her to do something that went against the very fabric of her moral values because it had suited him. He had thrown back the curtain and revealed a world where people used other people to get what they wanted. It wasn't a world she inhabited. He knew that because she had told him all about her friends in and out of school. Listening to her had been like lifting a chapter from an Enid Blyton book, one where good mates sat around drinking cheap boxed wine and discussing nothing more innocuous than the fate of the world and how best it could be changed.

Still, everything in life was a learning curve and being introduced to an alternate view would stand her in good stead.

'How is your sister faring in Ibiza?' he asked, an opportune reminder of why they were both here.

Violet smiled. 'Good,' she confided. 'Remember I told you about that job she wanted? The one at the tapas restaurant on the beach?' Despite the artificiality of their situation, she had found herself chatting to Damien a lot more than she had thought she might. Taking the lift down after visiting his mother, wandering out of the hospital together, he in search of a black cab, she in the direction of the underground...conversation was always so much less awkward than silence. And he was a good listener. He never interrupted and, when he did, his remarks were always intelligent and informative. He had listened to her ramble on about her colleagues at work without sneering at them or the lives they led. He had come up with some really useful advice about one of them who was having difficulties with a disorderly class. And he had cautioned her about worrying too much about Phillipa, had told her that she needed to break out of the rut she had spent years constructing and the only way to do that would be to walk away from over-involvement in what her sister was getting up to. If Phillipa felt she had no cushion on which to fall back, then she would quickly learn how to remain upright.

Had she mentioned Phillipa and the job at the bar? Damien thought. Yes. Yes, she had. Well, they saw each other every day. The periods of time spent in each other's company might have been concentrated, but they conversed. It would have been impossible to maintain steady silence when they happened to be on their own. Admittedly, she did most of the conversing. He now knew more about the day-to-day details of her life than he had ever expected to know.

'I remember.' No references needed for a bar job. Good choice.

'Well, she got it. She's only been there two days but she says the tips are amazing.'

'Let's hope she's not tempted to put her hand in the till,' Damien remarked drily but there was no rancour in his eyes as they met hers for a couple of seconds longer than strictly necessary.

'I've already given her a lecture about that,' Violet said huffily.

'And what about the partner in crime?'

'He wasn't a *partner in crime*.'

'Aside from the forging of references technicality.'

'He's working on restoring a boat with his friend.'

'He knows much about boat restoration?'

'Er...'

'Say no more, Violet. They're obviously a match made in Heaven.'

'You're so cynical!'

'Not according to my mother. She complimented me on my terrific taste in women and waxed lyrical about the joys of knowing that I'm no longer dating women with IQs smaller than their waist measurements.'

They had reached the café and he pushed open the door and stood aside as she walked past him. The brush of his body against hers made her skin burn. So his mother was pleased with her as a so-called girlfriend. She thought back to the eye-catching brunette on the magazine cover. He must find it trying to have pulled the short straw for this little arrangement. He could have been walking into a café, or into an expensive restaurant because hadn't he already told her that the women he dated wouldn't have been caught dead anywhere where they couldn't be admired, with a leggy brunette dangling on his arm. Instead of her.

He ordered them both coffee and then sat back in his chair to idly run his finger along the handle of the cup.

'Well?' Violet prompted, suddenly uncomfortable with the silence. 'I don't suppose we're here because you wanted to pass the time of day with me. It's been nearly two weeks. The new term is due to start in another ten days. Your mother seems to be doing really well. Have you brought me here to tell me that this arrangement is over?' She felt a hollow spasm in the pit of her stomach at the prospect of never seeing him again and then marvelled at how fast a habit, even a bad one, could be turned into something that left a gaping hole when there was the prospect of it being removed.

'When I told you that our little deal would be over and done with in a matter of days, I hadn't foreseen certain eventualities.'

'What eventualities?'

'The consultants agree that treatment can be continued in Devon.'

'And that's good, isn't it? I know your mother is very anxious about Dominic. She speaks to him every day on the telephone and has plenty of contact with his carers, but he's not accustomed to having her away for such a long period of time.'

'When did she tell you this?'

'She's phoned me at home a couple of times.'

'You never mentioned that to me.'

'I didn't realise that I was supposed to report back to you on a daily basis...'

'You're *supposed* to understand the limitations of what we have here. You're *supposed* to recognise that there are boundaries. Encouraging my mother to telephone you is stepping outside them.'

'I didn't *encourage* your mother to call me!'

'You gave her your mobile number.'

'She asked for it. What was I supposed to do? Refuse to give it to her?'

'My mother plans on returning to Devon tomorrow. She'll be able to attend the local hospital and I will personally make sure that she has the best in house medical team to hand that money can buy.

'That's good.' She would miss Eleanor Carver. She would miss the company of someone who was kind and witty and the first and only parent substitute she had known since her own mother had died. There had been no breathtaking revelations to the older woman or dark, secret confessions, but it had been an unexpected luxury to feel as though no one expected her to answer questions or be in charge. 'I guess you'll be going with her.'

'I will.'

'How is that going to work out for you and your work? I know you said that it's easy to work out of the office but is that really how it's going to be in practice?'

'It'll work.' He paused and looked at her carefully. 'The best laid plans, however…'

'I hate to sound pushy but would you be willing to sign something so that I know you won't go back on what you promised?'

'Don't you trust me?' he asked, amused.

'Well, you *did* put me in this position through some pretty underhand tactics…'

'Remind me how much your sister is enjoying life in sunny Ibiza…' Damien waved aside that pointed reminder of his generosity. 'Naturally, I will be more than happy to sign a piece of paper confirming that your sister won't be seeing the inside of a prison once our deal is over.'

'But I thought it was…' Violet looked at him in confusion.

'There's been an unfortunate extension.' He delivered that in the tone of voice which promised that, whatever he had to say, there would be no room for rebuttal. 'It seems that your avid attention and cosy chats with my mother on the phone have encouraged her to think that you should accompany me down to Devon.'

'What?' Violet stammered.

'I could repeat it if you like, but I can see from the expression on your face that you've heard me loud and clear. Believe me, it's not something I want either but, given the circumstances, there's very little room for manoeuvre.' Could he be treated to anyone looking more appalled than she currently was?

'Of course there's room for manoeuvre!' Violet protested shakily.

'Shall I tell her that the prospect of going to Devon horrifies you?'

'You know that's not the sort of thing I'm talking about. I…I…have loads to do before school starts…classes to prepare for…'

Damien waited patiently as she expounded on the million and one things that apparently required her urgent attention in London before raising his hand to stop her in mid-flow.

'My mother seems to think that having you around for a few days while her treatment commences would give her strength. She's aware that you start back at school in a week and a half.' She had no choice but to do exactly what he said; Damien knew that. When it came to this arrangement, she didn't have a vote. Still, he would have liked to have her on board without her kicking and screaming every inch of the way. And really, was it so horrific a prospect? Where his mother lived was beautiful. 'She's not asking you to ditch your job and sit by her bedside indefinitely.'

'I know that!'

'If I can manage my workload out of the office, then I fail to see why you can't do the same.'

'It just feels like this is…getting out of control…'

'Not following you.'

'You know what I mean, Damien,' Violet snapped irritably. 'I thought when I accepted this…this…*assignment*… that it was only going to be for a few days and it's already been almost two weeks…'

'This situation isn't open to discussion,' Damien said in a hard voice. 'You traded your freedom for your sister's. It's as simple as that.'

'And what about when I leave Devon? When do I get my freedom back?' Violet hated the way she sounded. As though she couldn't care less about his mother or her recovery. As though the last thing in the world she wanted was to help her in a time of need. And yet this wasn't what she had signed up for and the prospect of getting in ever deeper with Damien and his family felt horribly dangerous. How could she explain that? 'I'm sorry, but I have to know when I can expect my life to return to normal.'

'Your life will return to normal—' he leaned forward, his expression grim and as cold as the sea in winter '—just about the same time as mine does. I did not envisage this happening but it's happened and here's how we're going to deal with it. You're going to put in an appearance in Devon. You're going to enjoy long country walks and you're going to keep my mother's spirit fighting fit and upbeat as you chat to her about plants and flowers and all things horticultural. At the end of the week, you're going to return to London and, at that point, your presence will no longer be required. Until such time as I inform you that your participation is redundant, you remain on call.'

Violet blanched. What leg did she have to stand on? He was right. She had effectively traded her freedom for Phillipa's. While her sister was living a carefree existence in Ibiza, she was sinking ever deeper into a morass that felt like treacle around her. She couldn't move and all decision-making had been taken out of her hands.

'The more involved I get, the harder it's going to be to tell your mother…that…'

'Leave that to me.' Damien continued to look at her steadily. 'There's another reason she wants you there in Devon,' he said heavily. 'And, believe me, I'm not with her on this. But she wants you to meet my brother.' His mother had never known the reasons for his break-up with Annalise, nor had she ever remarked on the fact that, after Annalise, he had never again brought another woman down to the country estate in Devon. The very last thing he wanted was a break in this tradition, least of all when it involved a woman who was destined to disappear within days.

'That's very sweet of her, Damien, but I don't want to get any more involved with your family than I already am.'

'And do you think that *I* do?' he countered harshly. 'We both have lives waiting out there for us.' The fact that control over the situation had somehow been taken out of his hands lent an edge to his anger. When his mother had suggested bringing Violet to Devon, he had told her, gently but firmly, that that would be impossible. He cited work considerations, made a big deal of explaining how long it took to prepare for a new term—something of which he knew absolutely nothing but about which he had been more than happy to expound at length. He had been confident that no such thing would happen. His fake girlfriend would not be setting one foot beyond the hospital room.

His mother had never been known to enter into an argument with him or to advance contrary opinions when she knew how he felt about something. He had been woefully unprepared for her to dig her heels in and make a stance, ending her diatribe, which had taken him completely by surprise by asking tartly, 'Why don't you want her to come to Devon, Damien? Is there something going on that I should know about?'

Deprived of any answering argument, he had recovered quickly and warmly assured his mother that there was nothing Violet would love more than to see the estate and get to know Dominic.

'You will need a more extensive wardrobe than the one you have,' he informed her because, as far as he was concerned, there was nothing further to be said on the matter. 'You need wellies. Fleeces. Some sort of waterproof coat. I'm taking it that you don't have any of those? Thought not. In that case, you're going to go to Harrods and use the account I've already talked to you about.'

'Do you know something? I can't wait for all of this to be over! I can't wait for when I no longer have to listen to you bossing me about and reminding me that I'm in no position to argue!' Over the past few days she had been lulled into a false sense of security, of thinking that he wasn't quite as bad as she had originally thought. She had watched him interacting with his mother, had listened as he had soothed the same concerns on a daily basis without ever showing a hint of impatience. She had foolishly started feeling a weird connection with him.

'Is that how you treat everyone?' she blurted, angry with herself for harbouring idiotic illusions. 'Is that how you've treated all the women you've been out with? Is that how you treated Annalise?' It was out before she had a chance to rein it in and his eyes narrowed into chips of glacial ice.

'Was that another topic under discussion with my mother?'

'No, of course not! And it's none of my business. I just feel...frustrated that my whole world has been turned upside down...'

'Excuse me if I don't feel unduly sympathetic to your cause,' Damien inserted flatly. 'We both know what was at stake here. As for Annalise, that's a subject best left unexplored.' Without taking his eyes from her face, he signalled for the bill.

'You can't expect me to spend a week in your mother's company and not have an inkling of anything to do with your past.' She inhaled deeply and ploughed on. 'What do you expect me to say when she talks about you? It's going to be different in Devon. We'll have a great deal more time together. Your mother's already mentioned her once. She's sure to mention her again. What am I supposed to say? That we don't discuss personal details like that? What sort of relationship are we supposed to have if we never talk about anything personal?'

She stared at him with mounting frustration and the longer the silence stretched, the angrier she became. He might be the puppet-master but there were limits as to how tightly he could jerk the strings! She foresaw long, cosy conversations with his mother when her only response to any questions asked, aside from the most basic, would be a rictus smile while she frantically tried to think of a way out. She would be condemned to yet more lying just because he was too arrogant to throw her a few titbits about his past.

'I don't *care* what happened between the two of you. I just want to be able to look as though I know what your mother's on about if she brings the name up in conversation. Why are you so…so…*secretive*?'

Damien was outraged that she had the nerve to launch an attack on him. Naturally there was a part of him that fully understood the logic of what she was saying. Undiluted time spent with his mother in front of an open fire in the snug would be quite different from more or less supervised snatches of time spent next to a hospital bed during permitted visiting hours. Women talked and it was unlikely that he could be a stifling physical presence every waking minute of the day. That said, the implicit criticism ringing in her voice touched a nerve.

Bill paid, he stood up and waited until she had scrambled to her feet.

'Are you going to say anything?' She reached out and stayed him with her hand. 'Okay, so you've had loads of girlfriends. That's fine.'

'I was going to marry her,' Damien gritted.

Violet's hand dropped and she looked at him in stupefied silence. She couldn't imagine him ever getting close enough to any woman to ask for her hand in marriage. He just seemed too much of a loner. No…it was more than that. There was something watchful and remote about him that didn't sit with the notion of him being in love. And yet he had been. In love. Violet didn't know why she was so shocked and yet she was.

'What happened?' They were outside now, heading back towards the hospital. Her concerns about going to Devon had been temporarily displaced by Damien's startling revelation.

'What happened,' he drawled, stopping to look down at her, 'was that it didn't work out. I didn't share the details with my mother. I don't intend to share them with you. Any other vital pieces of information you feel you need to equip yourself with before you're thrown headlong into my mother's company?'

'What was she like?' Violet couldn't resist asking. In her head, she imagined yet another supermodel, although it was unlikely that she could be as stunning as the one on the cover of the magazine.

'A brilliant lawyer who has since become a circuit judge.'

Well, that said it all, Violet thought. It also explained a whole host of things. Such as why a highly intelligent male should choose to go out with women who weren't intellectually challenging. Why his interest in the opposite sex began and ended in bed. Why he had never allowed himself to have a committed relationship again. He had been dumped and he still carried the scars. She felt a twinge of envy for the woman who had had such power over him. Was he still in touch with her? *Did he still love her?*

'And do you bump into her? London's small.'

'Question time over, Violet. You now have enough information on the subject to run with it.' Damien's lips thinned as he thought of Annalise. Still hovering in the wings, still imagining that she was the love of his life. Did he care? Hardly. Did he bump into her? Over the years, with tedious and suspicious regularity. There she would be, at some social function for the great and the good, always making sure to seek him out so that she could check out his latest date and update him on her career. He never avoided her because it paid to be reminded of his mistake. She was a learning curve that would never be forgotten.

Violet saw the grim set of his features and drew her own, inevitable conclusions. He had been in love with a highly intelligent woman, someone well matched for him, and his marriage proposal had been rejected. For someone like Damien, it would be a rejection never forgotten. He had found his perfect woman and, when that hadn't worked out, he had stopped trying to find another.

What they had might be a business arrangement, but everything he had ever had with every woman after Annalise had been *an arrangement*. Arrangements were all he could do.

'I'll get some appropriate clothes,' Violet conceded. 'And you can text me with the travel info. But, at the end of the week, it's over for me. I can't keep deceiving your mother.'

'By the end of the week, I think you will have played your part and I will officially guarantee that your sister is off the hook.'

'I can't wait,' Violet breathed with heartfelt sincerity.

CHAPTER FIVE

THE HOUSE THAT greeted Violet the following evening was very much like something out of a fairy tale. Arrangements for Eleanor's transfer had been made at speed. Her circumstances were special, as she was the principal carer for Dominic, and Damien, with his vast financial resources, had made sure that once the decision to transfer was made, it all happened smoothly and efficiently.

In the car, Violet had alternated between bursts of conversation about nothing in particular to break the silence and long periods of sober reflection that the task she had undertaken seemed to be spinning out of control.

She was travelling with a stranger to an unknown destination, removed from everything she knew and was familiar with, and would have to spend the next few days pretending to be someone she wasn't. If she had known what this so-called arrangement would have entailed, would she have embarked on it in the first place? Regrettably, yes, but knowing that didn't stop her feeling like a sacrificial lamb as the powerful car roared down the motorway, eating up the miles and removing her further and further from her comfort zone.

While Phillipa was taking time out in Ibiza, doing very little in a tapas restaurant and no doubt enjoying the attention of all the locals as she wafted around in sarongs and summer dresses, here she was, sinking deeper and deeper into a situation that felt like quicksand, all so that her sister could carry on enjoying life without having to pay for the mistakes she had made.

'Maybe she *should* have had her stint in prison,' Violet said, apropos of nothing, and Damien shot her a sideways glance.

Locked in to doing exactly what he required of her, he could sense the strain in the rigid tension of her body. She would rather be anywhere else on earth than sitting here in this car with him. Naturally, he could understand that. More or less. After all, who wanted to be held hostage to a situation they hadn't courted, paying for a crime they hadn't committed? Yet was his company so loathsome that she literally found it impossible to make the best of a bad job? She was pressed so tightly against the passenger door that he feared she might fall out were it not for the fact that the doors were locked and she was wearing a seat belt.

There had been times over the past week and a half when some of her resentment had fallen away and she had chatted normally to him. There had also been times when, in the presence of his mother, he had touched her and his keenly attuned antenna had picked up *something*—something as fleeting as a shadow and yet as substantial as jolt of electricity. Something that had communicated itself to him, travelling down unseen pathways, announcing a response in her that she might not even have been aware of.

'You don't mean that,' he said calmly.

'Don't tell me what I mean! If it weren't for Phillipa I wouldn't be here now.'

'But you are and there's no point dwelling on what ifs. And stop acting as though you're being escorted to a torture chamber. You're not. You'll find my mother's estate a very relaxing place to spend a few days.'

'It's hardly going to be a *relaxing situation*, is it? I don't feel *relaxed* when I'm around you.' When she thought about seeing him for hours on end, having meals in his company, being submerged in his presence without any respite except when she went to bed, she got a panicky, fluttery feeling in the depths of her stomach.

Without warning, Damien swerved his powerful car off the small road. They were only a matter of half an hour away from the house and the roads had become more deserted the closer they had approached the estate.

'What are you doing?' Violet asked warily as he killed the engine and proceeded to lean back at an angle so that he was looking directly at her. In the semi-darkness of the car, with night rapidly settling in around them, she felt the breath catch painfully in her throat. Apprehension jostled with something else—something dark and scary, the same dark, scary thing that had been nibbling away at the edges of her self-control ever since he had told her about Devon.

'So you don't feel relaxed around me. Tell me why. Get it off your chest before we reach the house. Okay, you're not here of your own free will, but there's no point lamenting that and covering old ground. It is as it is. Have you never been in a position where you had to grit your teeth and get through it?'

'Of course I have!'

'Then tell me what the difference is between then and now.'

'You're scary, Damien. You're not like other people. You don't *feel*. You're so…so…*cold*…'

'Funny. Cold is not a word that any woman has ever used to describe me…'

Violet felt her heart begin to race and her mouth went dry. 'I'm not talking about…what you're like in bed with women…'

'Would you like to?'

'No!'

'Then how would you like me to try and relax you?'

Violet couldn't detect anything in his voice and yet those words, innocuous as they were, sent a shiver of awareness rippling up and down her spine. She had a vivid, graphic image of him relaxing her, touching her, making her whole body melt until she was nothing more than a rag doll. Was this the real reason why she was so apprehensive? Terrified even? At the back of her mind, was she more scared of just being alone with him than she was of playing a game and acting out a part in a place with which she was unfamiliar? Did her own responses to him, which she constantly tried to squash, frighten her more than *he* did?

It didn't seem to matter than he was cold, distant, emotionally absent. On some level, a part of her responded to him in ways that were shocking and unfamiliar.

She could feel the lazy perusal of his eyes on her and she wished she hadn't embarked on a conversation which now seemed to be unravelling.

'I'm just nervous,' she muttered in a valiant struggle to regain her self-composure. 'I'll be fine once we get there. I guess.'

'Try a little harder and you might start to convince me. You get along well with my mother. Is it Dominic?' The question had to be asked. He hadn't been in this position for a very long time. He had brought no one to Devon. He had vowed to never again put himself in the position of ever having to witness a negative reaction to his brother. However, this was an unavoidable circumstance and he felt the protective machinery of his defences seal around him like a wall of iron.

'What are you talking about?' Violet was genuinely puzzled.

'Some people feel uncomfortable around the disabled. Is that why you're so strung out?' It had taken Annalise to wake him up to that fact, to the truth that there were people who shied away from what they didn't know or understand, who felt that the disabled were to be laughed at or rigorously avoided. The ripple effect of those reactions were not contained, they always spread outwards to the people who cared. It was good to bring this up now.

'No!'

'Sure about that, Violet? Because you know me, you know my mother…the only unknown quantity in the equation is Dominic…'

'I'm *looking forward* to meeting your brother, Damien. The only person who makes me feel uncomfortable is *you*!' This was the first time she had come near to openly admitting the effect he had on her. She glared at him defensively, feeling at once angry and vulnerable at the admission and collided with eyes that were dark and impenetrable and sent her frayed pulses into overdrive.

All at once and on some deep, unspoken level, Damien could feel the sudden sexual tension in the air. Her words might say one thing but her breathlessness, the way her eyes were huge and fixed on him, the clenching and unclenching of her small fists…a different story.

He smiled, a slow, curving, triumphant smile. Whilst he had privately acknowledged the unexpected appeal she had for him, whilst he had been honest about the charge he got from a woman who was so different in every possible way to the type of women he had become used to, he had pretty much decided that a Hands Off stance was necessary in her case.

But they were going to be together in Devon and, like an expert predator, he could smell the aroma of her unwelcome but decidedly strong sexual attraction towards him. She was as skittish as a kitten and it wasn't because she was nervous about spending a week in the company of his mother. Nor was she hesitant about his brother. He had detected the sincerity in her voice when he had suggested that she might be.

He took his time looking at her before turning away with a casual shrug and turning the key in the ignition. Her presence next to him for the remainder of the very short drive felt like an aphrodisiac. Potent, heady and very much not in the plan.

The drive up to the grand house was tree-lined, through wrought-iron gates which he could never remember being closed. Having not been to the estate for longer than he liked to think, Damien was struck by the sharp pull of familiarity and by the hazy feelings he always associated with his home life—the sense of responsibility which was always there like a background refrain. Having a disabled brother had meant that any freedom had always been on lease. He had always known that, sooner or later, he would one day have to take up the mantle left behind by his parents. Had he resented that? He certainly didn't think so, although he *did* admit to a certain regret that he had failed to extend any input for so long.

Was it any wonder that his mother had been so distraught when she had been diagnosed, that she might leave behind her a family unit that was broken at the seams? He had a lot of ground to cover if he were to convince her otherwise.

'What an amazing place,' Violet murmured as the true extent of the sprawling mansion, gloriously lit against the darkness, revealed itself. 'What was it like growing up here?'

'My parents only moved in when my grandfather died, and I was a teenager. Before that, we lived in the original cottage my parents first bought together when they were married...'

'It must have seemed enormous after a cottage...'

'When you live in a house this size you get used to the space very quickly.' And he had. He had lost himself in it. He had been able to escape. He wondered whether he had been so successful at escaping that a part of him had never returned. And had his mother indulged that need for escape? Until now? When escape was no longer a luxury to be enjoyed?

Not given to introspection, Damien frowned as he pulled up in the large circular courtyard. The house was lit up like a Christmas tree in the gathering darkness and they had hardly emerged from the car with their cases when the front door was flung open and Anne, the house-keeper who had been with the family since time immemorial, was standing there, waving them inside.

Violet wondered what her role here was to be. Exactly. Sitting by a hospital bed, she had known what to do and the impersonal surroundings had relieved her of the necessity of trying to act the star-struck lover. A few passing touches, delivered by Damien rather than her—more would have seemed inappropriate in a hospital room, where they were subject to unexpected appearances from hospital staff.

But here she was floundering in a place without guide-lines as they were ushered into the grandest hall she had ever seen.

The vaulted ceiling seemed as high and as impressive as the ceiling of a cathedral. The fine silk Persian rug in the hall bore the rich sheen of its age. The staircase lead-ing up before splitting in opposite directions was dark and highly polished. It was a country house on a grand scale.

The housekeeper was chatting animatedly as they were

led from the hall through a perplexing series of rooms and corridors.

'Your mother is resting. She'll be down with Dominic for dinner. Served at seven promptly, with drinks before in the Long Room. You've been put in the Blue Room, Mr Damien. George will bring the bags up.'

Looking sideways, Violet was fascinated at Damien's indifference to his surroundings. He barely looked around him. How on earth could he have said that a person could become accustomed to a house of this size? She had initially been introduced to Anne as his girlfriend and now, as though suddenly remembering that she was trotting along obediently next to him, he slung one arm over her shoulder as the housekeeper headed away from them through one of the multitude of doors, before disappearing into some other part of the vast family mansion.

'An old retainer,' he said, dropping his arm and moving towards a side staircase that Violet had failed to notice.

'It's a beautiful house.'

'It's far too big for just my mother and Dominic, especially considering that the land is no longer farmed.' He was striding ahead of her, his mind still uncomfortably dwelling on the unexpected train of thought that had assailed him in the car, the unpleasant notion that the grand house through which he was now confidently leading the way had been his excuse to pull away from his brother. He had never given a great deal of thought to his relationship with Dominic. Was he now on some kind of weird guilt trip because of the circumstances? Had he shielded himself from the pain Annalise had inflicted on him when she had rejected his brother by pulling ever further away from Dominic? He should have been far more of a presence here on the estate, especially with his mother getting older.

'It would be a shame to sell it. I bet it's been in your

family for generations…' She was barely aware of the bedroom until the door was thrown open and the first thing that accosted her was the sight of a massive four-poster bed on which their suitcases had been neatly placed. While he strode in with assurance, moving to stand and look distractedly through the windows, she hovered uncertainly in the background.

'Well?' Damien harnessed his wandering mind and focused narrowly on her.

'Why are both our suitcases in this room?' Violet asked bluntly. She already knew the answer to that one, yet she shied away from facing it. She hadn't given much thought to the details of their stay. In a vague, generalised way, she had imagined awkward one-to-one conversations with Damien and embarrassing economising of the truth with his mother, along with stilted meals where she would be under scrutiny, forced to gaily smile her way through gritted teeth. She hadn't gone any further when it came to scenarios. She hadn't given any thought to the possibility that the loving couple might be put in the same bedroom. She had blithely assumed that such an eventuality would not occur because surely Eleanor belonged to that generation which abhorred the thought of cohabitation under their roof. Eleanor was a traditionalist, a widow who still proudly wore her wedding ring and tut tutted about the youth of today.

'Because this is where we'll be sleeping,' Damien replied with equal bluntness. His unaccountably introspective and dark frame of mind had not put him in the best of moods. Having questioned his devotion as a son and on-hand supportive presence as a brother, the last thing he needed was to witness his so-called girlfriend's evident horror at being trapped in the same bedroom as him.

'I can't sleep in the same room as you! I didn't think that this would be the format.'

'Tough. You haven't got a choice.' He began unbuttoning his shirt, a prelude to having a shower, and Violet's eyes were drawn to the sliver of brown chest being exposed inch by relentless inch. She hurriedly looked away but, even though she was staring fixedly at his face, she could still see the gradual unbuttoning of his shirt until it was completely open, at which point she cleared her throat and gazed at the door behind him.

'There must be another room I can stay in. This place is enormous.'

'Oh, there are hundreds of other rooms,' Damien asserted nonchalantly. 'However, you won't be in any of them. It's a few days and my mother has put us together. Somehow I don't think she's going to buy the line that we're keeping ourselves virtuous for the big day.' He pulled off his shirt and headed towards his case on the bed, flipping it open without looking at her. 'We have roughly an hour before we need to be downstairs for drinks. My mother enjoys the formal approach when it comes to dining. It's one of her idiosyncrasies. So do you want to have the bathroom first or shall I?'

Violet hated his tone of voice. It was one which implied that he couldn't even be bothered to take her concerns into account. He was accustomed to sharing beds with women, she thought with a burst of impotent anger. In his adult life, he had probably slept with a woman next to him a lot more often than he had slept alone. It wasn't the same for her. Did he imagine that she would be able to lie next to him and pretend that she was on her own? The bed was king-sized but the thought of moving in the night and accidentally colliding with his sleeping form was enough to make her feel like fainting.

'I hate this,' she whispered, filled with self-pity that the last vestige of her dignity was being stripped away from her. 'You'll have to sleep on the sofa.'

Damien glanced at the chaise longue by the window and wondered whether she was being serious. 'I'm six foot four. What would you suggest I do with my feet?' He raised his eyebrows and watched as she struggled in silence to come up with a suitable response. 'I've spent hours driving. I'm going to have a shower. Don't even think of trawling the house for another bedroom.'

With that, he vanished into the adjoining bathroom, leaving Violet to fight off the waves of panic as she stared at her lonesome suitcase on the bed. Everything about the bedroom seemed designed to encourage a fainting fit, from the grandeur of a bed that would have been better suited to the lovers they most certainly were not, to the thick, heavy curtains which she imagined would cut out all daylight so that the intimacy of the surroundings became palpable.

Wrapped up in a series of images, she almost forgot that he was in the shower until she heard the sound of water being switched off, at which point she raced to her suitcase, extracted an armful of clothes and then stood to attention by the window, with her back pointedly turned to the bathroom door.

She heard the click of the door opening and then she froze as his voice whispered into her ear, 'You can look. I'm decently covered. Anyone would think that you were sweet sixteen and never been kissed.'

He was laughing as she unglued her eyes from his bare feet and allowed them to travel upwards to where he was decently covered in no more than a pair of boxer shorts and his shirt, which he was taking his own sweet time to button up.

If he called that *decently covered* then she wanted to

ask him what she might expect of him when the lights were switched off.

'I'll meet you downstairs,' she said coolly, at which he laughed a bit more.

'You wouldn't have a clue where to go,' Damien pointed out. Her face was flushed. Her hair, which had started the journey in a sensible coil at the nape of her neck, was unravelling. He could feel his mood beginning to lift, which was a good thing because he was ill equipped for negative thoughts. 'You'd need a map to find your way round this house. At least until you've become used to it. Most of the rooms aren't used but good luck locating the ones that are.' He reached into the cupboard where a supply of clothes, freshly laundered, were hanging, awaiting his arrival.

Once again, Violet primly averted her eyes as he slipped a pair of trousers from a hanger. She backed towards the door but he wasn't looking at her.

Good heavens! She would have to get her act together if she was going to survive her short stay here. She couldn't succumb to panic attacks every time they were alone together! She would need immediate counselling for post-traumatic stress disorder as soon as she returned to London if she did! He wasn't even glancing in her direction. If he could be unaffected by her presence, then she would follow his lead and everything would be smooth sailing. Two adults sharing a room wasn't exactly a world-changing event, she told herself once she was in the bathroom, having checked the door three times to make sure that it was locked.

She took a long time. She had bought a couple of dresses so that she didn't have to spend the entire stay in jeans and sweaters. This dress, a navy-blue stretchy wool one with sleeves to her elbows, was fitted, although she couldn't quite see how fitted because there was no long mirror in the bathroom. Nor could she do much with her make-up because the ornate mirror over the double sink was cloudy with condensation. Her hair, she knew, was fit for nothing except leaving loose. Her curls were out of control, a tangle of falling tendrils which she impatiently swept back from her face before taking a deep breath and opening the bathroom door.

He was sprawled on the bed, the picture of the Lord of the Manor waiting for his woman to emerge. His trousers were on, although, her inquisitive eyes made out, zipped but with the button undone. His long-sleeved jumper was dark grey and slim-fitting, so there was no escaping the lean, hard lines of his body.

One arm behind his head, Damien watched her with brooding eyes. It was the first time he had ever seen her in a dress that actually fitted. More than that, it clung. To curves that did all the right things in all the right places and lovingly outlined the sort of breasts that mightn't work on a catwalk but sure as hell worked everywhere else. He forgot about any tension that might lie ahead. He forgot those vague, never disclosed concerns that he had turned a blind eye to his brother for too long. Hell, he forgot pretty much everything as his eyes raked over her body and he felt the pain of an erection leaping to attention. Which made him hurriedly sit up.

She was running her fingers through her hair and wincing as she tried to gently unravel some of the knots. Then, without saying a word, she flounced over to her case and excavated a pair of high-heeled shoes which she self-consciously slipped on with her back to him.

'I'm ready.' She smoothed nervous hands along the dress. This wasn't the sort of thing she ever wore. She had always favoured baggy. She wondered whether her stupid brain had actually paid attention to that passing compliment he had given her about her figure and then decided that if it had, she was pathetic. But she still felt a thrill of excitement as he lazily scrutinised her before shifting off the bed, taking his time and moving at an even more leisurely pace to retrieve his watch from the dressing table.

'I hope I look okay…' Violet was mortified to hear herself say and she was even more mortified when, with deliberate slowness, he eyed her up and down and then up and down again for good measure.

'You'll do. New dress?'

'You can have it back when this stint is over.'

'What would I do with it?'

'I just wouldn't want you to think that I wanted anything from you but my sister's freedom.'

'I've always found martyrdom an annoying trait.'

Violet seethed on the way down, through another wilderness of rooms. En route, he gave her a potted history of the house and the land around it. She thawed. She was reluctantly charmed at the thought of an unknown half Italian coming to live there and passing on the mansion to his children, wrenching it away from the exclusive grasp of the landed gentry.

By the time they were finally at the sitting room where drinks were being served, she was more relaxed, and then she fully relaxed as Eleanor was helped down to make her entry, accompanied by Dominic and a young girl who tactfully left, having settled Eleanor in the chair by the fire.

She forgot about Damien. She knew that she should be making conspicuous efforts to play the adoring girlfriend but she became wrapped up in Eleanor and Dominic. She had been warned about Dominic's disability. She hadn't been told that although he was in a wheelchair, although his speech was often difficult to understand and although his movements were not perfectly controlled, he was smart and he was funny and shy. She sat very close to him, sipping her wine and leaning in so that she could pick up everything he said while Damien and his mother conducted a conversation, the wisps of which came floating her way. The need to think about selling the house...the difficulties of managing the various floors even if she made a full recovery...the value of having somewhere closer to civilisation where doctors and the hospital were not an unsafe car drive away if the weather was inclement.

He was the background voice of reason, the head of the family making sensible decisions, although, sliding her eyes across to him, she was aware of the frustration etched on his features at his mother's vague, non-committal replies to his persuasive urgings.

Every family had its stories to tell and she wondered if this was his. If he was so embedded in his role as protector that he failed to recognise any form of mutiny in the ranks. He obviously didn't think that his brother should have any input because the conversation was dropped the minute they were at the dinner table.

A carer helped Dominic with his food while Eleanor fussed and explained to her that that was normally her job.

'I'm a pain in the ass,' Dominic stammered.

Violet laughed and looked across to Damien, who was seated opposite her. 'You have that in common with your brother,' she said tartly and then flushed when he looked back at her with a slow, appreciative smile. Her heartbeat quickened. His glance lingered just that bit too long and she returned it with just a little too much dragging intensity.

After that, she was conscious of every little movement he made and tuned in to every word he said, even when her attention appeared to be elsewhere. She was aware of the quality of the food and the fact that she was being treated like a valued guest because, despite what Damien had said, Eleanor had long dispensed with formalities when it was just herself and Dominic and the wonderful girl who helped with him. Then they ate in the kitchen with dishes served by the housekeeper straight from Aga to plate.

'My son would know that if he visited with a bit more regularity,' Eleanor said with asperity. 'Perhaps you could see that as your mission—to get him away from London and his never ending workload…'

Watching her, Damien was impressed at how well she fielded the awkward remark, which implied a future that wasn't on the cards. He took in the way she communicated with Dominic. With ease, not patronising, without a hint of indulgence or condescension. Nor did she look to anyone to rescue her from what she might have felt was an uncomfortable situation.

Sipping the espresso that had been brought in for him, he mentally began to compare her natural responses to those of Annalise but it was an exercise he killed before it could take root. Such comparisons, he knew, were entirely inappropriate. That said, he murmured softly as they walked back up the stairs, Dominic and his mother having retired for the night, 'Very good…'

'Sorry?' Violet wished she could have stretched the evening out for longer—for as long as she could, like a piece of elastic with no breaking point—because now she faced the prospect of the shared bedroom. He certainly wasn't going to sleep on the chaise longue. *She* could try to, but chaises longues had not been designed for deep REM slumber. She might embarrass herself by falling off. Worse, she might *hurt* herself by falling off.

'Your performance tonight. Very good.'

'I wasn't performing.' They were now at the bedroom door and she stood back as he pushed it open and waited for her to precede him. 'You know I like your mother and your brother's amazing.' He was pulling off the luxurious, ornate spread that had been thrown over the bed, dumping it in a heap in the corner of the room. Violet's hands itched to fold it neatly, a legacy of having an untidy sister behind whom she had long become accustomed to tidying up.

He was beginning to unbutton his shirt, eyes still firmly focused on her, pinning her into a state of near paralysis.

Why couldn't he have found somewhere else to sleep? Or found *her* somewhere else to sleep? Surely, in a mansion the size of a hotel, they could have had separate sleeping quarters without the whole world detecting it? Why was she being placed in this position? It felt as though every sacrifice was being made by *her* and she was the one who directly benefited from none of it.

Anger at her helplessness to alter the situation made her eyes sting. She clung to the anger like a drowning person clinging to a lifebelt.

'I can see why your mother was so worried about Dominic when she was diagnosed,' Violet imparted recklessly and she immediately regretted the outburst when he stilled.

'Come again?'

'Nothing,' Violet mumbled.

'Really?' He was strolling towards her, lean, dark and menacing, and Violet stood her ground, stubbornly defensive. 'If you have something to say, why don't you come right out and say it? Only start something, Violet, if you intend to see it through to the end.'

'Well, you don't seem to really communicate with him. You leave it all to your mother. I heard you talking about selling the house with her and yet you didn't say anything to Dominic about it, even though he would be affected as well…'

Damien stared at her with cold fury. Had he just heard

correctly? Was she actually *criticising* his behaviour? Coming hard on the heels of his own unexpected guilt trip, he could feel rage coursing through his veins like a poison. Was she deliberately needling him?

'I don't seem to communicate with him…' was all that managed to emerge from his incredulous lips.

'You talk around him and above him and when you *do* talk directly to him, you don't really seem to expect an answer, even though you look as if you do.'

'I can't believe I'm hearing this.'

'No one ever tells you like it is, Damien.'

'And you mistakenly think that you're in a position to do so?' He watched as she lowered her eyes, although her soft lips were still pinched in a stubborn line. 'This may come as a cruel shock, but you're over-stepping your brief…'

When had he stopped listening to what his brother had to say? Was it when they moved to the estate? When acres of space removed the need for physical proximity? And then later, in London…with trips back to the estate infrequent obligations…his mother usually amenable to taking a bit of time out in London, travelling without Dominic… had distance crept through the cracks until he had simply forgotten how to communicate? Or, worse, had he selfishly been protecting himself by unconsciously withdrawing? You couldn't feel pain at other people's thoughtless reactions if you just never put yourself in that position in the first place, could you?

'I know I am!' Violet flung at him defiantly. 'But you can't expect me to come here and have no opinions at all on the people I meet! And besides, what do I have to lose by telling you the truth? Once I leave here, I'll never see you again! And maybe it's time someone *did* speak their mind to you!' She had courted an argument. It seemed safer to get into that bed with her back angrily turned away from him. But the shutter that fell over his eyes sent a jolt of unhappiness through her. She fought it off because why did it matter what he thought of her in the long run?

'I think I'll go downstairs and catch up on work.' Damien turned away from her, walked towards his laptop, which he had left on the chest of drawers, and Violet was unaccountably tempted to rush into a frantic apology for having crossed the line.

'Don't,' he threw over his shoulder with biting sarcasm, 'wait up.'

CHAPTER SIX

WHEN DAMIEN HAD considered the challenge of setting his mother's fears to rest and allaying her worry that he would not be able to cope with Dominic in her absence, he had envisaged a fairly straightforward solution.

He would take time off work to come to Devon. He would dispatch Violet after her week and, henceforth, he would assume the mantle of responsible son and dependable brother. How hard could it possibly be? He might have been a little lax in his duties over the years, but that was not for lack of devotion to his family. His work, every minute of it, was testimony to his dedication. They wanted for nothing. His brother had the very best carers money could buy. His mother enjoyed help on every front, from garden to house. She fancied roses? He had ensured that a special section of the extensive cultivated land was requisitioned for a rose garden fit to be photographed in a magazine. When she had been complaining of exhaustion only months previously, before the reason behind that exhaustion became known, he had personally seen to it that one of the finest chefs in the area was commissioned to cook exquisite meals and deliver them promptly so that she could be spared the effort of doing so herself. On the rare occasions when she ventured up to London, theatre tickets had been obtained, opera seats reserved, tables at the best restaurants booked.

Unfortunately, his clear cut route now to a successful outcome was proving elusive.

He adjusted his tie, raked his fingers through his hair and then hesitated. He knew that Violet was more than happy to meet him in the sitting room. After five days, she knew that house better than he did. How had that transpired? Because she was involving herself with his family. She and his mother appeared to have become best buddies. From his makeshift office in the downstairs library, he had a clear view of the back garden and had spotted them out there in the cold, slowly strolling and chatting. About what? He had casually asked her a couple of days ago and she had shrugged and delivered a non-answer. Was he going to push it? No. Ever since she had decided that it was her right to speak her mind, she had defied all attempts to smooth the strained atmosphere between them. In company, she was compliant and smiling. The second they were alone together, he was treated to the cold shoulder despite the fact that he had magnanimously chosen to overlook her outrageous, uninvited criticism of him.

He pulled the chair over to the window and sat down. At six-thirty in the evening, the room was infused with the ambers and golds of what had been a particularly fine and sunny day. In an hour, they would be leaving for a local restaurant. This had not been of his choosing. He would have been more than happy to have had a meal in, relaxed for ten minutes and then retired to catch up on his emails. But his mother had suggested it, to take her mind off the treatment which was due to commence at the weekend.

Or maybe, he mused darkly, Violet had suggested it… who was to say? His mind idly wandered over the events of the past few days. The clever way she had bonded with

Dominic, involving him in the art preparation she was doing for her class, letting him guide her through some computer stuff for a website she wanted to set up to display the work of her more talented pupils. His mother had taken him to one side and confided that she had never seen Dominic so relaxed with anyone.

'You know how wary he is of people he doesn't know…' she had murmured.

He didn't, in actual fact. Which had only served as a reminder of what Violet had said about his communication skills.

He scowled and then looked up as the door to the adjoining bathroom slowly opened.

Immersed in her thoughts, with a towel wound turban style around her newly washed hair and another towel wrapped round her body, barely skimming her breasts and thighs, Violet was not expecting him. In fact, she didn't register him at all sitting on the chair in the far corner of the room.

She was thinking about the past few days. Having a view on Damien and his relationship with his family seemed to have been the catalyst for the one thing she had been determined to avoid, namely involvement. She had told him what she thought about his relationship with his brother and, in so doing, she had unlocked a door and stepped inside the room. She hadn't wanted to have opinions. She had simply wanted to do her time and then disappear back to her life. Instead, she was becoming attached and she had no idea where that was going to lead. Damien was barely on speaking terms with her. They communicated in front of an audience but once the audience was no longer around, the act was dropped and he disappeared into that office of his, only emerging long after she was fast asleep.

The bed which she had looked at with horror, which had thrown her into a state of panic because she had had visions of rolling over and bumping into him, had turned out to be as safe as a chastity belt. She was not aware of him entering the room at night because she was fast asleep and she was not aware of him leaving it in the morning because she was still sleeping.

She pulled the towel off her head and shook her hair, then she walked towards the bedroom door and locked it because you could never be too sure. Damien would already be downstairs. He would be making an effort.

Just like that, her mind leapt past her own nagging worries and zeroed in on Damien. She no longer fought the way he infiltrated her head. One small passing thought and suddenly the floodgates would be opened and she would lose herself in images of him. It was almost as if the connections to her brain were determined to disobey the orders given and merrily abandon themselves to reformatting her thoughts so that he played the starring role.

Without even looking in his direction, she was still keenly aware of everything he did and everything he said. There was no need to look at him because in her mind's eye she could picture the way he looked, his expressions, the way he had of tilting his head to one side so that you had the illusion that whatever you were saying was vitally important.

He had stopped trying to corner his mother into making a decision about the house and whether it should be sold.

He had begun asking her about small things, like books she might have read and committees she belonged to in the village.

His conversation with Dominic was no longer a few words, some polite murmurings, a hearty pat on the shoulder and then attention focused somewhere else. Over

dinner the evening before, she had heard him telling his
brother about one of his deals which had run into unexpected problems with the locals because a vital factory had
been denied planning permission, and the trouble they had
taken to accommodate their concern.

Violet would rather not have noticed any of these details. She would rather he remained the one-dimensional
baddy who barely had two words to say to her the second
they were alone. She didn't want to leave this house only
to find herself wondering how the rest of their lives all
turned out. She wanted to be able to put them all out of
her mind and yet, the more absorbed she became in their
dramas, the more difficult she knew that was going to be.

Still frowning, she dropped the towel to the floor and
stepped towards the wardrobe. Her hair felt damp against
her back and she lifted the heavy mass with one hand and,
at that very moment, she saw him.

For a few seconds Violet thought her eyes might be
playing tricks on her. She froze, her arm still raised holding her hair away from her body. Her brain refused to
accommodate the realisation that he wasn't safely downstairs but was, in fact, watching her as she stood in front of
him, completely and utterly naked. When it did, she gave
a squeak of absolute horror and reached for the discarded
towel, which she wrapped tightly around her body. She
was shaking like a leaf.

'What are you doing here?' She backed towards the
bathroom door but, before she could make it to the relative safety of the bathroom, he was standing in front of
her, barring her path.

For the first time in his life, Damien was lost for words.
What was he doing there? Did it make any difference that
it was his bedroom?

The thirty-second glimpse of her body had sent his libido into orbit. He was in physical pain and he fought to bring his senses back down to Planet Earth. The fluffy white towel was back in place, secured very firmly by tightly clenched fists, but in his mind's eye he was still seeing the voluptuous curves of her body. He had caught himself idly wondering what she looked like under the dresses and the jeans and the jumpers. Whenever he had entered the bedroom to find her asleep, the covers had been pulled tightly up to her neck as though, even in slumber, she was determined to make sure that she kept him out. The first time he had seen her in jeans, his imagination had been up and running and her deliberate attempts to keep him at arm's length had only served to increase its pace.

But nothing had prepared him for the mind-blowing sexiness of her curves. Her breasts, unrestrained by a bra, were far more than a generous handful. Her nipples were big pink discs that pouted provocatively and her stomach was flat as it planed downwards to the thatch of dark blonde hair between her thighs. All thoughts of self-denial were shattered in an instant. Every ounce of common sense that warned him against getting involved with a woman whose departure date from his life was any minute now, vanished like a puff of smoke.

'You have to go,' Violet said shakily. 'I want to get dressed.' She just couldn't look him in the face. Her body was burning at the thought of his eyes on it. Even with the towel secured around her, she still felt as though her nudity was on parade.

'I wanted to talk to you.'

'We can talk…later…your mother and Dominic…'

'Will be fine if they have to wait for us for a few minutes.'

He stood in front of her, as implacable as a solid wall of granite. Having made a concerted effort in the past few days to try and give her body as little option as humanly possible to feel any of that unnerving, unwelcome sexual awareness that seemed to ambush her at every turn, she was horribly aware of her racing pulses and the liquid heat pooling inside her. The silence stretched and stretched. She desperately wanted to get dressed and yet shied away from drawing attention to her nakedness under the towel.

'I need to get dressed,' she finally breathed and Damien stood aside.

Now that he had dropped all pretence of keeping life simple by not yielding to an attraction that seemed to have a will of its own, he could feel the stirrings of a dark, pervasive excitement coursing through him. Anticipation was a powerful aphrodisiac.

'Of course,' he murmured, stepping back further. 'We can talk later.' And they would.

Violet only realised that she had been holding her breath when she sagged against the closed bathroom door. Her breathing was thick and uneven. After days of standoff, she had felt those lazy eyes on her naked body and nearly collapsed. What did he want to talk to her about? She had heard the slam of the bedroom door, but she gave it a little while before poking her head out and establishing that the bedroom was empty.

She wanted to put that recollection of him sitting in that chair, looking at her as she blithely discarded the towel, to the back of her mind. Actually, she wanted to eradicate it completely, but it kept recurring as she got dressed and met the assembled party in the Long Room.

What had he thought of her? Had the reality of a body that wasn't stick-thin repulsed him? She had returned to her uniform of baggy clothes, a shapeless dress over which she had thrown a thick cardigan. The thought of drawing any more attention to herself made her feel sick. At least there would be more than just the four of them for the meal out. Eleanor had invited some of her friends. Damien's attention would be blessedly diluted. But, even amidst the upbeat conversation and the laughter, she was keenly aware of his eyes sliding over to her every so often. The conversation finally turned to Eleanor's treatment, which was due to start the following day.

'No one can tell me exactly how I'll be affected,' she confessed to one of her friends who had undergone a similar situation and was full of upbeat advice. 'Apparently, everyone reacts differently…but it'll be wonderful knowing that I'll have Dominic and Damien by my side…' She looked steadily at Damien. 'You *will* be staying on for a short while, won't you, darling?'

Damien smiled and gave an elegant, rueful and playfully resigned shrug. 'My office is up and running. It'll make a nice change looking through the window and not being treated to a splendid London view of office blocks…'

He did it so well, Violet thought, returning to her food. He was charm personified. Everyone was chuckling. There was general laughter when he launched into a wry anecdote about some of the urban myths surrounding a couple of the office blocks in the square mile.

When the laughter had died down, Eleanor turned to Violet. 'You must hate me for keeping Damien all the way down here in this part of the world…' she murmured.

Violet flushed. She hated those instances when she had felt horribly as though she was doing more than just play acting for a good reason, when she felt corralled into a corner from which she had no choice but to baldly lie.

'Oh, I shall be busy…you know…the new term starts soon and it's always hectic…' she offered vaguely.

'But you *will* come down on the weekends, won't you, my dear? You've been such a source of strength…'

'Well…sure, although…er…Damien mentioned something about having office stuff to do in London…in the coming weekends…'

'Did I?' Damien looked at her with a perplexed expression. 'I've been known to go to the office occasionally on a weekend, but…' he raised both hands in a gesture of amused surrender while keeping his eyes firmly pinned to Violet's flushed face '…even a diehard workaholic like myself knows when to draw the line…so I'll be down here unless something exceptional happens in London that requires my presence…'

'So that means that you'll be with us this weekend, my dear?' Eleanor was looking keenly at Violet's flushed face. 'I shall probably need some help around the house and it's so much nicer having someone around who knows us all rather than getting staff in. I do know you'll be busy at school…so please say if you'd rather not come…perfectly understandable…'

Violet felt the weight of expectation from everyone around the table and she sneaked a pleading glance at Damien, who returned her stare with an infuriatingly bland expression. 'I…' she stammered. 'I'm sure I should be able to…get away for the weekend…given the circumstances…' She smiled weakly. Even to her own ears, it was hardly the sound of excited enthusiasm but Eleanor was smiling broadly and reached over to pat her on her hand.

'Perfect! I shall probably be in a horizontal position most of the time but it should give you and Damien a really terrific opportunity to explore the village and the surroundings. I mean, you've hardly been out on your own since you got here and I may be an old lady but I'm not so old that I can't remember what it's like to be a couple of love birds…!'

Everyone laughed. Dominic said something salacious. Violet cringed.

She barely registered the remainder of the evening. She drank slightly more than was usual for her. By the time they eventually made it back to the house, it was after ten-thirty and her few glasses of wine had gone to her head.

'You need water,' Damien said, leading her towards the kitchen once Eleanor and Dominic had disappeared. 'And paracetamol…you drank too much.'

'Don't you dare lecture me on how much I drank, Damien!' She yanked her arm free of his supportive hand, stumbled, straightened and stopped to glare at him. 'How *could* you?'

Damien wondered whether she was aware that she was slurring her words. Ever so slightly. She had also, some-where along the line, hurriedly done up her cardigan but misaligned the buttons and her hair was all over the place as she had insisted on opening her car window for a spot of fresh air.

'You're going to have to sit down if you're going to ac-cuse me of something.' He led her towards a kitchen chair, sat her down and fetched her a glass of water and some tablets. 'Now…' he positioned his chair squarely to face her and leaned forward, resting his forearms on his thighs and staring at her with earnest concentration '…you were about to start an argument…'

Violet was mesmerised by his eyes. He hadn't shaved for the day and there was a dark shadow that promised stubble in the morning. She wanted to reach out and touch it. The temptation was so strong that she had to sit on her hand to suppress it.

'So tell me what I'm guilty of,' Damien prompted, 'but only when you've finished looking at me. I wouldn't want to rush that…'

Violet reddened and immediately looked away. 'So now I'm going to be coming here at the weekend,' she said in a rush. The feel of his eyes on her and the faint woody smell of his aftershave were doing disastrous things to her equilibrium, cutting a swathe straight through the cool detachment she had managed to maintain over the course of the past few days. After his reciprocal coldness, this sudden attention was as dramatic on her nerves as an open flame next to dry tinder.

'I do recall you agreeing to something of the sort.' Damien was enjoying her attention. Enjoying the way her eyes skittered away from his face but then were compulsively drawn back to stare at him. He realised how much he had disliked her coolness towards him. They might have found themselves sharing the same space for very dubious reasons, but proximity and their need to pretend had invested a certain edge to what they had. A little wine had now made her lower her defences and he liked that. A lot. He leaned a little closer, as though he didn't want to miss a single word of what she was saying.

'Are you telling me that you didn't mean it?' he asked in a vaguely startled voice, as though this angle had only now popped into his head. 'Perhaps I misconstrued the relationship you have with my mother. You two seemed to be getting along like a house on fire...'

'That doesn't have anything...to do with...anything...' Violet said incoherently. 'I *like* your mother very much. *That's* why I...why it's such *a mistake*...'

'Honestly not following you at all...'

'I was only supposed to be here until the end of the week...'

'You were. And you're free to go once your week here is over.' He sat back, angling his body to one side so that he could extend his legs. He linked his hands behind his head.

'You have a life happening back in London. Of course, I know that I could keep you hanging on, doing what I ask of you, because you would do pretty much anything to save your sister's skin, but...' He stood up and walked, loose-limbed, to fetch himself a bottle of water, which he drank in one go while he continued to stare at her.

'But?' Violet was still having trouble peeling her eyes away from him.

'But that could prove a never-ending situation. So once we're back in London, feel free to jump ship. I'll sign a guarantee that your sister won't be prosecuted. She will be free as a bird to roam the Spanish coastline doing whatever takes her fancy. And you can return to your life.'

'And what would you tell your mother?' Faced with the prospect of returning to her life, Violet was now assailed by a host of treacherous misgivings that this much-prized life, the one she had insisted was there, waiting to be lived, was not quite the glittering treasure she had fondly described. She didn't quite get it, but there had been a strange excitement to being in Damien's company. When she was around him, even when, as had been the case over the past few days, she was keeping her distance, she was still always so *aware* of him. It was as if her waking moments had been injected with some sort of life-enhancing serum.

'That's not your problem. You can leave that one to me.'

'I'd quite like to know,' Violet persisted. She should be grabbing at this lifeline. She knew that. 'I'm really fond of your mother, Damien. I wouldn't want to think...I wouldn't want her to...'

'Be unduly hurt? Become stressed out? Think badly of you? All of the above? Funny, but I wasn't getting the impression that you were overly bothered. After all, five seconds ago you were accusing me of deliberately blindsiding you by not announcing on the spot that you wouldn't be back here for weekends…'

'I thought you would *want* to start bracing your mother for…you know…the inevitable…'

'The day before she begins what could be gruelling treatment?'

'Well…'

'Dominic has become attached to you.'

'Yes…' Just something else to think about, just another link in the chain she would have to melt down when she walked away from his family.

'When my mother begins her treatment she'll probably be too weak to help with my brother…'

'He doesn't need *help* as such. I mean, he has his carers for the physical stuff…'

'But has always relied on my mother for everything else. If she's in bed, she won't be able to provide all of that.'

'Which could be where *you* step in,' Violet urged him.

Damien flushed darkly. This conversation wasn't meant to be about *him*. Her bright eyes were positively glowing with sincerity.

'I can't be on call twenty-four seven. I still have a business to run, even if it's from a distance.'

'You wouldn't have to *be on call* twenty-four seven. Dominic's perfectly happy doing his own thing. He's really got into that website I asked him to try and design… Besides, I've noticed…'

'What? What have you noticed?'

'You didn't like it the last time I spoke my mind.'

'Maybe I've realised that it's about time I stop trying to think of your mind as anything but a runaway train,' Damien mused under his breath.

'I don't think that's very fair.' All signs of tipsiness had evaporated. She felt as sober as a judge. Her hands were clammy as she rested them on her knees to strain forward.

'You speak your mind. Maybe I find that a refreshing change. So don't spoil the habit of a lifetime now by going coy on me.'

'Okay. Well, I've noticed that you're making a bigger effort with Dominic. I mean, when we got here, you were hardly on speaking terms with him.'

Considering he had asked her to speak her mind, Damien made a concerted effort to control his reaction to that observation. 'Go on,' he muttered tightly, through gritted teeth.

'You never really directly *talked* to him. You talked *at* him, then you turned your attention to someone else or something else. And yet,' she mused thoughtfully, 'your mother says you two used to be so close when you were growing up...'

So *that* was what they talked about, Damien thought tensely. They discussed *him*. He angrily swept aside the sudden undercurrent of guilt that had been his unwelcome companion over the past few days and rose to his feet.

'It's late. We should be heading up,' he said smoothly.

'*We*? Aren't you going to work?'

'I'll see you up to the bedroom first. My mother would be horrified if you missed your footing on the stairs because you had a little too much to drink and I wasn't there to do the gentlemanly thing and catch you as you fell...'

'You're annoyed with me because of what I've said...'

'You're entitled to have your opinions.'

'I never wanted to.' She rose a little clumsily to her feet and turned in the direction of the kitchen door.

'Never wanted to what...?'

His breath fanned her cheek as he leaned down to hear what she was saying.

'Have opinions. I never wanted to have opinions about you.' She felt giddy and breathless as he shadowed her out of the kitchen and into the series of corridors and halls that eventually led to the staircase up to the wing of the house in which they had been placed.

'I'm finding that so hard to believe, Violet,' he murmured in a voice that warmed every part of her. 'You *always* have opinions. When you first walked into my office, I took you for someone who had scrambled all her courage together to confront me but who, under normal circumstances, wouldn't have said boo to a goose. My mistake.'

Violet eyed the landing ahead of her. Bedroom to the right. She thought she had recovered from that momentary tipsiness induced by a little too much wine with dinner but now she felt dizzy and flustered and wondered if she had overestimated her sobriety after all.

She glanced down and her eyes flitted over his lean brown hand on the banister just behind her.

Her heart was beating wildly as they made it to the bedroom door.

'All teachers have opinions,' she managed in a strangled voice. She took a step back as he reached around her to push open the bedroom door.

'There's a difference between having opinions and being opinionated. You're opinionated.' His arm brushed her and, all at once, he felt himself harden at the passing contact. That forbidden excitement coursed through him, reminding him of what she had looked like standing in front of him, naked and unaware. He hadn't had a woman for over three months. His last relationship, short-lived though it had been, had crumbled under the combined weight of his unreliability and her need to find out where they were heading. Not even her stupendous good looks, her unwavering availability whatever the time of day or night, or the very inventive sex, could provide sufficient glue to keep them going for a little longer.

He firmly closed the door behind him and switched on a side light so that the bedroom was suddenly infused in a mellow, romantic glow.

'You're going downstairs to work now, aren't you?' Violet asked nervously and he gave her a rueful smile.

'I'm trying to kick back a little…I think it would reassure my mother that I'm capable of involving myself in family life and leaving the emails alone now and again… You do approve, don't you?'

Violet found herself in the unenviable position of having to agree with him, especially when she had stuck her head above the parapet to voice her positive opinions on just that point.

'So…if you'll excuse me, I'll go have a shower…' He began unbuttoning his shirt and was amused when she primly diverted her eyes. This was the very situation most women would have loved. Up close and personal with him in a bedroom. He caught the distinctly erotic aroma of inexperience and her shyness was doing amazing things for his already rampant libido.

He made sure not to lock the door but he took his time, washing his hair and emerging twenty minutes later to find her with all her accoutrements in her hands.

'Sure you don't need a suitcase to carry all that stuff through?' he enquired and Violet blushed.

'I wouldn't want to disturb you when I come out. Just in case you're sleeping.'

'Very thoughtful.'

Violet backed away, eyes pinned to his face, anywhere but his muscled body, which was completely naked but for the tiny towel he had slung around his waist and which was dipping down in a very precarious fashion.

Did he sleep in pyjamas? How would she know when he had spent the past few nights retiring to bed at after one in the morning and getting up before six to start his day? She certainly hadn't seen any lying about and she found that her mind was entirely focused on that one small technicality as she lingered in the bathroom for as long as she possibly could.

And for a while after she emerged into a pitch-black room, she actually breathed a sigh of relief that he was asleep. He was nothing more than a dark shadow on the bed. On the very *big* bed.

Barely daring to breathe, she slipped under the duvet and turned on her side away from him with movements that were exaggeratedly slow. *Just in case.*

'You never actually told me whether you'd decided to come next weekend or not. Our conversation must have become waylaid...'

Violet gave a squeak of horror that he was not only awake but, from the sound of his voice, bright-eyed and bushy-tailed. She heard him adjust his position on the bed and when he next spoke she knew that he was now facing her.

'I think we lost track of the point when you decided to congratulate me on my sterling efforts with my brother...' He reached out to place a cool hand on her shoulder and Violet's blood pressure soared into the stratosphere. 'I hate talking to someone's back.'

Violet froze. She felt trapped between a rock and a hard place. She was in this bed with this man and she either turned round to face him, thereby instantly diminishing the generous proportions of the bed, or else she remained as she was, with her back to him like a petrified object, desperately hoping that hand would go away and not do something more exploratory to urge her over onto her other side. She reluctantly shifted her position and was screamingly aware of the rustle of the duvet and the soft deflation of the pillow as her body shifted.

Her eyes had adjusted to the darkness in the bedroom and her mouth went dry when she realised that he was bare-chested. Propping himself up on one elbow, the duvet was down to his waist, allowing her an eyeful of his perfectly muscled, sinewy chest with its flat brown nipples and just the right amount of dark hair to make her breath catch painfully in her throat.

'That's better,' Damien said with satisfaction. 'Now I can actually see your face. So what's your decision to be?'

'Can't we discuss this in the morning?'

'I'm a great believer in not putting off for tomorrow what can be done today and that includes decisions.'

'I suppose it wouldn't hurt to come down next weekend,' Violet mumbled. Underneath the prim fleecy pyjamas, she could feel the heavy weight of her unconstrained breasts, which in turn made her remember that very moment when she had realised he had been watching her as she had emerged completely naked from the bathroom. Those twin attacks on her crumbling composure sent a wave of heat licking through her.

'My mother and Dominic will both be pleased.' Damien's voice was low and unbearably sexy. 'As,' he continued, 'will I...'

'You will? You don't mean that. You've barely spoken to me all week.'

'I might say the same for you. But we're talking now...'

'Yes...'

'Feels good, doesn't it?'

Violet could hear the rapid rush of her own breathing. His low, husky words were a backdrop to something else. She felt it with an instinct she wasn't even aware she possessed. He wasn't touching her but it felt as though he might be and, although she knew that he couldn't read her expression any more accurately than she could read his in the darkness, there was still a crackle of high voltage electricity between them that made the hairs on the back of her neck stand on end.

Was he going to make a move on her? Surely not! And yet…now was the time to briskly bring the conversation to an end by turning away. Sleep might be difficult to court with him lying right there next to her on the bed, but he would get the message that she had nothing more to say to him when she coldly turned away. And if she couldn't see him, then this weirdly unsettling *awareness* that was making her pulses race would be extinguished at source. He would probably be gone, as usual, before she woke up in the morning and they would be back to keeping a healthy distance from each other, only breaking it in front of his family.

Violet knew exactly what she should do and how she should react and instead, to her horror, she found herself reaching out to touch that hard, broad chest. Just one touch. Where on earth had that dangerous thought come from? How had it managed to slip through all the walls and barriers of common sense and self-protection she was frantically erecting?

And where had that soft gasping sound come from as her fingers rested briefly on his chest?

Damien felt a kick of supreme satisfaction. Never had a woman's touch felt so good. It was hesitant, timid, a barely-there sort of touch, and it ignited his blood, which was burning hot in his veins as he pulled her towards him…

CHAPTER SEVEN

HIS LIPS MET hers and Violet was lost. While a part of her knew that this shouldn't be happening, the rest of her clung to him with shameful abandon. She couldn't get enough of touching him. She wanted to explore every inch of his body and then begin all over again. The urge was nothing like anything she had felt before in her life. For her, love-making always seemed a calm, pleasant business, but then her one and only lover had started life as a friend. Damien was certainly no friend and this was not calm. She fever-ishly traced the muscled contours of his shoulders and she could feel him smiling against her mouth.

She ran her foot along his calf and shivered as her knee came into contact with the rigidity of his erection. When he flipped her onto him, she arched and threw her head back as he undid the buttons of her top, to reveal breasts that dangled tantalisingly by his mouth. She straightened to fling the constricting fleece off her.

She looked down at him, breathing hard, her hair tumbling past her shoulders. His skin was golden-brown, a natural bronze that contrasted dramatically against her own paleness. She reached out and flattened the palm of her hand against him and felt the ripple of muscle under her fingers.

He pulled her into him and half groaned as her breasts

squashed against his chest. This time, his kiss was long, lingering and never-ending. It was a kiss that was designed to get lost in. It was a kiss that allowed no room for thought.

The warm fleece of her pyjama bottoms felt itchy and uncomfortable. Her underwear was damp with spreading moisture. She parted her legs and, through the fleece, she felt the hard jut of his erection.

'We shouldn't,' she moaned, instantly negating that passing thought by moving sinuously against him.

'Why? We both want it...'

'Because you want something doesn't mean that you should just go right ahead and have it...'

'Are you telling me that you want to stop?' She could no more do that than he could. Damien was aware of this with every fibre of his being. He pulled her back down against him, stifling any protest she might have come up with, and Violet ran her fingers through his hair. She loved the feel of its silky thickness. Touching him like this...it felt decadent, taboo, weirdly wicked. Even though she was supposed to be his girlfriend...

She felt like a Victorian maiden on the verge of swooning when he eased her up and hooked his fingers into the waistband of the pyjamas. Her breasts were tempting and luscious, but first...

He tugged the bottoms and watched with satisfaction as she quickly slipped them off. When she reached to do the same with her panties, he stayed her hand. He could see the dampness darkening the crotch as she straddled him and he placed his palm against the spot and moved it until he could feel the wetness seeping through to his hand.

'Enjoying yourself?' Anticipation was running through his veins. Making his blood boil. He intended to take things slowly, but it was hard. All he could think of was her settling on him, feeling her softness sheathing him and her tightness as she moved on him. 'Touch me.'

Violet quivered. The underwear had to come off. She was going crazy. She swung her legs over the side of the bed and kicked it free, then turned back to see him watching her with a little smile as he touched himself. He was huge. A massive rock-hard rod of steel nestled in whorls of dark hair. She was mesmerised by the sight of his hand lightly circling himself, moving lazily, biding his time until she could pleasure him.

'I'd rather *you* were doing this...'

Violet made her way over to him so that she was within touching distance...within licking distance...

Damien groaned and flung his head back, eyes closed, enjoying her tongue and mouth on him. He curled his hands into her hair, cupping her head. He had to steel himself against a powerful urge to let go, to release himself. He was in the process of physically losing control and he almost failed to recognise that fact because it was not something with which he was familiar. For him, making love had always been a finely tuned art form, where mutual pleasure rose along a predictable, albeit pleasurable, incline.

With a shudder, he reluctantly pulled her away from him and took a few seconds to gather himself.

Violet experienced a heady feeling of power. That this beautiful, desirable alpha male had to steady himself because of her...

She revelled in the unusual situation of really and truly, for the first time in her life, letting herself go. She felt as though she had had years of always having to be the one in control. Even in her one and only relationship, she had remained that person—the person who always thought before acting, the person who was always responsible. In

giving Phillipa permission to be exactly the person she
wanted to be, Violet, without knowing it, had tailored her
own responses, had become the one who held back because
someone had to, in the absence of parents.

Now…

She licked his rigid shaft once again and felt the rough-
ness of veins against her tongue, a contrast to the silky
smoothness at the top.

She had a moment's hesitation as her ever present common sense cranked into gear.

What was going on here? So yes, he was an intensely
attractive man. It was perfectly understandable that she
might be attracted to him. Attraction and lust had nothing to do with love and affection. She knew that now. But
why on earth did *he* find *her* attractive? He was a man
used to supermodels. She had seen pictures of them and,
on his own admission, his first impressions of her had
hardly been positive. So was he here now because a certain amount of boredom had met a similar amount of curiosity and the two, in this strangely charged situation, had
combined to produce desire? Had the charade of playing
their respective parts spilled over into reality?

For whatever reason, this man wanted her and for even
more nebulous reasons, and against her better judgement,
she wanted him. She knew what she should do. But suddenly she thought of her sister, flitting around in Ibiza,
doing exactly what she wanted to do while she, Violet,
remained behind to pick up the pieces. She thought of
herself, always travelling in the slow lane, always taking
care, while the fast-paced rush of the unexpected and the
novel flew past her, leaving her in its wake.

Why, she wondered with a spurt of rebellion, shouldn't
she jump on the roller coaster for once in her life? Why

should she hold back at this eleventh hour? Would it be fair to herself? It certainly wouldn't be fair to *him*.

So what they had wouldn't last but what did she stand to lose? Damien meant nothing to her emotionally. He turned her on but she would always be able to walk away from lust because, sooner or later, her common sense would once again kick in, telling her that it was time to move on. When that time came, she would get back out there and jump back into the dating game, find herself a nice guy. She would never look back and have regrets that she had had her one window to be reckless and she had chosen to primly shut it and walk away.

She raised her head to meet his eyes and read the naked desire there.

'You're fabulous,' he said roughly, and Violet smiled and blushed because she couldn't think of a time when anyone had called her that.

'You're just saying that…'

'Don't tell me you haven't driven your fair share of men crazy before…' He raised himself, pulled her towards him and kissed her with driving urgency, stifling any confirmation. He didn't want to think of her with any other man. It was an unsettling and momentary pull of possessiveness that was completely alien to him.

His mouth never left hers as he found one breast and massaged its plumpness, finding the erect peak of her nipple to tease it until she was squirming.

In shocking detail, his voice rough and uneven, he told her exactly what he wanted to do with her, where he wanted to touch her, what he wanted her to feel.

Violet's skin burned hotly with the thrill of what he was saying. True, her experience when it came to the opposite sex was limited to one guy, but even so nothing could quite have prepared her for this sensory overload. His husky sex talk was doing all sorts of things in her mind while his hand, which had moved from her breast to caress the fluffy downy hair between her legs, was having a similar effect on her body.

She writhed and moaned softly, lowering herself to rake her teeth along his shoulder. He flipped her over so that he was now on top of her and she watched the progress of his dark head as he trailed a blazing path with his mouth along her shoulders to clamp on her nipple. Her nails dug into his shoulder blades then moved to tangle into his hair so that she could urge his mouth harder on her sensitised nipple.

He told her to tell him what she liked. Violet blushed furiously and thought that that was something she would never be able to do in a million years.

'So...' Damien was inordinately thrilled at her shyness. On so many levels he had been spot on when he had told her that she made a refreshing change. He had raised himself up now, his powerful body over hers, his hardness pressed against her, which made her desperate to open her legs and guide him inside. He laughed when she tried and told her that he was having none of that. Yet.

'You don't talk during sex...' He slipped two fingers inside her, felt her wetness and began teasing her, rubbing the throbbing little bud of her clitoris until she was gasping, only to move his attention elsewhere so that she didn't peak.

'Damien...'

'How do you expect me to know what turns you on if you don't tell me...?'

'You *know* what turns me on... You're...you're...'

'Doing it right now?'

'Please...'

'I like it that you're begging me...do you enjoy it when *I* talk...?' He whispered a few more things in her ear and Violet groaned. 'Well...?' His exploring fingers drove deeper inside her and she tightened her legs.

'Yes,' Violet whispered, then she shot him a devilish smile, 'although right now...there's other stuff I'd like you to do...'

'Tell me...'

'I...I can't...' She felt as green as a virgin.

'Of course you can,' Damien coaxed. It was taking a massive amount of willpower to maintain this leisurely pace. Her body pressed against his was beyond a turn-on and the slippery wetness between her legs was something he could barely think about because, if he did, he knew that he would lose control.

'I like it when you...suck my nipples...they're very sensitive...' Violet could feel her skin burning as though she was on fire. She felt forward and wanton and thoroughly debauched and she wondered how it was that she had never, ever been tempted to let go like this before. For a second she panicked at the notion that a man with whom she had nothing in common had been the one to rouse her to these heights.

'Your wish is my command...and I have other things in store for you...'

Violet decided not to think. She immersed herself in sensation after sensation as he suckled on her nipples, his tongue darting and rubbing and licking and then she gasped, shocked, as his wandering mouth travelled southwards. When she stammered that she had never...he couldn't possibly mean to...he laughed, deep-throated and amused, and proceeded to precisely what she had never...

His head between her legs made her want to cry out loud. Of their own volition, they parted to accommodate his ministrations and he was very thorough. He teased her with his tongue until she knew that she couldn't stand it any longer, then he angled his big body so that she could pleasure him just as he was pleasuring her.

Her legs were spread wide as he continued to feast on her. His tongue probed every bit of her and she did likewise to him, taking his bigness into her mouth, tasting it in every way possible. Only when she knew that they were both about to tip over the edge did he raise himself up, pulling apart only to ask her if she was protected. He was breathing heavily.

Why on earth would she be? Violet wanted to ask. But she knew that, for Damien, his relationships would always have been with women who travelled prepared. She was certain that had they fallen into bed in his house or flat or apartment, or wherever it was he lived, there would be ample supplies of condoms in a bedside cabinet. She shook her head. She searched his face for signs of impatience and frustration but there were none. Instead, he rubbed himself against her and murmured that full intercourse would have to wait.

'There are other ways to keep busy...'

Violet was lost for words at his generosity. She wasn't completely naive. She knew that a lot of men would have been angry, enraged even, to have had their pleasure curtailed, even if it wasn't the woman's fault. A lot of men were selfish. Contrary to first impressions, Damien clearly was not one of those men.

Something shifted inside her but it was something she didn't stop to analyse. Just at that moment, her brain wasn't up to doing anything analytical. Not when he was touching her once again, burying his head between her thighs, relentlessly teasing her throbbing clitoris with his tongue.

Their bodies seemed to fuse into one and when, finally, she climaxed, thrusting up against his greedy mouth, she felt utterly spent. She blindly reached for him, felt his hardness and curved her languorous body so that her mouth met it, so that she could take him to the same heights to which he had taken her.

Their bodies were slick with perspiration and the room filled with the miasma of sex. He tugged her off him before he came and she felt his ejection on her face and body. It mirrored her own wetness that glistened on his face. When they kissed as he returned to Planet Earth, it was the most sensuous thing she had ever done. She felt giddy from such complete loss of her self-control.

'I think tomorrow we might pay a visit to the chemist…' Damien was on top of the world. What was it about this woman? They hadn't even indulged in full intercourse and why kid himself, no amount of inventive touching could compare to the unique sensation of penetration. Yet he was infused with a feeling of absolute well-being. On a high. He wanted to start all over again, touching, tracing her body with his hands, tasting…

He pulled her against him and relished the softness of her full breasts squashed against his chest.

'I don't know how this happened…'

'Are you saying you wish it hadn't?'

'No,' Violet admitted truthfully, 'but I'm not the kind of girl who falls into bed with men…'

'Not even with the boyfriend you happen to be deeply in love with?'

It took a couple of seconds for it to register that he was teasing her. 'Ha, ha, very funny…' she said weakly. *But what happens next?* she wanted to ask. Except the question seemed strangely inappropriate.

'This complicates things…' she said instead.

It was precisely why he had made such a big effort not to go there. Even when he had acknowledged that he was attracted to her, even though he was a man who had never missed a step between attraction and possession, it was precisely why Damien had stepped back. Because he had acknowledged that to sleep with her would be to complicate an already complicated situation.

Now, with her sexy, luscious body pressed against his, there was no room in his head for thoughts of complications.

'That's one way of looking at it. On the other hand, you could say that it makes the situation much more interesting.'

'I'm not an interesting person.'

'Leave the character assessment to me...' He smoothed his hand over her thigh, slipped it underneath, sandwiching it between her legs, his own personal hand warmer.

Violet knew exactly what sort of character assessment he was talking about. It had nothing to do with her personality.

'So we're here...and we're sleeping together. You might say it adds a great deal more veracity to the situation. No need to pretend...'

Except, Violet thought, they were *still* pretending. Pretending an emotional connection that was absent, even though there was now a physical one.

'You're still frowning.'

'I can't help it.'

'Live for the present.'

'I've never been good at doing that. When our parents died, I was left in charge of Phillipa and the last thing I could afford to do was live for the present.'

'I get that,' Damien murmured. He wasn't one for soul-searching conversations but he was feeling incredibly relaxed. 'With a sister like her, you had to carry worries about the future for both of you.' He gently parted her legs and slipped his finger along the crease that protected her femininity like the petals of a flower.

'I can't...talk when you're doing that...'

'Fine by me. Touching and talking don't go hand in hand. At least...not unless the talking's dirty...which I've discovered turns you on...'

'But we have to talk...'

'Wouldn't you rather...'

'Damien!' She could feel her body tensing and building up to a climax. His caressing hand was doing all sorts of things to her and yet there was stuff that needed to be said.

'I know. Irresistible, isn't it? And you can feel how much it's turning me on as well...'

Violet wondered how it would be were they to make love fully, properly... Her imagination soared as the rubbing movements against the pulsating bud of her clitoris got faster and faster and when she came it was an explosion that left her drained.

She curled against him. 'What happens now...?' She hadn't wanted to pose the question but it was one that needed to be asked.

Damien stilled. Questions of that nature always left him cold. However, in a strange way, this was a far more straightforward situation. 'You come up next weekend. As agreed. But I won't be working till one in the morning and leaving the bedroom by six. It has to be said that the prospect of sojourns in the countryside has taken on a distinctly upbeat tempo.'

'But I'm not your real girlfriend...'

'Where are you going with this?'

'Do we communicate during the week?' She worried her lower lip as she tried to get her head round a relationship that wasn't a relationship. 'Or do we just become involved when we're here? I mean,' she added, just in case he got it into his head she would spend Monday to Friday pining for his company and putting her life on hold, 'what if I meet someone…? I have quite a busy social life. Teachers like going out after school. Most of us feel we need a drink after a day in the company of high energy kids.'

'Meet someone?' He shifted so that he could look down at her.

'I've been thinking about getting back into the dating scene. For some reason, it's always been difficult with Phillipa around. I guess she just took up so much of my energy. I spent so much time worrying about what she was getting up to and listening to her personal sagas that there never seemed to be much time left over for myself. With Phillipa in Ibiza now…'

Damien's brain had come to a screeching halt at the words *getting back into the dating scene*. They had just made love! He was outraged. How could she even be contemplating the prospect of some other guy when she was lying next to him, her body still hot and flushed after her climax that he had given her?

'Sorry, but that's not going to happen.' He flung himself back and stared up at the ceiling with its ornate mouldings which he could hardly make out in the darkness. He felt her shift next to him so that she, likewise, was staring up at the ceiling.

'I'm not following you…'

'Explain to me how, on the one hand, you say that you don't climb into bed with random men whilst on the other telling me that you want to start going to nightclubs and sleeping with whoever takes your fancy at the time…'

'That's not at all what I said!'

'No? It sounded very much like that to me. And I am very much offended that you would even think of raising a subject of this nature after we've spent the past hour and a half making love. In fact, you shouldn't even be *thinking* about other men. Right now, *I* should be the only man on your mind.'

'The game's changed,' Violet said calmly on a deep breath, 'and now there are different rules.'

'Enlighten me.'

'Why do you have to be so arrogant?'

'It's one of the more endearing aspects of my personality. You were going to tell me about these new rules.'

'I… For some weird reason I find I'm attracted to you.' She took a deep breath. 'You've told me that I should live in the present and I guess this is my one-off opportunity to do that. I never expected it to happen, but there you go.'

'So…other guys…out of the question. Nightclubs and sex after two drinks…likewise out of the question.'

'In which case, the same rules apply to you.'

Damien rolled to his side and looked at her. In accordance with a serious conversation, she had tucked the duvet right up to her neck.

'Gladly.' He pulled the duvet down, exposing her breasts and he gently nuzzled a rosy tip until it stiffened against his tongue. 'Gladly?' Violet tugged him up so that he was looking at her, although her body was aching for him to carry on doing what it had been doing so well.

'I'm a one woman kind of man…'

Violet wondered whether that was because he happened to be temporarily stuck far away from the action but then she conceded that, however arrogant and infuriating he could be, his ground rules would be fair.

'And besides…' he nibbled her lower lip, tugging it gently between his teeth '…this works…'

'You said you first thought that getting involved like this…'

'Falling into bed together and making love until we're too exhausted to move…'

'…would complicate things.' Violet didn't know what she wanted him to say. She had knowingly thrown caution to the winds and yet she still felt confused. She had never felt so physically satisfied—*never ever*—and yet the road ahead still seemed opaque and clouded with uncertainty. He might not want to put a label to what they now had, but effectively they were an item. For real. And yet why didn't it feel that way? And did she really expect him to set those niggling anxieties to rest?

'I wasn't thinking out of the box. I've found that women seem to associate fun in bed with meeting the parents and eventually shopping for a wedding ring. You…' seemingly of its own volition, his hand caressed her breast; he couldn't get enough of her '…fall into a different category. You know how the ground lies. I'm not looking for any kind of commitment. Been there, done that, won't be revisiting that particular holiday hotspot in the foreseeable future. But what's going on right now…mind-blowing…and I'm not one to throw around superlatives lightly…' He shot her a smouldering smile that made her toes curl. 'I won't be casting my net anywhere else and, if it makes you happy, you can communicate with me all you want to during the week. In fact, you'll need to be updated on my mother's progress. I'm sure she'll also get in touch. It would be abnormal for you to be ignorant of how she is doing. So I'm guessing all your questions have been sorted…'

They were having fun. Plus it was convenient. But he was trusting her not to get emotionally wrapped up. When he said that they would communicate during the week, she knew that their conversations would be about Eleanor, that there would be a specific reason for them to happen in the first place. They wouldn't be passing the time chatting about nothing much in particular. Violet decided that she was fine with that. She had never been the sort of person who kept the various sections of her life neatly boxed away and separated. This was how it was done. Of course, it would take a little getting used to but she would do it because, like it or not, she was greedy for the physical exhilaration he had introduced into her life, which, on that level, now seemed bland and nondescript in comparison.

She parted her legs and felt his hardness rub against her. No penetration but the sensation produced was still powerful and she moved in time to increase the pressure.

'And when things fizzle out between us…' she volunteered breathlessly.

'It's called the natural course of events.'

She could hardly imagine him being so deeply in love with a woman that he would want to take it to the very limit, that he would propose marriage. She couldn't get her head around the notion of him offering commitment rather than talking about the natural course of events. For a man as intensely proud and intensely passionate, she could understand how he could have been permanently damaged by the most significant relationship in his life going belly up. Eleanor had never broached the subject of Annalise again and neither had she. Damien's past was none of her business. This was the here and now. Everything he said made sense. This was her one opportunity to ditch her comfort zone and there was no point having a mental debate on the pros and cons of the clauses attached.

'We'll go our separate ways but as long as we're lovers you'll find, my darling, that I am exceedingly generous…'

'Your money doesn't mean anything to me.' She tried not to feel hurt at the implication that she could be shoved into the predictable mould of one of his women, eager to take whatever gifts were on offer. 'That's not why…I don't care if you own the Bank of England. I don't want anything from you.'

Damien thought that whilst she might say that now, her tune would change the second he presented her with her very first diamond-encrusted bracelet or top-of-the-range sports car.

'Frankly, my mother would expect it.'

'She already knows that I'm not the materialistic kind.'

'More confidences exchanged during one of your cosy tête-à-têtes?' But he liked her protestations of wholesomeness. What guy in his position wouldn't? Even if, sooner or later, the moral high ground took a bit of a beating? Greed and avarice were frequent visitors to his life. It was nice not to have them knocking on the door just yet.

'We don't *just* talk about you!'

'I'm hurt. I thought I was never far from your thoughts…' He moved fractionally against her and she squirmed and her eyes fluttered. To stop herself from losing control altogether once again, she reached down and firmly held him in her hand. The steel thickness of his girth made her shudder with wicked pleasure.

'You're not *in* my thoughts,' Violet denied vigorously. Having someone in your thoughts implied a *connection*. Even jokingly, she didn't want to go there, didn't want to let him think that he might be anything more to her than she was to him. 'You crop up in conversation with your mother because you're the person we have in common and, under normal circumstances, a girlfriend would be really happy to hear her stories about the guy in her life from his mother. It's natural that your mother would want to talk about you. Now, though, we talk about other things. Art, the garden, life in a small community, the treatment and what it might involve…and I don't just have conversations with your mother. I talk a lot to Dominic as well. He has a lot to say. You just have to be patient. He gets frustrated because he can't communicate as fluently as he'd like, but he's smart.'

Damien gently removed her hand from him. Reluctantly. Of course, warning bells shouldn't be ringing. They were, after all, singing from the same song sheet but still…just in case…

'Don't get too wrapped up, Violet.'

'What do you mean?'

'I mean…we might become more involved with one another than either of us anticipated or probably even wanted, and your role might have been extended beyond what I envisaged, but don't start nurturing ideas of permanence.'

'I wouldn't do that!' She pulled away from him. 'And you don't have to warn me! You've already made the parameters of what we have perfectly clear. I understand, Damien. It suits me! I'm not an idiot.'

'But you're forming links with my family,' Damien said drily.

'I'm *having conversations*!' But she could detect the coolness in his voice. This wasn't a gentle caution. This was a warning shot across the bows, a blunt reminder that she was not to go beyond the Keep Out signs he had erected around himself. If she did, and the message was clear though unspoken, she would be ditched. He would enjoy her but that was as far as things would go. In short, *don't start getting any ideas…*

'I'm a big girl. I know how to take care of myself. And because the women you've dated in the past might have wanted more from you than you were prepared to give, that's not the case with me. I've always been careful. I'm just having a go at what it feels like not to be careful for once in my life. And do you always have a list prepared of dos and don'ts when you start a…something? With a woman? Or is this specially for me because I happen to have met your family?'

Violet knew that she shouldn't be pursuing this. This wasn't part of her decision to *be daring for once in her life*.

'I'm always upfront when it comes to women. I let them know that I'm not in it for the long-term.'

'Because you've been hurt once doesn't mean that you have to spend the rest of your life keeping your distance.'

'Come again?' Damien said coldly.

'I'm sorry. I shouldn't have said that.' But had he laid down loads of rules and regulations for Annalise? No. She wasn't in the same category—of course she wasn't—but neither did she need to be subjected to a hundred and one boundary lines because he thought she was too gullible or too stupid to know how the land lay.

'Let's move on from this conversation, Violet. My past is not fertile ground for discussion.' And he was willing to let it go. His magnanimity surprised him because he categorically did not invite anyone's opinions on certain aspects of his life. Naturally, he didn't want to engineer an argument. He hadn't enjoyed the past few days of awkwardness. And also, for once, he was thinking with that part of his body which he always had under control. Never had elemental desire been so important a factor in his response.

'As I said, I understand the parameters and it suits me.'

'You're using me, in other words.' His voice was light and amused.

'No more than you're using me.'

Not quite the response he had expected. He gave a low laugh. Fair's fair, he thought. Wasn't it? He'd never had any woman admit to using him before. So what if the feeling didn't sit *quite right*? He wanted her. She wanted him. Trim away the excess and that was all that mattered.

CHAPTER EIGHT

DAMIAN REACHED INTO his jacket pocket and flipped open the lid of the black and gold box which had been nestling there for the past three hours.

A necklace with a teardrop pendant, a blood-red ruby, surrounded by tiny diamonds. He had chosen it himself. Well, why not? Suitable recompense for the past three and a half months, during which Violet had proved herself a superb and satisfying lover. He always gave gifts to his lovers. She might have thwarted every attempt he had made thus far on that front, rebutting his offers of a car, *because who needed to become snarled up in traffic, not to mention contributing to global warming whilst having to pay the Congestion Charge the second you needed it for anything really useful?* an expensive weekend in Vienna now that his mother seemed to be responding so well to her treatment programme, *can't, too much work, sorry,* some really expensive kitchen equipment because he had seen what she had, *no, thanks, a girl becomes accustomed to working with old, familiar pots and pans and ovens and fridges and microwaves...*

But this necklace was a fait accompli. She would have no choice but to accept it.

He snapped shut the lid of the box and returned it to

his jacket pocket before sliding out of his car and heading up to her house.

He had grown accustomed to the confined space in which she lived. Literally two-up, two-down. Phillipa was still doing whatever she was doing in Ibiza. He couldn't imagine the claustrophobia of actually having to share the place with another adult human being. Personally, it would have driven him mad. He was used to the vast open-plan space of his five-bedroom house in Chelsea. When he had moved there years ago, he had hired a top architect who had re-configured the layout of the house so that the rooms, all painted stone and adorned with a mixture of established art and newer investment worthy pieces, flowed into one another.

Violet's house was more in the nature of a honeycomb. Two weeks previously, he had offered to have the whole thing gutted and redone more along his tastes, but predictably she had looked at him as though he had taken leave of his senses and laughed. Alternatively, he had said, they could just spend more time at his place. He was now splitting his time between London and the West Country. Why not make love in luxury? But she had told him, in the sort of semi-apologetic voice that managed to impart no hint of remorse, that she didn't like his house. Something about it being sterile and clinical. He had refrained from telling her that she was the first woman to have ever responded to opulence with a negative reaction.

He pressed the doorbell and instantly lost his train of thought at the sound of her approaching footsteps.

From inside the house, Violet felt that familiar shiver of tingling, excited anticipation. After the first month, and once he had ascertained that Eleanor was responding well, Damien had split his time. He always made sure to spend weekends in the country and often Mondays as well, but he was now in London a great deal more and Violet liked that. On all levels, what she was doing was bad for her. She knew that. She didn't understand where this driving, urgent chemistry between them had sprung from and even less did she understand how it was capable of existing in a vacuum the way it did, but she was powerless to fight it. Having always equated sex with love, she had fast learned how easy it was for everything you took for granted to be turned inside out and upside down.

She had also fast learned how easy it was to lose track of the rules of the game you had signed up to.

When had she started living her week in anticipation of seeing him? Just when had she sacrificed all her principles, all her expectations of what a relationship should deliver on the high altar of lust and passion and sex?

She had told herself that she was throwing caution to the winds. That most of her adult years had been spent being responsible and diligent and careful so why on earth shouldn't she take a little time out and experience something else, something that wasn't all wrapped up with *doing the right thing*? She had practically decided that she *owed* herself that. That she was a grown woman who was more than capable of handling a sexual relationship with a man to whom she was inexplicably but powerfully attracted.

So how was it that it was now so difficult to maintain the mask of not caring one jot if he never discussed anything beyond tomorrow? If he assumed that whatever they had would fizzle out at some point? More and more she found herself thinking about Annalise, the wife that should have been but never was. He never mentioned her name. That in itself was telling because three weeks ago, on one of their rare excursions out for a meal at a swanky restaurant in Belgravia, he had bumped into a woman and had afterwards told her that he had dated her for a few months. The woman had been a flame-haired six-foot beauty, as slender as a reed and draped over a man much shorter and older. Afterwards, Damien had laughed and informed her that the man in question was a Russian billionaire, married but with his wife safely tucked away in the bowels of St Petersburg somewhere.

'Don't you feel a twinge of jealousy that he's dating a woman you used to go out with?' Violet had asked, because how could any man not? When the woman in question looked as though she had stepped straight off the front cover of a high-end fashion magazine? Damien had laughed. Why on earth would he be jealous? Women came and went. Good luck to the guy, although he had enough money to keep the lady in question amused and interested.

'Was she too expensive for you?' Violet had asked, which he had found even more amusing.

'No one's too expensive for me. I dumped her because she wanted more than money could buy.'

Violet had thought that that had said it all. The woman in question had wanted a ring on her finger. Damien, on the other hand, had wanted casual. Which was what he wanted with her and the only woman to whom those rules had never applied was the one woman who had broken his heart.

And yet, knowing all that, she could still feel herself sliding further and further away from logic, common sense and self-control. Forewarned wasn't forearmed.

She pulled open the door and her heart gave that weird skippy feeling, as though she were in a lift that had suddenly dropped a hundred floors at maximum speed.

It was Thursday and he had come straight from work, although his tie was missing and his jacket was slung over his shoulder.

'Damien…'

'Missed me?' Deep blue, hooded eyes swept over her with masculine appreciation. No bra. Ages ago, he had told her that it was an entirely unnecessary item of clothing for a woman whose breasts were as perfect as hers. At least indoors. When *he* was the male caller in question…

He had been leaning indolently against the doorframe. Now he pushed himself off and entered the tiny hallway, his eyes glued to her the whole time.

His smile was slow and lazy. With an easy movement, he tossed his jacket aside, where it landed neatly on the banister, then he wrapped his arms around her, drew her to him so that he could try and extinguish some of the yearning that had been building inside him from the very second he had set foot in his car. Her mouth parted readily and he grunted with pleasure as his tongue found hers, clashing in a hungry need for more.

Violet braced her hands against his chest and stayed him for a few seconds. 'You know I hate it when the first thing you do the very second you walk through the front door is…is…'

'Kiss you senseless…?' Damien raked his fingers through his hair. Frankly, he wasn't too fond of that particular trait himself. He didn't like what it said about his self-control when he was around her, but he chose to keep that to himself. 'Is that why the last time I came, we didn't even manage to make it up the stairs?' he said instead. 'In fact, if I recall…your jumper was off on stair two, I had your nipple in my mouth by stair four and by stair eight, roughly halfway up, I was exploring other parts of your extremely responsive body…'

Violet blushed. As always, it was one thing saying something and another actually putting it into practice.

Right now, although he had done as asked and had

drawn back from her, the one thing she wanted to do was pull him right back towards her so that they could carry on where they had left off.

It was only a very small consolation that these little shows of strength helped her to maintain the façade of being as casual about what they had as he was. She knew that she had to cling to them for dear life.

'I'm going to cook us something special.' She led the way to the kitchen and retrieved a cold bottle of beer from the fridge, which he took, tilting his head back to drink a couple of long mouthfuls.

'Why?'

Violet contained a little spurt of irritation. Shows of domesticity were never appreciated. He had never said so but, tellingly, his chef would often prepare food, which he would bring with him, stuff that tasted delicious and required an oven, a microwave and plates, or else takeaways were ordered when they had been physically sated. The ritual of eating was usually just an interruption, she sometimes felt, to the main event.

'I'm trying it out as a meal for my class to learn,' she lied and he shrugged and swallowed a couple more mouthfuls of beer before retreating to the kitchen table, where he sprawled on one chair, pulling another closer and using it as a footrest.

Violet bustled. Now that they weren't tripping over themselves, tearing each other's clothes off in a frantic race to make love, she wished that they were. Her body tingled at the knowledge that he was looking at her. She loved it when his eyes got dark and slumberous and full of intent.

'Tell me how your mother's doing,' she said, to clear her head from the wanton desire to fling herself at him and forget about the meal she had planned.

She listened as he told her about recent trips into the

village, her upbeat mood, which so contrasted with her despair when she had initially told him about the situation, recovery that was exceeding the doctor's expectations...

Violet half listened. Her mind was drifting in and out of the uncomfortable questions she had recently started asking herself. Occasionally she said something and hoped for the best. She was a million miles away when she jumped as Damien padded up towards her and whispered into her ear, 'Must be a complicated recipe, Violet. You've been staring into space for the past five minutes.'

Violet snapped back to the present and turned to him with a little frown. 'I've got stuff on my mind.'

'Anything I'd like to hear about?'

She hesitated, torn between not wanting to rock the boat and needing to say what she was thinking.

'No. Just to do with school.' She cravenly shied away from doing what she knew would ruin the evening.

'What can I do to take your mind off it...?' Just like that, Damien felt his tension evaporate. He thought he might have been imagining the thickness of the atmosphere, her unusual silence. He turned her back to the chopping board, where she had been mixing a satay sauce, and wrapped his arms around her from behind. 'Looks good. What is it?' He slipped one big hand underneath her loose top and did what he had been wanting to the moment he had set foot through the front door. He caressed one full breast, settling on a nipple, which he rubbed gently but insistently with the pad of his thumb. With his other hand, he dipped a finger into the sauce, licked some off and offered the rest to her. Violet's mouth circled round his finger and she shivered at the deliberate eroticism in the gesture.

She moved across to the kitchen sink, carrying some dishes with her, and he released her, but only briefly, before resuming his position standing right behind her.

Outside, with the days getting longer, darkness was only now beginning to set in. Her view was spectacularly unexciting. The back of the house overlooked the wall of another house; the outside space comprised of a pocket-sized back garden just big enough for Phillipa to lie down in summer and spend the day tanning without having to dismantle the washing line.

Their bodies, merging together, were reflected hazily back to them in the windows overlooking the garden and their eyes tangled in the reflection as he slowly pushed up her jumper until she could see both their bodies and the pale nudity of her breasts. She gasped and fell back slightly against him as he began massaging them, rhythmic, firm movements that pushed them up, making her large nipples bulge and distend.

'Damien…no…someone might see us…' Although that wasn't really a possibility. The one thing about the house and its location was that it was surprisingly private, given the fact that it was in London, where privacy was a rarity. The small back garden was fully enclosed with a fence and a fortuitous tree in the back garden of the neighbour opposite ensured limited view.

Damien continued rubbing her breasts, filling his hands with the heavy weight of them, bouncing them slightly, as though evaluating their worth.

'Get naked for me,' he murmured, nipping her neck and then trailing hot kisses along it.

'Get…what…?'

'Don't pretend you didn't hear. Get naked for me. Take your clothes off. Scratch that. Maybe I'll let you get away with just wearing an apron…'

'I'm not dressing up for your enjoyment!' But already the thought of his dark, intense eyes following her naked body as she moved around the kitchen was making her feel hot and bothered.

'I'm not asking you to dress up. I'm asking you to dress down…' He shifted her jumper up, over her breasts, and Violet responded by spinning round to face him, her bare breasts pushing against the hard wall of his chest.

She began unbuttoning his shirt. From a position of relative inexperience only months ago, she had grown in confidence. He might not have had it at his disposal to offer anything most women would have expected of a proper relationship, but he certainly had it within him to turn her into a woman who was no longer tentative when it came to responding in ways that would pleasure her.

She shoved her hands under his shirt and felt the abrasive rub of his chest, not smooth and androgynous, but aggressively masculine with its dark hair. Slowly, she pushed the shirt off his broad shoulders, running her hands expertly along the contours of his muscles until the shirt had joined her jumper on the kitchen floor.

He propped himself against the counter, caging her in, and took his time kissing her until her whole body was burning up and she could feel the damp heat pooling between her legs.

'Those jogging bottoms do nothing at all for your superb figure… They should be banned from your wardrobe…' He slipped his fingers underneath the stretchy waistband and tugged them down, allowing her to wriggle out of them, keeping his arms on either side of her so that her movements were restricted. When he looked down, he could see her generous breasts shifting as she moved, soft and succulent. Unable to resist, he captured one and lifted it until her nipple was pouting directly at him. Reluctantly he decided that a full-on assault would have to wait. He wanted to take his time. She had been in his head for days; frankly, from the last time he had seen her, which had been the previous week, and he wasn't going to rush things. He had spent hours fantasising about the next time they met and he intended to see at least some of those fantasies translated into sexy reality.

'Same goes for the underwear...'

'But it's beautiful lacy underwear...' Violet protested with mock hurt. 'Brand new! And very expensive...not the sort of underwear a hard-working teacher can afford too much of...'

'I'll buy you the store. Then you can save your hard-earned salary for other things...'

Violet traced the outline of his flat brown nipples, moistened her fingers with her tongue, traced them again, and relished the way he flexed in immediate, gratifying response.

'I like the underwear,' Damien asserted huskily as he looked down at the lacy lavender piece of nothing. 'I just don't like it on you at this particular moment in time...' He pointedly tugged the lace, then, without giving her time to protest, knelt in front of her.

Looking down with a little gasp, Violet saw the dark bowed head of a supplicant. Even if he was very far from being one. It was an incredible turn-on.

He gently urged her thighs slightly apart and then peeled the underwear back, revealing the lushness of her hair.

With a shudder, she braced herself against the counter, head flung back, knowing that if she wasn't careful she would come in seconds. As his tongue slipped into the groove of her wetly receptive sex, she could hear the faint slick sounds as he licked and explored, with his finger still holding the underwear to one side.

She clenched her fists and gritted her teeth in a mammoth effort not to come against his questing mouth.

She reached down to tug his hair and, on cue, he straightened. Her hands scrabbled helplessly at his trousers and he gave a deep throaty laugh and began to unzip them.

'We haven't made it to the food,' he murmured.

'But at least we're not on the staircase…' As if that said anything, as if it implied any more restraint. It didn't. She was as desperate for him now as she always was when he came through her door.

'No. The kitchen. Lots of scope for being inventive… although would you rather we ate the food than tried playing with it…?' Damien laughed at her shocked expression. She had only had one other lover. He had managed to get that out of her ages ago and, from the sounds of it, that one lover had hardly been sizzling in the bedroom stakes. Every time they made love, he felt as though he was coming to her as her first and the feeling that generated was beyond satisfaction. 'Okay,' he drawled, 'maybe next time. I could teach you some very inventive things that can be done with champagne and cherries…'

He removed his trousers and underwear in one smooth movement. The kitchen was warm and fragrant with the food that had already started cooking. Outside, night had finally drawn in. With the lights off, they were just two shadows touching, feeling and responding to one another.

He breathed in her uniquely feminine scent, something to do with a light floral perfume she wore. It wouldn't have suited everyone but it damn well suited her. Even when they were apart, he could recall the smell and it always managed to get him aroused. How was that possible? He half closed his eyes and was relieved that she couldn't witness that momentary lapse of self-control.

For a few seconds a streak of anger flared inside him. A confused, chaotic anger that resented the peculiar hold he sometimes thought she had over him. He lifted her, taking her by surprise, and sat her on the counter, shoving aside the remnants of food and cutlery still to be cleared.

'What are you doing?' Violet's voice was breathless as her rear made contact with the cool surface of the kitchen counter.

'I'm taking you.'

'But…'

He didn't say anything, instead holding her with one hand while he bent to retrieve the wallet from his trousers, home of at least one extremely useful condom if memory served him right. He was hard and erect, throbbing with an urgent need to sink into her body and feel it wrap itself around him like a glove.

Her hands were on his shoulders and her short pearly nails were digging into his flesh. Leaning back, her breasts were thrust out, nipples standing to attention. He paused briefly to take one into his mouth, sucking hard on it until she was whimpering and crying out and could no longer keep still. His leisurely lovemaking plan had taken a nose-dive. Pushing open her legs and angling her just right so that she was ready to receive him, he entered her.

Pleasure exploded in her like a thunderbolt. She could feel every magnificent inch of him as he moved inside her, strong, forceful and with deepening intensity.

This was almost rough and yet it felt so good. She heard herself crying out and the sound seemed to be coming from someone else.

'Talk to me!' he demanded, curling his long fingers into her hair, tugging her into looking at him. Which she did, through half closed eyes because she was pretty much beyond focusing on anything but what he was doing to her.

'Damien!' He talked dirty to her but it was something she had not done in return. Some lingering element of prudishness always seemed to stand in the way.

'Tell me how you're feeling with me inside you!' He emphasised the order with a powerful thrust that made her slide a little way back on the counter.

Violet shivered with heady abandon. She clutched him and told him exactly what he was demanding to know. How it felt to have him in her, filling her up, taking away her ability to think. Her breasts ached for him. She wanted his mouth on them. She just couldn't get enough of him...

To her own ears, every word she uttered seemed to plunge her deeper and deeper into a vulnerable place. Would he pick that up? Was that finely tuned instinct of his sharp enough to pick up what wasn't being said behind the graphic descriptions? That she literally couldn't get enough of him, and not just on the physical, carnal plane, addictive though that was? That, for her, want was very much interlinked with need, which was dangerously close to...

Violet clamped shut her mouth, allowed herself to be carried away to oblivion. She cried out mindlessly as wave upon wave of glorious, unstoppable sensation ripped through her perspiring body, and he echoed her.

When he withdrew from her, turning to deposit the used condom in the bin, she scrambled off the counter and, for a few seconds, barely remembered the train of thought that had been running through her head just before she had climaxed.

It was a luxury that wasn't destined to last long. She went upstairs for a quick shower. She desperately needed some time to herself, time for her thought processes to be followed through to their natural conclusion, even though the conclusion might not be one she wanted to reach.

She had fallen in love with him. How had that happened? Shouldn't there have been a natural progression of steps to get from A to B? Where was the calm, peaceful contentment she had always associated with falling in love? She had been swept along on a roller coaster ride and now she felt ambushed by an emotion that had crept in without her noticing, without her being able to take the necessary precautions. Whilst she had been racing with the devil and calling it *experience*, a *one-off*, love had been quietly settling like cement and now she felt constricted, unable to move and as fragile as a piece of spun glass.

She went downstairs to find that he had tidied the kitchen, which surely must have been a first for him, and waiting for her with a glass of wine in his hand. His trousers were back on, as was the shirt, although he hadn't bothered to do up the buttons on the shirt which hung rakishly loose, revealing a sliver of bronzed torso.

'Full marks for the appetiser...' Damien sipped some of his wine and regarded her over the rim of the glass. If she had used a shower cap, it hadn't done its job. Damp tendrils clung to her cheeks. She looked clean and rosy and unbelievably sexy, especially with the V-necked striped T-shirt she had put on, which allowed a generous view of her cleavage. It was a constant source of mystery that her appeal hadn't diminished over the course of time. Why was that? Was it because he was fully aware that they came from opposite ends of the pole? That, for a man like him—a man who didn't want commitment—he had found his match in a woman who probably *did* want commitment but not with a man like him? Could that be it?

Violet's eyes skittered away from his beautiful, sinfully sexy face. Every compliment he paid her had to do with sex, with her body, with the physical. She could see now that that had been the start of her downfall. Those husky words of rampant appreciation, delivered with intent, had arrowed in on a part of her that had always been insecure and found their mark. Like a flower coming into bloom, she had opened up and grown in an area of her life that had been stunted and underdeveloped. He had made her feel like a woman, a powerful, beautiful, engaging woman, and she had run with the sensation. She had let him in and, without even realising it, had seen beyond their differences to all the things about him that were strangely endearing.

'Damien…we need to…to talk…'

He continued to smile that crooked little half smile of his but his eyes were suddenly watchful. Women wanting *to talk* was usually synonymous with women *saying things he didn't want to hear.*

'I'm listening.' He strolled across to one of the kitchen chairs and sat down, looking at her carefully as she shuffled to the chair opposite him, so that the width of the table was separating them.

'It's been a while, Damien. Your mother has responded really well to treatment and is out of the danger zone. I agreed to all of this…pretending, the charade…for my sister and then I carried on with it for myself, because I was talked into putting sexual attraction above everything else…'

'Ah. I get it. Are we going to start on a blame game, Violet? With me cast in the role of seducer of innocent girls? If that's the case, then I suggest you have a rethink before you get on your soapbox.'

Violet had forgotten this side to him, the side that could withdraw and grow cold. The fact that it was still there, right beneath the surface, was a timely reminder of why it was so important to begin detaching herself from this relationship, if indeed relationship was what it could be called.

'I wasn't going to do that.'

'No?' Damien drawled. He hadn't been expecting this, not after having had mind-blowing sex, and tension lent a hard, mocking edge to his voice. 'Because no one pointed to a bed and then held a gun to your head while you got undressed.'

'I know that! Why are you being so…so horrible?'

'I'm just waiting to hear what you have to say and reminding you that you were an eager and willing volunteer when it came to sex.' She couldn't meet his eyes. What the hell was going on? How could everything change in a matter of seconds? His confusion angered him because it was yet another niggling reminder that he was not as much in control with this woman as he would have liked to have been.

'I'm saying that I think it would be a good idea if we… we…took a step back…' Violet lowered her eyes and frowned into the glass of wine which had somehow found its way in front of her.

'A step back…'

'Your mother is more than stable enough to deal with our relationship hitting the rocks. She's back to doing stuff with Dominic, can go out in her garden now and again… I feel that the time has come for us to get back to our normal lives…'

'And between us making love in the kitchen and you going to have a shower…you've reached this decision *when…? Exactly…?*'

'I don't have to give you any explanations of when or why I've reached my decision, Damien. It's over. I'm not like you. I can't carry on sleeping with you, knowing that it's something that's not going anywhere.'

'Where do you want it to go?' Damien asked, as quick as a flash.

'I don't want it to go anywhere!'

'And what if I tell you that I don't want what we have to end yet? Doubtless my mother is strong enough to recover from a crash and burn relationship, even if she's unduly fond of you, but it's long ceased to be about my mother, as you well know.' Suddenly restless, he vaulted to his feet, glass in one hand, and began to pace the tiny kitchen. He'd never been dumped by a woman. Pride alone should have had him gathering his jacket and heading for the door. Hadn't he made it his mission to avoid the hassle of the demanding woman? And what was she demanding anyway? She had always made it quite clear that they were poles apart, that he was not the blueprint of the kind of man she would ever consider settling down with.

So…was it money? Underneath all the protestations of not being materialistic, had she become used to the opulence that surrounded him wherever he went? Had she glimpsed a vision of how life could be if she could get access to his? He stifled a sudden feeling of intense disappointment. He was a realist and this was the explanation that made the most sense.

His brain locked into gear. He still wanted her and, whether she admitted it or not, she was still hot for him. So maybe she didn't feel as though she had a stake in their relationship. She made a big song and dance of not wanting to accept anything from him but, in so doing, did she feel that she was utterly disposable? That, despite his offers to buy her no less than he would have bought for any of his lovers, he found her in any way less attractive? If only… Just thinking about the way her breasts spilled heavily out of her bra was enough to engage his mind for a few seconds on a completely different path. If he had felt, in any way, that the sex was beginning to wane, he might have shrugged and taken his leave but he was an expert when it came to gauging responses. He couldn't remember a time when the woman had been the flagging partner and it wasn't the case now. Nor was he about to give up a sex life that was second to none.

'There's something I want you to see.'

Violet was taken aback by a remark that seemed to come from nowhere. 'What is it?'

'Wait here.' In the heat of the moment, he had forgotten the costly item of jewellery nestling in its classy black and gold box. His fait accompli present. Whoever said that the Great One didn't work in mysterious ways?

She was still sitting in the same position in the kitchen when he returned and extended his hand. 'For you,' he informed her solemnly. 'I hear what you're saying and this is just a small measure of what you mean to me…'

Violet took the box but already she could feel her skin beginning to get clammy. *What he meant to her.* How many times had she told him that she didn't want anything from him? She lifted the lid of the box and stared down at an item of jewellery that she knew would have been spectacularly expensive. What she meant to him would never be love, it certainly wasn't durability. She was his willing plaything and her worth could be counted in banknotes. She fought down the stupid urge to cry over a piece of jewellery that would have had any other woman shrieking in delight.

'I don't want it.' She stuck it back in the box, snapped shut the lid and handed it to him.

'What do you mean? I know you've made a big deal about not accepting anything from me, but you want to know what this…what we have…means to me…take it in the spirit with which it was given.' He obviously wasn't about to relieve her of the necklace.

'I think it's time we called this a day, Damien.' It hurt just saying that but say it she knew she had to. In that single gesture he had made her feel sordid and cheap.

'Where the hell is this coming from?'

'I can't be bought for a few weeks or months of sex

until you get tired of me and send me on my way with… with *what*…? Something even bigger and more expensive? A really huge pat on the back, it was nice knowing you goodbye gift?'

Damien wondered how long she had been contemplating the outcome of their relationship and working herself up to wanting more. Was she holding him to ransom or did she genuinely want out and if she did genuinely want out, how was it that she was still on fire for him? No, that made no sense.

But if she wanted more, if she wanted a passport to a lifestyle she could never have attained in a million years, then was it so inconceivable that he give it to her…?

'I don't want to buy you,' he murmured. 'I want to marry you…'

'SORRY?' THERE WAS a rushing sound in her ears. She thought it might have temporarily impaired her hearing.

'You say you can't be in a relationship if you think it's not going anywhere. Curious considering we embarked on this relationship in the expectation that it wouldn't go anywhere.'

'I didn't think a game of make-believe would…would…' Violet was still grappling with what he had said. Had he actually asked her to marry him? Had she imagined the whole thing? He certainly didn't have the expectant, love struck look of a man who had just voiced a marriage proposal.

'Nor did I. And yet it did and now here we are. Which brings me back to my marriage proposal.'

So, she hadn't been imagining it. And yet nothing in his expression gave any hint that he was talking about anything of import. His eyes were unreadable, his beautiful face coolly speculative. Violet, on the other hand, could feel a burning that began in the pit of her stomach and moved outwards.

Marriage? To Damien Carver? The concept was at once too incredible to believe and yet fiercely seductive. For a few magical seconds, her mind leapfrogged past all the obvious glitches in his wildly unexpected proposal. She was in love with the man who had asked her to marry him! Even when she had been going out with Stu, even though they had occasionally talked about marriage, she had never felt this wonderful surge of pure happiness.

Reality returned and she regretfully left her happy ever after images behind. 'Why would you want to marry me?'

'I'm enjoying what we have. I'm not getting any younger. Yes, at the time we started out on our charade, I had not given a passing thought to settling down, even though I realised that that was what my mother wanted…'

*Too hurt by past rejection to go there again…*went through Violet's head.

'Now I can see that it makes sense.'

'Makes sense?'

'We get along. You've bonded with my family. They like you. My mother sings your praises. Dominic tells me that you're one of a kind, a gem.' He paused, thought of Annalise with distaste, wondered how he could ever have been so naive as to think that only idiots viewed disability as an unacceptable challenge. He remembered how he had borne the insult delivered to his brother as much as if it had been directly delivered to him. Annalise might have been attractive and clever, but neither of those attributes could have made up for her basic inability to step out of the box. Her neatly laid out future had not included hitches of that nature. Over the years, he had bumped into her, sometimes coincidentally, occasionally at her request. She never mentioned Dominic but she always made a point of informing him how much she had grown up. The fact that Violet naturally and without trying had endeared herself to his mother and his brother counted for a great deal.

'You've asked me to marry you because I get along with your family?'

'Well…that's not the complete story. There's also the

incredible sex…' He scanned her flushed cheeks with lingering appreciation.

'So let me get this straight. You've asked me to marry you because I've been accepted by your family, because we get along and because we're good in bed together. It's not exactly the marriage proposal I dreamed of as a girl.' She kept her voice steady and calm. Inside, her heart was hammering as she absorbed the implications of his proposal. This wasn't about love or a starry-eyed desire to walk off into the sunset with her, holding hands, knowing that they were soulmates, destined to be together for the rest of their lives. This was a marriage proposal of convenience.

'And what when we get tired of one another? I mean, lust doesn't last for ever.' And without love as its foundation, whatever was left when the lust bit disappeared would crumble into dust. When that happened, would he decide that being stuck in a loveless marriage was maybe not quite the sensible option he had gone for? Would his eyes begin to wander? Would he see that other options were available? Of course he would and where would that leave her? Nursing even more heartbreak than if she walked away now with her pride and dignity intact.

'I don't like hypothesising.' Why hadn't she just said yes? He was giving her what any other woman on the planet would want. He knew that without a shred of conceit. He had a lot to offer and he was offering it to her, so what was with the hesitancy and the thousand and one questions? Would he have to fill out an informal questionnaire? To find out if he passed with flying colours?

'I know, but sometimes it's important to look ahead,' Violet persisted stubbornly. In some strange way, this marriage proposal was the nail in the coffin of their relationship. At least as far as she was concerned. She might have wondered aloud where they were going, but she knew, deep down, that she would have been persuaded to carry on, just as she knew that, in carrying on, she would have clung to the belief that her love was returned, that it was just a question of time. She would have allowed hope to propel her forward. But he had proposed what would be a sham of a marriage and she knew, now, exactly where she stood with him.

He liked her well enough but primarily he liked her body. And the added bonus was that she got along with Eleanor and Dominic. When the scales were balanced, he doubtless thought that they weighed in favour of putting a ring on her finger.

'It's not necessary to look ahead,' Damien countered, but sudden unease was stirring a potent mix of anger and bewilderment inside him. 'And I'm not sure where the cross-examination is leading.'

'I can't accept your offer,' Violet said bluntly. 'I'm sorry.'

'Come again?'

'*You* might think we're suited, but I don't.'

'Do we or do we not have amazing sexual chemistry? Do I or do I not turn you on until you're begging me to take you?'

'That's not the point.'

'So you're back to this business of looking for your soulmate. Is that it?'

'There's nothing wrong in thinking that when you settle down you'll do so with the right guy…'

'Do you know the statistics when it comes to divorce? One in three. May even be one in two and a half. For every woman with stars in her eyes and dreams of rocking chairs on verandas with her husband when they're eighty-four with the great-grandchildren running around their feet, I'll show you a hundred who have recently signed their divorce papers and are complaining about the cost of the lawyer's fees. For every child at home with both parents, I'll show you a thousand who have become nomads, travelling between parents and inheriting an assorted family of half-siblings and step-siblings along the way.' He raked impatient, frustrated fingers through his hair. She had made noises about wanting more, and he had blithely assumed that the more she claimed to be wanting was with *him*. It hadn't occurred to him that the more she wanted was with someone else. There was still this amazing, once in a lifetime buzz between them. Was it his fault that he had interpreted that in the only way that seemed possible? And yet here she was, turning him down flat.

'I know that,' Violet said, her mouth stubbornly downturned. Of course, every argument he might use to persuade her that tying the knot was a sensible outcome to their relationship would be based in statistics. In the absence of real emotion, statistics would come in very handy.

She was also aware that sex was only part of the drive behind his proposal. Eleanor's illness had shattered the complacent world he had established around himself and forced him into re-evaluating his relationship with his brother and, by extension, his mother. It had been easy for him to justify his interaction with them and convince himself that there was nothing out of kilter by throwing money in their direction. They had wanted for nothing. Damien had not told her that himself. She had garnered that information via Eleanor, passing remarks, rueful observations… However, as everyone knew, money was not the be-all and end-all when it came to relationships and he had been helped in his fledgling attempts to rebuild what had been lost thanks to her. She knew that without having to be told. She had not entered this peculiar arrangement ever thinking that it would extend beyond the absolutely necessary and yet it had and now all of that had entered the murky mix of logic and rationale that lay behind his proposal.

She didn't want to end up being the convenient other half in a relationship where she would inevitably be taken for granted, nor was it fair on either Eleanor or Dominic for her to slot into their lives where she would eventually pick up the slack, enabling Damien to return to his workaholic life which had no room for anyone, least of all a wife. Even a wife he might temporarily be in lust with.

And yet when she thought of waking up next to him, being able to turn and reach out and touch his warm, responsive body…every morning…

When she half closed her eyes she could recall the feel of his mouth all over her body, kissing and licking and exploring, and a treacherous little voice in her head insisted on telling her that that could be hers. Lust could last a very long time, couldn't it? It could last for ever. It could turn into something else. Couldn't it?

And yet he had approached her the way a person would approach a mathematical equation that needed solving. And that wasn't right. Not when it came to marriage.

But she still had to take a deep breath and steel herself against being sidetracked. Especially when he was sitting right there in front of her, his hands loosely linked, his body leaning towards her, his dark, sinfully beautiful face stirring all sorts of rebellious thoughts inside her.

'But—' she inhaled deeply '—I'm on the side of the minority who actually have working marriages and kids with both parents.' She plucked at her jumper with nerveless fingers. 'And please stop looking at me as though I'm mad. There are some of us out there who prefer to dream rather than just cave in and think that we're never going to be happy…'

'No one's talking about being happy or not being happy...' Damien interrupted impatiently. 'Where did you get that idea from? Did I ask you to marry me with the sub-clause that you shouldn't hold out for happiness?' He wondered why he was continuing to pursue this. She had turned him down and it was time now to take his leave. And yet, although he could feel the sharp teeth of pride kicking in, something was compelling him to stay. Was it because he was keenly aware of how awkward it was going to be breaking the news of their break-up to his mother and Dominic? Made sense. Who liked to be the harbinger of bad news, as he undoubtedly would be? Were it any other woman, he would have left by now. Actually, were it any other woman he would not have proposed in the first place.

'We're not suited. Not in any way that makes sense for a long-term relationship. We might enjoy...you know... the physical side of things...' At this point, she felt faint at that physical side of things no longer being attainable. No more of that breathless excitement. No more melting as their bodies united. But, much more than that, no more heady anticipation knowing that the man she loved was going to be walking through her front door, taking her in his arms... How had she only managed to now work out what should have been obvious from the start? That so much more than just her body looked forward to seeing him? That he had awakened a side to her that she never knew existed and something like that didn't happen in a vacuum? That she just didn't have the sort of personality that could lock away various sides of herself and only bring them out when appropriate?

She had sleep walked herself into loving him and it was a feeling that would never be returned. No amount of persuasive arguments about divorce statistics could change that.

'You're repeating yourself. I don't think there's much point to my remaining here to listen to any more of the same old.' He made to stand and a wave of sickening panic rushed through her at speed, with the force and power of a tsunami.

'But I know you agree with me!' Desperate to keep him with her just a little bit longer, Violet sprang to her feet and placed a restraining hand on his arm.

He looked down at it with withering eyes. 'Our days of touching are over. So…if you don't mind?' He raised one cool eyebrow and Violet removed her hand with alacrity.

'We would end up in a bitter, corrosive relationship if we got married,' she gabbled on, clasping her hands tightly together because she wanted to reach out again and pluck at him to stay. His face was stony. 'I'm sorry I ever said anything about…about… We'd be far better off staying just as we are…' Violet knew that she was backtracking and that there was desperation in that but there was a void opening up in front of her that she knew would be impossible to fill. It was dark and bottomless and terrifying. So what if they just carried on the way they were? Would it be the end of the world? And wouldn't it be better than this? Being a martyr? Hadn't she agreed with him once that martyrdom was cold comfort?

'I don't think so,' Damien said coolly, as he began getting his things together. 'That window's closed, I'm afraid.'

Violet fell back and looked at him in numb silence until he was ready to leave.

'I'll tell my mother this weekend that things didn't work out between us.'

'Let me come with you.' She could feel tears pushing to the back of her eyes.

'What for?'

'I'd like to explain to her myself that…that…'

'There's nothing to explain, Violet. Relationships come and go. Fortunately my mother is in a better place. She'll be able to cope with the disappointment. I wouldn't lose sleep over that if I were you.'

Violet could feel him mentally withdrawing from her at a rate of knots. She hadn't complied and there was no room for anyone in his life who didn't comply.

'Of course I'm going to lose sleep over it! I'm very fond of both Eleanor and Dominic!'

Damien shrugged as though it was of relatively little importance one way or the other. He was moving towards the door. Where was the necklace? No matter. He wanted to tell her that she could consider it a suitable parting gift but he knew he would have to listen to a lecture on all the things money, apparently, couldn't buy. He gritted his teeth at the uncomfortable notion that he would miss those lectures of hers, which had ranged from the ills of money to the misfortune of those who thought they needed it to be happy. She was adept at pointing out all the expensive items that had brought nothing but misery to their owners. She always seemed to have a mental tally at the ready of famous people whose lives had not been improved because they were rich, and had been prone to loftily ignoring him when he pointed out that she should stop reading trashy magazines with celebrity gossip. In between the fantastic sex, which had evolved from their charade in a way that had taken him one hundred per cent by surprise, he was uncomfortably aware that she might have got under his skin in ways he hadn't anticipated.

'In that case,' he returned with supreme indifference, 'I suggest you go see your local friendly doctor and ask him to prescribe you some sleeping pills.'

'How can you be so…so…unsympathetic?' She was traipsing along behind him to the front door. Before she knew it, he was pulling it open, one foot already out as though he couldn't wait to leave her behind.

'There's no point in you having any involvement with me or my family from now on. My mother would be far happier were she spared the tedium of a post-mortem.'

And with that he was gone, slamming the door behind him in a gesture that was as final as the fall of the executioner's axe.

Left on her own, Violet suddenly realised just how lonely the little house was without the promise of his exciting, unsettling presence to bring it to life. She lethargically tidied up the kitchen but her thoughts were exclusively on Damien. She had backed him into a corner and it was no good asking herself whether she had done the right thing or not. You couldn't play around with reality and hope that it might somehow be changed into something else.

But neither could she put thoughts of him behind her as easily as she might have liked. School was no longer gloriously enjoyable because she was busy looking forward to seeing him. There were no little anecdotes saved up for retelling. She spent the following week with the strange sense of having been wrapped up in insulation, something so thick that the outside world seemed to exist around her at a distance. She listened to everyone laughing and chatting but it was all a blur. When Phillipa phoned in a state of high excitement to tell her that she and Andy were getting married at the end of the year, on a beach no less, and would she come over, help her choose a dress or at least a suitably white sarong and bikini, she heard herself saying all the right things but her mind was cloudy, not operating at full whack, as though she had been heavily sedated to the point where her normal reflexes were no longer in proper working order.

Several times she wondered whether she should call Eleanor. But was Damien right? Would his mother be happier to accept their break-up without having to conduct a long conversation about it? Furthermore, what would she say? She had no idea what Damien would have told her. For all she knew, he might have told her that she was entirely to blame, that she had turned into a shrew, a harpy, a gold-digger. It was within his brief to say anything, safe in the knowledge that he wouldn't be contradicted.

And yet she couldn't imagine him being anything other than fair, which, reason told her, was ridiculous, considering the way their relationship had commenced. He had blackmailed her into doing what he wanted. Since when had he turned into a good guy? He had drifted into a sexual relationship for no better reason than she had made a change from the sort of women he usually dated, but he had nothing to offer aside from a consummate ability to make love. So how was it that she had managed to fall in love with him? For every glaring downside in his personality, her rebellious mind insisted on pointing out the good things about him—his wit, his sincere attempts to do what was right for his family, his incredible intellect, which would have made a lesser man sneering and contemptuous of those less gifted than he was, and yet, in Damien's case, did not.

The decision to call Eleanor or not was taken out of her hands when, a week and a half after Damien had walked out of her house, Eleanor called.

She sounded fine. Yes, yes, yes, everything was coming along nicely. The prognosis was good…

'But my son tells me that the two of you have decided to take a break…'

So that was how he had phrased it. Clever in so far as he had left open the possibility that the break might not be permanent. His mother's disappointment would be drip-fed in small stages, protecting her from any dramatic stress their separation might have engendered.

'Um…yes…that's the…er…plan…'

'I confess that I was very surprised indeed when Damien told me…'

'And I'm so sorry I wasn't there to break the news as well, Eleanor.' Violet rushed into apologetic speech. 'I wanted so much to…er…'

'I'd never seen Damien so relaxed and happy.' Eleanor swept past Violet's stammering interruption. 'A different man. I've always worried about the amount of time he devotes to work, but you must have done something wonderful to him, my darling, because he's finally seemed to get his perspective in order… He hasn't just made time for me, but he's made time for his brother…'

'That's…great…'

'Which is why I'm puzzled as to how it is that suddenly you and he are…taking a break…especially when I can see how much the two of you love one another…'

'No! No, no, no… Damien just isn't…he's…we…'

'You're stumbling over your words, my darling,' Eleanor said gently. 'Take your time. You love my son. I know you do. A woman knows these things when it comes to other women…especially an old lady like me…'

Violet lapsed into temporary defeated silence. What could she say to that? Even with Eleanor talking down the end of a phone, she still had the uncanny feeling that the older woman was seeing right into the very heart of her. 'You're not old,' she finally responded. 'And I'm so glad the treatment's going well…'

'Is that your way of changing the conversation?' Eleanor asked tartly. 'Darling, I do wish we could have sat down and talked about this together, woman to woman. Somehow, hearing it from Damien…well, you know what men are like. He can be terribly tight-lipped when it comes to expressing anything emotional…'

'That's true…'

'So why don't you pop over to his place, say this evening…around eight…? We can…chat…'

With unerring ability, Violet realised that Eleanor had found her Achilles heel. She would have thought that Hell might have frozen over before she faced Damien again. She just wanted to somehow try and get him out of her system and paying him a visit was the last thing destined to achieve that goal. But she was very fond of his mother and Eleanor, despite her cheerful optimism about her health, did not deserve to be stressed out.

She was also still in the throes of guilt at not having spoken to the older woman yet.

'You're in London?'

'Flying visit. Check-up… So, darling, I really must dash now. I'll see you shortly, shall I? Can't tell you how much I'm looking forward to that! Don't think that I'm going to allow you to creep out of my life that easily.'

Those two, Eleanor thought with satisfaction as she peered through the window of her chauffeur-driven car on her way back down to Devon, needed to have their heads banged together. Or at least made to sit and really talk because she refused to believe that whatever had taken place between them couldn't be sorted with a heartfelt conversation. And who better to engineer that but herself? If, at the end of it, things were over, then so be it but Damien had been so sketchy in his details, so alarmingly evasive…and men so often didn't recognise what was best for them…

Violet was disconnected before she had time to start thinking on her feet. Was, for instance, Damien going to be present? Would there be an awkward three-way conversation where they both tried desperately to undo what they had so carefully knitted together at the very beginning? She assumed not. She assumed that Eleanor had invited her for a one to one. She had no idea what she would say to the other woman. She would have to be vague. Her fingers itched to dial Damien's mobile and ask him what he had said to his mother but she felt faint just at the thought of hearing that deep, dark, sexy drawl down the end of the line.

Several hours later, standing in front of the imposing Georgian block, some of which had been converted into luxury apartments, others remaining as vast houses, such as his, Violet had to fight down a sickening attack of nerves.

The road where he lived was a statement to the last word in opulence. Gleaming back wrought-iron railings guarded each of the towering white-fronted mansions. The steps to each front door were identical in their scrubbed cleanliness and the front doors were all black with shiny brass knockers for appearance only as a bank of buzzers was located at the side.

She had only been to his place a handful of times but she remembered it clearly. The exquisite hall with its flag-stoned floor, the pale walls, the blond wooden flooring that dominated the huge open spaces. Everything within those mega-expensive walls was of the highest standard and state-of-the-art. There was no clutter. She had always found its lack of homeliness off-putting. Now, as she dithered in front of the imposing black door, she had to take some deep breaths to steady her nerves, even though she was nearly a hundred per cent certain that he would not be at home. A cosy chat with Eleanor and she would be on her way. Her uneasy conscience that she hadn't contacted the older woman would be put to rest. They would meet in the future, of course they would, and it would be fine just as long as Damien wasn't around, and maybe, down the line, he could be around because she would have moved on from him.

She pressed the buzzer and settled back to wait because she was certain that Eleanor would not be moving at the speed of light to get to the door, however keen she was to see her.

It had been a lovely day which had mellowed into a cool but pleasant evening. In this expensive part of London, there were few cars and even less foot traffic and she was idly watching a young woman saunter past on the opposite side of the wide, tree-lined road, attempting to infuse a reluctant puppy with enthusiasm for a walk it clearly didn't want, when the door was pulled open behind her.

The greeting died on her lips. For a few seconds her heart seemed to arrest. Damien framed the doorway. He was wearing a pair of faded black jeans that hugged his long, muscular legs and a white T-shirt, close-fitting enough to outline the strong, graceful lines of his body. Memories of touching that body rushed towards her in a tidal wave of hot awareness. In only a matter of a few months, he had guided her down myriad sensual roads never explored before. Her mouth went dry as she thought of a few of them.

'What are you doing here?' she asked inanely.

'It's my house and, funny…I was just about to ask you the same thing.' He half stepped out, pulling the door behind him and blocking out the light from the hall.

'I came to see your mother.' She just wanted to stare and stare and keep on staring. Instead, she looked down at her shoes, some sensible black ballet pumps that worked well with her skinny jeans. She had stopped dressing to hide. It was one of his many lasting legacies to her—the self-confidence to be the person she was.

'And that would be…? Because…?' Damien leant indolently against the doorframe and folded his arms. His fabulous eyes were veiled and watchful as he stared down at her. However, his nerves were taut and he was angry with himself for the seeping away of his self-control. There was nothing left to be said on the subject of their non-relationship. He had offered her marriage. She had thrown his offer back in his face and he was not a man who allowed second bites at the cherry.

He wondered why she had come. Had she had second thoughts? Had she come round to all the advantages marriage to him would provide? His mouth curled with derision. He shifted as his body refused to cooperate and jumped into gear as his eyes unconsciously traced the sexy outline of her breasts underneath the figure-hugging top she was wearing. But hell, she could wear something only seen on someone's maiden aunt and yet have any red-blooded male spinning round in his tracks to stare. He couldn't understand how he could ever have credited her with being anything but sex on legs. He must have been blind and those tight jeans…that jumper. He wanted to pounce and rip them off her so that he could touch what was underneath. Given the circumstances, it was an entirely inappropriate reaction and he was furious with himself for even allowing his mind to travel down those pathways.

'Because your mother phoned and asked me to come here,' Violet muttered. She balled her hands into fists. So he didn't even have the simple courtesy to ask her inside. He would rather conduct a hostile conversation on his doorstep.

'Pull the other one, Violet. My mother left to return to Devon hours ago. So tell me why you imagine she would be waiting here for you? No, don't bother to answer that. I wasn't born yesterday. I *know* what you're doing here.'

Violet's mouth dropped open and she looked at him in bewilderment. At the same time, it was dawning on her that she had been coaxed into coming to his house by Eleanor, who had schemed for...what, exactly? A heartfelt talk where their so-called differences would be ironed out? And a reconciliation might take place? If only she knew the truth of their relationship.

'And you can forget it.'

'Forget what?'

'Any plan you might be concocting to show up here unannounced and resume where we left off.'

'I wasn't doing any such thing!' Violet gasped.

'Expect me to believe that? When you're dressed in the tightest clothes possible? Showing off your assets to maximum advantage?' He pictured her in the unflattering dress she had worn that very first time when she had hesitantly walked into his office and scowled because the image didn't dispel his reaction to her body.

'You're being ridiculous! Your mother asked me over here. She said she wanted to chat and I felt guilty because I should have called her, I should have made contact!'

Damien was fast reaching the same conclusion as Violet had only seconds before. She hadn't come here to try and entice him back into the bedroom. Having recognised that, he had to firmly bank down the fleeting suspicion that he rather enjoyed the notion of her making a pass at him. Naturally, he would have rejected it. But not before he felt immense satisfaction at having her plead with him for a second chance.

'You're impossible!' Violet could scarcely believe the accusations flying at her. Admittedly, there was some small chance that he might have jumped to the wrong conclusions, but how on earth could he think that she had *dressed to impress*? She was suddenly aware of the tightness of her clothes where she hadn't been before. Her breasts were heavy and aching within the constraints of her lacy bra and, as her eyes travelled upwards, doing a reluctant, hateful tour of his impressive body, she could feel herself getting damp between her thighs. She recalled his fingers down there, his mouth sucking and licking until she was writhing for more.

'You have an ego as big as a cruise liner if you imagine that I would come here to…to…make a pass at you! You're the most arrogant man I've ever met!' She longed to inform him, coldly, that she had moved on, but she couldn't bring herself to utter such a whopper.

As she stood there, floundering in front of his assessing eyes, she heard a voice behind him. A woman's voice. Coy and cajoling. For a few seconds she froze and then her eyes widened as the owner of the voice materialised into view.

How on earth could he have dared to accuse her of wearing tight clothes? The leggy brunette with the short, silky bob was clad in white jeans that fitted like a second skin and a small white vest that left very little to the imagination. She was as slender as a reed and Violet could only stare as the brunette sidled up to Damien and slipped her arm through his.

'Aren't you going to introduce us, darling? Though I guess there's no need. You must be Violet…' The pale blue eyes were glacially cold as she stretched out one thin arm in greeting. 'I'm Annalise…'

CHAPTER TEN

IT WAS RAINING by the time Violet made it back to her house. A fine, needle-sharp drizzle that she barely noticed. She took the Tube and bus back to her house on autopilot. She couldn't think straight and her heart was thumping like a steam engine inside her chest, making it uncomfortable to breathe.

She wanted to block out images of Damien with Annalise. She tried hard to tell herself that it didn't matter, that he was a free man who could do whatever he liked with whomever he liked. Unfortunately, no amount of cool logic could paper over the devastation she felt nor could it stop the flood of painful speculation that assailed her, wave upon wave, upon wave until she wanted to pass out.

He was back with his ex, back with the only woman he had never been able to forget, the only woman to whom he had wanted to commit, fully and without reservation or a list of sensible reasons why the match could work out. It certainly hadn't taken him long to reconnect. Was it because her rejection of his proposal had put things into perspective for him? Made him wake up and realise that marriage was more than a list of dos and don'ts? Had that propelled him to seek out Annalise? Had it reminded him that, in his carefully controlled world, there was still one woman who had broken through the boundaries and that he needed to find her and tell her? They certainly had looked very cosy with one another.

And Annalise was much more his style than she, Violet, could ever hope to be. Tall, skinny, beautiful. Nor did she look like a typical bimbo. No, she looked like one of those rare, annoying breeds—a true beauty who also had brains.

She couldn't look at herself in the mirror as she banged about in the bathroom, getting ready for bed. She didn't want to see the comparisons between her and his ex. Thinking about comparisons drained her of all her self-confidence. Had he only really seen her as a novelty? The broad bean versus the runner bean? Had he fallen into bed with her because she had been *there*? Available and eager? Was he any different from any other man in a situation where opportunity was handed to him on a plate? No one could accuse him of being the sort of guy who took relationships seriously, who held out for the right woman. He was a red-blooded male with a rampant libido who took what he wanted. And she had been there for the taking. And then he had proposed because it was convenient. He was never going to fall in love; he had done that with Annalise, so why not hitch up with the woman who had won his family's approval? Noticeably, he had only proposed when he had woken up to the reality that she might walk out on him.

She climbed into bed and tried to read and only realised that she had actually fallen asleep when she was awakened by two things.

The first was the sound of the rain. It had progressed from a persistent drizzle to the wild rapping of rain against her windows. She had left one window slightly ajar and the voile curtain was blowing furiously under the force of the wind. When she went to close it, she realised that the chest of drawers just underneath was splattered in rainwater but she had no intention of doing anything about that just at the moment.

Because, competing with the howling of the wind and the rain, was the thunderous sound of someone banging on her front door.

Outside, dripping water, Damien was cursing the English weather. Between eight, when he had opened his front door to Violet, and midnight, when he had finally managed to get rid of Annalise, the rain had picked up. Now, at a little after three-thirty, the only thing that could be said in favour of his jumping in his car and coming here was the fact that the roads had been traffic-free.

He noticed that one of the lights in the house had now been turned on and breathed a sigh of relief. He really didn't want to remain outside her house for the remainder of the night, although he would have, had she not answered the door.

Violet had stuck on her bathrobe to see who was at the door. Her immediate thought when she had heard the banging was to imagine that it was someone trying to break in but, almost as soon as she thought that, she realised that it was a ridiculous supposition because since when did intruders give advance notice of their intention by banging on doors?

So was it someone who needed help? She knew her neighbours. The old lady living next door was quite frail. Was there something wrong? She tried and failed to imagine small Mrs Wilson, in her late eighties, having the strength to venture out of her house in the early hours of the morning to bang on a door.

As she hurried downstairs, switching on lights in her wake, she could feel her heart pounding because, of course, there was someone else it might be, but, like her scenario involving the polite burglar knocking to warn her of his imminent break-in, the thought that it might be Damien was too far-fetched to be worth consideration.

The safety chain was on and as she opened the door a crack she knew instantly that the one man she had least expected was standing outside. There was a storm raging outside her house, or so it seemed. The wind was sending his trench coat in all directions and the rain was whipping down at a slant. His feet were planted squarely on the ground but, as she pulled the door open a little wider, he placed his hand against the doorframe to look down at her.

He was drenched. Soaked through.

'What do you want?' Violet wrapped the robe tightly around her. 'What are you doing here?'

'Violet, let me in.'

'Where's your girlfriend, Damien? Is she waiting in the car for you?' She could have kicked herself for mentioning Annalise but, at this point, she really didn't care.

'Let me in.'

'I don't know why you've come but I don't want you here.'

'Please.'

That single word stopped Violet in her tracks. She could feel the rain beating down towards her and she stepped back into the house to avoid being soaked.

'I have nothing to say to you.'

'Maybe there are things that *I* need to say to you.'

But, tellingly, he hadn't followed her into the hall. He remained standing on the doorstep, getting drenched. Was he *hesitant*? Violet thought in some confusion. Surely not! Hesitancy was one of those emotions he didn't do. Along with love. And yet he was still standing there, getting wet and looking at her.

'What could you possibly want to say to me, Damien? I just came to see your mother. I didn't come to try and start back what we had! You're out of my life and if I was a little…a little…disconcerted, it was because I hadn't expected to be confronted with your girlfriend! Quick work, Damien!'

'Ex. Ex-girlfriend. Please let me in, Violet. I'm not going to barge my way into your house and if you tell me that you don't want to see me again, then I'll go.'

Tell him to go and she would never see him again. Of course, that would be for the best. They really had nothing to say to one another. Less than nothing. Maybe he had braved the foul weather because he felt badly, because he wanted to explain to her, face to face, how it was that Annalise was back in his life. Perhaps he thought that he might be doing her a favour by playing the good guy and filling her in. And still, painful though that thought was, her mind seized up when she thought of him disappearing back into the driving rain and vanishing out of her life for good, without saying what he had to say.

'It's late.' She stood aside and folded her arms as he dripped his way into her hall and removed the trench coat. His hair was plastered down and he raked his fingers through it, which just scattered the drops of water.

'Perhaps I could have a towel…'

'I suppose so,' Violet muttered a little ungraciously.

She returned a few minutes later to find him in the same spot, standing in the hall. Where was the guy who had never hesitated to make himself at home? Where was the self-assured man who knew the layout of her kitchen, who might be expected to make himself a cup of coffee?

She watched in silence as he roughly dried himself. He made no attempt to remove his jumper, which clung to him, and she bit back the temptation to tell him to take it off because if he didn't he would catch cold.

'I'm sorry you had to find Annalise in my house,' Damien said heavily.

Violet broke eye contact and headed towards the kitchen. He might be comfortable having a conversation neither of them wanted in the middle of her hallway, but she needed to sit down and she needed something to do with her hands. She was aware of him following her. It might be after three in the morning but every sense in her was on red alert.

'It was unexpected, that's all.' She busied herself with the kettle, mugs, spoons, keeping her back to him because she was scared that if he saw her face he would be able to read what was going on in her mind. 'Like I said…'

'I know. My mother got you there on false pretences. I spoke to her. She…thought that a little bit of undercover matchmaking wouldn't go amiss…'

'And did you tell her about Annalise?'

'No. There *is* no Annalise.'

And he didn't know what had possessed him to open the door to her when she had showed up the previous evening. He had opened the door and he had invited her in. She had heard about Violet. Friend of a friend of a friend had seen them together at a restaurant…there were rumours…gossip, even…she was curious…he could talk to *her*…after all, they had a history…they were connected… weren't they…?

At that point, Damien knew that he should have escorted her out. It was quite different bumping into her at a random company affair or even occasionally meeting her in a public place where, like a masochist, he could be reminded of his narrow escape, but letting her into his house had not been a good idea.

And yet hadn't there been a part of him that had *questioned* whether Annalise might not be reintroduced into his life? Violet had walked out and he hadn't known what to do with the chaos of his emotions when she had left. Hadn't a part of him bitterly wondered whether Annalise, who could never wield the sort of crazy control over him that Violet had, might not just be the better bet? He had had his marriage proposal chucked back in his face. Annalise…well, he could buy her and what you could buy, you could control.

He had let her in and the moment of questioning had gone as quickly as it had arrived. But she was in his house and, foolishly, he had prevaricated about throwing her out. Would it have been asking too much of fate to step aside for a while and not steer Violet towards his doorstep?

'What do you mean?' Clasping her cup of coffee between her hands, she stalked out towards the sitting room. She hadn't offered him anything to drink. It was meant as a pointed reminder that she had only allowed him in under duress, but really, if he thought that he could somehow try and come up smelling of roses, then he was mistaken.

She sat down and when she looked up it was to find him hovering by the door.

'You might as well sit down, Damien. But I'm tired and I'm not in the mood for a conversation.'

'I know.' He removed the jumper, which was heavy and wet, and carefully put it over one of the radiators, then he prowled over to the window, parted the curtains a crack and peered outside into the bleak rainy night. 'I didn't invite her,' he offered at last. 'She showed up.'

'It's none of my business anyway.'

'Everything I do should be your business,' Damien muttered, flushing darkly. 'At least, that's what I'd like.' He thought that this must be what it felt like to indulge in a dangerous sport, one where the outcome was a life or death situation. 'And I would understand if you don't believe me, Violet.'

'I don't understand what you're saying.' Violet's voice was wary. She couldn't tear her eyes away from him. He was even more compelling in this strangely vulnerable, puzzling mood. It was a side to him she had never seen before and it threw her. He circled the room, one hand in his trouser pocket, the other playing with his hair, before finally standing directly in front of her so that she was forced to look up at him.

'Would you mind sitting down? I'm getting a crick in my neck looking up at you.'

'I need you to sit next to me,' Damien told her roughly. 'There are things I need…to say to you and I need to have you…next to me when I say them…' He sat on the sofa and patted the spot next to him. 'Please, Violet.' He grinned crookedly and looked away. 'I bet you've never heard me say *please* so many times.'

'I can't do this. Just tell me why you've come. You didn't have to. I know we had…something. You probably feel obliged to explain yourself to me. Well, don't. So we broke up and you've returned to the love of your life.' Violet shrugged. The vacant space on the sofa next to him begged her to fill it but she wasn't going to give in to that dangerous temptation. He had this effect on her…could make her take her eyes off the ball and she wasn't going to fall victim to that now.

'I told you Annalise was my ex and she still is.'

'And this is the ex you've seen on and off over the years?'

'Sometimes it pays to be reminded of your mistakes.'

'I beg your pardon?'

'I can't talk when you're sitting on the other side of the room. It's hard enough…as it is… I don't usually…'

He raked his fingers through his hair and realised that he was shaking.

Reluctantly, Violet went to perch on the sofa. Just closing this small gap between them made her stomach twist in nervous knots.

'Once upon a time,' Damien said heavily, 'I fancied myself in love with Annalise. I was young. She was beautiful, clever…ticked all the boxes. It was a whirlwind romance, just the sort of thing you read about in books, and I proposed to her.'

'You don't need to tell me any of this,' Violet interjected stiffly and yet she wanted to hear every word of it.

'I need to and I want to. You'd be surprised if I told you that I've never felt the slightest inclination to share any of the details of my relationship with Annalise with anyone.'

'I wouldn't be surprised. You keep everything locked up inside.'

'I do.'

'You're agreeing with me. Why?'

'Because you're right. I've always kept everything locked up inside. It's why no one has ever known what Annalise really meant to me.'

And he was about to tell her. Yet the details so far weren't adding up to the love of his life and she fought to subdue the tendril of hope unfurling inside her that there might be another side of the story. Ever since she had met him, her placid life had become a roller coaster ride, hope alternating with despair before rising again to the surface like a terrible virus over which she had no control. Did she want to get back on that ride? Did she want to nurture that tendril of hope until it began growing into something uncontrollable? She could feel tears of frustration and dismay prick the back of her eyes. She curled her fingers in her

lap and was shocked when he reached out and slowly un-
curled them so that he could abstractedly play with them.

It was just the lightest of touches but it was enough to
send her body into wild shock.

'Annalise turned me down because she couldn't cope
with the prospect of being saddled, at some point in time,
with a disabled brother-in-law.'

'What?' This was not what she had been expecting to
hear and she leaned forward to catch what he was saying.

'She met Dominic and I knew instantly that she couldn't
cope with his condition. For Annalise, everything was
about perfection. Dominic was not perfect. She knew that
at some point I would be responsible for him. She had visions of him living with us, her having to incorporate him
into the perfect world she was desperate to have.'

'That's…that's awful…' Violet reached out and rested
her hand on his arm and felt him shudder.

'From that moment onwards, I knew that never again
would I put myself in a position of vulnerability. I enjoyed
women but they had their place and I made damn sure
that they never overstepped it. And just in case I was ever
tempted to forget, I made sure that Annalise was never
completely eliminated from my life.'

'And yet she was there tonight. In your…in your
house…'

'You turned me down. I asked you to marry me and
you turned me down.'

Because you couldn't love me! Despite everything he
had said, he still didn't love her. He was just explaining
why he couldn't. She would do well to remember that and
not get swept away by this strange mood he was in and
his haltering confidences.

'When Annalise showed up on my doorstep, I let her in
because I was…not myself. No, that doesn't really explain

it either. I was going out of my mind. Had been ever since we broke up. I told myself that it was for the best, that you could damn well go your own way and find out first-hand that there was no such thing as the perfect soulmate, but I couldn't think straight, couldn't function… I resented the fact that even when you were no longer around, you were still managing to control my behaviour.'

Violet was finding it impossible to filter the things he was telling her.

'I am ashamed to say that I briefly considered Annalise a known quantity and that maybe the devil you know… Of course, it was just a passing aberration. I got rid of her as fast as I could and then I waited…for normality to return. It didn't.'

'So you came here…to tell me what? Exactly?' She pinned her mouth into a stubborn line but she had broken out in a fine film of nervous perspiration. She tried to ignore the way he was still toying distractedly with her fingers and the way their bodies were leaning urgently towards each other, radiating a fevered heat that made her want to swoon. His familiar scent filled her nostrils. Once, she had found him devastatingly attractive. Having slept with him, knowing the contours of his lean, hard body, the body along which she had run her hands and her mouth so many times, made him horribly, painfully irresistible. Familiarity hadn't bred contempt. The opposite. It had ratcheted up the level of his sexual pull to the extent that she could barely think of anything else as she continued to stare at him, pupils dilated, dreading the way her body was reacting in ways her brain was telling it not to.

'That I proposed to you because…it made sense. I didn't realise…' He withdrew his hand to tousle his dark hair. 'I didn't think that I might have needed you in my life for reasons that didn't make any sense. That you'd climbed under my skin and it wasn't just to do with the good sex.'

'What was it to do with?'

'I'm in love with you. I don't know when that happened or how, but…'

'Say that again?'

'Which bit?'

'The bit about being in love with me.' A feeling of being on top of the world, of pure joy, filled her like life-saving oxygen. She felt heady and giddy and euphoric all at the same time. 'You didn't say,' she told him accusingly, but she was half laughing, half wanting to cry. 'Why didn't you say?'

'I didn't know…until you left…'

She flung herself into his arms and sighed with pure contentment when he wrapped his arms around her and held her close, so close that she could hear the beating of his heart. 'You were so arrogant,' she told him. 'You forced me into an arrangement I hated. You broke all the rules when it came to the sort of guy I could ever be interested in. You didn't want any kind of long-term relationship and I've never approved of men who move from woman to woman. And, as well, I was convinced that you were still wrapped up with Annalise, that you'd never let the memory go, that she was the ex no one had ever been able to live up to. On all fronts you were taboo, and then I met your family and I got sucked in to you…to all of you…and it was like being in quicksand. When you proposed, when you listed all the reasons why marrying me would make sense, I finally woke up to the fact that the one reason why anyone should get married was missing. You didn't love me. I thought you didn't know how and you never would and I couldn't accept your offer, knowing that the power balance would be so uneven. I would forever be the helpless, dependent one, madly in love with you and waiting for the time when you got tired of me physically and the axe fell.'

'And now?'

'And now I'm the happiest person in the world!'

'So if I ask you again to marry me…this time for all the right reasons…'

'Yes! Yes! Yes!'

Damien shuddered with relief. He felt as if he'd been holding his breath ever since he'd walked into the house. His arms tightened around her and he breathed in the fresh floral smell of her hair. 'You've made me the happiest person in the world as well…' Then he gave a low rumble of laughter. 'And I don't think my mother or Dominic will mind too much either…'

EPILOGUE

THEY DIDN'T MIND. Not when Damien and Violet showed up, surprising both Dominic and Eleanor, the following day.

'Of course,' Eleanor said smugly, 'I knew it was just a case of getting you two together so that you could sort out your silly differences. Damien, darling, I love you but you can be stubborn and there was no way that I was going to allow the best thing that ever happened to you to slip through your fingers. Now, let's discuss the wedding plans… Something big and fancy? Or small and cosy…?'

'Fast,' was Damien's response.

They were married six weeks later at the local church close to his mother's house. Dominic was the best man and he performed his duties with a gravity that was incredibly touching and, later, at the small reception which they held at the house, he was cheered on to speak and, bright red, raised his glass to the best brother a man could have.

Phillipa didn't stop teasing her sister that she had managed to beat her down the aisle. 'And you'll probably be preggers by the time I make my vows in my white sarong and crop top!' she wailed, which, as it turned out, was exactly what happened.

On a hot day, watching her sister and her assortment of new-found friends, with the sound of the surf competing with the little band drumming out the wedding march as

Phillipa took her vows, Violet leaned against her husband, hand on the gentle swell of her stomach, and wondered whether it was possible to be happier.

From those inauspicious beginnings, the relationship she never thought would happen had blossomed into something she could not live without, and the man who had fought against becoming involved had turned into the man who frequently told her how much he loved her and how much he hated leaving her side.

'I've come to terms with the value of delegation,' he had confided without a shade of regret, 'and when my son is born...'

'Or daughter...'

'*Or daughter*...I intend to explore its value even more...'

Thinking about what else they explored now brought a hectic flush to her cheeks and, as if reading her mind, Damien leant to whisper in her ear, 'Okay. The ceremony is over. What do you say to us staying for the meal and then heading back to the hotel? I think I need to remind myself of what your nipples taste like... I'm getting withdrawal symptoms...'

Violet blushed and laughed and looked up at him. 'That would be rude...' she said sternly, but already her mind was leaping ahead to the way her developing body fascinated him, the way he lavished attention on her breasts, even more abundant now, and suckled on her nipples, which were bigger and darker and a source of never-ending attention the minute her clothes were off. She felt the heat pool between her legs when she thought of them lying in the air-conditioned splendour of their massive curtained bed, his head on her stomach while he stroked her thighs with his hand, then tickled the swollen, engorged bud of her clitoris, which she would swear was even more sensitive now.

'But I'm sure Phillipa will understand…' she conceded as he planted a fleeting kiss on the corner of her mouth. 'After all, we pregnant ladies can't stay in the heat for too long…'

* * * * *

TROUBLE ON
HER DOORSTEP

NINA HARRINGTON

Nina Harrington grew up in rural Northumberland, England, and decided at the age of eleven that she was going to be a librarian – because then she could read all of the books in the public library whenever she wanted! Since then she has been a shop assistant, community pharmacist, technical writer, university lecturer, volcano walker and industrial scientist, before taking a career break to realise her dream of being a fiction writer. When she is not creating stories which make her readers smile, her hobbies are cooking, eating, enjoying good wine—and talking, for which she has had specialist training.

CHAPTER ONE

Tea, glorious tea. A celebration of teas from around the world.
There is no better way to lift your spirits than a steaming hot cup of builders' brew. Two sugars, lots of milk. White china beaker. Blend of Kenyan and Indian leaf tea. Brewed in a pot. Because one cup is never enough.

From *Flynn's Phantasmagoria of Tea*

Tuesday

'LADIES, LADIES, LADIES. No squabbling, please. Yes, I know that he was totally out of order but those are the rules. What happens in the Bake and Bitch club…?'

Dee Flynn lifted her right hand and waved it towards the women clustered about the cake display as though she was conducting a concert orchestra.

The women put down their tea cups, glanced at one another, shrugged their shoulders and raised their right hands.

'Stays in the Bake and Bitch club,' a chorus of sing-song voices replied, a second before they burst into laughter and sank back into their chairs around the long pine table.

'Okay. I might not be able to snitch, but I still cannot

believe that the faker tried to pass that sponge cake off as his own work,' Gloria sniggered as she poured another cup of Darjeeling and dunked in a homemade hazelnut biscotti. 'Every woman at the junior school bake sale knew that it was Lottie's triple-decker angel drool cake and you can hardly mistake that icing. We all know how hard it is to make, after last week's efforts.'

'Hey! Don't be so hard on yourself,' Lottie replied. 'That was one of my best recipes and chiffon sponge is not the easiest to get right. You never know; I might have become one dad's inspiration to greater things.'

A chorus of 'Boo,' and 'Not likely,' echoed around the table.

'Well, never mind about dads wanting to show off at the school bake sale in front of the other fabulous baked creations you gals create. We have five more minutes before your cakes come out of the oven so there is just enough time for you to taste my latest recipe for a February special. This is the cake I am going to demonstrate next week.'

With a flourish reserved for the finest award-winning restaurants where she and Dee had trained, Lottie Rosemount waited until every one of the girls had stopped talking and was looking at the cake plate at the centre of the table, before whipping away the central metal dome and revelling in the gasp of appreciation.

'Individual cupcakes. Dark chocolate and raspberry with white-chocolate hearts. And just in time for Valentine's Day. What do you think?'

'Think?' Dee coughed and took a long drink of tea. 'I am thinking that I have a week to come up with the perfect blend of tea to complement chocolate and raspberries.'

'Tea? Are you joking?' Gloria squealed. 'Hell no. Those cupcakes are not meant to be washed down with tea around the kitchen table. No chance. Those are after-dinner bedroom dessert cakes. No doubt about it. If I am lucky, I might get to eat half of one before my Valentine's Day dinner date gets really sweet—if you know what I mean. Girl, I want me some of those. Right now.'

A roar of laughter rippled like a wave around the room as Gloria snatched up a cupcake and bit into it with deep groans of pleasure, before licking her fingers. 'Lottie Rose-mount, you are a temptation. If I made those cupcakes I know that I would get lucky, and just this once I would not think about the risk of chocolate icing on the bedclothes.'

Dee sniggered and had just pulled down a tea caddy of a particularly fragrant pomegranate infusion when she heard the distinctive sound of the antique doorbell at the front door of the tea rooms.

Lottie looked up from serving the cupcakes. 'Who can that be? We've been closed for hours.'

'Not to worry. I'll get it. But save one of those for me, can you? You never know—my luck might change and a handsome new boyfriend might turn up out of the blue just in time for Valentine's Day. Miracles can happen.'

Dee skipped out of the kitchen across the smooth wooden floorboards in her flat ballet pumps, and in three strides was inside the tea rooms. She flicked on the lights and instantly the long room was flooded with warm natural light which bounced back from the pistachio-and-mocha painted walls and pale wood fittings.

Lottie's Cake Shop and Tea Rooms had only been open a few months and Dee never got tired of simply walking up and down between the square tables and comfy chairs, scarcely able to believe that this was her space. Well, Lottie and Dee's space. They had each put up half of the money to get the business started. But they were partners sharing everything: tea and cake; both crazy, both working at the thing they loved best. Both willing to invest everything they had in this mad idea and take a risk that it would work.

Big risk.

A shiver ran across Dee's shoulders and she inhaled sharply. She needed this tea shop to work and work brilliantly if she had any hope of becoming a tea merchant in her own right. This was her last chance—her only chance—of creating some sort of financial future for herself and for her retired parents.

But suddenly the ringing bell was replaced by a hard rapping on the front door and she looked up towards the entrance. 'Hello? Is someone there?' A male voice called out from the street in a posh English accent.

A tall dark figure was standing on the pavement on the other side of the door with his hands cupped over his forehead, peering at her through the frosted glass of the half-glazed door.

What a cheek! It was almost nine o'clock at night. He must be desperate. And it was lashing down with rain.

She took a step forward then paused and sniffed just once before striding on.

After a lifetime of travel she was not scared of a stranger knocking on her door. This was a London high street, for goodness' sake, not the middle of some jungle or tropical rain forest.

With a lift of her chin and a spring in her step, Dee turned the key in the lock in one smooth movement and pulled the front door sharply towards her.

A little too sharply, as it turned out.

Everything from that moment seemed to happen in slow motion—like in some freeze-framed DVD where you could scarcely believe what had happened, so you played the same scene over and over again in jerky steps, just to make sure that your memory was not playing tricks on you.

Because as she flung open the door, the very tall man just raised his arm to knock again and, in that split second he leant forward, he found the door was missing.

But his body carried on moving, carrying him forward into the tea room. And directly towards Dee, who had stepped backward to see who was knocking so loudly.

A pair of very startled blue-grey eyes widened as he tumbled towards her, the bright light almost blinding him after the gloomy dark street outside.

What happened next was Dee's fault. *All of it.*

Either time slowed down or her brain went into over-drive, because suddenly she had visions of lawyers claiming compensation for broken noses and bruised elbows. Or worse.

Which meant that she could not, dared not, simply leap out of the way and let this man, whoever he was, fall forward, flat on his face and hurt himself.

So she did the only thing she could think of in that split second.

She swept his legs out from under him.

It seemed to make perfect sense at the time.

Her left leg stepped forward to his left side as she reached up and grabbed hold of the soggy right sleeve of his rather elegant long dark-wool coat and pulled him towards her.

Then she swept her right leg out, hooked her ballet pump behind his left ankle and flipped him over sideways. By keeping a tight hold on his coat sleeve, even though it was wet and slimy, she took his weight so that instead of falling flat on his back his besuited bottom hit the wooden floor instead.

It was actually a rather good side judo foot sweep, which broke his fall and took his weight at the same time. Result!

Her old martial arts tutor would have been proud.

Shame that the two middle buttons on what she could now see was a very smart cashmere coat popped open with the strain and went spinning off onto the floor under one of the tables. But it was worth it. Instead of flying across the floor to join them, her male visitor sat down in a long, heavy slow slump instead. No apparent harm done.

Dee's fingers slowly slid away from the moist fabric of his coat sleeve and his arm flopped down onto his knees.

She closed the front door and then sat back on her ankles on the floor so that she could look at him from about the same height.

And then look again.

Oh, my. Those blue-grey eyes were not the only thing that was startling. For a start he seemed to be wearing the kind of business suit she had last seen on the bank manager who had grudgingly agreed to give the bank loan on the tea room. Only softer and shinier and much, much more expensive. Not that she had much experience of men in suits, but she knew fabric.

And then there was the hair. The sleet had turned to a cold drizzle and his short dark-brown hair was curled into moist waves around his ears and onto his collar. Bringing into sharp focus a face which might have come from a Renaissance painting: all dark shadows and sharp cheekbones. Although the baggy tired eyes could probably use some of her special home-sewn tea bags to compensate for his late nights in the office.

Blimey! She had just swept the legs out from under the best looking man she had seen in a long time and that included the boys from the gym across the street, who stoked up on serious amounts of carbs before hitting the body-sculpting classes.

Men like this did not normally knock on her door.... ever. Maybe her luck *had* finally changed for once.

A smile slid across Dee's mouth, before the sensible part of her brain which was not bedazzled by a handsome face decided to make an appearance.

So what was he doing here? And who was he?

Why not ask him and find out?

'Hello,' she said, peering into his face and telling her hormones to sit down. 'Sorry about that, but I was worried that you might hurt yourself when you fell into the shop. How are you doing down there?'

How was he doing?

Sean Beresford pushed himself up on one elbow and took a few seconds to gather his wits and refocus on what looked like a smart café or bistro, although it was hard to tell since he was sitting on the floor.

Looking straight ahead of him, Sean could see cake stands, teapots and a blackboard which told him that the all-day special was cheese-and-leek quiche followed by an organic dark-chocolate brownie and as much Assam tea as he could drink.

Sean stared at the board and chuckled out loud. He could use some of that quiche and tea.

This was turning out to be quite a day.

It had started out in Melbourne what felt like a lifetime ago, followed by a very long flight, where he had probably managed three or four hours of sleep. And then there had been the joy of a manic hour at Heathrow airport where it soon became blindingly obvious that he had boarded the plane, but his luggage had not.

One more reason why he did not want to be sitting on this floor wearing the only suit of clothes that he possessed until the airline tracked down his bag.

Sean shuffled to a sitting position using the back of

a very hard wooden chair for support, knees up, back
straight, exhaled slowly and lifted his head.

And stared into two of the most startling pale-green
eyes that he had ever seen.

So green that they dominated a small oval face framed
by short dark-brown hair which was pushed behind neat
ears. At this distance he could see that her creamy skin was
flawless apart from what looked like cake crumbs which
were stuck to the side of a smiling mouth.

A mouth meant to appease and please. A mouth which
was so used to smiling that she had laughter lines on either side, even though she couldn't be over twenty-five.

What the hell had just happened?

He shuffled his bottom a little and stretched out his legs.
Nothing broken or hurting. That was a surprise.

'Anything I can get you?' The brunette asked in a light,
fun voice. 'Blanket? Cocktail?'

Sean sighed out loud and shook his head at how totally
ridiculous he must look at that moment.

So much for being a top hotel executive!

He was lucky that the hotel staff relying on him to sort
out the disaster he had just walked into straight from the
airport could not see him now.

They might think twice about putting their faith in Tom
Beresford's son.

'Not at the moment, thank you,' he murmured with a
short nod.

Her eyebrows squeezed tight together. She bent forward
a little and pressed the palm of one hand onto his forehead,
and her gaze seemed to scan his face.

Her fingers were warm and soft and the sensation of
that simple contact of her skin against his forehead was so
startling and unexpected that Sean's breath caught in his
throat at the reaction of his body at that simple connection.

Her voice was even warmer, with a definite accent that told him that she has spent a lot of time in Asia.

'You don't seem to have a temperature. But it is cold outside. Don't worry. You'll soon warm up.'

It he did not have a temperature now, he soon would have, judging by the amount of cleavage this girl was flashing him as she leant closer.

Her chest was only inches away from his face and he sat back a little to more fully appreciate the view. She was wearing one of those strange slinky sweaters that his sister Annika liked to wear on her rare weekend visits. Only Annika wore a T-shirt underneath so that when it slithered off one shoulder she had something to cover her modesty.

This girl was not wearing a T-shirt and a tiny strip of purple lace seemed to be all that was holding up her generously proportioned assets. At another time and definitely another place he might have been tempted to linger on that curving expanse of skin between the top of the slinky forest-green knit and the sharp collar bones and enjoy the moment, but she tilted her head slightly and his gaze locked onto far too many inches of a delicious-looking neckline.

It had been a while since he had been so very up close and personal to a girl with such a fantastic figure and it took a few seconds before what was left of the logical part of his brain clicked back into place. He dragged his focus a little higher.

'Nice top,' he grinned and pressed his hands against the floor to steady his body. 'Bit cold for the time of year.'

'Oh, do you like it?' She smiled and then looked down and gasped a little. In one quick movement she slid back and tugged at her top before squinting at him through narrow eyes. Clearly not too happy that he had been enjoying the view while she was checking his temperature.

'Cheeky,' she tutted. 'Is this how you normally behave in public? I'm surprised that they let you out unsupervised.'

A short cough burst out of Sean's throat. After sixteen years in the hotel trade he had been called many things by many people but he had never once been accused of being cheeky.

The second son of the founder of the Beresford hotel chain did not go around doing anything that even remotely fell into the 'cheeky' category.

This was truly a first. In more ways than one.

'Did you just deck me?' he asked in a low, questioning voice and watched her stand up in one single, smooth motion and lean against the table opposite. She was wearing floral patterned leggings which clung to long, slender legs which seemed to go on for ever and only ended where the oversized sweater came down to her thighs. Combined with the green top, she looked like a walking abstract painting of a spring garden. He had never seen anything quite like it before.

'Me?' She pressed one hand to her chest and shook her head before looking down at him. 'Not at all. I stopped you from falling flat on your face and causing serious damage to that cute nose. You should be thanking me. It could have been a nasty fall, the way you burst in like that. This really is your lucky day.'

'Thank you?' he spluttered in outrage. Apparently he had a cute nose.

'You are welcome,' she chuckled in a sing-song voice. 'It is not often that I have a chance to show off my judo skills but it comes in handy now and then.'

'Judo. Right. I'll take your word for it,' Sean replied and looked from side to side around the room. 'What is this place?'

'Our tea rooms,' she replied, and peered at him. 'But

you knew that, because you were hammering at our door.'
She flicked a hand towards the entrance. 'The shop is
closed, you know. No cake. No tea. So if you are expecting to be fed you are out of luck.'

'You can say that again,' Sean whispered, then held up
one hand when she looked as though she might reply. 'But
please don't. Tea and cakes are the last thing I came looking for, I can assure you.'

'So why were you hammering on the door, wearing a
business suit at nine on a Tuesday evening? You have obviously come here for a reason. Are you planning to sit on my
floor and keep me in suspense for the rest of the evening?'

His green-eyed assailant was just about to say something else when the sound of female laughter drifted out
from the back of the room.

'Ah,' she winced and nodded. 'Of course. You must be
here to pick up one of the girls from the Bake and Bit…
Banter club. But those ladies won't be ready for at least
another half-hour.' One hand gestured towards the back
of the room where he could hear the faint sound of female
voices and music. 'The cakes are still in the oven.' Her
lovely shoulders lifted in an apologetic shrug. 'We were
late getting started. Too much bit…chatting and not enough
baking. But I can tell someone you are here, if you like.
Who exactly are you waiting for?'

Who was he waiting for? He wasn't waiting for anyone. He was here on a different kind of mission. Tonight
he was very much a messenger boy.

Sean reached into the inside breast pocket of his suit
jacket and checked the address on the piece of lilac writing paper he had found inside the envelope marked
'D S Flynn contact details' lying at the bottom of the conference room booking file. It had been handwritten in dark-

green ink in very thin letters his father would instantly have dismissed as spider writing.

Well, he certainly had the right street and, according to the built-in GPS in his phone, he was within three metres of the address of his suspiciously elusive client who had booked a conference room at the hotel and apparently paid the deposit without leaving a telephone number or an email address. Which was not just inconvenient but infuriating.

'Sorry to disappoint you, but I am not here to pick up anyone from your baking club. Far from it. I need to track someone down in a hurry.'

He waved the envelope in the air and instantly saw something in the way she lifted her chin that suggested that she recognized the envelope, but she covered it up with a quizzical look.

That seemed to startle her and he could almost feel the intensity of her gaze as it moved slowly from his smart, black lace-up business brogues to the crispness of his shirt collar and silk tie. There was something else going on behind those green eyes, because she glanced back towards the entrance just once and then swung around towards the back of the room, before turning her attention on him again.

And when she spoke there was the faintest hint of concern in her voice which she was trying hard to conceal and failing miserably.

'Perhaps I could help if you told me who you were looking for,' she replied.

Sean looked up into her face and decided that it was time to get this over with so he could get back to the penthouse apartment at the hotel and collapse.

In one short, sharp movement he pushed himself sideways with one hand, curled his knees and effortlessly got back onto his feet, brushing down his coat and trousers with one hand. So that, when he replied, his words were more directed towards the floor than the girl standing watching him so intently.

'I certainly hope so. Does a Mr D S Flynn live here? Because, if he does, I really need to speak to him. And the sooner the better.'

CHAPTER TWO

Tea, glorious tea. A celebration of teas from around the world.
'A woman is like a tea bag: you never know how strong it is until it's in hot water.' Eleanor Roosevelt.
From *Flynn's Phantasmagoria of Tea*

'WHAT WAS THAT name again?' Dee asked, holding on to the edge of the counter for support, in a voice that was trembling way too much for her liking. 'Mr Deesasflin. Was that what you said? Sounds more like a rash cream. It is rather unusual.'

A low sigh of intense exasperation came from deep inside his chest and he stopped patting down his clothes and stretched out tall. As in, very tall. As in well over six feet tall in his smart shoes which, for a girl who was as vertically challenged as she was, as Lottie called it, seemed really tall.

Worse.

He was holding the envelope that she had given to the hotel manager the first time she had visited the lovely, posh, boutique hotel to suss out the conference facilities.

They had gone through everything in such detail and double-checked the numbers when she had paid the deposit on the conference room in October.

So why was this man, this stranger, holding that envelope?

Dee racked her brains. Things had been pretty mad ever since Christmas but she would have remembered a letter or call from the hotel telling her that it had been taken over or they had appointed a new manager.

Who made house calls.

Oh no, she groaned inside. This was the last thing she needed. Not now. *Please tell me that everything to do with the tea festival is still going to plan...please?* She had staked her reputation and her career in the tea trade on organizing this festival. And the last of her savings. Things had to be okay with the venue or she would be toast.

'Flynn. D. S.' His voice echoed out across the empty tea room, each letter crisp, perfectly enunciated and positively oozing with annoyance. 'This letter was all that I could find in the booking system. No name or telephone number or email address. Just an address, a surname and two initials.'

What? All that he could find?

Great. Well, that answered that question: he was from the hotel.

She was looking at her gorgeous but grumpy new hotel manager or conference organizer.

Who she had just sideswiped.

Splendid. This was getting better and better.

The only good news was that he seemed to think that his client was a man, so she could find out the reason for his obvious grumpiness without getting her legs swiped from under her. With a bit of luck.

As far as he knew, she was just a girl in a cake shop. Maybe she could keep up the pretence a little longer and find out more before revealing her true credentials.

'You don't seem very pleased with this Mr Flynn person.' She smiled, suddenly desperate to appear as though she was just an outside party making conversation. 'They must have done something seriously outrageous to make you come out on a wet night in February to track them down.'

Ouch. That was such a horrible expression. The idea that he had made it as far as the tea rooms and was actually hunting her was enough to give her an icy cold feeling in the pit of her stomach which was going to take a serious amount of hot tea to thaw out.

From the determined expression on his face, right down to the very official business suit and smart haircut, this man spelt 'serious'.

As serious as all of the finance people who had tried their hardest to crush her confidence and convince her that her dream was a foolish illusion. She had been turned down over and over again, despite the brilliant business plan she had worked on for weeks, and all the connections in the tea trade that she could ever need.

The message was always the same: they could not see the feasibility of a new tea import business in the current economy. All of the statistics about the British obsession with tea and everything connected with it had seemed to fly over their heads. Not enough profit. Too risky. Not viable.

Was it any wonder that she had gone out on a limb and offered to organize the tea festival so that she could launch her import business at the same time?

Lottie had been her saviour in the end and had pulled in a few favours so that the private bank her parents used was aware that it was a joint business with the lovely, seriously wealthy and connected Miss Rosemount as well as the equally lovely but seriously broke Miss Flynn.

Come to think of it, the banker had been a girl in a suit. But a suit all the same.

'On the contrary, Mr Flynn has not done anything. But I do need to speak to him as soon as possible.'

'May I take a message?' she asked in her best 'innocent bystander' voice, and smiled.

He paused for a second and she thought that he was going to slide over to her counter but he was simply straightening his back. Oh lord. Another two inches taller.

'I am sorry but this is a confidential business matter for my client. If you know where I can find him, it is important that we talk on a very urgent matter about his booking.'

A cold, icy pit started to form in the base of Dee's stomach and something close to panic flitted up like a bucket of cold water splashed over her face.

She blinked, lifted her chin and stuck out her hand. 'That's me. Dervla Skylark Flynn. Otherwise known as Dee. Dee S Flynn. Tea supplier to the stars. I'm the person you are looking for, Mr...?'

He took two long steps to cross the room and shake her hand. A real handshake. His long, slender fingers wrapped around her hand which Dee suddenly realized must be quite sticky from dispensing cake and biscuits and clearing away bowls covered in cake batter.

His gaze was locked on her face as he spoke, and she could almost see the clever cogs interconnecting behind those blue eyes as he processed her little announcement, took her word that she was who she said she was and went for it without pause.

Clever. *She liked clever.*

'Sean Beresford. I am the acting manager of the Beresford Hotel, Richmond Square. Pleased to meet you, Miss Flynn.'

'Richmond Square?' She replied, trying to keep the

panic out of her voice. 'That's the hotel where I booked a conference room for February. And...'

Then her brain caught up with the name he had given her and she inhaled through her nose as his fingers slid away from hers and rested lightly on the counter.

'Did you just say Beresford? As in the Beresford family of hotel owners?'

A smile flickered across his lips which instantly drew her gaze, and her stupid little heart just skipped a beat at the transformation in this man's face that one simple smile made.

Lord, he was gorgeous. Riveting.

Oh, smile at me again and make my blood soar. Please?

And now she was ogling. How pathetic. Just because she was within touching distance of a real, live Beresford did not mean that she had to go to pieces in front of him.

So what if this man came from one of the most famous hotel-owning families in the world? A Beresford hotel was a name splashed across the broadsheet newspapers and celebrity magazines, not *Cake Shop and Tea Room Weekly*.

This made it even more gut-clenching that he had just been in close and personal contact with her floorboards.

'Guilty as charged,' he replied and touched his forehead with two closed fingers in salute. 'I am in London for a few months and the Richmond Square hotel is one of my special projects.'

'You're feeling guilty?' she retorted with a cough. 'What about me? You almost had an accident here tonight. And I could have dropped you. Oh, that is so not good. Especially when you have come all the way from the centre of London late in the evening to see me.'

Then she shook her head, sucked in a long breath and carried on before he had a chance to say anything. 'Speaking of which, now we have the introductions sorted out, I think you had best tell me what the problem is. Because I am starting to get scared about this special project you need to see me about so very urgently.'

He gestured towards the nearest table and chairs.

'You may need to sit down, Miss Flynn.'

A lump the size of Scotland formed in her throat, making speech impossible, so she replied with a brief shake of the head and a half-smile and gestured to one of the bar stools next to the tea bar.

She watched in silence as he unbuttoned his coat, scowled at the missing buttons then sat down on the stool and turned to face her, one elbow resting on the bar.

Nightmare visions flitted through her brain of having to tell the tea trade officials that the London Festival of Tea was going to going to be cancelled because she had messed up booking the venue, but she fought them back.

Not going to happen. That tea festival was going ahead even if she had to rent the damp and dusty local community centre and cancel the bingo night.

She had begged the tea trade organization to give her the responsibility for organizing the event and it had taken weeks to convince the hardened professionals that she could coordinate a major London event.

Everything she had worked for rested on this event being a total success. *Everything.*

Suddenly the room started to feel very warm and she dragged over a bar stool and perched on it to stop her wobbly legs from giving way under her.

Focus, Dee. Focus. It might not be as bad as she was thinking.

'I only took over the running of the hotel today so it has taken me a while to go through all of the paperwork. That's why I only started working through the conference-booking system this afternoon. I apologize for not calling in earlier but there has been a lot of catching up to do and I didn't have any contact details.'

She swallowed down her anxiety. 'But what happened to the other manager? Frank Evans? He was taking care of all my arrangements in person and seemed very organized. I must have filled in at least three separate forms before I paid the deposit. Surely he has my contact details?'

'Frank decided to take up a job offer with another hotel company last Friday. Without notice. That's why I came in to sort out the emergency situation at Richmond Square and get things back on track.'

She gasped and grabbed his arm. 'What kind of emergency do you have?' Then she gulped. 'Has something happened? I mean, has the hotel flooded or—' she suddenly felt faint '—burnt down? Gas explosion? Water damage?'

'Flooded?' he replied, then tilted his head a tiny fraction of an inch. 'No. The hotel is absolutely fine. In fact, I went there straight from the airport and it is as lovely as ever. Business as usual.'

'Then please stop scaring the living daylights out of me like that. I don't understand. Why is there a problem with the booking?'

'So you met Frank Evans? The previous manager?'

She nodded. 'Twice in person, then I spoke to him several times over the phone. Frank insisted on taking personal responsibility for my tea festival and we went over the room plans in detail. Then we had lunch at the hotel just before Christmas to make sure that everything was going to plan. And it was. Going to plan.'

'In any of those meetings, did you see him recording any of your details on a diary or paper planner? Anything like that?

'Paper? No. Now that you mention it, I don't remember him taking any notes on paper. It was all on his notebook computer. He showed the photos of the layout on the screen. Is that a problem? I mean, isn't everything loaded onto computers these days?'

There was just enough of a pause from the man looking at her to send a shiver across Dee's shoulders.

'Okay; I get the picture. How bad is it?' she whispered. 'Just tell me now and put me out of my misery.'

'Frank may have taken your details but he didn't load them onto the hotel booking system. If he had, Frank would have found out that we were already double-booked for the whole weekend with a company client who had booked a year in advance. So you see, he should never have accepted your booking in the first place. I am sorry, Miss Flynn, I have to cancel your booking and refund your deposit… Miss Flynn?'

But Dee was already on her feet.

'Stay right where you are. I need serious cake washed down with strong, sugary tea. And I need it now. Because there is no way on this planet that I am going to cancel that booking. No way at all. Are we clear? Good. Now, what can I get you?'

'I don't understand it. Frank seemed so confident and in control,' Dee said in a low voice. 'And he loved my oolong special leaf tea and was all excited about the conference. What happened?'

Sean was siting opposite and she watched him sip the fragrant Earl Grey that Dee had made for him. Then took another sip.

'This is really very good,' Sean whispered, and wrapped his fingers around the china beaker.

'Thank you. I have a wonderful supplier in Shanghai. Fifth-generation blender. And you still haven't answered my question. Is it a computer problem? It was, wasn't it?

Some crazy, fancy booking system that only works if you have a degree in higher mathematics?'

She waved the remains of a very large piece of Victoria sandwich cake through the air. 'My parents were right all along: I should never trust a man who did not carry paper and pen.'

She paused with her cake half between her mouth and her plate and licked her lips.

'Do you have paper and a pen, Mr Beresford?'

He reached into the inside pocket of his suit jacket and pulled out a state-of-the-art smart phone.

'Everything I type is automatically synched with the hotel systems and my personal diary. That way, nothing gets lost or overlooked. Which makes it better than a paper notepad which could be misplaced.'

Dee peered at the glossy black device covered with tiny coloured squares and then shook her head. 'Frank didn't have one of those. I would have remembered.'

'Actually, he did. But he chose not to use it.' Sean sighed. 'I found it still in the original packaging in his office desk this afternoon.'

'Ah ha. Black mark for Team Beresford Hotels. Time for some staff training, methinks.'

'That's why I am back in London, Miss Flynn.' Sean bristled and put away his phone and started refastening his remaining coat buttons. 'To make sure that this sort of mistake does not happen again. I will personally arrange to have your deposit refunded tomorrow so you can organize a replacement venue at your convenience.'

She looked at him for a second then took another swig of very dark tea before lowering her large china beaker to the table. Then she stood up, stretched and folded her arms.

'Which part of "I am not cancelling" did you not understand? I don't want my deposit back. I want my conference suite. No, that's not quite right.' Her eyebrows squeezed tight together. 'I *need* my conference room. And you…' she smiled up at him and fluttered her eyelashes outrageously '…are going to make sure I get it.'

Sean sighed, long and low. 'I thought that I had made it clear. The conference facilities at the Richmond Square had already been reserved for over a year before Frank accepted your booking. There are four hundred and fifty business leaders arriving from all over the world for one of the most prestigious environmental strategy think-tank meetings outside Davos. Four days of high-intensity, high-profile work.'

'Double-booked. Yes. I understand. But here is the thing, Sean; you don't mind if I call you Sean, do you? Excellent. The lovely Frank made my copies of all of those forms I signed on his very handy hotel photocopier and, as far as I know, my contract is with the Beresford hotel group. And that means that you have to find me an alternative venue.'

'But that is quite impossible at this short notice.'

And then he did it.

He looked at her with the same kind of condescending and exasperated expression on his face as her high school headmistress had used when she'd turned up for her first big school experience in London after spending the first fifteen years of her life travelling around tea-growing estates in India with her parents.

'Poor child,' she had heard the teacher whisper to her assistant. 'She doesn't understand the complicated words that we are using. Shame that she has no chance in the modern educational system. It's far too late for her to catch up now and get the qualifications she needs. *What a pity she has no future.*'

A cold shiver ran down Dee's back just at the memory of those words. If only that teacher knew that she had lit a fire inside her belly to prove just how wrong she had been to write her off as a hopeless case just because she had been outside the formal school system. And that fire was still burning bright. In fact, at this particular moment it was hot enough to warm half the city and certainly hot enough to burn this man's fingers if he even tried to get in her way.

This man who had fallen into her tea rooms uninvited was treating her like a child who had to be tolerated, patted on the head and told to keep quiet while the grown-ups decided what was going to happen to her without bothering to ask her opinion.

This handsome man in a suit didn't realize that he was doing it.

And the hair on the back of her neck flicked up in righteous annoyance.

She had never asked to come to London. Far from it. And what had been her reward for being uprooted from the only country that she had called home?

Oh yes. Being ridiculed on a daily basis by the other pupils because of her strange clothes and her Anglo-Indian accent, and then humiliated by the teachers because she had no clue about exam curricula and timetables and how to use the school desktop computers. Why should she have? That had never been her life.

And of course she hadn't been able to complain to her lovely parents. They were just as miserable and had believed that they were doing the right thing, coming back to Britain for the big promotion and sending her to the local high school.

Well, that was then and this was now.

The fifteen-year-old Dee had been helpless to do anything about it but work hard and try to get through each day as best as she could.

But she certainly did not have to take it now. She had come

a long way from that quiet, awkward teenager and worked so very hard to put up with anything less than respect.

Maybe that was why she stepped forward and glared up into his face so that he had to look down at her before he could reply.

'Exactly. There is no way that I could find another hotel that can cope with three hundred international tea specialists less than two weeks before the festival. Everywhere will be booked well ahead, even in February.'

She lifted her cute little chin and stared him out. 'Here is a question for you: would you mind reminding me exactly how many hotels the Beresford hotel group runs in London? Because they seem to be popping up everywhere I look.'

'Five,' he replied in a low voice.

'Five? Really? That many? Congratulations. Well, in that case it shouldn't be any trouble for you to find me a replacement conference room in one of the four other hotels in our fine city. Should it?' she said in a low, hoarse voice, her eyes locked onto his. And this time she had no intention of looking away first.

The air between them was so thick with electricity that she could have cut it with a cake knife. Time seemed to stretch and she could see the muscles in the side of his face twitching with suppressed energy, as though he could hardly believe that she was challenging him.

Because she had no intention whatsoever of giving in.

No way was she going to allow Sean Used-to-having-his-own-way Beresford to treat her like a second-class citizen.

And the sooner he realized that, the better!

Sean felt the cold ferocity of those pale-green eyes burn like frostbite onto his cheeks, and was just about to tell her what an impossible task that was when there was an explosion of noise and movement from behind his back. What seemed like a coach party of women of all shapes and ages burst out into the tea rooms, laughing like trains, gossiping and competing with one another in volume and pitch to make their voices heard above the uproar.

It felt like a tsunami of women was bearing down on him.

All carrying huge bags bursting with what looked like cake tins and mystery utensils and binders. Sean stepped back and practically squeezed himself against one wall to let the wall of female baking power sweep past him towards the entrance and out into the street.

'Ah, Lottie. There you are!' Dee Flynn cried out and grabbed the sleeve of a very pretty slim blonde dressed in a matching navy T-shirt and trousers. 'Sorry I did not get back to serve more tea. Come and meet Sean. The London Festival of Tea is going to have a new exciting venue and Sean here is the man who is in charge of finding the perfect location. And he is not going to rest until he has found the perfect replacement.'

She grinned at him with an expression of pure delight, with an added twist of evil. 'Aren't you, Sean?'

CHAPTER THREE

Tea, glorious tea. A celebration of teas from around the world.

There are many different kinds of tea, but they are all derived from just one type of plant: *Camellia sinensis*. The colour and variety of the tea (green, black, white and oolong) depends on the way the leaves are treated once they are picked.

From *Flynn's Phantasmagoria of Tea*

Wednesday

'SO HOW ARE you enjoying being back in London?' Rob Beresford's voice echoed out from the computer screen in his usual nonchalant manner. His eyebrows lifted. 'Same old madness?'

'Nothing that boring.' Sean snorted and pointed to the bags under his eyes. 'Still shattered. Still jet-lagged. Still wading through the mess Frank Evans got himself into at Richmond Square. I still can't believe that the man we trusted to run our hotel just took off and left this disaster for someone else to sort out.'

Sean's half-brother sat back in his chair and gave a low cough. 'Now, who does that remind me of? Oh yes, your ex-girlfriend. I caught up with the lovely Sasha at the catering-strategy forum last week. She asked me to say hi, by the way. Now, wasn't that sweet? Considering that she dumped you with zero notice. I could almost dislike her if it wasn't for her fantastic figure.' Rob gave a low, rough sigh. 'And that tan… She's looking good, brother. The Barbados hotel seems to be suiting her very nicely and the clients love her.'

'Thanks for the update.' Sean coughed and then squinted towards the computer screen. 'And she did not dump me. It simply wasn't working out for either of us. Trying to co-ordinate our diaries so that we were in the same time zone for more than a few days had stopped being funny a long time before we called it a day. You know what chaos it was last year! You were there, working the same hours as I was.'

Sean turned back to shuffling through a file on the desk. Sasha had been on the fast-track Beresford Hotels management programme and he had been working so hard that he hadn't even noticed that they barely saw one another face to face any more.

Until he'd come back to her apartment at one a.m., exhausted after two weeks on the road solving all the teething problems for a hotel opening, to find Sasha sitting waiting for him.

He had just missed her birthday dinner, the one he had promised that he would be there for. Not even the private jet could fly in tropical storms.

It was a pity that it hadn't been the first time that he'd missed her birthday. They had both worked like crazy over the Christmas and New Year holiday, but February should have been down time. Until the new hotel they were opening in Mexico had flooded only days before the grand opening and a holiday became a distant memory.

They had talked through the night but in the end there had been no escaping the truth. He was the operations troubleshooter and Tom Beresford's son. It was his job to be on stand-by and cope with emergencies. No matter what else was happening in his life. Or who. And she'd wanted more than he was prepared to give her.

It had been crunch time. He could either decide to give her the commitment she needed and deserved or they could walk away as friends who had enjoyed a fun and light hearted relationship and leave it like that.

He had not even bothered to unpack.

'Ah, but I still managed to find the time to enjoy the company of a few lovely ladies,' Robert replied. 'Unlike some people. But that's past history. So last year! Come on; you were in Australia for six weeks scouting for new locations! You must have spent some time at the beach.'

Robert Beresford sat back with his hands clasped behind his head. 'I am having visions of lovely ladies in very small bikinis on golden sands and surf boards. Classy. You have just made my day.'

'I know. I can see you drooling from here,' Sean shook his head. 'That was the plan. Two glorious weeks in Melbourne in February. Two weeks to sleep, soak up the sun and generally have some down time before starting the Paris assignment.'

He waved the conference-booking file at the screen. 'That *was* the plan. And now I am in London instead. Remind me again why I am the one who gets called in to pick up the pieces when the brown stuff hits the fan?'

'Who else is the old man going to call? I am only interested in the food and drink side of this crazy business, remember? There has to be someone in the family who can squeeze into a super-hero costume and fly in to save the day and Annika is way too stylish to wear underpants over her tights.'

Sean laughed out loud and flicked open the event files.

'Now, that is just being mean. I caught those last restaurant reviews. The food critics are crazy about that new fusion franchise you brought in. Kudos.'

Rob saluted him with a hat-tip. 'I'll tell you all about it when we meet up for the conference on Friday. Right? And try and relax. You'll have that mess sorted out by then. You always do. Shame that you can't take some down time before starting the new job. But you never know. You might find some sweet distraction while you are in London.'

Then Sean's gaze caught the lilac envelope that he had popped onto his desk to be filed. He quickly stole a glance at the file he had updated the minute he had got back to his hotel room the previous evening. Complete with the photo of Dee he had clipped from a London newspaper article from the previous October about the opening of Lottie's Cake Shop and Tea Rooms.

The two girls were standing outside the cake shop in what looked to be a cold autumn day.

Dee grinned out to the photographer with a beaming smile which was a lot warmer than the one he had been on the receiving end of. But her colour scheme was just as alarming.

She was wearing a short, pleated green skirt in a loud check-pattern tweed and a knitted top in fire-engine red partly covered with a pretty floral apron. Her blonde friend, Lottie, was in navy trousers and top with the same apron and compared to Dee looked elegant, sedate and in control while Dee looked…like a breath of fresh air. Animated, excited and alive.

That was the strange thing. Even in a digital scan from a newspaper this girl's energy and passion seemed to reach out from the flat screen, grab him and hold him tight in her grasp. She was looking at him right in the eyes. Just as she had in the flesh. No flinching or nervous sideways glances. Just single-minded focus, with eyes the colour of spring-green leaves; it was quite impossible to look away.

But not cold. Just the opposite, in fact. Even when she'd been challenging him to come up with a replacement venue that sexy smile was warm enough to turn up the heat on a cold winter's evening. Or was it that slippery one-shoulder sweater that she had been almost wearing?

He had vowed never to get involved in another relationship after Sasha, and no amount of bar crawling with Rob had persuaded him to change his mind. But there was something about Dee that seemed to get under his skin and he couldn't shake it off.

Maybe it was getting very up close to a client when he had no clue who she was?

It was usual practice in Beresford hotels for the conference manager to take a photo of their client so that the team could recognize who they were dealing with.

Sean blinked and cricked back his neck, which was stiff from stress and lack of sleep. Jet lag. That was it. He had a workload which was not funny and two weeks in London before heading to his new job in Paris. He didn't have time to sort out double bookings and track down conference space in the London hotels.

If only Frank had followed procedures!

'You wouldn't be calling me Superman if you had seen me last night,' he chuckled, then blinked and looked up at the monitor, where Rob was tapping his pen and looking at him with a curious expression.

'Do tell.'

'A girl with green eyes and a wicked judo throw brought me to my knees. That's all I am going to say.'

Rob snorted and sat forward with his elbows on the desk, and that gleam in his eyes which had got both of them into trouble on more than one occasion. 'Now that really is being mean. I need facts, a photograph and vital statistics. Sounds like the kind of girl I would like to meet. In fact, here is an idea—free, gratis and no charge. Bring this green-eyed fiend to the management dinner on Friday night. If you think you can handle it? Or should I have security on standby?'

'What…so you can ogle the poor girl all evening? No way.'

'Then give me something to report back to Annika in the way of gossip. You know she is always trying to set me up with her pals. It's about time our sister focused on you for a change. Are you planning on seeing this girl again?'

Sean checked the clock on the computer screen.

'As a matter of fact, I am meeting up with her this morning. Our latest client has given me a mission and I have a feeling that this lady is not going to fobbed off with anything but the best. In fact, come to think of it, I might need that super-hero costume after all.'

'How about this one?' Dee called out as Lottie swept by with a tray of vanilla-cream pastry slices. '"Flynn's Phantasmagorian Emporium of Tea".'

Then she leant back and peered at the words she had just written in chalk on the 'daily specials' blackboard next to the tea and coffee station.

'It has a certain ring to it and I can just see it on a poster. Maybe dressed up in a Steampunk theme. I like it!'

Lottie gave two short coughs, continued filling up the tiered cake stand on the counter then waved to two of their favourite breakfast customers as they strolled out onto the street.

'You also liked "Flynn's Special Tea Time Fantasies", until I pointed out that some folks might get the wrong idea and think you are selling a different kind of afternoon fantasy experience where you are not wearing much in the way of clothing. And I don't know about you, but I am not quite that desperate to sell your leaf teas.'

'Only people with that kind of mind.' Dee tutted. 'Shame on a nice well-brought-up girl like you for thinking such things.'

'Just trying to keep you out of mischief. Again.'

Dee felt the weight of an unexpected extra layer of guilt settle on her shoulders and she slipped off her stool and gave Lottie a one-armed hug. She had been so focused on organizing the festival that Lottie had done a lot more work than she should have done in the shop. 'Thanks for putting up with me. I know I can be a tad obsessive now and then. I don't know what I would have done without you these past months. Organizing this tea festival has already taken so much of my time; I'm sure that you have done more than your fair share in the shop.'

'That's okay.' Lottie grinned and hugged her back. 'It takes one obsessive to know one, right? Why else do you think I came to you the minute I had the idea for a cake shop? I needed someone who loved tea.'

Lottie stood back and nodded towards the blackboard with the daily specials. 'Tea. Cake. Gotta be a winner.' Then she turned back to the cake stand. 'Turns out that I was right.'

'Any chance that you could sprinkle some of that business-fairy dust in this direction? I am going to need something to give my own special blend of afternoon tea that special oomph, or I'll never make any money out of the tea festival.'

Dee slumped down on her stool and stared out at the breakfast customers who were slurping down her English breakfast tea with Lottie's almond croissants and ham and cheese paninis.

Lottie strolled over and sat down next to her before re-plying. 'I know that I promised not to get involved, be-cause we agreed that it is important that you do this on your own, but what about all of the exhibitors who will be selling their teas and chinaware and teapots and special tea kettles and the like? Surely they're giving you a fee or a cut in any sales they make on the day?'

'They are. But it's just enough to cover the money I spent on the deposit for the hotel. Beresford is really ex-pensive, even for one day. But I thought that a big interna-tional hotel chain like Beresford wouldn't let me down, so it was worth paying for the extra security just to make that there wouldn't be any last minute hassles with the venue. Hah! Wrong again.'

Dee started tapping her tea spoon on the counter. 'After Mr B left I called Gloria to ask if the church hall might be available. The ladies' lunch club loved my last demon-stration on tea tasting. I thought that Gloria could put a good word in for me and I might even get it for free. But do you know what? Even the church hall is fully booked for the rest of the month.'

'I thought you said that it was damp and there were mouse droppings in the kitchen,' Lottie replied as she cut two large slices from a coffee-walnut layer cake and taste-fully arranged them on the cake stand.

'Yes and yes. Small details. But that settles it; Sean Beresford is going to have to find me a mega replacement venue. Whether he likes it or not.'

'Well, you did have one bonus. The lovely Sean. In the flesh. I didn't think that the millionaire heirs to the Beres-ford hotel chain turned up in person to break bad news, so he scores a few points on the Rosemount approval board. And, oh my—tall, dark and handsome does not come close.

And he seemed very interested in you. I think that you might be on to a winner there.'

The memory of a pair of sparkling blue eyes smiling down at her tugged at the warm and cuddly part of Dee's mind and her traitorous heart gave just enough of a flutter to make her cover up her smirk with a quick sniff.

Dee pressed her lips together and shook her head. 'Charlotte Rosemount, you are such a total romantic. Can I remind you where that has taken us in the past? I lost track of the number of frogs we had to kiss back at catering college before you finally admitted that not one of those boys was a prince. And then you had the cheek to set me up with Josh last year.'

'It was a simple process of elimination!' Lottie grinned and then twisted her face into a grimace. 'I did get it wrong about Josh, though. He looked so good on paper! His dad was even a director at the tea company and he had the looks to die for. But sheesh, what a loser he turned out to be.'

'Exactly!' Dee nodded. 'And it took me six months to find out that all he wanted was a stand-in girl until someone more suitable came along. No, Lottie. Handsome hotel owners do not date girls who deck them. Well-known fact. Especially girls who give them extra work and refuse to go along with their get-rid-of-the-annoyance-as-quickly-as-possible schemes.'

'Perhaps he likes a girl who can stand up him. You are a change from all of the gold-diggers who hit on him on a daily basis. And he liked your Earl Grey.'

'Please. Did you see him? That suit cost more than my last shipment of Oolong. That is a man who fuels up on espressos and wouldn't let carbs pass his lips. He will pass the problem on to someone else to sort out, you wait and see. Big fish, small pond. Passing through on the way to greater things. Just like Josh. I think he only turned up to tell me so that he could tick me off his to-do list.'

'But he is trying to find you a replacement venue. Isn't he?'

'His assistant is probably run off her feet at this minute calling every hotel in London which is still available on a Saturday two weeks before the event. The list will be small and the hotels grotty. And he is not getting away with it. I need a high-class venue and nothing else will do.'

Lottie was just about to reply when the telephone rang on the wall behind them and the theme song for *The Teddy Bears' Picnic* chimed out. She scowled at Dee, who shrugged as though she had not been responsible for changing the ring tone. Again.

'Lottie's Cake Shop and Tea Rooms,' Lottie answered in her best professional voice, and then she reached out and grabbed Dee by the sleeve, tugging hard to make sure that she had her full attention. 'Good morning to you, too, Sean. Why yes, you are in luck, she is right here. I'll just get Dee for you.'

Lottie opened her mouth wide, baring her very white teeth, and held out the telephone towards Dee, who took it from her as Lottie picked up a menu and fanned her face. The message was only too clear: hot.

Dee looked at the caller ID on the phone for second longer than necessary and lifted her chin before speaking.

Time to get this game of charades started the way she wanted.

'Good morning, Flynn's Phantasmagorian Emporium of Tea. Dee speaking.'

There was a definite pause on the other end of the phone before a deep male voice replied. *Excellent.* She had put him off his stride and victory was hers.

Shame that when he replied that deep voice was resonant, disgracefully measured, slow and confident. It seemed to vibrate inside her skull so that each syllable was stressed and important.

'That's quite a name. I am impressed. Good morning to you, Miss Flynn.'

The way he pronounced the end of her name was quite delicious. 'I have just made it up, and that's the idea. And how are you feeling this morning, eh? I hope that there is no bruising or delayed mental trauma from your exciting trip to the tea rooms yesterday evening. I wouldn't like to be responsible for any lasting damage.'

She almost caught the sound of a low chuckle before he choked it. 'Not at all,' Sean replied in a voice that was as smooth as the hot chocolate sauce Lottie made to pour over her cream-filled profiteroles.

'Excellent news.' Dee smiled and winked at Lottie, who was leaning against her shoulder so that she could hear every word. 'So, does that mean you have found me a superb replacement venue that will meet my every exacting need?'

'Before I answer that, I have a question for you. Are you free to join me for a breakfast meeting this morning?'

Dee held out the phone and glanced at Lottie, who rolled her eyes with a cheeky grin, stifled a laugh and headed off into the kitchen, leaving Dee to stare at the innocent handset as though it were toxic.

'Breakfast? Ah, thank you, but the bakery opens at six-thirty, so Lottie and I have already had our breakfast.'

'Ah,' he replied in a low voice. 'Misunderstanding. I didn't mean eating breakfast together, delightful as that would be. But it would be useful to have an early morning meeting to go through your list of exhibitors and put a detailed profile together, so that my team can work on

the details with the venue you decide on. Pastries and coffee on the house.'

Dee squeezed her eyes tightly shut with embarrassment
and mentally kicked the chair.

Sean Beresford had not only made her toss and turn
most of the night, worrying about whether the event was
going to happen, but apparently those blue-grey eyes had
snuck in and robbed her of the one thing that was going
to get her through the next two weeks: the ability to think
straight.

Of course, a breakfast meeting wasn't about bacon butt-
ies and wake-up brews of tea that would stain your teeth.
She knew that. Even if she had never been to one in person.

How did he do it? How did he discombobulate her with
a few words? Make her feel that she was totally out of her
depth in a world that she did not understand?

It was as though he could see through the surface barriers she had built up and see straight through to the awkward teenager in the hot-weather cotton clothes on her first
day in a London high school. In November.

She had known from the first second she had stepped
inside that narrow off-grey school corridor that she was
never going to fit in and that she was going to have to start
her life from scratch all over again. She was always going
to be the outsider. The nobody. The second best. The girl
who had to fight to be taken seriously in anything she did.

But how did Sean see that? Did she have a sign painted
in the air above her head?

This had never happened to her before with any man.
Ever. Normally she just laughed it off and things usually
turned out okay in the end.

Usually.

Dee inhaled a deep breath then exhaled slowly. Very
slowly.

Focus. She needed to focus on what was needed. That was it. Concentrate on the job. Her entire reputation and future in the tea-selling business was dependent on it. She couldn't let a flash boy in a suit distract her, no matter how much she needed him to make her dream become a reality.

Dee looked out of the tea-room window onto the busy high street; the first sign of pale winter sunshine filtered through the half-frosted glass. The sleet had stopped in the night and the forecast was for a much brighter day.

Suddenly the urge to feel fresh air on her face and a cool breeze in her hair spiralled through her brain. She quickly glanced at the wall clock above the counter. It was just after nine. Swallowing down her concerns, Dee raised the phone to her mouth.

'I can be available for a briefing meeting. But pastries and coffee? That's blasphemy. Do I need to bring my own emergency supply of tea?'

'Better than that. Following our meeting, I have set up appointments for you at three Beresford hotels this morning. And they all serve tea.'

Dee caught her breath in the back of her throat. Three hotels? Wow. But then her brain caught up with what he was saying. He had set up appointments for *her*. Not *them*.

Oh no. She was not going to let him get away with that trick.

'Ah no, that won't work. You see, I still don't feel that the Beresford management team is fully committed to fixing the problem they have created. It would be so reassuring if one of the directors of the company would act as my personal guide to each of the three venues. In person. Don't you agree, Sean? Now, where shall I meet you?'

CHAPTER FOUR

*Tea, glorious tea. A celebration of teas from around
the world.*
Do you add the milk to your tea? About two-thirds
of tea drinkers add the milk to the cup before pouring in the hot tea. Apparently this is an old tradition from the early days of tea drinking, when fine
porcelain was being imported from China and the
ladies were terrified the hot tea would crack the very
expensive fragile china.

From *Flynn's Phantasmagoria of Tea*

Wednesday

DEE STEPPED DOWN from the red London bus and darted
under the narrow shelter of the nearest bus stop. The show-
ers that had held off all morning had suddenly appeared
to thwart her. Heavy February rain pounded onto the thin
plastic shelter above her head in rapid fire and bounced
off the pavement of the smart city street in the business
area of London.

Typical! Just when she was determined to make a good
impression on Sean Beresford and prove that she was totally in control and calling the shots.

She peered out between the pedestrians scurrying for

cover until her gaze settled on a very swish glass-plate entrance of an impressive three-storey building directly across the road from her bus stop. The words Beresford Hotel were engraved on a marble portico in large letters.

Well, at least she had found the hotel where Sean had asked her to meet him. Now all she had to do was step inside those pristine glass doors and get past the snooty concierge. Today she was a special guest of the hotel management, so she might be permitted entry.

What nonsense.

She hated that sort of false pretension and snobbery. In India she had met with some of the richest men and women in the land whose ancestors had once ruled a continent. Most of the stunning palaces had been converted into hotels for tourists but they still had class. Real class.

She could handle a few London suits with delusions of grandeur.

Dee took another look and sighed out loud as the rain faded and she could see the exterior more clearly.

This was one part of town she didn't know at all well. Lottie's Cake Shop and Tea Rooms were in smart west London and she rarely went further east than the theatres around Soho and Covent Garden. The financial and banking part of the City of London past St Paul's Cathedral was a mystery to her.

At first sight the outside of the hotel looked so industrial. Metal pipework ran up one side of the wall; the lift was made of glass and looked as though the architects had glued it to the outside of the stone block building.

There was nothing welcoming or friendly about the entrance at all.

Just the opposite, in fact. It was imposing. Cold. Austere. Slippery and grey in the icy rain.

Where was the connection to that warm and commu-

nal spirit that came with the ritual of making tea for people to enjoy?

It was precisely the kind of building she avoided whenever possible. In fact, it gave her the shivers. Or was that
the water dripping down onto her jacket from the back of
the bus shelter?

Dee closed her eyes and, ignoring the two other ladies
waiting at the bus stop, exhaled slowly, bringing her hands
down from her cheeks to her sides in one slow, calm, con-
tinuous motion.

If there was ever a time to be centred, this was it.

This had been her decision. She was the one who had
volunteered to organize the London Festival of Tea. Nobody had forced her to take on all of the admin and co-
ordination that came with pulling together dozens of
exhibitors, tea growers and tea importers looking for any
excuse to show and sell their goods.

But there was one thing that Dee knew for certain.

This was her big chance, and maybe even her only
chance, to launch her own business importing tea in bulk
from the wonderful tea estates that she knew and understood so well, and the passionate people who ran them.

This was her opportunity to show the small world of the
tea trade that Dee Flynn was her father's daughter and had
learnt a thing or two after spending the first fifteen years
of her life travelling the world from tea plantation to tea
plantation. Peter Flynn might have retired from the world
of tea importing, but his little girl was right up there, ready
to take over and make a name for herself as an importer.

Just because her parents had found out the hard way
that there was a big difference between importing tea other
growers had produced and running your own tea plantation, it did not mean to say that she was incapable of running a business.

And she was determined to prove it.

Of course, that had been last summer while she'd been working for a big tea-packaging company. Before Lottie had asked her to help her run the tea rooms in her cake shop. Her life had certainly been a lot simpler then.

But she had done it. No backing out. No giving in. No staying put in a nice, safe job in the back room of the tea importers while her so-called boyfriend Josh took the credit for the work she had done.

Josh had been so kind and attentive that her good nature had stepped in the first time he had struggled over a technical report. He really did not have a clue about the tea and had really appreciated her help. For a few months Dee had actually believed that they could have a future together, and the sex had been amazing.

Pity that it had turned out that Josh was waiting for his real girlfriend to come back from her gap year travelling in nice four-star hotels. Walking in on the two of them in bed last August had not been her finest moment.

Past history. Done and dusted. No going back now. And good luck to them both. They were going to need it.

Dee blinked her eyes open and smiled across the street as the rain shower drifted away and she could see patches of blue in the sky above the hotel roof.

Idiot! She was overreacting.

As usual.

This was probably where Sean had his office. There was no way that he could offer her a conference room in a hotel this swanky. This was a five-star hotel for bankers and stockbrokers, not rough and ready tea growers and importers who were likely to drop wet tealeaves on the no-doubt pristine hand-woven carpet.

She was just been silly and she was exhausted from the worry.

Time to find out just what Sean had come up with.

With a quick laugh, Dee shook the rain from the sleeves of her jacket and dashed out onto the pavement in a lull in the traffic as the lights turned to red and the queue of people at the crossing ran across the busy road.

In an instant she was with them, her boots hitting the puddles and taking the splashes, but she made it.

Taking a breath, Dee lifted her chin, chest out, and rolled back her shoulders as she stepped up to the hotel entrance. For the next few hours she would be D S Flynn, tea importer, not Dee from the cake shop.

Stand back and hear me roar.

She flashed a smile at the doorman, who held the heavy glass door open for her, but the frosty look he gave her almost sent her scurrying back outside, where it would be warmer.

With one bound she was inside the impressive building. Shaking off the rain, she looked up and froze, rocking back on her heels, trying to take in what she was looking at.

White marble flooring. Black marble pillars. Tall white orchids in white ceramic bowls shaped like something from a hospital ward. And, in the centre of the reception area, a large sculpture fabricated from steel wire and white plastic hoops hung from the ceiling like an enormous deformed stalactite.

Well, that was one spot she wouldn't be walking under. If that monstrosity fell on her head, the tea festival would be the least of her problems.

Ha. So the interior *did* match the outside.

The only warmth in this room was the hot air blasting out from vents high in the walls.

Dee gazed around the reception area, from the black leather sofas in the corner to the curved white polymer reception desk.

There was no sign of Sean, but she was five minutes early.

Dee started to stroll over to the reception desk but changed her mind. The rail-thin receptionist with the stretched-back, shiny, straight ponytail and plain black fitted suit was collecting something from a large printer on the other side of the desk and probably had not even noticed her coming in.

It might be more interesting to watch Sean work from this side of the desk. As a hotel guest. People-watching was one of her favourite pastimes. And free!

Dee strode over to a black high-back chair and slid as gracefully as she could onto the narrow seat. The stainless-steel legs were about the same thickness as the heels on some of Lottie's designer shoes and she didn't entirely trust the chair to take her weight.

Comfort had clearly not been one of the design specifications for this place.

She stroked the skirt of her cotton dress down over her warm leggings and neatly clasped her hands in her lap.

A butterfly feeling of nerves fluttered across her stomach and into her throat as the heat from the vents started to blow on her shoulders.

Memories of sitting on a hard bench at a railway station at a tiny Indian stop waiting for her parents to come and collect her flitted through her brain. Those had been the days before mobile phones, and her parents would not have used one even if they could, so all she'd been able to do was sit there and wait with her luggage and presents. And wait, worrying that something had happened to them, alone in the heat and crush of the ladies' waiting room, for long hour after hour before the kindly station master had offered to phone the tea estate for her.

It turned out that her dad had been working on a problem with one of the shipping agents and had forgotten that she was flying back from London to spend Christmas with them and that they had agreed that she should take the train to the nearest station that day.

Work had always come first.

Even for those who loved her best in this world.

It had been two years since she had last seen them. She couldn't afford the air fare when she needed every penny for the tea rooms and they certainly couldn't spare any cash to fly back to see her now they were retired.

But it would have been fun to have them here for the tea festival at a Beresford hotel of all places. They would have found this all very grand, and probably have been a bit intimidated, but she had promised to send them photos of the event and write a long letter telling them how it had gone.

And they certainly would have been impressed with Sean Beresford. Now, there was a man with a good work ethic! Her dad would like that.

With those good looks and all the money he wanted, Sean would have pre-booked dinner-and-drinks dates already scheduled into his electronic diary to share with his no-doubt lovely girlfriend.

In fact that might be her now, at the reception desk. All polished and groomed; pretty and eloquent. A perfect choice for the second in line to the Beresford hotel fortune.

Sean would probably be astonished that Dee had taken the trouble to look him up on the Internet. For research purposes, of course.

It was amazing the amount of celebrity gossip his father Tom and brother Rob featured in, but Sean? Sean was mostly photographed shaking hands with some official or other at the opening ceremony of the newest Beresford hotel.

Perhaps he did have some hidden talents.

Dee shuffled out of her padded jacket and picked up a brochure about the hotel spa treatments. She was just considering having hot rocks placed on certain parts of a girl's body which were not supposed to have hot rocks on them when there was a blast of cool air from the front entrance and she shivered in her thin dress as she turned to see who had let the cold in.

It was Sean.

Only not the Sean who had sat on her floor the previous evening. This version of Sean was a different kind of man completely.

He stood just inside the entrance shaking the water droplets from a long, navy waterproof raincoat—a different one from last night, but just as elegant. She could tell because the smiling doorman was helping his boss out of his damp coat and she caught a glimpse of a pale-blue silk lining with a dark-blue tartan stripe. Very stylish. Classy. Smart. A perfect match for the man who wore it.

Sean's face was glowing from the cold wind and rain and he ruffled his hair back with his right hand like a male fashion model on a photo-shoot. The master of the ship. Lord of all he surveyed.

He looked taller somehow. More in control. Last night he had invaded the tea rooms and entered a foreign territory with strange new customs and practices. But here and now the difference shone out. This was his space. His world. His domain. Confidence and authority seemed to emanate out from him like some magical force-field.

No wonder the doorman was happy to take his coat; there was absolutely no mistaking that he was the boss.

She envied him that confidence and physical presence that came from a wealthy family background and the education to match. He had probably never known what it was like to be ignored and sidelined and made to feel second rate. It was as if they were from different worlds.

Sean rolled back his shoulders, picked up his briefcase and strode out towards the reception desk. And as he turned away Dee sucked in the breath that had been frozen in her lungs.

The fine navy cloth of his superbly cut business suit defined the line of his broad shoulders. From the way his legs moved inside those trousers, she wouldn't be in the least bit surprised if Sean made regular use of the gym facilities she had just been reading about in the hotel magazine.

That confident stride matched his voice: rich, confident and so very self-assured of his identity. He knew who he was and liked it.

This version of Sean could have graced the cover of any business magazine. He was the personification of a city boy. A man used to being in authority and calling the shots.

The second son and heir.

A man who would never know what it felt like to have to cash in his pension fund and savings to pay the staff wages.

A lump formed in Dee's throat and she turned her gaze onto what passed for the floral display on the coffee table.

Her sweet, kind father had been too soft-hearted to cut the wages for the estate workers when it had become obvious that his dream tea plantation on Sri Lanka was not able to pay for itself. Those wages paid for health care and made it possible for the workers' children to go to school. How could he take that away from them? How could he be responsible for ruining so many people's lives? But, even when they were selling their possessions, her parents had kept reassuring her that she shouldn't worry, they would get their savings back. It would all work out for the best in the end.

Dee exhaled very, very slowly and focused on the pattern of the marble floor tiles beneath her boots.

Past history.

And it was not—*not*—going to happen to her.

History was not going to repeat itself.

She was not going to lose her tea shop or let her dream slip away. With her contacts and experience, she had the technical ability to go right to the top. Now all she had to do was make it happen. No matter how scared she was.

She had worked so hard to get to this point, she could not afford to let her foolish pride get in the way.

Even if it meant asking for help now and then.

A rustle of activity across the room broke the hushed silence of the reception area and she looked up just as Sean turned away from the desk and saw her.

There must have been something about her that amused him, because she felt those blue eyes scan her entire body in a flash, from the toes of her practical red boots to the top of her head, before they slid down to her face. His gaze seemed to lock onto hers and stay there, unmoving, as though he was trying to decide about something.

Whatever it was, the corner of his mouth slid into a lazy smile which reached his eyes as they locked with hers and held them tight.

The heat of that smile warmed the air between them faster than the hot-air vent behind her legs.

The few hotel guests and staff milling around disappeared and all Dee could see was the handsome man in a suit and tie standing at the reception desk.

It was as though they were the only people in the room.

Dee had often wondered what it would feel like to be the star of the show and the centre of attention. To have people adore you and admire you because you are so very special.

Well, now she knew.

It felt…wonderful.

Instead of squirming away into a corner out of embarrassment, she stretched her head high and stared right back at Sean.

Her blood was thumping in her veins, filling every cell of her body with confidence and life.

And something else. Because, the longer he smiled at her, the more she recognized that tell-tale glint of animal attraction in his eyes. Attraction which had nothing to do with the suit and everything to do with the man wearing it.

Elemental. Raw. Alive.

A look that was flicking switches she had locked down into an off position ever since she'd found Josh in bed with a pretty blonde and decided to focus on her career plans and put herself first for once.

How did he do that? How did he make her want to flick her hair, run out to the nearest department store and buy the entire lingerie department and latest beauty products?

Was there an executive training course for that? Or did it come naturally?

One thing was for certain: this hotel was looking better by the minute.

Sean could not resist smiling as he crossed the floor to where Dee was sitting. She was sitting looking up at him with a look of total innocence and sweet charm. As though she had not planned her outfit today with one single purpose in mind: to knock any chance of sensible thought out of his brain.

A printed floral dress above grey leggings which seemed to have tiny hearts embroidered on them. And her hair? Short, cropped into a pixie style. Textured into a mass of tight brunette curls which any man within a thousand feet would want to run his fingers through and tousle up a bit.

But it was her eyes that captivated him.

Who was he kidding? Those pale-green eyes reached out, grabbed him by the man-parts and tugged him to her with a steel cable that just got tighter and tighter the closer he came.

After Sasha he had set his female-resistance setting on high. But there was something about Dee that was simply irresistible.

She looked like a bright spring flower against the monochrome hotel design scheme. And just as fragile. Slender and small. A greenhouse blossom which could be knocked over in the slightest cold breeze.

No way. This tiny girl was the one who had stopped him falling flat on his face last night. Then had beaten him up verbally.

'Fragile' was not how he would describe her.

Interesting was more like it. Intriguing. Enchanting.

Who was she? Apart from a tea fanatic?

'Good morning, Miss Flynn.' He smiled and stepped forward and held out his hand. 'I am so sorry to have kept you waiting.'

'Actually, I was early,' she replied and her long slender fingers wrapped around his with a firm positive grip before sliding away. 'Couldn't wait to hear what you have lined up for me.'

Completely inappropriate images of what those fingers would feel like on other parts of his body flicked like a video show through Sean's mind and he gave a low cough and took a tighter hold of his briefcase.

He pointed the flat of his right hand towards the office suite. 'I have booked one of the breakout rooms. Shall we?'

'Breakout rooms?' Dee laughed as she got to her feet

and flung her coat over one arm. 'That sounds ominous. Is that where your hotel guests organize the escape committee?'

'Just the conference delegates.' Sean smiled. 'And only when they have had enough of the speakers. Most of the business meetings we hold here need separate rooms where they can hold workshops and seminars away from the main group. It works well.'

'Workshops,' Dee repeated and followed him down a wide corridor fitted with an oatmeal carpet. 'Right. I don't think that I shall be needing any of those.'

'Understood.' Sean nodded and held open the white polymer door to the only small meeting room that was available for the next hour on a busy week day. 'After you.'

Her reply was a quick nod as he stood back, waited for her to step inside, then turned and followed her in.

Only Dee could not have taken more than two steps into the room when she whirled around to face him so quickly that he had to lean back slightly to stop her from swinging her bag into his chest.

Her eyes were wild, flashing green and he could see her breathing fast and light, the pulse throbbing in her neck.

They were so close that he could have reached out and touched her face, or fastened up the top button on her cotton dress which was gaping open slightly as it stretched taut from her coat and bag, revealing that same creamy, clear skin that he had seen last night when she'd worn the one-strap jumper.

'Is something wrong?' Sean asked and looked over her shoulder at the perfectly orderly and clean meeting room with its cluster of tables and chairs.

Dee took one step closer and pressed both hands against the front of his shirt. He inhaled a heady mix of bakery sweetness and spice blended with a spicy floral perfume with a touch of musk which surprised him by being so girly. Sweet. Aromatic. Personal.

She smelt wonderful, but when she lifted her head to reply her gaze darted from side to side with alarm and there was just enough of a quiver in her voice for his every nerve to stand to attention.

'There are no windows in this room. Not one. I can't stay here. No way. No how. No discussion. Borderline claustrophobia. Had it for years. Nothing I can do.'

Then she shuddered and his hands automatically reached out and rested on her hips to steady her, hold her, warm her and sooth away whatever problem was causing her such clear distress.

'Sean, I am really sorry, but I hate this hotel. Do you have another one? Because I have to get out of here. Right now.'

CHAPTER FIVE

Tea, glorious tea. A celebration of teas from around the world.
On a cold winter's day? A piping-hot infusion of ginger and lemon will do the trick. Fruit and flower combinations are brilliant at lifting the spirits.

From *Flynn's Phantasmagoria of Tea*

Wednesday

SEAN ALMOST HAD to snatch his raincoat from the hotel doorman before dashing out onto the pavement. But it was worth it, because Dee was still waiting to cross the busy road, her attention focused on shrugging into her duvet jacket, her bag clenched tight between her knees.

'Dee. Wait a moment. What about our meeting?'

Her head swivelled back towards him and she looked from side to side for a moment before she realized who was calling out. Instantly her shoulders seemed to slump and she fastened up her jacket and slung her bag over one shoulder.

'Meeting? Can we do it over the phone? I really don't want to go back inside.'

She shrugged her shoulder bag higher and sighed out

loud. 'I think that I've embarrassed myself enough for one morning. Don't you?'

Then she pulled a dark-green and gold knitted cap out of her jacket pocket and pulled it down over her pixie cut. 'Right now I am far more interested in finding the nearest piece of park, grass, garden, anything in fact, that will make me forget the white holding cell that I have just been in. Okay?'

Then she noticed the crossing light had turned green and she turned on the heels of her ankle boots and strode forward, her cotton dress swinging from side to side above the grey-patterned leggings.

Her outfit was the perfect match for her personality: stylish, modern and surprisingly sexy. Just like the woman wearing them. The ankle boots were just short enough to display a finely turned ankle and toned calf muscles.

And just like that his libido switched up another level.

What had he told Rob? That he had missed his two weeks in the sun? Well, maybe he could find some of that life and colour right here in London in the shape of Dee Flynn.

He rarely met women outside work, and never dated guests or his employees, so his social life had been pretty static ever since the disaster with Sasha.

But there was something about this girl that screamed out that her open, friendly manner was real. Genuine. And totally, totally original. Which in his world was a first.

She knew exactly who she was and she knew what she wanted. Yet she was prepared to tell him that she had a problem with closed, windowless spaces and she had to change the rules to deal with it.

Sexy and confident inside her own skin.

And she was totally unaware of how rare a thing that was, especially in the hotel business, where most people had hidden agendas. Her goal was simple: she had placed her trust in the hotel and they had let her down. And she needed him to put that right. Because it was personal. Very personal.

Was that why he had taken time out today to meet her when his conference team were perfectly capable of finding a replacement venue in one of the other Beresford hotels in this city?

She marched ahead, then stopped and looked up at the street names high on the wall of the buildings on either side, hesitant and unsure.

'Looking for somewhere in particular, or will any stretches of grass do?'

Dee whirled around to face him, her eyebrows squeezed together, her hands planted firmly on her hips. 'I have no clue where I am. Seriously. I left my street map back at the shop and was too frazzled to jump on the next bus. I would probably end up even more lost. And shouldn't you be back doing your hotel management thing?'

She waggled her fingers in the direction of the hotel with a dismissive sniff.

'What? And leave my special client lost in a strange part of the city? Tut tut. That would be a terrible dereliction of my duties. Please. Allow me to be your tour guide.'

He closed the gap between them on the narrow pavement outside the smart row of shops and waved his right hand in the air. 'As it happens, I know this area very well even without a map. And you wouldn't want to see me get into trouble with the senior management, would you?'

'Is this all part of the Beresford hotel's five-star service?' She asked with just enough of an uplift in her voice to tell him that she was struggling not to laugh.

'What do you think?' he asked, and was rewarded with

a knowing smile before she squeezed her lips together, a faint blush glowing on her neck.

Her gaze scanned his face, hesitant at first, but the longer she looked at him, the more her features seemed to relax and she lifted her chin before replying in a low, soft voice which to his ears was like the rustle of new leaves in the trees that lined the street. The relentless noise of the buses, taxis and road traffic faded away until all he could focus on was the sound of her words. 'I think I would like to see the river. Do you know how to get there?'

Sean nodded, and soon they were walking side by side along the wide, grey stone pavement that ran along beside the river Thames.

'Okay, what was it that made you hate my hotel so much that we had to dash out into the rain?' Sean asked.

Dee winced. 'Do you really want to know? Because I am famous for being a tad blunt with my opinions when asked questions like that.'

He coughed low in his throat and took a tighter grip on his briefcase. 'I noticed. And, yes, I do want to know.' Then he glanced over at her and gave a small shrug. 'It's my job to keep the guests happy and coming back for more. So fire away; I can take it.'

Dee stopped walking and dropped her head back, eyes closed. Her chest lifted and fell inside her padded jacket a couple of times.

'I'm so glad that the rain stopped. I like rain. Rain is good. Snow too. But cold sleet and grey skies? Not so much.'

Then she opened her eyes and looked up at him. 'What were you like when you were fifteen years old?'

The question rocked Sean a little and he took a second before replying. 'Fifteen? Living in London, going to school then working in the kitchens at my dad's first hotel: loading dishwashers, peeling veg, helping to clean the rooms. My brother and sister did the same. We are a very hands-on family and there was no special treatment for any of us. We had to learn the hotel business from the bottom up. Those were the rules. And why do you want to know that?'

'I was born in north-east India. At a tea plantation where my dad was the general manager. He worked for a big firm of Scottish tea importers who owned most of the tea gardens in that district of Assam. And don't look at me like that. I am simply answering your question the long way round.'

'Are you always so curious about other people's lives?' Sean asked.

'Always, especially when I can see the worry on your face. No doubt you have some terribly important business meeting that you should be attending at this very minute instead of putting up with me. As a matter of interest, how long had you given me in your whizzy electronic diary this morning? Just for future reference?'

Sean lifted both hands in the air and gave a low chuckle. 'A whole fifty minutes. So we are still on the clock. Please, carry on. Your delightful childhood in sunny India. That must have been very special.'

She grinned, shook her head, then carried on walking. 'You have no idea. Both of my parents were working estate managers so I was left with my nanny and the other kids to run feral across a huge farm most of the time outside school. It was paradise. I only went down with serious diseases twice and grew up speaking more of the many local languages than English. I loved it.'

'When did you leave?'

'We moved four times to different estates in fifteen years and that was tough. But they all had the same problems and my dad had a remarkable talent for turning the businesses around. He seemed to have a knack for dealing with people and helping them with what they needed. Mostly better education for their children and health care.' Then her voice faded away and she looked out over the wide, grey river in a daze. 'They respected him for that. I'm sure of it.'

'Did you come back to England for your education?' Sean asked and stepped closer to avoid a couple of joggers.

Dee stopped and turned back to face him, and her eyebrows squeezed together as she focused on his question. 'Partly. But mainly because the firm promoted my dad to be a tea broker. We came back to London when I was fifteen.' Then she exhaled and blew out hard. 'Total culture shock. I had been here for holidays many times, but living here? Different thing.'

Then she paused and licked her lower lip. 'That was when I realized how much I had taken the outdoor life for granted. Being cooped up in a classroom with only a couple of small windows to let in air and light started to be a real problem, and my schoolwork suffered. I found that the only lessons where I could relax were the cookery and art classes where we were taught in a lovely sunlit studio extension at the back of the school.'

She looked up at him through her eyelashes, which he realized were not black but more of an intense dark brown.

'I was okay there. Big open patio doors. Lots of space. And colour; lots of colour. The gardens were planted out in wonderful displays of flowering shrubs and plants. Tubs and hanging baskets. Planters everywhere.'

Then she pressed her lips together tight. 'In fact, that studio was just about as opposite as you could get to that windowless, airless cube of a white room we have just escaped from.'

She titled her head to one side and blinked. 'Human beings are not supposed to be in spaces like that meeting room of yours. Seriously. What was the designer thinking? Monochrome, hard surfaces. No colour or texture. No living plants. If I was a business person, it would be the last place on the planet where I would want to go to work.'

Then she winced and flashed him a glance. 'Sorry, but you did ask. And I am sure that the bedrooms are very nice and cozy.'

'Actually, they are exactly the same. We market the style as minimalist couture. No pictures on the walls and all-white polymer surfaces and sealed tiling.'

'What about the food?' Dee asked in a low, incredulous voice.

'Micronutrients, hand-harvested seafood and baby organic vegetables. It is very popular with the ladies who lunch.'

'Not the same ladies who come into our tea rooms. Those girls can eat! We are run off our feet keeping up with the demand. But I am starting to get the picture. Oh, Sean! I don't envy you that job. How do you survive? Oh no—I've just had a horrible thought. Wait. Wait just one minute.'

Sean stopped walking and Dee stomped up to him, close enough that she had to look up into his face.

'Please tell me that this other hotel is not the same! I'm not sure that I could stand another minimalist venue. Forget the breakfast meeting. All I want is a replacement venue, Sean.' And she clutched hold of the lapels of his raincoat. 'Somewhere with windows and light and air where people can enjoy tea. Because you have to understand, that's what tea is all about. Having fun and sharing a drink with friends and family. The ceremony and the rituals are optional extras. And you can't do that in a cement basement garage. Please give me some light and space. Is that too much to ask?'

Her bright eyes were shining. Her hands were on his coat, so it made perfect sense for his right hand to rest lightly on her hip.

'As it happens, this hotel is the first one on my list of options. They have a vacancy a week Saturday and can easily fit the numbers you gave on the booking form.'

He flicked his head over his right shoulder. Dee's stunning green eyes widened in surprise and she took a small gasp of astonishment.

'This was the first of the Beresford luxury five-star hotels. Art deco. Original stained glass. Plenty of natural light, and the conference suite opens up onto the lawns leading down to the river. It's also the same place where I cut my teeth as a junior manager so I think I know it pretty well. And not a minimalist detail in sight. In fact, I would go as far as to say it is old school. So. What do you think?'

'Think? I am too stunned to think. Wow. You can officially consider yourself forgiven.'

And, without asking permission or forgiveness, she leant up on the tips of her shoes and tugged his lapels down towards her so that he was powerless to pull back even if he wanted to.

The quick flutter of her warm breath on his cold cheek happened so fast that, when her soft and warm lips pressed against his skin, the fragile sensation of that tender, sweet kiss was like liquid fire burning her brand onto his skin and in a direct line to his heart.

To Dee it was probably nothing more than a quick, friendly peck on the cheek but when Sean looked into those smiling green eyes he saw his world reflected back at him.

He should have looked away. Made a joke, stepped back and pointed out some of the famous London landmarks that were on the other side of the Thames. But for the first time since Sasha the only thing Sean was interested in was the warm glow and welcome that a pair of captivating green eyes held out to him.

Tantalizing. Alluring. He was held tight in their grasp and that suited him just fine. Forget the cold wind. Forget that they were on a public footpath. Forget that she was a client.

All that he could think about was the red glow on her cheeks, and when she tilted her face to one side the first real smile of the day creased the corners of her mouth and lingered there for a moment before reaching her eyes.

Sean lifted his hand and popped a stray strand of hair back under her knitted hat with one finger. He made sure that the knuckles of that hand traced a feather-light track along cheekbones which were so defined and yet so soft that his skin ached to do it again to make sure that he had not mistaken the sensation.

Instantly her head lifted just a little and those eyes recognized a shift in the electricity in the air between them. It had that same power as the energy bolt he had felt when he first saw her in the hotel, but here it was magnified a hundred times.

It seemed only natural to drop his briefcase to the floor, slip both hands behind the back of Dee's head and cradle her skull. When he bent down and pressed his cheek against her temple, he could feel her breath on his skin, and each breath he took was warmed by the scent of the woman he was holding so close to his chest.

His mouth slid slowly down to her lips, making her take a sharp gasp that told him everything he needed to know.

This was a woman designed for pleasure, and given the chance he wanted to be the one to show her just how good that pleasure could be.

Shame that two cyclists just happened to be speed-racing past them at that very second, laughing loudly, followed by a woman on a mobile phone with a tiny yapping dog on a lead.

Perhaps this was not the place. Dee certainly thought so; she let him go so quickly that he almost overbalanced but held it together by keeping a tighter grip on her waist.

Dee grinned back at him, and suddenly it was as if the sunlight in the break in the clouds above their heads was focused on the genuine warmth of her delight. The grey was gone, replaced by an infectious smile which seemed to reach down inside his very being and twist by several hitches that steel wire of attraction that bound them together.

Irrepressible, fun, real. His sunshine on a grey day.

This was what he wanted. This was what he needed in his life.

This was probably why he stepped back, slid his hand from her hip and held his elbow out towards her.

'May I have the pleasure of being your personal hotel guide on this fine February morning, Miss Flynn?'

Dee looked at his elbow, eyebrows high, as though she was getting ready to give him her very best snarky remark, then flashed him a blushing half-smile.

'Well, if you can stand the scurrilous gossip this will create, I may be prepared to risk it,' she replied and threaded her hand through the crook of his elbow. 'Although, there is something you should know.'

'You have a jealous boyfriend at home who is going to track me down and sort me out if I make a move?' Sean chuckled as they strolled up the path away from the river, Dee leaning slightly into his shoulder because of the height difference.

'Hah! Very amusing. Not a bit. No boyfriend, jealous or

otherwise. I am working on my master plan to take over the tea trade one festival at a time. No time for boyfriends; hell, no. They are far too distracting to a lady entrepreneur like myself.'

'Of course. I completely understand. Today Lottie's Cake Shop and Tea Rooms, tomorrow the world. I can see it now. And a great idea for a franchise.'

'I know. But the tea shop is only one of my many talents.' Dee coughed dismissively. 'I was quite serious this morning when I answered the shop phone. The tea-import business is at the very early stages and I am taking my time to think about the name of the company and how to brand myself. So important, don't you agree?'

Sean opened his mouth to answer then looked down at this girl who was capable of rendering him silent.

Then he looked at her again in silence before replying. She was serious. Totally, totally serious.

And his interest in her just ramped up another notch.

'I do agree. The right name and brand are crucial for creating the perfect image for your company. It has to be unique, creative but easy to recall. Not easy. Which is why there are a lot of companies making serious money working for clients who have exactly that problem.'

His reward was a short nod. 'I had a feeling that you would appreciate my business sense, which is why I plan to launch my new company at the tea festival. That way I get the perfect feedback direct from the experts in the trade. It's an ideal opportunity.'

Then she looked up at him with a sly glance.

'Ah. So this is not just about the tea. Now I understand; you are taking a chance. That's quite something. Brave.'

'Daft more like,' she replied and flashed him a light, quizzical glance though her eyelashes. 'As a matter of interest… Were you…planning to make a move? Just curious.'

'Might be. Miss Curious.'

'Not Miss Anything. The name is Dee, but my friends call me Dee.'

Then she bumped her head against his side. 'Dee.'

Sean slid his hand down his side and clasped hold of her fingers. 'My friends call me Sean. Conventional, but I like it.'

'Sean,' she whispered and the sound was carried away in the breeze like the sound of the wind in the trees. 'I like it too.'

He grinned and took a tighter hold of her fingers. 'Let me show you my hotel. Somehow, I think it might be a perfect match. Ready to find out?'

'Prakash! What on earth are you doing here?'

A slim, elegantly dressed man with a Beresford hotel name-pin on his lapel and a lively open smile turned towards them in the foyer of the stunning hotel. But he did not have a chance to reply because Dee squealed and practically pounced on him, pressing her chest against his suit before pecking his cheek.

Then she stood back and covered her mouth with her hand.

'Oh no, you're working here. Sorry, Prakash. Especially since your boss is right here with me. Do you know Sean?'

Sean stepped forward and in an instant scanned the employee name-badge and mentally made the connections.

'Prakash.' He nodded. 'Of course.' They exchanged a hearty handshake. 'Haven't you just graduated from the management academy? I know my father was very impressed with the whole team.'

'Thank you, Mr Beresford. It was tough but I learnt a huge amount.'

'But what are you doing here?' Dee pressed, looking into her friend's startled face as she grabbed his arm. 'Last time I saw you was when we graduated from catering college and you were all set to run your parents' chain of family restaurants.'

Ah. So they'd been at catering college together. That would explain why Prakash Mohna was looking shell-shocked. He was probably terrified that Dee was going to start sharing some scandalous student prank that they had got up to.

As though a hidden sensor in the back of Dee's head had detected that Sean was thinking of her, when she turned his way her face twisted into an expression that screamed out: *go on, say something snarky about students.*

'Actually, I am the new conference manager. Started yesterday,' Prakash blustered.

'Conference manager.' Dee laughed and thumped him on the shoulder. 'That's brilliant news. Because I, Miss Dee Flynn of Flynn's Phantasmagorian Tea Emporium, need a conference room. In a hurry. Sean here—' she flicked her head over her shoulder in his direction '—found out that I had been double-booked at another Beresford hotel. And several hundred tea lovers are going to descend on London looking for a tea festival a week on Saturday. Do you think that you can help me out? Because otherwise we'll be setting up the stall in this gorgeous foyer.'

Her college friend flashed Sean a look of sheer panic before licking his lips and waving down a hallway. 'Why don't we check the booking system and find out?'

'Is it computerized?' Dee winced.

'Well, yes, but we also have the printed booking sheet as back-up,' Prakash replied, obviously confused, then he nodded. 'Don't tell me that you are still a complete technophobe? Dee!'

She held up both hands in protest. 'Not a bit. I have a laptop. Lottie has set it up for me and I run my world-class tea empire from the comforts of my own home. Progress has been made.'

Then she turned and opened her mouth to say something with that glint in her eye which told Sean that she couldn't resist giving him a sly dig, but Sean saw it coming and cut it off.

'Human error caused the double booking at Richmond Square, so we are going to have to convince Dee that our systems can handle it.'

Sean looked up at Prakash who had pressed a finger to his lips as though he was finding the fact that his boss and his pal from catering college were on first-name terms very amusing.

'I checked the system this morning, Prakash, and we had a cancellation which might fit the bill. Why don't I leave you to look after Dee and sort out the details while I take care of some other business? I'll be just over here if you need me.'

Sean looked up from the reception desk as Dee's laughter echoed out across the marble foyer. She was strolling out of the main conference room with her arm looped around Prakash's elbow.

Right now Prakash seemed to be doing a fine job of charming their latest client and keeping her entertained.

Strange that every time he looked up Dee just happened to glance in his direction and then instantly turn away. With just enough of a blush on the back of her neck to tell him she was only too aware that they were sharing the same breathing space.

Sean paused. For a moment there he thought… Yes, he was right. They were chatting away in what sounded like Hindi.

Of course. She had grown up in India. Nevertheless, it was still impressive.

Dee Flynn was certainly an unusual girl. In more ways than one.

He had made a mistake when he'd walked into the cake shop last night and taken her for a baker or shop assistant.

This girl was a self-employed tea entrepreneur who was organizing what sounded like a very impressive festival on her own.

That took some doing.

She couldn't be a lot older than his half-sister Annika, who had grown into a lovely and talented photo-journalist. But when it came to organisation? Not one of her strengths, and Annika was happy to admit that, even to him.

Even their father had been impressed with how the shy little blonde girl had blossomed into a lovely teenager and confident, beautiful woman with straight As, and a first-class honours degree from a famous university under her belt.

It was an education designed to open doors. And it had.

He loved Annika and was the first to admit that she had achieved her success by working as hard as he had to make it happen. Yet he did wonder sometimes how things would have turned out for them all if their father had not been there to pay for the private education, with a solid back-up plan and financial edge to give them the support they needed.

Things might have been different for all of them if his father had not insisted that all of his children should grow up together: same school, same house most weekends and holidays.

Three children with three different mothers living in the same house had not always been easy—especially for his stepmother—and they had fought and bickered and had vicious pillow fights just like any other children. But Tom Beresford had forged them into a family and he had done it through love and making sure that each one of them knew that he would always be there for them. The one constant in each of the children's lives.

For that, he was prepared to forgive his dad's woman-ising ways. Rob never stopped teasing him that his little brother was letting the side down by staying faithful to every one of the lovely women who had agreed to put up with a light and fun relationship with him while it lasted.

Sean Beresford did not do long-term commitment. He had seen first-hand the fallout from that kind of life when you were working twenty-four-seven, and he was deter-mined to learn from his father's mistakes.

But to succeed on your own? With parents who worked overseas? That took a different skill set.

Dee was definitely a one-off.

Suddenly aware that he had been totally focused on Prakash and Dee, Sean bent his head over the conference-centre booking system and one thing was only too obvi-ous: Prakash was not going to be very busy for the next few weeks. Far from it. Compared to the previous year, bookings over the winter had fallen by over forty per cent and were only picking up now for spring weddings and business meetings. Summer was busy most weeks but the autumn was a disaster.

Something was badly wrong here. The recession had hit some London businesses more than others, and large conferences were a luxury many companies could no lon-ger afford. Events booked a year in advance were regu-larly being cancelled.

Sean stretched up and ran his fingers along the back of his neck, anxious not to make a fool of himself. But the girl in the flowery cotton dress and leggings distracted him by strolling across through to the other room, totally confident and completely at ease, with Prakash and his assistant making notes as they walked.

Their half-whispered words tickled the back of his neck and Sean yearned to drop everything and join in the conversation instead of focusing on the work.

Well, at least they would have one happy customer.

The conference centre at this luxury hotel was in a different league from the facilities at Beresford Richmond Square, which was designed for large seminar groups. Most of the time companies booked the whole hotel for the event and organized special catering and personalized planning.

That did not happen too often in a hotel this size… Maybe that was something he could look at?

Sean quickly checked the hotel brochure. Conference delegates could have a ten per cent discount if they stayed here. At Richmond Square it was fifty per cent. And he already knew that this hotel was never fully booked. Ever.

Perhaps he should be thanking Dee for giving him an idea.

He looked up as the door to one of the ground-floor meeting rooms opened and a stream of hotel guests walked past him towards the sumptuous buffet he had already spotted being laid out.

Slipping in right behind them, Dee smiled back at him over one shoulder and waltzed into the dining room with Prakash leaving Sean to stare after her. And the way her dress lifted in the air conditioning as her hips swayed as she walked.

Suddenly light-headed, Sean blinked. Food. Now, that was an idea.

Sean stood in silence as the chatting, smiling strangers filled the space his newest client had left in her wake, and watched as Dee looked over her shoulder with a wry smile, shrugged her shoulders, then turned to laugh at something Prakash said, before they were swallowed up by the businessmen who were clearly desperate for brunch after a hard morning.

The last thing he saw was the slight tilt of her head and a flash of floral cotton as she sashayed elegantly away from him. Every movement of every muscle in her body was magnified, as though a searchlight was picking her out in the crowd for him alone.

This was a girl whom he had only met in person for the first time yesterday.

Strange that he was even now reliving the moment when her body had been pressed against his arm.

Strange how he was still standing in the same spot five minutes later, watching the space where she had last stood. Waiting. Just in case he could catch a glimpse of her again.

The prettiest woman in the room.

And a very, very tantalising distraction.

Sean breathed out slowly through his nose and turned away.

Before Sasha, the old Sean would have already flown in his lady and made dinner reservations, or drinks that would stretch out into the evening with a long, slow languorous seduction as a nightcap.

But now? Now long-term relationships were for men who stayed longer in one place than a few days or weeks at most. Men who were willing to commit fully to one woman and mean it.

His gaze flicked up to the place where Dee had just been and lingered there longer than it should have.

They were different people in so many ways, yet there was something about Dee that made him want to know her better. A lot better.

He would love to have the luxury of being able to take personal time in London, but that was impossible if he wanted to get his job done before leaving for Paris. Even if that temptation came in the shape of a tea-mad beauty who was different from any other girl that he had met for a long time.

A cluster of older men in suits burst into the reception area, blasting away his idle thoughts in a powerful rush of financial chatter and cold air.

Sean gave a low cough and straightened his back as he nodded to the guests.

Nothing had changed. The work had to come first.

He owed it to his father and the family who were relying on him to get things back on track. There was no way that he could let them down. Not now. Not ever.

Not after all that his father had done for him. For all of them.

Sean looked up at the screensaver on the computer: *The Beresford Riverside. A Beresford Family Hotel.*

There it was. The Beresford family. His rock when things had collapsed around him when his mother had been taken ill. His rock when his father had remarried but kept the children together, making sure that they all felt loved and cherished.

His family was all he had. And he was not going to let them down.

Dee was a lovely girl and a new client. He had been friendly and gone beyond the call of duty. The last thing either of them needed was a long-distance relationship which was bound to end in heartbreak and tears—at both ends of the telephone. From now on he had to keep his guard.

His family had to come first.

It was time to get back to work.

CHAPTER SIX

Tea, glorious tea. A celebration of teas from around the world.
You can't have a cup of tea without something to go with it: from tiny fairy cakes and English cucumber-and-salmon sandwiches to seafood accompanied by warm green tea in Japan. Tea and food are perfect partners.

From *Flynn's Phantasmagoria of Tea*

Wednesday

DEE GAVE PRAKASH a quick finger-wave and then stood on tiptoe and peered over the top of the frosted glass barrier which separated guests from hotel staff.

Sean was sitting in exactly the same position as she had left him well over an hour ago. A plate with the remains of a sandwich sat next to his keyboard, an empty coffee cup on the other.

'You missed a great meal,' she said, but Sean's focus did not waver from the computer monitor. 'In fact, I am officially impressed. So much so, that I have just come to a momentous decision.'

He flashed her a quick glance, eyebrows high. And

those blue eyes seemed backlit with cobalt and silver. Jewel-bright.

'Okay, Mr B. You win,' Dee whispered in a high musical voice. 'You have pulled out the big guns and wowed me with the most fantastic hotel that I have ever stepped into in my entire life. And the conference suite is light, airy and opens out onto the gorgeous grounds. I am powerless to resist.'

Dee lifted her head and pushed out her chest so that she could make the formal pronouncement with the maximum splendour. 'I accept your offer. The Beresford Riverside *is* going to be the new home of the annual London Tea Festival. Congratulations.'

Then she chuckled and gave a little shoulder dance. 'It is actually happening. I can't wait. Can*not* wait. Just can't. Because this festival is going to be so mega, and everyone is going to have the best time.' Then she clasped her fingers around the top of the barrier and dropped her chin onto the back of her hands so that Sean's desk was practically illuminated by the power of her beaming grin.

Sean replied by sitting back in his swivel chair and peering at her with one side of his mouth twisted up into a smirk. 'Let me guess—Prakash introduced you to the famous Beresford dessert buffet in the atrium restaurant.'

'He did.' Dee grinned then blinked. 'And it is spectacular. But how did you know that?'

He shook his head then pointed the flat of his hand towards her and pulled the trigger with his thumb before sliding forwards again. 'The last time I saw someone so high on sugar and artificial colours was at my sister Annika's fourth birthday party. And I know that you don't drink coffee, so it can't be a caffeine rush. How many of the desserts did you sample?'

Dee pushed out her lower lip. 'It seemed rude not to

have a morsel of all of them. And they are so good. Lottie would be in heaven here. In fact, I might insist that she comes back with me and tries them all for research purposes.'

'Better give me some warning in advance so I can tell the dessert chef to work some overtime,' Sean muttered.

Then he stood up and stretched out his hand over the top of the glass. 'Welcome to the Beresford Riverside, Miss Flynn. We are delighted to have your custom.'

Dee took Sean's hand and gave it a single, firm shake. 'Mega.' She smiled and clutched onto the edge of the conference brochure tight with both hands. 'Righty. Now the room is sorted, we can get started on the rest of the organization.'

'Don't worry about that,' Sean replied and walked around to her side of the barrier. He reached into the breast pocket of his suit jacket, pulled out a business card and held it out towards her. 'Prakash will make sure that you have a great event. I wish you the very best of luck, Dee. If there is anything else you need, please get in touch.'

Dee glanced at the business card, then up into Sean's face, then back at the card.

And just like that, the joyous emotional rush of finding this fabulous venue and knowing that her fears had been unfounded was swept away in one spectacular avalanche that left her bereft and mourning the loss.

This was it.

She was being dismissed. Passed off. Discarded.

So that was how it worked? She'd been given the personal attention and star treatment by one of the Beresford family for just as long as it took to get her booking sorted out. Then she was back in line with all of the other hotel guests. Business as usual. Fuss and bother all sorted out.

She was being discarded as not important enough to invest any more time on.

Just as her parents had been.

She had been forced to stand back and watch her parents lose their tea gardens when the money had run out and the powers that be had refused to wait until the tea could be harvested and sold before pulling the plug.

A one-family tea-growing business had not been a priority customer. Not worth their time. Not worth their money. Not worth spending time to get to know who they were and how they had invested everything they had in that tea garden.

She had been a teenager back then and struggling to cope with the relentless exhaustion of training in a professional kitchen after she'd left catering college, powerless to do anything to help the people she loved most.

Her parents had come through it. They had survived. But their dreams had been shattered and scattered to the winds.

Well, history was definitely not going to repeat itself when it came to her life.

Nope. Not going to happen. Not when she was around.

What made it even worse was that it was Sean who was giving her the big brush-off. What had happened to the man who'd been happy to give her a cuddle only a few hours ago after listening to her life story? Now that same Sean was only too willing to pass her off onto an underling to deal with, so that he could get rid of her and get back to his real job.

No doubt there was some terribly important business meeting that required his attention and he could not possibly waste any more time with the simple matter of a conference booking.

It was such a shame. Because, standing there in his fitted suit, pristine shirt and those cheekbones—lord, those cheekbones—he looked delicious enough to eat with a spoon and a dollop of ice-cream on the side.

Shame or no shame, she recognized the signs only too well. And if he thought for one second that he could get rid of her that easily, he was badly mistaken.

'Oh no,' Dee said in a loud voice which echoed around the reception area, making several of the men in suits glance in their direction. 'Big misunderstanding. I obviously have not made myself clear. No business card; I am not going down that route.'

Then she tilted her head slightly to one side and shrugged before carrying on in a low, more intimate voice, confident that she now had his full attention.

'You screwed up. Big time. So now I have to reprint all of my promotional materials and contact loads of exhibitors to let them know about the new venue. Posters, flyers, postcards to tea merchants and tea fanatics. All have to be done again. Then I have to go back to all of the tea shops and online tea clubs with the new details with only a week or so to go. That's a lot of work to get through, and I have a full-time job at Lottie's.'

She pressed her lips together and shook her head. 'Prakash is a pal, but he does not have the level of authority to spend the cash and resources to make all of those things happen and happen fast. It seems to me to point one way. I am going to need that five-star Beresford service from the man at the top.'

Dee fluttered her eyelashes at his shocked face and there was a certain glint in those blue eyes that was definitely more grey than azure. 'You are not off the hook yet, Mr B. In fact, I would say that this is only the start of the project. Now, here is an idea. Shall we talk though the next steps on the way back to your office? You must be very excited about this opportunity to demonstrate your commitment to customer service. And there is an added bonus: we will be working together even longer! Now, isn't that exciting?'

Sean shrugged into his coat and double-checked the long string of emails before popping his smart phone into his pocket. Apparently the Beresford hotels around the world did not have anything so urgent that he needed to jump on a plane and take off at a minute's notice. So, no excuse. He glanced back towards the conference centre.

Dee was still talking to the scariest office manager in the company, and from the laughter coming out of her office they were getting on like a house on fire.

It was first time he had ever heard Madge laugh.

Almost six feet tall and built like a professional rugby player, his very well-paid, über-efficient and organized manager terrorised the reception areas on a daily basis, ruthlessly checking every guest bill, and even his brother Rob had been known to hide when he heard that Madge was chasing up his expenses.

This was turning out to be one hell of a day of firsts and it was not over yet.

Of course, he had tried to convince Dee that he was already committed to making her event a success.

Sean had introduced Dee to three of the full-time conference organizers who took care of event management, and both of the office admin ladies who provided the VIP business concierge service. They had demonstrated their fax and photocopying equipment; their digital scanners and super-fast laser colour printers; their spreadsheets and floor plans; their menu cards and delegate stationery.

And Dee had smiled, thanked them for their time, promised each of them free tea samples and refused to budge one inch.

In fact, if anything the list of items she had written out in her spidery handwriting on the conference pad she had snatched from his desk was getting longer and longer by the minute.

Madge would sort it out, he had no doubt about that, and he had already asked her to make it her top priority.

But there was no getting away from the fact that Dee Flynn was not a girl who gave up easily.

Sean chuckled low in his throat and shook his head. He could not help but admire her for having the strength to stand up and demand what she believed he owed her.

Problem was, from everything he had seen so far, she had no intention of making his life any easier. At all.

In any way.

Because, every time he looked up and saw her with Prakash or one of the team, his brain automatically retuned to the sound of her musical voice and the way she jiggled her shoulders when she got excited. Which was often.

And when those mesmerising eyes turned his way?

Knockout.

Of course, Dee was not the only reason he found it difficult to settle at the Riverside.

It was always strange coming back to this hotel where he had found out the hard way that washing frying pans and loading dishwashers in a kitchen that could serve four hundred hot meals was not for wimps.

Rob's fault, of course. From the very moment that his older half-brother Rob had announced that he wanted to follow his passion and learn to cook professionally, their father had insisted that he should learn his trade from the bottom up, starting in the hotel kitchens and going to the local catering college. No free rides. No special favours or dispensations from the award-winning chefs the Beresford hotels employed, who had learnt their trade through the classic apprentice system, working their way through gruelling long hours at kitchens run by serious taskmasters.

If that was what his eldest son and heir truly wanted to do, then their father had said he would support Rob all the way. But he was going to have to prove it in a baptism of fire. And, where Rob had gone, his little brother Sean had wanted to follow.

Somewhere in the London house their father had a photograph of Rob in his kitchen whites, standing at a huge stainless-steel sink sharpening a knife on a steel, with his brother Sean at his side scrubbing out a pan as though his life depended on it. Rob could not have been more than nineteen at the time, but he looked so deadly serious. Skinny, unshaven and intense. There were only a few years between them in age but sometimes it felt a lot more.

They had both come a long way since then. A very long way.

The sound of a woman's laugh rang out from the office and his body automatically turned as Dee and Madge strolled down the corridor together.

Now, there was a killer team. Dee was probably five feet and a few inches tall in her boots, but looked tiny compared to Madge, who towered above her in smart heels.

Amazing. Madge even smiled at him after shaking Dee's hand and waving her off as though they were best pals who had known one another for years.

Dee seemed to accept this sort of miraculous behaviour as completely normal, and a few minutes later she had found her jacket and they were outside the hotel and heading for the taxi rank.

Only, before the doorman could hail a black cab, Dee rested her hand on Sean's coat sleeve and asked, 'Do you mind if we walk? The rain has stopped, the sun is coming

out and I am so busy in the tea rooms I just know that I'll
be cooped up for the rest of the day.'

Sean made a point of checking his wristwatch. 'Only
if we go a different route this time. I make it a rule not to
go the same way twice if I can avoid it.'

'Fair enough,' Dee replied, shuffling deeper into her
jacket. 'And, since you're my tour guide, I shall rely on
you completely.'

'You didn't give me a lot of choice,' he muttered, but
she heard him well enough.

'You can stop pretending that you are put out by my
outrageous request for personal attention. You love it! And
I love your hotel. It is gorgeous. Lucky girl; that's me.'

Sean nodded. 'You were very lucky to find the two-day
slot you wanted at this much notice. That is certainly true.'
He gestured to a side street and they turned away from
the busy street down a two-way road lined with stately
white-painted Regency houses. 'But, as a matter of interest, what was your back-up plan in case of some emergency? Your Plan B?'

Dee chuckled and shook her head. 'I didn't have one.
There is no Plan B. No rescue mission. No back door. No
get-out clause. No security exit.'

Sean blew out hard. 'I don't know whether that is brave
or positive thinking.'

'Neither,' she replied with a short laugh. 'I don't have
anything left in the piggy bank to pay for a back-up plan.
Everything I have is in the tea rooms and this event. And
I mean everything. If this festival doesn't bring in a return, I shall be explaining to the bank why they won't be
receiving their repayment any time soon. And that is not
a conversation I want to have.'

Then she threw her hands in the air with a flourish.
'That's why I was having a mini melt-down last night.

But no longer. Problem solved. I only hope that Prakash enjoys his job long enough to stay around.'

'What do you mean?'

'I was only talking to Prakash for a fairly short time, but it's obvious that he feels like a tiny cog in a big machine where nobody knows his name or what he wants from the job. It seems to me that you and your dad and brother have created a training system which is incredibly impersonal and cold.'

Then she paused and twisted one hand into the air. 'Not deliberately. I don't mean that. But you are all so busy.'

Dee gave a small shrug. 'Maybe you could take a few tips from a small business and talk to Prakash and the new graduates one to one, find out what they need. It would make a change from a big, flashy presentation in a huge, impersonal lecture theatre. It might work.'

'That's an incredibly sweet idea, Dee, and maybe it would work in a cake shop, but we have hundreds of trainees. It would take weeks of work to get around all of them and then process the responses. It is simply not doable. I wish it was. But that's business.'

'No, Sean. You can talk to your graduates for days and give the all of the motivational speeches you like but when they are back in their jobs they have to want to do their best work and be inspired by you and your family. Because you motivate them. Not because they feel they have to perform to bring in a pay cheque. Totally different.'

Then Dee shrugged with a casual smile that left him speechless. 'And who would have guessed that your Madge is a total tea addict? And that girl knows her leaves! Only the finest white tea for her. I am impressed. And I hope you don't mind, but I did give her a voucher for a free cream tea if she came to Lottie's.'

'Mind? Why should I mind if you give away free samples?' Sean replied as he dodged a kamikaze cyclist who served around them. 'But you should try our traditional afternoon tea. It is very popular with the guests—and you seemed to enjoy our desserts.'

'Oh, the food would be amazing. That's not the problem. It's the tea you serve.' She winced as though there was an unpleasant odour. 'It's very nice—and I know the warehouse where you buy it from, because I used to work there—but for a five-star hotel? I have to tell you that you have been fobbed off with stale old tea that has been sitting in those boxes for a very long time. It's certainly not up to the standard I expected. Why are you looking at me like that?'

'Fobbed off? Is that what you said?' Sean replied, coming to a dead halt.

'Now, don't get upset. I just thought that I should point it out. For future reference.'

'Anything else you would like to mention?' Sean asked in a voice of disbelief. 'I would hate for all that great free advice to be burning up inside without an outlet. Please; don't hold back. Fire away.'

He ignored her tutting and tugged out his smart phone; his fingers moved over the keys for a second. 'There. The food and beverages director has been alerted to your concerns. And Rob Beresford is not a man who lets standards slip. What?'

Dee was standing looking at him with her mouth half hanging open. 'Wait a minute. Beresford; of course. I never made the connection. Are you talking about the celebrity chef Rob Beresford? The one who runs that TV programme sorting out rundown restaurants in need of a makeover?'

'One and the same. And it's even worse than that. He is my half-brother. And the man may look laid-back, but underneath that slick exterior he is obsessed with the quality of everything we serve and as sharp as a blade.'

A ping of reply echoed out from the phone. Sean snorted and held the phone out to Dee, who looked at it as if he were offering her a small thermonuclear device. 'I thought that might push his buttons. He needs your mobile number. Expect a call very soon.'

Dee stared at the phone and shook her head very slowly. 'I don't have a mobile phone. Never had one. No clue how to use one.' Then she looked up at Sean and chuckled. 'I could give him the number for the cake shop, but Lottie would probably put the phone down on him thinking it was a prank call. Would email be okay?'

Sean stood in silence for a few seconds.

'No mobile phone?'

She shook her head again. 'I live above the shop and rarely travel. My friends know where I live. No need.'

'Tablet computer? Or some sort of palm top?' She rolled her eyes and mouthed the word 'no'.

Sean took back his phone and fired off a quick message, then laughed out loud when the reply came whizzing back.

'Have I said something to amuse you? My life's mission is now complete,' Dee whispered and looked up and down the street as Sean bent over his phone as though she were not there. Then she spotted something out of the corner of her eye just around the next corner, glanced back once to check that Sean was fully occupied and took off without looking back.

Sean did not even notice that she had walked off until he had exchanged a couple of messages with Rob, who thought that the whole thing had to be one huge practical joke, and couldn't believe that a girl who was willing to criticize his tea supplier didn't have a phone. So he came up with another idea instead.

An idea so outrageous that Sean was sure Dee would turn him down in a flash, but hey, it was worth a try.

'Well, it seems that you were right, it really is your lucky day. I have a rather unusual request from my brother. Rob is flying in on Friday for... Dee?'

Sean turned from side to side.

She had gone. Vanished. Taken off. Left him standing there, talking to himself like an idiot. What was all that about?

The girl was a mirage. A mirage who he knew had not retraced her steps to the hotel—he would have spotted that—so she must have gone ahead.

One more thing to add to his new client's list of credentials: impatient. As well as a technophobe.

Sean strolled down the street, and had only been gone a few minutes when he turned the corner and walked straight into one of the local street markets that were famous in the area. Once a week stallholders selling all kinds of handmade goods, food, clothing, books, ornaments, paintings and everything else they had found in the attic laid out their goods on wooden tables.

A smile crept unbidden across Sean's face.

His mother used to love coming to these markets and he used to spend hours every Saturday trailing behind her as she scoured the stalls for what she called 'treasures'. Her collections: postcards of London; Victorian hand-painted tiles; antique dolls with porcelain faces; handbags covered with beads and sequins, most of them missing; cupboards-full of old white linen bedding which had always felt cold and scratchy when he was a boy. But to her eyes, glorious items which were simply in need of a good wash and a good home.

Each item had its own story. A silver snuff-box must have been owned by someone important like Sherlock

Holmes, while a chipped tin car had once been the treasured toy of a refugee who had been forced to leave everything behind when his family had fled. Just as she had done when she'd escaped persecution when she'd been a small girl, arriving in London with her journalist parents and only a small suitcase between them. Simply glad to be safe from the political persecution from the new regime in their corner of Eastern Europe.

The horror of being forced to flee from your home to avoid arrest was one thing. But to start again and make your life a success in a new country was something special. Sean admired his mother and his grandparents more than he could say. They had taught him that hard work was the only way to make sure that you were never poor or hungry again. To build a legacy that nobody could take away from you.

No wonder his dad had adored her.

His dad usually had been working all hours of the day and night at one or another of the hotels, but if he was home when they got back, carrying their bags of assorted 'treasures', he'd used to laugh like a train and go through every single one and pretend to love it.

Happy days.

Happier days.

Sean inhaled a couple of sharp breaths.

It had been years since he had been to a street market and even longer since he had thought about coming here with his mother as a boy. Most of the time he would much rather have been playing football with his mates from school. But now? Now they were treasured memories.

Long years filled with good times and bad. Hard, physical work had helped to block out the bad. Long years when he'd usually been so exhausted that he collapsed into bed at night without the luxury of dreams.

Not much had changed there. He was still working so hard that sometimes the days just melted together into one huge blur.

When was the last time he had walked anywhere? He always caught a black cab or had a limo waiting to take him to some airport. There was no down time. There couldn't be. His work demanded his full attention and he didn't know how to give anything else but his best.

He had paid the price for the hugely successful company expansion.

Only, at moments like this, he wondered if maybe the cost was too high.

Sasha had been the last of a long line of short-term relationships. His friends had stopped calling because there was always some excellent reason why he couldn't make their dinner or meet up for drinks.

All he had left was his family.

Sean stood in silence, overwhelmed by the sights, sounds and smells of the street market, and allowed all of those happy memories to come flooding back.

The sun broke through the clouds and filled the space with light and a little warmth. The birds were singing in the London plane trees which lined the street and, for the first time in months, he felt a sense of contentment well up inside him.

Shockingly new. Depressingly rare.

But for once he did not over-analyze how he felt or push it away.

He simply gave in to the sensation and enjoyed the moment. Each breath of the heady air seemed to invigorate him. The long-standing stiffness in his neck and shoulders simply drifted away. Gone.

He felt engaged and buoyant at the same time.

He shook his head and sighed. Maybe there was something to be said for leaving the hotel now and again.

And he knew precisely who to blame.

The girl who was strolling down between the market stalls, oblivious to the world, a grin on her face and a skip in her steps. Living in the moment and loving it.

Gorgeous, astonishing and totally pushing all of his buttons.

Dee Flynn was turning out to be the best thing that had happened to him in quite a while.

Forget the rules. Forget over-analyzing his schedule and responding to every email that came in. Time to take some of that personal time he was due and had never taken. And he knew who he wanted to share it with.

Dee dropped her head back and felt the sun on her face.

Oh, that felt so good.

Okay, it was a pale imitation of the sun she had grown up with, but right now she would take whatever sun she could get.

'Sunbathing already? Does this mean that you plan to strip off any time soon? Because if you do I can sell tickets and talk up the tea festival at the same time.'

Dee chuckled from deep in her chest.

Sean. His voice was deep, slow and as smooth as fine chocolate. Unmistakable.

She couldn't be angry with this man. Not when the sun was shining and she had a new venue which was ten times more impressive that the Richmond Square hotel—not that she would tell him that, of course.

She lifted her head and turned to face him. And blinked.

Sean was smiling at her with his hands behind his back and a look on his face that made the hairs on the back of her neck stand on end. Tiny alarm bells started to sound inside her head, and as he stepped closer she fought the sudden urge to buy something from the haberdashery stall. Buttons. Ribbons. Anything.

He had something on his mind and she knew before he opened his mouth that it would involve her stepping outside her comfort zone in a serious way.

This must be how antelopes felt before the lion pounced.

'Sorry I spent so long on the phone. Rob had come up with a few ideas about how to make the best use of your advice,' Sean said and then paused.

One more step and he had closed the distance between them, but before she could respond his hand whipped out from behind his back. He was holding the most enormous bunch of tulips that she had ever seen. And he was holding them out towards her.

No—make that bunch*es*. Lipstick-red tulips that called out to be sniffed; yellow tulips still in bud; and her favourite tulip: stripy parrot blossoms in glorious shades of white and red with splashes of orange and flame. All set off by swords of dark-green leaves with pristine, clean-cut edges.

Without a moment's hesitation she clutched the flowers from his fingers and gathered them into her arms and up to her face.

It was spring in a bouquet.

It was heaven.

'I thought that you might like them,' Sean said with a smile in his voice.

She blinked up into his face, and was totally embarrassed to find that she could hardly speak through the closed sore throat that came with the tears that ran down her cheek.

'Hey,' he said in a voice so warm and gentle that it only

made her cry more. 'It's okay. If you don't like them, the flower stall has a great selection of daffodils.'

He ran his hand up and down her arm and bent lower to look into her face. His blue eyes showed such concern that she sniffed away her stupid tears and blinked a couple of times.

'I love them. Thank you. It's just that...'

'Yes. Go on,' he replied, his gaze never leaving her face.

'This is the first time anyone has bought me flowers. Ever. And it is a bit overwhelming.'

Sean looked at her with an expression of complete bewilderment. 'Please tell me that you are joking. Never? Not one boyfriend? Impossible.'

'Never.' She nodded, reached into her pocket for a tissue and blew her nose in a most unladylike fashion.

'Well, that is totally unacceptable,' Sean said and stood back up to his full height. 'You've clearly been treated most shamefully and, as one of the many single men who would love to buy you flowers on a regular basis, I apologize for the oversight.'

Then he smiled with a smile that could have melted ice at fifty paces and which reached his eyes before he opened his mouth.

'Perhaps we can help you to feel more appreciated. Are you doing anything this Friday evening?'

Dee reared back a little and tried to reconnect her brain. 'No. I don't think so. Why?'

'Prakash and the other management graduates are meeting the hotel managers at a company dinner on Friday. Rob is flying in from New York and would love to meet you and talk tea.'

Then Sean lifted her hand that was not busy with the flowers, turned it over and ran his lips across the inside of her wrist, sending all chance of sensible thought from her brain.

'And I...' he kissed her wrist again, his hot breath tingling on the tiny hairs on the back of her hand, his gaze never leaving her face '...would love you to be my date for the evening.'

He folded her fingers into her palm but held her hand tight against his coat, forcing her to look into those blue eyes.

And she fell in and drowned.

'Say yes, Dee. You know that you want to. It's going to be a very special night.'

Words were impossible. But somehow she managed a quick nod.

That was all it took, because the next thing she knew she was walking down past the market stall in the afternoon sunshine with one arm full of tulips. And Sean Beresford was holding her hand.

It was turning out to be quite a day.

CHAPTER SEVEN

Tea, glorious tea. A celebration of teas from around the world.
Visualize a hot summer afternoon. Birds are singing and there is a warm breeze on your face. Scones and jam (no wasps allowed) and refreshing, delicious green tea in a floral-pattern china cup. Bliss.

From *Flynn's Phantasmagoria of Tea*

Thursday

'I DON'T UNDERSTAND the panic. So you're going on a date. With a multi-millionaire. To a management dinner, where all the Beresford hotel bosses will be lined up to kiss Sean's father's feet.' Lottie nodded slowly. 'That makes perfect sense to me. There was bound to be some intelligent man out there who could recognize a goddess when he saw one.'

Lottie waggled the plastic spatula she was holding over the bowl of blueberry-muffin batter in front of Dee's floral-print slimline trousers and canary-yellow long-sleeved top. 'Goddess. Obviously.'

Then she went back to folding in the vanilla and almond extracts and extra fresh blueberries for a few seconds before lifting her head and adding, in a dreamy, faraway voice, 'Why, yes, I did know Miss Flynn before she became the tea consultant to the international hotel chains around the world. But we both knew even then that she was destined for greatness. She had that spark, you see. Special. And she still sends me a Christmas card every year from her Caribbean tax haven. Just for old times' sake.'

Dee gave Lottie a squinty look as she packed napkins into the dispensers on the tables. 'Very funny. Laugh all you like. I'm having a screaming panic attack here. See these bags under my eyes? Haven't slept a wink.'

'I'm not laughing, I'm celebrating,' Lottie retorted as she spooned the batter into paper cases in the muffin tin. 'Sean obviously likes a girl who knows what she wants and can stand up for herself. I know these management types from my old job. They are always looking for something or someone to give them a buzz. You will be fine.'

'A buzz?' Dee groaned. 'I am not trained to give anyone a buzz. Ever. All I know about is tea!'

'Well, for a start that's not totally not true,' Lottie replied as she sprinkled cinnamon and crystallized brown sugar mixed with chopped pecans over the tops of the muffins. 'Who was the star of the celebration-cake contest? And your eggs Benedict are the best. I can only dream of making a hollandaise sauce that good. Remember what I told you when I called you at the tea warehouse and asked if I could buy you lunch? Universities do not award first-class degrees just for turning up. If I am going to set up a business with someone, I only work with the best.'

'True. Three first-class degrees in a class of forty-two.'

'Damn right,' Lottie said as she popped the muffin trays into the oven and set the timer. 'You, me and Luca Calavardi.' She stood up and pressed a sugary hand to her chest. 'Oh, my. Now you've done it. Reminded me about the lovely Luca.'

'Oh, stop. He was fifty-six, happily married with children and grandchildren, and only came on the course because he was fed up with being a sous chef all his life. That man had forty years of catering experience under his belt and we had four months.'

'All the more reason to feel proud of what we achieved. Right? Sean is a lucky man, and you are going to knock their socks off. You wait and see. And in the meantime...' Lottie grinned and looked over Dee's shoulder as the doorbell chimed. 'We have our first customer of the morning. They will probably want tea and plenty of it. Go to it, girl. Show them what you can do.'

Dee popped the last napkin holder onto the tray with a snort and walked out of the kitchen and into the tea rooms. But, instead of her usual customers, a short man in a biker's jacket with a motorcycle helmet over one arm was standing at the counter.

'Delivery for—' he glanced at the screen of a palm top computer '—Miss D Flynn. Have I got the right address?'

'That's me. You have come to the right place.' Dee smiled and leant on the counter with both elbows. 'What delights do you have in your bag today?'

The courier flashed Dee a withering glance, then dived into his rucksack and pulled out a small package the size of a book which he passed onto the counter. Dee barely had time to scratch her name with the stylus onto the computer screen before he was out of the door.

'And thank you and goodbye to you too,' Dee said as she turned the box from side to side. Too small for tea samples or festival flyers. Too large for a personal letter.

Intriguing.

A small, sharp knife and a whole bag of foam curls later, Dee stood in silence, peering at an oblong box. It was covered in fluorescent-pink gift paper with a dark-blue ribbon tied in an elaborate bow on the top. There was a small pink envelope tucked into the ribbon and she hesitated for a moment before opening it up and reading the note.

With thanks for a lovely morning. Operating instructions are included and my personal number is number one on the list.
Prakash is next.
Have fun.
Sean.

Dee had a suspicion she knew exactly what was inside the gift box but she tugged away the ribbon and peeked inside anyway.

Staring back at her from a whole pack of scary accessories and manuals was a very shiny, very elegant version of the smart phone that Sean had been using yesterday. But with pastel-coloured flowers in shades of pink and cream printed onto the silver cover.

'Oh my,' Lottie whispered over her shoulder. 'Please excuse my drool. Your boy has very good taste in toys. Am I allowed to be jealous?'

Dee shook her head. 'I know. And it would be churlish to send it back. But…I'm not sure how I feel about Sean sending me personal gifts. I've only known him two days.'

'Think of it this way—it gives him pleasure to send you a phone, and you need one to keep in touch with the hotel if you are out and about doing your organizing thing. It's a winner. Go on, have a play.'

Lottie finished drying her hands and pointed to the shiny silver button. 'That's the power button.' Then she stood back and smiled before giving Dee a quick one-armed hug. 'There you are. He took your photo yesterday when you hit the streets. You look so sweet carrying those tulips.'

Then Lottie gave a quick chuckle. 'Might have guessed. Dee, darling, I hate to state the obvious but that boy is smitten with you. Totally, totally smitten. And, the sooner you get used to the idea that you are being wooed, the better!'

'Wooed! Have you been sniffing the brandy bottles again? I haven't got the time be wooed by a Beresford. I have a tea festival to organize.'

'Wooed. Whether you like it or not. And, actually, I kind of like it. Sean and Dee. Dee and Sean. Oh yes. And that's my oven timer. Have fun with your phone.'

Dee watched Lottie jog back into the kitchen and waited until her back was turned before picking up Sean's note and reading through it again with a silly grin on her face. He had written it himself, using a pen on paper. That must have been a change for him. The man seemed to live for his technology.

Her foolish and very well hidden girly heart leapt a few beats as she scanned down to the photo he had taken when she'd stopped at one of the market stalls to look at the antique silver teapots.

The girl smiling back at her with her arms full of tulips looked happy and pretty.

Was that how Sean saw her? Or as a girl who had a problem with enclosed spaces who could deck him any time of the day or night?

Her finger hovered over the menu button. She was so tempted so call him right there and then and spend five minutes of easy, relaxed chatter like they had enjoyed the day before. Talking about their lives and how much he missed London sometimes, just as she missed warm weather and the mountains.

Two normal people enjoying a sunny winter's morning. Getting to know one another.

How had that happened?

Dee licked her lips and was just about to ring when a group of women swooped in and headed straight towards her. Customers!

Perhaps Lottie was right. Perhaps she was being wooed. Strange how much she rather liked that idea.

Sean looked out over the London skyline from the penthouse apartment at the Beresford hotel Richmond Square and watched the planted arrangements of ferns and grasses thrash about in the winds that buffeted his high-rise balcony.

No spring flowers or tulips here. Not on a cold evening three storeys above the street level where he had strolled with Dee the previous day.

But she was still with him, and not only in a photo on his phone.

No matter where he went in the Beresford Riverside he could almost hear the sound of laughter and easy chatter. Even Madge had smiled as he'd passed her office.

But it was more than that. Sean felt as though he had been infected with the Dee virus which coloured everything he did and made him see it in a new light.

He had spent the day getting to know the new hotel management trainees. They were a great group of young and not so young graduates: bright, keen and eager to learn. The future lifeblood of Beresford hotels.

It had been a pleasure to take them through some of the Beresford training materials, materials written and tested by experts in the hospitality industry and used in the hotels around the world. And yet, the more time he'd spent standing at the front of the minimalist meeting room at Beresford City, working through the elegant presentation materials while the graduates had scribbled away taking notes, the more his brain had reworked what she had said to him.

Was it really the best way to engage with his staff and motivate them?

Frank Evans was not the only hotel manager who had left Beresford hotels in the last twelve months, and they needed to do something different to keep the staff that were crucial to any hotel business. And it was not just the investment the family made in their training and development; it was that precious connection between the manager, his staff and the hotel guests. That kind of connection took years to build up and could transform customer service.

But it had to come from the top.

Perhaps that was that why he had turned off the projector after a couple of hours and herded these intelligent adults out onto the footpath to the Riverside hotel. He'd let them talk and chatter away as they'd walked, and he'd listened.

It was a revelation. A twenty-minute stroll had given him enough material to completely change his view on how to retain these enthusiastic new employees and make them feel engaged and respected.

The rest of the afternoon had been amazing. He had felt a real buzz and everyone in the room had headed back to their hotels exhausted and dizzy with new ideas and bursting with positivity.

He couldn't wait to tell Dee all about it.

He couldn't wait to see Dee and share her laughter. Up close and personal.

Sean flicked open his notebook computer and smiled at the new screensaver he had loaded that morning.

Dee's sweet, warm smile lit up the penthouse. Her green eyes sparkled in the faint spring sunshine under that silly knitted hat as she clasped the red and yellow tulips to her chest.

She was life, energy and drive all in one medium height package.

The kind of girl who would enjoy travelling on rickety old railways, and always be able to find something interesting to do or someone fascinating to talk to when their flight was delayed. Dee was perfectly happy to spend her days serving tea to real people with real lives and real problems.

She was content to work towards her goal with next to nothing in the way of backing or support, making her dream come true by her own hard work.

His mouth curved up into a smile. He hadn't forgotten the hit in his gut the first time that he had looked into those eyes only a couple of days ago. The touch of her hand in his as they'd walked along the London streets like old friends, chatting away.

Sean turned his screen off, got up, walked over to the window and looked out over the city where he had grown up.

Where was his passion? He was a Beresford and proud to be part of the family who meant everything to him. There had hardy been a day in his life when he had not been working on something connected to the hotels.

Sasha had accused him of putting his work before everything else in his life, blaming him for not having time for a relationship.

But she had been wrong. Sasha had never understood that it was not the work that drove him. It was the love for his family, and especially his commitment to his father.

That was the fuel that fed the engine. Not money or power or success. They came with the job.

When his mother had died of cancer a few short months after that first visit to the doctor, he had shut down, blocking out the world, so that he could grieve alone and in silence. His father was the only person who had been able to get through to him and prove that he had a home and a stable base where he was loved unconditionally, no matter what happened or what he chose to do.

The family would be there for him. His father and his half-brother Rob: Team Beresford.

Damn right. His father might have remarried when he'd gone to university, and he had a teenaged sister on the team now, but that had only made it stronger.

So why was his mind filled with images of Dee, her smile, the way her hair curled around her ears and the small brown beauty spot on her chin? The curve of her neck and the way she moved her hands when she talked?

Magic.

Sean ran his hands over his face.

Was it a mistake inviting Dee to the management dinner and introducing her to the family?

Paris was a short train ride from central London and Dee would love it there.

Maybe he could take a chance and add one more person to Team Beresford?

Only this time it would be for totally selfish reasons. *His own.*

Dee locked the front door, turned the lights off one by one and then slowly climbed the stairs to the studio apartment where she lived above the tea rooms.

What a day!

She never thought that she would be complaining about the tea rooms being busy but they had been going flat out. It was as if the rays of sunshine had encouraged half the tea-drinking and cake-eating population of London out of their winter hibernation in time for a huge sale at a local department store. And they all wanted sustenance, and wanted it now.

The breakfast crew had scarcely had time to munch through their paninis and almond croissants before the first round of sales-mad shoppers had arrived, looking for a carb rush before they got down to the serious shopping, and the crush had not stopped since.

Ending with the Thursday evening young mums' club who held their weekly get-together in the tea rooms between seven and nine p.m. while their partners took care of the kids. And those girls could eat!

Lottie had gone into overdrive and a production line of cakes, muffins and scones had been emerging from the tiny kitchen all day. The girl was a baking machine in the shape of a blonde in whites.

And the tea! Lord, the tea: white; green; fruit infusions; Indian extra-strong. Pots. Beakers. And, in one case, a dog dish for a guide dog. She must have hand-washed at least sixty tea cups and saucers by hand because the dishwasher had been way too busy coping with the baking equipment.

They had never stopped.

But there were some compensations.

Whenever she had a moment it only took one quick glance at the huge display of bright tulips which Lottie had moved onto the serving counter to put the smile back on her face. Sean!

Dee padded through the small sitting room into her bedroom, unbuttoning her top as she went, and collapsed down on her single bed.

She slipped off her espadrilles and dropped her trousers and top into the laundry basket before flopping back onto the bed cover, arms outstretched.

Bliss! The bedroom might be small but Lottie had agreed to a rent which was more than affordable. And it was hers. All hers. No need to share with a nanny or friend or relative, as she'd had to for most of her life growing up. This was her private space and she treasured it.

She bent forwards and was rubbing some life back into her crushed toes when the sound of Indian sitar music echoed around the room and made her almost jump out of her skin.

Dee scrabbled frantically from side to side trying to work out where the song was coming from for a few seconds, before she realized it was bellowing out from the phone that Sean had sent over that morning.

Dee picked it up and peered at it before pressing the most obvious buttons and held it to her ear. 'Hello. This is Dee. And I should have known that you would set my ringtone to something mad.'

'Hello, this is Sean,' a deep, very male voice replied with a smile in his voice. The same male voice that had kept her awake most of the previous night, reliving the way it had felt to saunter down the streets with Sean holding her hand.

Which was so pathetic it was untrue.

It was her choice not to have a boyfriend. And just because he had asked her to be his date at a company dinner did not mean that they were dating. Not real dating. His brother wanted to talk to her about tea. It was a business meeting.

She had tried that line on Lottie, who had still been laughing and muttering something about her being delusional when she'd staggered home.

'I was wondering how you were getting on with your new phone. Do you like it?'

She snuggled back against the headboard and smiled. 'I do like it. It was one of those unexpected gifts that take you by surprise and then make you smile. Thank you. Sorry I haven't had time to call. We have been really busy.'

'No problem. And you can change the ringtone to anything you like. There are several to choose from on the special options menu.'

Dee held the phone at arm's length and made a scowl before holding it closer. Suddenly she felt as though she was being asked to sit an exam and she had not had time to study the subject.

'Sean. It is flowery and shiny, and there are so many touch-screen buttons that working out which one to use is going to take me the rest of the day. If I can stay awake that long. I'm long past the tired stage.'

'I know what that feels like.' He breathed out hot and fast. Then his voice faded away until he was speaking in little more than a whisper that reached down the phone and sent tendrils of temptation into her mind, mesmerizing, tantalizing and delicious. 'So here is an idea—have dinner with me tonight. I know a few restaurants in your part of town and we can have a great meal and a glass of wine while I squeeze in a master class on how to use your phone.'

Just the way he breathed out the word 'squeeze' was so suggestive that Dee almost dropped her new phone.

Dinner?

Oh, that sounded good.

But she was shattered and full of cake.

And not sure that she could sit opposite Sean Beresford without pouncing on him, which would be bad news for both of them.

'That sounds great, Sean, but work has been mad and I ate earlier. And now you have made me feel extra guilty for not calling to thank you.'

'No need. This is the first real break that I've taken all day. And if anything I should be thanking you.'

'Why? Talk to me. After all, that's why you sent me this phone. Wasn't it?'

A gentle laugh echoed down the phone that warmed her in places that even her best hot tea could not reach. It was a laugh designed to tantalize any female within earshot and make her skin prickle with awareness. Right down to her toes. Pity that it was a sensation she liked more than she would ever be willing to confess to a man like Sean. He would enjoy that far too much.

'I was giving a presentation to our new group of trainee hotel managers this morning and after thirty minutes in the all-white holding cell, as you described it so delightfully, I began to understand what you meant by an airless, windowless room. So do you know what I did?'

'You went to the park and sat on benches and fed the ducks.' Dee smiled. 'The wannabe managers had to train the ducks to race for the food and the trainee with the fastest duck got the best job in the hotel chain. Was that how it worked?'

'Ah. Duck training and Pooh sticks are only used in the advanced management courses. These were first-year students. If it had not been raining, I might have given them a treasure map to follow around London, but that option was out. So I decided to take your advice instead and I moved the whole group to the conservatory room at the Riverside, opened every door to the lawns and turned the presentation into a discussion about hotel design and meeting customer expectations. It was fascinating. And useful. Every one of those trainees seemed to come to life in the conservatory. They were transformed from sitting in total silence to being open and chatty and much more relaxed. You should have seen their faces when I told them why we had moved.'

Dee sucked in a breath. 'Did you mention my name so that they could pin it to a dart board for target practice?'

'Not specifically.' He laughed. 'You were a valued event planner who gave me feedback on the repressive feeling of the breakout rooms. But they totally got it, in a way that I couldn't have predicted. Instead of telling them about the impact of room design, they described how they felt in the two spaces and worked it out for themselves. It was brilliant. Thanks.'

'Ah. So that is the real reason for this call. It's confession time. What you really want to say is that you listened to my whining about how intelligent people shouldn't be packed into closed box rooms and then pretended that you had come up with the idea all by yourself. Is that right?'

'Drat, you have seen through my evil plans,' Sean replied in a low, hoarse voice which sent shivers down her back. She imagined him sitting in his office in the minimalist hotel surrounded by all-white marble and smooth, plastic surfaces, and instinctively pulled the silky cover over her legs.

'Are you still at work?' she asked, daring to take the first move.

'I just got back to the penthouse at Richmond Square. The view from up here is fantastic. Pity you aren't here to share it with me. Floor-to-ceiling windows. Breathtaking skyline. I have a feeling you might enjoy it.'

Dee closed her eyes to visualize how that might look and took a couple of breaths before replying. 'Sorry to disappoint you, but I would hate to be one of those girls who only suck up to you because they want to share the view from the penthouse over breakfast.'

The second the words were out of her lips, she winced in

embarrassment. What was it about this man that caused apparently random sounds to emerge from her mouth which bypassed the brain?

'You could never disappoint me. And, as it happens, I know how to make breakfast without needing to call for room service.'

I bet you do.

'I told you that you were cheeky.' Dee smiled and nibbled at one corner of her little fingernail. 'But I may have been mistaken about that.'

'So you do make mistakes?' Sean hit right back across the net. 'And just when I thought that you had all of the answers.'

'Cheeky does not come close. Brazen might be a better description. Does this wonderful breakfast include tea?'

'Dee,' he replied in his rich, deep, sensual tone that reached down the phone and caressed her neck, 'for you, it would include anything you like. Anything at all.'

Suddenly she was glad that she was lying down because her legs seemed to turn to jelly and her throat went dry.

Closing her eyes should have helped but all she could hear was his lazy, slow breathing in her ear which did nothing at all to calm her frazzled brain.

A handsome man who she liked far more than she ought to was holding something out to her on a velvet cushion, gift-wrapped and sumptuous, and she already knew that it would be astonishing.

And terrifying. She was going to have to face him in less than twenty-four hours and somehow she had to get a hold on this out-of-control attraction before it spiralled away into something more elemental which could only ever be a short-term fling.

So she did what she always did when someone came

too close. She put a smile in her voice and hit him right back between the eyes.

'Would that be part of the Beresford five-star service or the VIP special?'

His open and carefree laughter was still ringing in her ear when she said, 'Goodnight, Sean. See you tomorrow.' And she pressed the red button then turned the phone off.

Goodnight, Sean. Sleep tight.

CHAPTER EIGHT

Tea, glorious tea. A celebration of teas from around the world.
Finding the perfect tea to drink with your meal is just as tricky as matching food and wine. One tip: green tea flavoured with jasmine is wonderful with Chinese food but serve it weak and in small cups, and add more hot water to the pot as you drink. And no hangover!

From *Flynn's Phantasmagoria of Tea*

Friday

IT WAS ALMOST six on the Friday evening before Dee was finally satisfied that all of the leaf-tea canisters were full, the tea pots were all washed and ready for the Saturday rush and that everything the tea rooms needed for an eight a.m. start was in place.

But she still insisted on helping Lottie load the dishwashers, then cleaned the floor and generally got in the way of the last-minute customers, until Lottie had to physically grab her shoulders and plop her into a chair with a steaming cup of chamomile until the closed sign was up on the door.

Whipping away her apron, Lottie poured a cup of

Assam and collapsed down opposite Dee with a low, long sigh before stretching out her legs.

Her fingers wrapped around the china cup and Lottie inhaled the aroma before taking a sip. Her shoulders instantly dropped several inches.

'Oh, I am so ready for this. When did Fridays get so mad?'

'When you decided to have a two-for-one offer on afternoon cream teas, that's when. I have never served so much Indian tea in one session. How many batches of scones did you end up making?'

Lottie snorted. 'Six. And four extra coffee-and-walnut cakes, and three chocolate. And I gave up counting the sandwiches. But the good news is…it worked. The till is full of loot which I will be taking to the bank before the lovely Sean picks up his princess to take her to the ball.'

'The ball? I'm not so sure that I would call a management dinner a "ball". But the food should be good and apparently all the Beresford clan will be there en masse to toast the staff. So there's a fair chance I will score a free glass of fizz.'

Lottie cradled the cup in both hands and sat back in her chair. 'Ah. So that's what the problem is,' she said, then blew on her tea before taking a long sip. 'For the next few hours you are going to be up close and personal with Sean's father and his swanky brother and sister, and you're feeling the pressure. I see.'

'Pressure? I don't know what you mean. Just because his dad founded a huge chain of luxury hotels, and Sean's older brother, Rob the celebrity chef, is flying in from New York especially for the occasion, it doesn't mean that the family will be snooty and look down their noses at me.' Dee flashed a glance at Lottie. 'Does it?'

'No, not at all. Why should they? And if my experience

of management meetings is anything to go by, the owners will be way too busy talking to the staff and making sure they feel the love to worry about extra guests.'

Then Lottie leant her elbows on the table and grinned. 'Think of it this way—you are going to a great night out in a lovely hotel on the arm of a handsome prince. You are a goddess! What can possibly go wrong?'

Dee choked on the tea that went down the wrong way and had to grab a couple of napkins to stop her from spraying Lottie with chamomile through her nose.

'Are you kidding me?' she spluttered. 'I have a long list of things that could go wrong, and the more I think about it the more opportunities I have to put my foot in it. Everything from what I am going to wear, which is a nightmare, right through to my total inability to control the words that spill out of my mouth.'

Her hands came up and made circles in the air. 'And, when it does all go wrong, I can wave goodbye to my free conference centre and any chance I have of finding a replacement venue at this short notice for the tea festival and—' she swallowed '—show Sean up at the same time. Now, isn't that something to look forward to?'

She slid her cup out of the way and dropped her head forward until it rested on the table. 'I am doomed.'

Lottie shook her head and smiled. 'What rubbish. Do you remember that first day we met in catering college? I had come straight out of the business world, had no clue what to expect and turned up to the first morning wearing a designer skirt-suit, four-inch heels and a silk blouse. I thought that the first morning would be paperwork and class schedules, just like university. Instead of which, I spent the whole day gutting fish and making white sauces.'

Dee put her head to one side and sniffed. 'It was a different look, I'll give you that.'

'So you said—right before you passed me your new chef's coat and trousers.'

'I had spares. You hadn't,' Dee replied, sitting up, her shoulders slumped. 'The funniest thing was when you had them bleached and starched at some posh dry cleaners overnight. It was hilarious.'

'It was kind of you to offer me them in the first place. Which is why it is time for me to return the favour. I cannot believe I am saying this, because I think all your clothes are brilliant and suit you perfectly, but if you're worried about not having a cocktail dress to impress Sean's family then I can probably help you out.'

'You're going to lend me one of your fancy posh frocks?' Dee asked in a quiet voice, eyebrows high.

Lottie nodded her head. Just once.

Dee propped her chin up with one finger and looked up at Lottie through her long, brown eyelashes.

'And the shoes and bag to match?'

'Natch!' Her friend slurped down the last of her tea and rolled her shoulders back. 'Good thing we take the same shoe size. Come on; we have a lot to do and not much time to do it in. You, my girl, are going to take time out and celebrate just how much you've achieved whether you like it or not. Let the makeover begin.'

An hour later Dee paced up and down on the bedroom carpet in bare feet, her hands on her hips as she moved from her bed to the wardrobe, then back to the bottom of her bed again.

It was quiet in her bedroom. A chilly, gentle breeze fluttered the edge of the heavy curtains, bringing with it the welcome sound of chatter and traffic from the street below. The sound of normal people living normal Friday-evening lives.

But inside the room the atmosphere was anything but calm.

She stretched out her hand to lift the black fitted cocktail dress from the hanger, then froze. *Again*.

She blinked at the dress hanging on the wardrobe door for several seconds, nodded, then slipped her feet into Lottie's favourite stiletto-heeled sandals and tried a few tenuous steps. Lottie had told her that she should practise walking in them in case she had to take the stairs in the hotel. Four-inch heels with a platform slab under the toes were going to take some getting used to.

Two steps. Three. Then her right foot toppled over sideways on the slippery couture leather and she had to grab hold of the wardrobe door before she almost twisted her ankle as it bent over.

These were not shoes! They were instruments of torture, which had clearly been designed by men who hated their mothers and were determined to make all women suffer as a result. That was the only possible explanation!

And it did not matter one bit if they had pristine red soles if she couldn't walk in them.

Her shoulders slumped and she rested her forehead on the waxed oak panel, not caring that she might destroy the make-up which had taken Lottie an hour to put on, wipe off, then put on again in a different way.

She was terrified that she was sending out the wrong message. Or was it the right message?

She had been aiming for elegant and attractive, while the girl who stared back at her from the mirror looked like a stranger. Some clone from a fashion magazine. Not her. Not Dee Flynn, the wannabe tea merchant.

This wasn't working.

She had been mad even to think that she was ready to

go out on a date with Sean Beresford. Even if it was for only one evening.

She tottered to her bed in one shoe, fell backwards and let her arms dangle over the sides.

She was just about to make herself a laughing stock in exchange for a few canapés and a glass of fizz in a luxury hotel.

Dee bit down on the inside of her lip. Deep inside, where she kept her dreams and most sacred wishes, she knew that she had every right to stride into that hotel in these high-heeled shoes with her head high and stun the lot of them, including Sean. Strong, and confident that she was the equal of anyone there.

She had worked for this success and deserved to be treated like a goddess.

Drat Sean for reminding her that she still had a long way to go.

Dee closed her eyes, her throat burning and tears stinging at the sides of her eyes.

She was pathetic.

This handsome and attentive man had chosen her to be his date for the evening. Which was so amazing that she still couldn't believe it.

The past few days had passed in a blur of activity and mad work.

Sean had kept his word, and Prakash and Madge were now her official best friends in the whole world. Nothing was too much trouble. Extra power points for the hot-water heaters? No problem. Portable kitchen equipment, refrigerators and study tables appeared out of nowhere like magic.

Apparently the word had come down from on high that, whatever Miss Flynn needed for her festival of tea, the team had to make sure happened.

Especially when the boss, the one and only Mr Sean

Beresford, had seemed to find his way into the conference area several times during the day, just to make sure that everything was on track.

Oh, it was on track. *In more ways than one.*

Strange how many times in the day he'd found a way to brush against her hand with his, or look over her shoulder at some suddenly vital piece of information on the floor plan.

She'd had to stop the tickling, of course. That had got completely out of hand and she'd had to scold him about being professional in front of his staff.

Of course, he had insisted on regular tea breaks. Just the two of them, sitting around an elegant table in the hotel dining room, chatting about her critique of the quite good tea the hotel served. And all the while he'd told her anecdotes about his work in the hotel trade which had her clutching her stomach with laughter, and family stories about the antics his brother and sisters got up to.

And maybe it was just as well that she had been kept busy. It had kept her mind from mulling over all of those intimate moments they had shared since he had walked into the tea rooms: the sly glances that set her pulse racing and the gentle touch of his hand on her back or arm. His kindness. His quiet compassion. His humour.

A girl could fall for a man like that.

Hell. She was already halfway there.

Then her smile faded. This evening was turning into a date with Sean when she should be focusing on taking her dream one step closer to being a reality.

And that sent a cold shiver across her shoulders.

She couldn't let the exhibitors down. Some of the tea merchants were coming a long way to show London what tea was all about.

And she couldn't let Sean down either.

No wonder she had the jitters.

Dee stole another glance at the dress hanging outside the wardrobe.

Lottie had done a fantastic job and the girl in the mirror looked every bit the type of sophisticated, elegant girl that Sean was used to having on his arm.

It was the world that Lottie had been born into. A world of luxury and privilege where eating dinner in a Beresford hotel costing hundreds of pounds was something her family did without thinking.

Lottie had her own problems to deal with, no doubt about that, but she could never truly understand what it felt like always to have been the new girl with the second-hand school uniform and the strange accent. Never feeling as though she fitted in. No matter what she did to change her clothes, her hair and the way she spoke, she was always going to be different. And her parents had loved that about her. Loved that she was unique.

Pity that as a teenaged girl going to a city high school the last thing the fifteen-year-old Dee Flynn had wanted to be was unique.

Strange. She thought that she had conquered that particular battle years ago when her flair for catering had taken her higher than she had ever expected.

But that was not the only reason for the jitters.

For the next few hours she would be dealing with Sean's father and his wife Ava, their daughter Annika and Sean's older brother Robert—the professional celebrity chef and current pin-up for a lot of trainee chefs at catering college. And Sean—the blue-eyed boy who had come to her rescue.

How was she going to make polite chit chat with Sean when they had become…what? Event planners? Friends? Or as close to it as you could be when you had spent half the week together.

Dee wrapped her arms around her bare waist, squeezed her eyes tightly shut and relived, once more, the sensuous pleasure of his gentle kiss in the park and the touch of his hand on the small of her back. All of those subtle moments where she had felt him next to her.

No matter that those thoughts had made for very little sleep the night before. In an hour or so she would be seeing him again. Holding him. Just being in the same room within touching distance.

Delicious.

Her eyes flicked half-open and she glanced across at the brightly coloured tulips which she had popped into a plain white milk-jug on her desk. She could smell their fragrance anywhere in the room, and just seeing the blossoms reminded her of Sean all over again.

His laugh. His smile. The expression of pure pleasure and delight on his face when he'd telephoned his brother the other day and talked to her about his family. They truly were the most precious people in the world to him. He loved his family. And they loved him right back.

It would be so special to be on the receiving end of that kind of devotion.

Had it only been a few days since Sean had walked into the tea room? It felt so much longer. And like the tulips he would fade and go out of her life. Back to his hotel chain, bottomless wallet and first-class everything. Back to the life she would never have.

A low groan of exasperation escaped her lips, and she would have wiped her eyes but Lottie had just spent her evening using make-up brushes Dee had not known existed to create the face that she was wearing. She dared not mess it up.

She dared not mess any of this evening up.

Too much was at stake. The tea festival was serious

business and people were relying on her to do the very best she could.

But why now? Of all the times she could have chosen to have a crush, why did it have to be now, and why, oh why, did it have to be on Sean Beresford—the big-city hotel executive with the shiny, shiny lifestyle and looks to die for? The man who was in line to run the Paris branch of the Beresford hotel empire?

Fate had certainly played her a blinder of a hand. And Sean was currently holding all of the aces.

Sean could make her laugh like no other man, and discombobulate her with equal ease. But she dared not tell him. Could not tell him. Letting him know how attracted she was would only lead to heartbreak, disaster and embarrassment on both sides. He had his life and she had hers, and never the twain would meet. Wasn't that how the poem went?

One evening—that was their deal. Sean had kept his side of the bargain. Now it was time for her to keep hers.

Shame it was so hard to remember that fact when he was so close.

She smiled and slipped off the bed.

Maybe Lottie was right—maybe it was time to celebrate everything that she had achieved and take time out to enjoy herself.

Why shouldn't she enjoy his company for this evening? He had asked her to be his date. And that was precisely what she was going to be.

His date. Yes. That was it. Tonight Sean would be her date who she could rely on not to let her down. Even if it did mean never letting him out of her sight.

Sean rang the doorbell of Lottie's Cake Shop and Tea Rooms. Twice. And heard the bell tinkle inside the shop.

There was a bustle of movement from behind the front door and he could see a dark shape slip forward; as he lifted his chin, the ornate half-glass door opened inwards.

A woman dressed in black was standing just a few feet away: slender, medium height and absolutely stunning.

So stunning that he had to do a double take for his brain to recognise who was standing in the doorway smiling at him with a quizzical look on her face.

It was Dee Flynn. Only not the hard working, tea-obsessed version of Dee he had half the week with.

She had been transformed into a completely different person.

This Dee was dressed in a black cocktail dress: sleeveless, with a high collar tied behind her neck with a ribbon. And a low-cut back. Totally hot.

Sean had seen enough French couture dresses, and had bought enough fashion for Sasha and Annika to know the real thing when he saw it.

The dress fitted her perfectly, the fabric draped close to her waist then flaring out over the slim hips to just above the knees.

Sheer black stockings covered long, slim but muscular legs.

Silk shoes with heels so high that for the first time during the week she came almost to his height.

In a flash he could suddenly feel the life force of this woman emanate towards him, and her energy sparkled like the jewels in the gold bracelet on her wrist. Intoxicating, invigorating and bursting with confidence.

She was effervescent, hot and so attractive he had to fight down that fizz of testosterone that clenched the muscles under his dress shirt and set his heart racing just at the sight of her.

'Hello,' he said, suddenly keen to break the silence and

stop the ogling. 'I thought it might be safer to stand outside just in case you had your judo costume stashed behind the counter. Last time I barely made it out alive.' Then he grinned. 'You look amazing, by the way.'

'Why, thank you. You don't look too bad yourself.' She nodded with her head towards the counter. 'Do you want to come in out of the cold? I just need a minute to get my coat.'

'No problem; we have plenty of time. No need to rush.' He smiled and followed her into the warmth of the tea rooms. He was happy to be able to spend a few extra minutes alone with Dee before they joined the noisy crush of hotel guests and the management team, who were probably just hitting the bar back at the hotel.

Dee smiled back at him then swivelled towards the back of the room. Then, as he watched in horror, she flung both of her arms out into the air and launched herself towards the counter, as her right foot twisted over sideways and the girl literally fell off her shoe.

Sean leapt forward and grabbed her arm so that she wouldn't fall, and heard her slow hiss of pain as she winced and exhaled sharply.

'Are you okay?' he asked, looking into her face in concern.

Her response was an exasperated sigh followed by a sharp nod. 'Fine. Just dandy. My ankle will survive. Unlike my dignity.'

Then she turned her back on him, feeling stupid and humiliated, and scrabbled to slip the silly shoe back onto her foot and fasten the strap tighter. But her trembling fingers let her down and the shoe fell to the floor.

Before Dee could reach down to scoop it up, she sensed his presence seconds before a strong hand slid onto each side of her waist, holding her firm. Secure.

She breathed in a heady fragrance of fresh citrus aftershave and testosterone that was all Sean, which made it impossible for her to resist as he moved closer behind her until she could feel the length of his body from chest to groin pressed against her back.

His arms wrapped tighter around her waist, the fingers pressing oh, so gently into her rib cage and Dee closed her eyes, her pulse racing. It had been a long time. And he smelt fabulous. Felt fabulous.

Sean pressed his head into the side of her neck, his light stubble grazing against her skin, and her head dropped back slightly so that it was resting on his.

Bad head.

Bad heart.

Bad need for contact with his man.

Bad, full-stop.

One of his hands slid up the side of her dress and smoothed her hair away from her face so that he could press his lips against the back of her neck.

'Is there a rule somewhere that dictates that lovely ladies lose all sensible parts of their brain at the sight of shoes they can't actually walk in? Because it does seem to be a very common affliction. I see it everywhere I go. Sad, really.'

Dee tried to pretend that it was perfectly normal to have a conversation with her back pressed against the pristine dinner suit of the most handsome and desirable man she had ever met.

'Absolutely,' she whispered. 'They belong to Lottie, and she promised me that these were the latest thing in limo shoes. Dancing was out unless I wanted permanent disfigurement, but standing in one place could work. Would you mind holding me up here a little longer? I have a small problem standing up straight in Lottie's stilettos and talking at the same time, and you might not be there to break my fall when I try to make it as far as the car.'

He chuckled deep in his chest as though suppressing a smile, and the sound reverberated across her collarbone, down her spine and into regions which were previously closed to reverberations of any kind.

Sean continued to breathe into her neck, and one of his hands slid up from her waist to move in small circles on her shoulder. The room began to heat up at a remarkably rapid rate.

She clasped hold of the serving counter as Sean gently, slowly, slowly, slid down the length of her body until he could reach down and pick the sandal from the floor.

It was quite remarkable that he also needed to touch the inside of her leg with his fingertips as he did so, sending shivers up and down her spine, which made it seriously difficult to breathe, focus and talk at the same time.

'Over the years I have been dragged by the ladies in my family around every fashion shop and footwear retailer in London at one time or another so I could carry their loot home. And we never, ever, bought shoes which they didn't try on in the shop and at least totter a few steps in. Walking any distance—now, that was different.'

She slowly lifted one of Sean's hands from her waist, and pushed gently away from him, instantly sorry that she had broken the touch, but Sean had other ideas and held her even tighter this time as she turned to face him.

Without her shoes, her head came up to his chest and she leant back against the counter so that she could look into the smiling, quizzical, handsome face of a truly nice man.

His eyes never blinked or left hers, and her breathing seemed to match his; it was a few seconds before he broke the silence.

'Did I mention that I am a hotel manager? Yes? I did? Well, we have these terribly practical health and safety standards which mean that I cannot condone any footwear which is likely to lead to personal injury. Not in our hotels.'

He took a step back and held both of her arms out wide as his gaze stayed locked onto her wonky feet.

He flicked one hand in the air and tutted. 'My hands are tied. No choice—you can either slip your shoes off and go barefoot the whole evening, or you pop back inside and change into something you can walk in and stand in for several hours. What's it to be?'

CHAPTER NINE

Tea, glorious tea. A celebration of teas from around the world.
The tea a person chooses to drink for pleasure is as unique as their fingerprint. Personal and special. And a true insight into their character.

From *Flynn's Phantasmagoria of Tea*

'I HOPE THAT you are not going to inspect the contents of my entire wardrobe,' Dee snorted as Sean bounded up the stairs from the tea shop to her apartment and followed her along the narrow corridor. 'Because I'm going to tell you now that my selection of footwear suitable for a conference dinner is rather limited.'

'Not at all.' Sean smiled, enjoying the view as Dee skipped up the stairs in front of him and trying not to ogle too blatantly. The memory of her judo training was still too fresh to forget in a hurry. 'Your delightful choice of clothing has been inspired this week and I expect nothing less.'

Dee came to a dead stop outside a white-painted door and he held onto the bannister as she looked down at him with something close to nervousness in her eyes.

'What is it?' he asked with a smile. 'Worried that I will reveal the terrors of your boudoir to the world?' He pressed his right hand to his chest, lifted his head and said in a

clear voice, 'As a true gentleman, I promise that your secrets are safe with me.'

Dee lifted both eyebrows high. 'No doubt. But that's
not the problem. It's just that—' she coughed and Sean
caught a shy blush at the base of her neck '—Lottie is the
only person who has seen my bedroom before, and I am
actually quite shy about showing my space to other people.
In fact, I think it might be better if you wait downstairs. I
shouldn't be too long.'

Sean shook his head very slowly. 'Not a chance. I'm
not going anywhere.'

Dee sighed and folded her arms. 'Has anyone ever told
you that you are annoyingly stubborn?'

'Frequently. It is one of my finer qualities,' he replied
in a light, lilting voice. 'Once I make my mind up about
how to do something or a particular plan—that's it. My
plans are not for changing.'

She gazed at him for a few seconds before slowly un-
folding her arms.

'This tea festival has a lot to answer for,' Sean heard
her mutter, but she turned and opened her bedroom door,
swinging her shoes in one hand.

Sean stood at the door and took a breath as he tried to
take in what he was looking at.

For a small bedroom Dee had managed to squeeze in a
wide pale-wood wardrobe and a table under the window.
An upright bookcase stacked with papers, magazines and
books of all sizes took up the rest of the wall as far as her
bedside cabinet.

The walls had been painted in a warm shade of cream.
All of the soft furnishings in the room were variations of
shades of lavender and primrose yellow, including a cream
quilted bed-cover embroidered with tiny blossoms.

The whole room was calm, orderly, clean, serene and

tranquil. Feminine without being over-the-top girly or pretty. It was the type of colour scheme and arrangement several of his interior designers had introduced for the new boutique-hotel range his sister was running.

Sean realized with a shock that it was the exact opposite of what he had been expecting. Shame on him for making judgements about the choices Dee would make in her home. Shame on him for judging her. Full-stop.

A smile crept up on him unannounced.

Dee Flynn was turning out to be one of the most astonishing people that he had ever met.

'You can come in if you promise not to touch anything or criticize,' Dee said as she lifted a silk kimono from the bed, swung open her wardrobe door and pulled out a hanger.

'Thank you. This is...a lovely room.'

She coughed and whirled around to face him.

'Don't sound so surprised. What exactly were you expecting? Did you think I had made a nest of straw from old wooden tea chests or something?'

Sean held up both hands. 'Not a bit. I simply didn't think that you would go for a Scandinavian colour scheme with an English twist. Most of your clothes seem bright and Far Eastern. I thought you might have chosen an ethnic style—something bright. That's all.'

'Ah, you were expecting to see rainbow colours and dark wood. I see what you mean. This must be really quite shocking. But you forget that this is where I come to relax at the end of the day. I need this quiet space to help me centre myself and calm down and focus. Otherwise, I think I really would go nuts with the chaos that is my daily life.'

'Well, I know what that feels like. Especially with jet lag,' Sean replied and squeezed past her and picked up a silver-framed photograph from her computer desk.

A tall, slender, grey-haired man in white tunic and trousers was standing with one hand resting on a wooden balcony, the other hand across the shoulders of a dark-haired woman wearing a bright azure top and wrap skirt. All around them was exuberant green foliage, and a riot of flowering plants of all shapes and colours spilled out from pots and planters.

'Are these your parents?' he asked, and gestured with his head towards the photo.

Dee put down a shoe box and came and stood next to him.

'Yup. That's Mum and Dad on the veranda of the house they are renting in Sri Lanka. They love it there and I certainly cannot see them coming back to the UK now that they are both retired, especially in winter. The lifestyle is so different for retired people in a hot climate. And they can make their pension go a long way.'

'Do you see them often?'

'Once a year I save up for a flight and set up some appointments at the tea plantations. It's an amazing treat, and tax deductible. Actually, the owner of the estate where my folks live will be at the tea festival next week. It will be nice to see him again, even if he is a tough negotiator when it comes to his best tea. Mum and Dad get on with him and he treats the estate workers very well.'

'So you only see them once a year? That must be tough. Do they have Internet?'

She threw back her head and laughed out loud. 'Oh please, don't make me laugh. It took Lottie an hour to put this make-up on and she will go mad if I wipe it all off. But in answer to your question...' she dabbed the corner of her eyes with a tissue '...my folks are anti-technology in a big way. That place they are renting has a generator which breaks down at regular intervals but they get by without it most of the time. So, no—no Internet, computer, mobile phone or anything close to what they think is the curse of western culture. But they do write lovely letters. And for that I am thankful.'

Then she paused. 'And I'm talking way too much and not looking for shoes and we have a deadline. Righty; how about these?'

Dee turned and was about to dive into the shoebox when Sean stepped closer and took a gentle hold of both of her arms and smiled. 'I would much rather listen to you talking about your parents all evening than face the trainee managers. My seminar on time management and productivity can wait until tomorrow. Because right now I have a much more pressing task. I owe you a huge apology, Miss Flynn.'

She cleared her throat and stared back at him wide-eyed. And blinked. Twice. Then waited in silence for him to finish.

'When I fell into the tea shop the other evening and you decked me so delightfully, I filed you neatly away into a box labelled "sexy baker lady" who was responsible for my undignified first view of the tea rooms sitting on my butt. Ah; don't tut at me like that, because as it happens my view has changed.'

He flashed her a quick wink. 'Not about the sexy— that's still up there—but I was temporarily blinded by the force of your exuberance into thinking that you might be exactly what you appear to be.'

Sean shook his head, looked around the bedroom and exhaled slowly as he moved his head from side to side. 'Wrong. A thousand times wrong. Every day this week you have turned up to work wearing a riot of colour and pattern which has livened up my life and that of everyone you have met. But I am starting to see that that is only one tiny part of who you are.'

Then he stepped closer, then closer still, until he was totally inside her personal space, their bodies almost touching, tantalizingly close. So close that there was scarcely enough room for his hands to slide lightly onto her hips.

'You fascinate me, Dee Flynn. How many sides to you are there? And, more importantly, why are you keeping them hidden? Tell me, because I would really love to know.'

'Why do I wear bright clothing? That's easy, Sean. It's human nature to judge a book by its cover. You look at the clothes people are wearing and you make an instant judgement about who they are and what they do and where they fit in this crazy world. Especially in Britain, where the class system rules whether we like it or not.'

Her gaze scanned his body from head to toe.

'Look at you—you go to work in a smart suit and shiny black shoes every day. I've never seen you in jeans and a T-shirt. Perhaps you don't own those things. Perhaps this is who you are. And that's fine. You own that suit; it's gorgeous. And it's your job.'

Dee gave a small shrug. 'But the rest of us? The rest of us are doing the best we can to build bridges with people and make connections. I designed most of my day clothes, and they are friendly, open and welcoming for when I am working in the tea rooms. I love wearing them and it gives me pleasure. Practical too. They fit my personality. They express who I am. They are honest and real.'

'So why are you wearing black this evening?'

Dee slid out of his arms, paced over to the window and drew back the curtain so that the cool night air played on her bare arms.

'Isn't it obvious, Sean?'

'Not to me. Talk to me, Dee. Why black?'

She seemed to hesitate for a few seconds before whirling back towards him, and he was shocked to see tears in the corners of her glistening eyes.

'I didn't want to show you up. There; that's it. Happy now?'

Each word hit him right between the eyes like a high-velocity ice cube that melted the second it reached his heart, which burned hot and angry.

No other woman had ever done that for him.

Wanted that for him.

She was not wearing this lovely couture outfit to impress the big cheeses—she was wearing it so that she did not embarrass him.

And it blew him away.

Sean ran his fingers along the slippery silk fabric of her silk kimono strewn on the bedcover. For once in his life, words were impossible.

He slipped his dinner jacket onto the back of the small desk-chair and took a second before turning back to face his amazing woman.

'Not many people surprise me, Dee,' he managed to say. 'Not after a lifetime working in the hotel trade.'

Then he smiled and tapped the end of her nose with his forefinger. 'You don't need a little black dress to make you feel special. You could wear an old bath towel and still be gorgeous. Look at you. No, don't pull away like that. I think that it's time that you saw yourself through my eyes.'

'What are you doing? We're going to be late,' Dee protested.

'Then we are going to be late. You are more important than a room full of hotel management any day of the week. Okay? Besides, you have already pointed out that I have that stubborn streak, remember? I am not leaving this room until you have changed out of this dress and put on something which you love. Something you have chosen. Something you feel wonderful and special in. Then I might help you to choose the shoes.'

'You want me to change? Into what? This dress was really expensive. I don't have anything in my wardrobe to match it.'

'I didn't ask for an expensive dress to keep me company this evening. I asked you—Dervla Skylark Flynn. Not some designer clone. In fact, here is a challenge. What's the one outfit you possess which is the exact opposite of a black designer dress? Come on, you must have one.'

She snorted and shook her head. 'You mean my sari? I can't wear that to a hotel dinner when all of your clan will be there.'

'Yes.' He smiled. 'You can.' And then he bit down on his lower lip and stepped in closer. So close that his chest was pressed against hers as he held her tight around the waist with both hands flat on her back.

'But first we have to get you out of this dress. And, since I am the one who is insisting on it, I feel that it is my duty to help you.' His lips brushed lightly across her forehead. 'Every...' he moved onto her temple '...inch...' then her neck, nuzzling into the space below her ear with his cheek '...of the way.'

Dee closed her eyes and revelled in the glorious sensation of his cheek against hers, the feeling of his hot breath on her neck, the gentle friction of his hair on her ear. Whatever cologne or aftershave he was wearing should have been labelled with a hazard code and stored away in a bomb-proof box, because her sensitive nose and palate were overwhelmed with the rich, aromatic aroma blended with a base note that was nothing to do with a chemical laboratory and everything to do with the man who was wearing it.

Of course, she could feel the sensation of his fingers moving on her back but pressed so tight against his body it was suddenly irrelevant—the only thing that mattered was Sean and this moment they were together. Future. Past. Nothing else mattered but this moment. It was glorious.

So when he slowly, slowly inched his head away from her it was a shock. She eased open her eyes to find that his breathing was as fast as hers and she could see the pulse of the blood in the vein in his neck. Those blue eyes were wide, and the pupils startling deep and dark pools. Dark water so deep that she knew that she could dive into them and never find the bottom.

The intensity of that look was almost overwhelming and so mesmerizing that she could not break away.

No other man had ever looked at her like this before but she recognized it for what it was, and her heart sang. *It was desire.*

Seduction burned in Sean's eyes. Hot and passionate and all-consuming.

His desire for her.

And it astonished her.

Astonished her so much that she forgot to be scared of all of the chaos that love, desire and passion could bring and focused on the joy instead.

He wanted her.

He wanted her badly.

And the huge red switch marked 'danger' that had been buried under a lifetime of disappointment and making do with second-hand love suddenly and instantly flicked up and turned green.

She wanted him right back. On her single bed. And wearing Lottie's posh frock. Forget slow, she wanted fast. She wanted it all and she wanted it now.

It was almost a relief to turn in the circle of his arms

so that she could not feel the burning heat of his intense gaze scorching her face.

But that was nothing compared to what she saw when she opened her eyes fully.

She was standing in front of her full-length bedroom mirror on the wardrobe door with Sean standing behind her.

Instinctively she lifted both hands and pressed them to her chest as Sean slid Lottie's black dress away from her shoulders on each side. He had unzipped it as she enjoyed him. Now it was free and all that was holding it up, and protecting her modesty, were her two hands.

Dee stared at the girl in the mirror. Her hair was messed up, her eyes and skin glowing, and there was a handsome man with tight curled brown hair kissing her naked neck and, oh lord, her shoulders.

It was getting very hard to breathe but she could not look away, dared not look away, from the view in the mirror.

Sean was looking at the back of her neck as though it was the most beautiful and fascinating thing that he had ever seen, his fingertips stroking her skin from the innermost curve of her neck and along her collarbone. She could feel the heat from his touch, and the sensation of those fingertips was almost too much for her to tolerate.

A shiver of delicious excitement ran across her back and she saw Sean smile back at her in the mirror.

Lottie Rosemount had a lot to answer for. The mocha lace bra and shorts-style pants she was wearing had been a Christmas present from her, but not even the lovely Lottie could have anticipated that they would be on display in this way when Dee had slipped into them straight out of the shower only an hour earlier.

Slowly Sean brought his hands to the front, laid them

over hers and whispered in her right ear in a voice that she could have spread on hot crumpets.

'I want you to see yourself the way I see you. You don't need the dress.'

Dee smiled back at the man in the mirror as he slowly unfurled one finger at a time until only her palms were holding the couture dress against her bra.

'Do you trust me, Dee?'

Speech was impossible but she hesitated. This was it. If she wanted a way out, this was the time to say something or do something to take back control. Instead of which her head lifted and fell in a simple yes, and she was rewarded by a truly filthy grin.

And just like that she grinned back and pulled her hands away so that the dress fell to the floor in a heap around her feet.

She would have bent down to pick it up but that would have meant bending down while Sean was still holding her tight around the waist.

Bad idea! Such a bad idea!

So instead she swallowed down a sea of doubt and looked back at the mirror and the girl who was standing there in her underwear, with Sean's arms around her waist and his chin resting on her shoulder.

'Tell me what you see,' he whispered.

Her head dropped back and she half-closed her eyes, surrendering her entire body to his hands as they moved in firm and gentle circles in a delicious blissful movement.

Dee dared to open her eyes and watch the scene in the mirror.

Sean stroked and caressed her breasts through the flimsy fabric of her bra, lifting up her left breast then the right. He was slow and gentle, as though he was not in the slightest rush and they had all night to explore one another's bodies.

She felt Sean unclip her bra but did nothing to stop him and leaned back against him, feeling her bare skin on the crisp, white dinner shirt and not caring that she was probably creasing it.

The window was still slightly open and the chilly breeze wafted in, making her nipples stand proud inside her bra, pushing against the lace.

Sean noticed. She could see his reaction, feel the rise and fall of his chest and the pressure against her back from his trousers.

But instead of going for her nipples the pads of his soft fingertips expertly stroked down from her collarbone down over the top of her cleavage, as though he knew instinctively that was the most sensitive part of her neck.

Then her breasts. Exposed to the air, the dark skin around her nipples was already raised and ready. His fingers stroked all along the length of the side of her breast, moving into a more circular pressure, but then he looked up into the mirror.

But then his fingers paused, and every inch of her skin screamed out for release as he wrapped his arms around her waist and rested his chin on her shoulder so that they were both staring into the mirror at the same time.

'We need to be somewhere. And I need to get some air. Cold air.'

He pressed his lips to her throat and grinned. 'The sacrifices I make for my family. Oh yes...' And with one last, long, shuddering sigh he slipped back, picked up his jacket and walked slowly out of the bedroom.

CHAPTER TEN

Tea, glorious tea. A celebration of teas from around the world.
Tea is a natural product, hand-picked and completely free from artificial colours and preservatives, but rich in minerals and antioxidants. And best of all? Calorie-free.
Perfect for when you need to slip into that little black dress.

From *Flynn's Phantasmagoria of Tea*

Friday

SEAN SAUNTERED CASUALLY into the white marble reception area of the most prestigious Beresford hotel in London, the flashguns lighting up his back.

He might be the youngest director in the family firm but this was the one time a year he was willing to put his Armani tux on show for the press and wear his family pride on his sleeve.

Glancing around the room, he gave a quick wave to the management training team who were already lining up the latest graduates to chat to his father, who was greeting the hundred or so specially invited guests in person, same as always.

Tom Beresford. Straight-backed, tall, dark and impressive. The poster boy for every self-made multi-millionaire who had learnt his trade the hard way. The company PR machine loved to repeat the story about the boy who had started work at fourteen, washing dishes in the kitchens where his mother was the head chef, his father serving in the army overseas. His wages had been a hot meal every day and enough cash to pay his bus fare to school.

The weird thing was, it was all true. Except for one thing: he had been thirteen when he'd started, and barely tall enough to stand at the sinks, but had told the hotel he was older to get the work.

By eighteen he'd been working for the hotel and studying at college and at twenty-one had his first job as deputy manager. The rest was history.

Of course, the PR experts did not go into quite so much detail when it came to his father's complicated personal life, which was way more tabloid fodder than inspirational reading for young managers. He had certainly enjoyed female company as a single man—and when he was not so single.

Not that he could get away with that now. His lovely third wife Ava had been by his side night after night for the past eighteen years, just as she was greeting the guests tonight, and Sean knew that his father adored her.

He was still the man who had read him bedtime stories every night all dressed up in his dinner suit before heading to the hotel to work.

'Hey, handsome. Feeling lonely?'

Sean laughed out loud as his teenage half-sister Annika hooked her arm around his elbow and leant closer to give him a hug.

He replied by lifting the back of her hand to his lips then glancing up and down her gorgeous aqua cocktail dress. 'Why look at you, pretty girl. All grown up and everything.'

He was rewarded with a soft kiss on the cheek.

'Charmer! But you scrub up nicely. New suit?'

'Had it for months. All ready for the Paris job. New dress?'

'Had it a day.' She sniffed and looked around. 'What have you done with Dee? I noticed that fabulous sari she was wearing when she came in with Rob and then she seemed to disappear. You were very brave, letting him escort your lady friend. Rob is a scamp.'

Then Annika's voice faded away and she gave a small cough. 'Oh my. I think I think you'd better go to the rescue. Don't you? See you later.' And with that she released his hand to move to the cluster of new arrivals who had packed the reception area behind him.

Sean followed the direction of Annika's gaze and stood there, chuckling.

Judging by the number of people clustered around the buffet table, there was obviously something exciting going on. Sean could see Rob's head in the crowd but Dee had emerged from the tea rooms wearing far more practical flat gold sandals. Practical, but it also meant that in a room of tall men she was the orchid shaded by the tall trees.

Except that this was one girl who would always stand out in a crowd.

Especially when she was wearing a gold silk sari, gold jewellery and an azure-and-gold bodice which revealed a tantalizing band of the same taut skin he had admired back in the bedroom.

She took his breath away.

This was no clone. This was a real woman showing that she could act the part when she needed to, and revealing yet another side to her personality that he could never have imagined existed.

He had spent the week learning about one side of Dee Flynn. The woman who had taken a risk with her friend and transformed a simple patisserie into something spectacular. Doing what she loved to do, capitalizing on her passion. On her own terms.

When had he last met a woman like that? Not often. Maybe never. Oh, he had met plenty of glossy-haired girls with high IQs who had claimed they were doing what they truly loved, but so few people knew what they wanted in their twenties that it was astonishingly rare.

He had known precisely what he wanted from the first day he'd walked into his dad's hotel. His career path had been as clear as a printed map. He was going to do exactly what his father had done, start at the bottom and work his way up, even if he was the son of the owner of the hotel chain.

Dee Flynn had done the same.

Maybe that was why he connected with the tiny woman he was looking at now.

They were different from other people.

Different and special.

He was in awe, and ready to admit that to anyone.

Sean stood in silence as the chatting, smiling men and women in business suits who worked for his family filled the space that separated them. But his gaze was locked on one person. And it was not Rob, who seemed to be holding court.

He could hear his brother's familiar roar of laughter warm the room, but Sean's ears were tuned only to Dee's sweet laugh which was like a hot shower.

His senses were razor-sharp. And, as the cluster broke up, he caught sight of her.

She was looking around the room. Looking for him.

She winked at him with a wry smile, shrugged her shoulders and then turned to laugh at something Rob said before they were swallowed up by the trainees and older managers enjoying the delicious food and drink, only too happy to meet the celebrity chef Rob Beresford in person.

The last thing he saw was the slight tilt of her head and a flash of gold silk as she sashayed elegantly away from him.

Dervla Flynn was turning out to be one of the most remarkable women he had ever met in his life, and the last ten minutes had only served to increase his admiration.

He was totally in awe.

Then she slipped out of view as Rob and the whole entourage joined his father in the dining area, leaving him alone with his thoughts.

Strange that he was even now reliving that moment when her body had been pressed against his arm.

Strange how he was still standing in the same spot five minutes later, watching the space where she had last stood. Waiting. Just in case he could catch a glimpse of her again, the most beautiful woman in the room.

For that he was prepared to wait a very long time.

It seemed like ten minutes had gone by, but when the sitar music sang out from the mobile phone in her embroidered bag Dee was shocked to see that she had been swept up with Rob and his dad, talking food and drink, for over an hour.

There was a text message on the screen:

Ready to escape the noise and crush and get some air? Meet you at the elevator in five minutes. Sean

Sean! She had been so engrossed that she had only spent ten minutes with her date the whole evening. Quickly gathering up her skirts, Dee excused herself and skipped up the steps, and instantly caught sight of Sean, who was beckoning to her.

In a moment he had drawn her into the lift and pressed a card into a slot on the lift button before giving her a quick hug.

'Do you remember that penthouse suite I was trying to talk you into? Well, I seem to recall that this hotel has a private penthouse worth seeing. If you are willing to risk it?'

'Risk it?'

'It's the eighteenth floor, which means a quick trip inside a lift,' he whispered, and grinned at her shocked reaction. 'But it does have a balcony.'

And what a balcony!

Dee stepped out onto a long, tiled terrace, and what she saw in front of her took her breath away.

The rain had cleared to leave a star-kissed, cool evening. And stretched out, in every direction, was London. Her city. Dressed and lit, bright, shiny and sparking with street lamps, advertisements and the lights from homes and offices.

It was like something from a movie or a wonderful painting. A moment so special that Dee knew instinctively that she would never forget it.

She grasped hold of the railing and looked out over London, her heart soaring, all doubt forgotten in the exuberant joy of the view.

It was almost a shock to feel a warm arm wrap a coat around her shoulders and she turned sideways to face Sean with a grin, clutching onto his sleeve.

'Have you seen this? It's astonishing. I love it.' Dee breathed.

'I know. I can see it on your face.'

Then he moved closer to her on the balcony, his left hand just touching the outstretched fingers of her right hand.

But Sean was looking up at the stars.

'Last February it was snowy and cloudy for the whole of the three weeks that I was back in London. But tonight? Tonight is perfect.'

'This is amazing. I had no idea that you could see skies like this in London. I thought the light pollution would block out the stars.'

And she followed his gaze just in time to see a shooting star streak across the sky directly above their heads, and then another, smaller this time, then another.

'A meteor shower. *Sean! Look!*'

'What is it, Dee?' he asked, his mouth somewhere in the vicinity of her hair. 'Have you made a wish on a shooting star? What does your heart yearn to do that you haven't done yet?'

'Me? Oh, I had such great plans when I was a teenager and the whole world seemed to be an open door to whatever I wanted. My parents loved their work, and I was so happy for them when they decided to retire and run their own tea gardens. Warmth. Sunshine. They could not have been happier.'

She wrapped her arms tight around her body. 'But then the hard reality of running a business in a recession where tea prices are falling hit. And they lost it. And they lost everything they had dreamt of. And it was so hard to see them in pain, Sean. So very hard.'

'But they stayed. Didn't they?'

She nodded. 'They won't come back unless they have to and if they did… It would break them. And that is what scares me.'

She lifted her head and rested it on Sean's chest. 'I know that I am in a different place in my life, and there are lots more opportunities out there for me, but do you know what? I am not so very different from my folks. I want my own business so badly and I don't know how I could cope if my dream fell apart. Six months ago I was working for a big tea importer and going to night school to study business most evenings and weekends. But Lottie changed that when she asked me to join her in the tea rooms. The time seemed so right. I have volunteered to run the festival and I felt ready to do anything.'

'You are ready. I know it.'

She looked up into his smiling face but stayed inside the warm circle of his arms.

'How do you know what your limits are?'

'You don't. The only way to find out is by testing yourself. You would be astounded at what you are capable of. And if you don't succeed you learn from your mistakes and do what you have to do to get back up and try again until you can prove to yourself that you can do it. And then you keep on doing that over and over again.'

'No matter how many times you fall down and hurt yourself?'

'That's right. You've got it.'

Dee turned slightly away from Sean and looked out towards the horizon, suddenly needing to get some distance, some air between them. What he was describing was so hard, so difficult and so familiar. He could never know how many times she had forced herself to smile after someone had let her down, or when she had been ridiculed or humiliated.

Dee blinked back tears and pulled the collar of his jacket up around her ears while she fought to gain control of her voice. 'Some of us lesser mortals have been knocked down so many times that it is hard to bounce back up again, Sean. Very hard. Can you understand that?'

Sean replied by wrapping his long arms around her body in a warm embrace so tender that Dee surrendered to a moment of joy and pressed her head against his chest, inhaling his delicious scent as her body shared his warmth.

His hands made lazy circles on her back in silence for a few minutes until he spoke, the words reverberating inside his chest into her head. 'Better than you think. Working in the family business is not all fun. I have been in these hotels all my life one way or another. And I still have a lot to learn.'

Dee shuffled back from him, laughed in a choked voice and then pressed both hands against his chest as she replied with a broken smile.

'So that makes two of us who are stuck in the family trade. Am I right?'

'Absolutely. How about a suggestion instead? I know a couple of venture-capital guys who have money to invest in new business ideas. All I have to do is make a few phone calls and… What? What now?'

'I don't want to carry any debt. No maxed-out credit cards; no business loans; no venture capital investment. That's how my dad got into so much trouble and there is no way that I am going there. So thank you, but no. I might be hard up, but I have made some rules for myself. I have already maxed out my credit on my share of the tea shop. I can't handle any more debt.'

Sean inhaled very slowly and watched Dee struggle with her thoughts, her dilemma played out in the tension on her face.

She was as proud as anyone he had ever met. Including himself. Which was quite something.

And just like that the connection he had sensed between

them from the moment he had laid eyes on her in the tea rooms kicked up a couple of notches.

And every warning bell in his body started screaming 'danger!' so loudly that in the end he could not ignore it any longer. And he pulled away from her.

She shivered in the cool air, fracturing the moment, and he grabbed her hand and jogged back across the balcony. Sean slid open the patio doors and wrapped his arm around her waist, hugging her to him, the luxurious warmth from the penthouse warming their backs.

'Oh, that's better. Won't you get into trouble with the boss for wasting heat? Oh—you are the boss! Well, in that case, carry on.'

'We should be getting back to the others,' Sean whispered, only his voice sounded low and way too unconvincing. 'They might be missing us.'

She must have thought so too, because she took a last step and closed the distance between them and pressed the palms of both of her hands flat against the front of his white dinner shirt. He could feel the warmth of her fingertips through the fine fabric as she spread her fingers out in wide arcs; the light perfume enclosed them.

'This has been a magical evening. Thank you for inviting me,' she whispered.

Every muscle in his body tensed as she moved closer and pressed her body against his, one hand reaching in to the small of his back and the other still pressed gently against his shirt. He tried to shift but she shifted with him, her body fitting perfectly against his, her cheek resting on his lapel as though they were dancing to music which only she could hear.

So he did the only thing he could.

He kissed her.

She lifted her head and her hair brushed his chin as she

pressed tentative kisses onto his collarbone and neck. Her mouth was soft and moist and totally, totally captivating.

With each kiss she stepped closer until her hips beneath the sari were pressed against his and the pressure made him groan.

'Dee,' he hissed, reaching for her shoulders to draw her away. But somehow he was sliding his hands up into her hair instead, holding her head and tilting her face towards him. Then he was kissing her, his tongue in her mouth, her taste surrounding him.

He stroked her tongue with his and traced her lower lip before sucking on it gently. She made a small sound and angled her head to give him more access.

She tasted so sweet, so amazing. So giving.

She gazed at him with eyes filled with such delight, as if she was expecting some suggestive comment about the fact that this penthouse came with a king-sized bed...

And that look hit him hard.

He did not just want Dee to be his stand-in date for tonight. He wanted to see her again, be with her again. He wanted to know what she looked like when she had just made love. He wanted to find out what gave her pleasure in bed, and then make sure that he delivered precisely what the lady ordered.

She was as proud and independent as he was. And just as unforgiving with anyone who dared to offer her charity or their pity.

By some fluke, some strange quirk of fate, he had met a woman who truly did understand him more than Sasha had ever done. And that was beyond a miracle.

Could he take a chance and show her how special she was? And put his heart on the line at the same time?

He slid a hand down her back to cup her backside, holding her against him as he flexed his hips forward, and one hand still in her hair. She shuddered as he slid his hand in slow circles up from her back to her waist, running his hands up and down her skin which was like warm silk, so smooth and perfect. He ducked his head and kissed her again, his hands teasing all the while until he was almost holding her upright.

When their lips parted, Dee was panting just as hard as he was. She looked so beautiful, standing there with her gold sari brilliant against the night sky, her cheeks flushed pink and the most stunning smile on her face.

His response was to wrap his arms around her back and, holding her tight against him, rested his chin on her top of her hair.

Eyes closed, they stood locked together until he could feel her heart settle down to a steady beat.

All doubt was cast aside. Her heart beat for him, as his heart beat for her.

Dee moved in his arms and he looked down into her face as she smiled up at him, not just with her sweet mouth but with eyes so bright, fun and joyous that his heart sang just to look at them. And it was as though every good thing that he had ever done had come together into one moment in time.

And his heart melted. Just like that.

For a girl who was just about as different from him and his life as it was possible to be.

And for a girl who had made her tiny flat the size of the hotel's luggage store into a home and was willing to share her joy with him. And who wanted nothing in return but a chance to see a meteor shower from a penthouse balcony.

God, he admired her for that…. Admired her?

Sean stopped, his body frozen and his mind spinning. He didn't just admire Dee, he was falling for her.

Just when he thought that he had finally worked out

that he had nothing to give to any woman in the way of a relationship.

Think! He had to think. He could not allow his emotions to get the better of him.

If he cared for her at all then he should stop right now, because the last thing Dee needed was a one-night stand which would leave her with nothing but more reasons to doubt her judgement.

He wouldn't do that to her. Hell, he wouldn't do that to himself. It would only be setting them up for heartbreak down the road.

'I think we might want to rethink the whole getting back in time for dessert...' She grinned as though she had read his mind.

'Right as always,' he replied, and stroked her cheek with one finger. 'God, you are beautiful. Do you know that?'

Dee blushed from cheek to neck. It was so endearing that he laughed out loud, slid his arms down to her waist and stepped back, even though his body was screaming for him to do something crazy. Like wipe everything off the dining-room table and find out what came next.

He sucked in a breath.

'You are not so bad yourself. I had no idea that hotel managers were so interested in astronomy.' And then she bit down on her lower lip and flashed him a coquettish grin. 'Or did I just get lucky? You are one of a kind, Sean.'

Lucky? He thought of the long days and nights he had spent working for the company to the exclusion of everything else in his life, including the girls who had cared about him. Sasha had lasted the longest.

He had sacrificed everything for the family hotel chain. Everything.

Now as he looked at Dee he thought about what lay

ahead, and the hard, cold truth of his situation emptied a bucket of ice water over his head.

His hands slid onto her upper arms and locked there, holding her away from him and the delicious pleasure of her body against his.

'I am not so sure about the "lucky" bit, Dee. Right now I am in London for a few days to sort things out and run a few classes, then Paris for a month at most. Then I'm off to Canberra…and my diary is full for the next eighteen months. Constant pressure. And all the while I feel as though I am running and running and not getting anywhere.'

'Then maybe you should stand still long enough to look around and see what you have achieved,' she said. Dee tilted her head to one side. 'Somewhere along the way to being the best, I think you forgot the fun part. But I think that funny and creative side of Sean is still inside you, all ready to get excited about new things and have the best time of his life.'

Stretching up onto tiptoes, she kissed him on the lips. 'You deserve it.'

She stepped back and patted him twice on the chest. Then she laughed. 'And now it is time to head back down stairs before I embarrass myself even more.' And she moved a step backwards with a smile.

He frowned, nodded just once and muttered something under his breath along the lines of what he did for the firm. Then he lifted his head, turned towards the door and presented the crook of his arm for her to latch onto. 'Shall we go to the ball, princess? Your audience awaits.'

CHAPTER ELEVEN

*Tea, glorious tea. A celebration of teas from around
the world.*
Astrologers have long used tea leaves to predict the
future. Try it for yourself by leaving a little tea in the
bottom of your tea pot with the tea leaves. Stir the
brew three times, empty the tea pot into your saucer, then inspect the pattern the leaves make in the
cup. Each specific pattern has a special meaning.

From *Flynn's Phantasmagoria of Tea*

*Friday
A week later*

SEAN STROLLED INTO the bar at the Beresford Riverside and
nodded to the head barman who was serving after-dinner
drinks to guests wandered in from the dining room.

The light strains of a cocktail piano could just be heard
in the background against the chatter and laughter from
the guests.

He quickly scanned the bar and lounge area to see if
Dee was still there. She had called him a couple of times
during the afternoon to let him know that Prakash and his
team had done an amazing job and all of the last minute
worries that had kept her awake were sorted.

The tea festival was all set to go tomorrow.

Then he heard her laughter ring out from a table of Japanese guests who had clustered around the tables next to the long patio doors which led onto the landscaped gardens.

Ribbons of white outdoor lights trailed over the budding branches of the cherry trees which Dee had enjoyed over the past few days.

The first smile of the day slid over his mouth. Hell. His first smile all week. Last minute presentations, flying visits to France with his dad and two days scouting for locations in Scotland meant that he had hardly seen Dee since the night of the dinner.

He missed her like crazy.

Dee was sitting at the table, and spread out in front of her was what looked like a makeshift kitchen. White saucers from the kitchen were scattered all around her, and on each was a tiny sample of what looked to Sean like clippings from the evergreen plants outside in the garden but were no doubt some example of specialist tea leaves.

Whatever they were, the hotel guests seemed enthralled. They were picking up the saucers, sniffing, tasting and chatting away with enormous enthusiasm and clear delight. Nodding, delighted, bewitched.

Because at the centre of it all was Dee.

Sean paused at the bar and leant on the rail, happy just to watch the woman he had come to find.

Her long, sensitive fingers flitted above the table gesturing here and there, no doubt on some terribly important point about growing conditions and water temperature, and he could see the glint of gold in the bangles around her wrists.

She was wearing what for Dee probably passed for quite a conservative outfit of a fitted jacket in a knitted navy fabric which clung to her curves as she moved. But of course that was offset by a stunning scarf which shimmered in shades of blues and greens, highlighting her fair complexion, and even though her head was down he knew that those pale-green eyes were going to be totally enchanting.

This was the real Dee. Sharing her passion and enjoying every second of it.

The Dee he had fallen for the minute he had looked up from a tea room floor and was sucked into oblivion by those eyes. Why wouldn't he? She was stunning.

Recognition came flooding in, and instead of pushing it away Sean held it in his mind and treasured it like a precious gift that he had never expected to receive but adored.

He was falling for Dee Flynn. In a big way. This was way beyond attraction. He cared about her and wanted to be with her, in every way possible.

And the very idea shocked him and terrified him so badly that he could only stand there and take it like a sock in the jaw.

His life had been a roller coaster for so many years, he had forgotten what it felt like to make connections with people and form bonds that went beyond business transactions, contracts and meetings in windowless white rooms.

But why now?

He slid silently onto a high-boy leather bar stool.

This was the way he was going to remember her.

He had only been standing there for a few minutes in silent ogling when he saw her head lift and her back straighten.

Almost as if she knew that he was watching her. So that, when she stood up and looked over her shoulder at him, he should have been ready for the impact that seeing her smile transform into a grin that was laser-focused on him would cause.

Impossible. Nothing could have prepared him for the blast of that smile.

She had never looked lovelier. And she literally took his breath away.

Mesmerized, Sean could only watch as she excused herself with several deep bows to the guests, who returned her bows with gentle warm waves and smiles.

Oh yes, she was good.

She skipped between the tables and was at the bar in seconds.

Instantly she flung her arms around his neck as he bent down to kiss her on the cheek, much to the amusement of the hotel guests.

'You have been away far too long, Sean Beresford.'

'Agreed. Only, I think your fan club are taking our photograph on their smart phones.'

Dee peeked around Sean's back and waved back. 'Oh no, those are proper cameras. We are probably already online. But I'm not in the least ashamed. This has been a brilliant afternoon.' And, just to prove it, she went up on tiptoes and pecked him on the lips so lightly that he barely had time to register the sensation of her warm, full lips on his before she stepped back into her shoes.

'I hardly dare to ask,' he replied, but kept his arms tight around her waist. 'But could it be anything to do with the party of visiting Japanese academics?'

Dee pressed one finger to her bottom lip and tried to look innocent, but failed.

'You do know that they brought their own tea with them, don't you? The word is out Mr B—there is not one hotel in the whole of London who serves speciality Japanese green tea of the quality your guests demand and in the way they like. I think this is quite shocking news. Just imagine the impact on the hotel trade. If only you knew someone who could import some of that fine tea for you. Just imagine what a difference it could make. Now... I wonder what we can do about that?'

Then she fluttered her eyelashes at him in the most outrageous, over-the-top way and a bubble of laughter burst up from deep inside his gut and exploded into a real belly-laugh. The kind of laugh which turned heads and made the barman look at Sean over the top of his spectacles.

And why not? It had been far too long since he had laughed out loud—really laughed.

He had almost forgotten what it felt like, which was more than sad. It was a judgement of the life that he had chosen for himself and had never stopped to question—a roller coaster of work and travel, then more work and more travel, which never stopped long enough for him to get off and see the view now and then. It was too fast, and the highs and lows were so exhilarating, that it was impossible to look anywhere else but straight ahead because he never knew what was going to happen next.

It was a life that was as addictive as it was exhausting. A rush of daily adventure and excitement that called for his total focus and attention.

That was why he had been so attracted to Sasha.

They loved the hotel trade, and the rush of pulling off seemingly impossible projects and delighting his father and their hotel guests along the way. Sasha had been on her own roller coaster and at first they had been side by side, project to project. But slowly their tracks had simply drifted apart, further and further away, until they hadn't been able to see one another. Both of them had been strapped in and going for the adventure of their lives.

It was true. His life was one long roller-coaster ride. He had jumped on when he was sixteen and was still strapped in at thirty-one.

Almost half of his life.

Strange. He had never thought of it that way until now.

And he knew exactly who he had to thank for that.

The girl with the twinkling green eyes who was grinning up at him.

The girl who had swept into his life like a warm breeze on a cold day.

The girl who he was going to leave behind, and sooner than he had planned.

Sean slid one of his hands from her waist and onto the bar so that he could lean forward slightly. He inhaled the light floral fragrance that she was wearing like the aroma of a fine wine. Intoxicating and provocative. Heady and enticing. Daring him to find out if her skin tasted as delicious as the aroma promised.

'I still haven't forgiven you for texting me when you knew that Tuesday was our Bake and Bitch Club night. The girls were scandalized by that sort of suggestive language.'

'How could I forget our first anniversary? And you did call me brazen last week. I have a reputation to maintain, young lady,' he whispered into her ear in a voice that was not meant to be overheard, especially by the hotel staff.

Her eyes met his without hesitation or excuse. Beguiling. Honest. True. And, oh, so magical.

'I know. And I am certainly not complaining,' she said.

Sean swallowed down a lump in his throat.

Dee was so close. So very close. Her gaze was locked onto his face, as though it was the most fascinating thing that she had ever seen, and he almost flinched with the loss when a guest sidled up behind them at the bar.

'That colour looks great on you.' He smiled. 'Stylish and...' He paused and, when he was sure that she was looking at him, silently mouthed the word 'hot' before slipping off the bar stool and grabbing her hand.

Her eyebrows lifted and she replied with a girly giggle and a small shoulder-wiggle, which was so endearing that he had to distract himself by focusing on the way her fingers felt clasped inside his.

Time to move to something less likely to scandalize his staff.

'I think it's about time you showed me what you have been up to in my conference suite. Don't you?'

Dee paused outside the main doors to the conference room where she had spent most of the day with Prakash, and a stream of porters, delivery drivers and other people who she had never met before but who somehow seemed to be able to transform her sketches and lists into reality.

She raised one hand, palm upwards. 'Now, it might come as a bit of a shock. So prepare yourself.'

Sean nodded just once. 'I have been through everything, from Mardi Gras to beer festivals. I can handle it.'

Dee stretched out her hand towards the brass door plate, then lifted it back and whirled around on her heel. 'First of all, I should say that Prakash and the team were amazing. Just amazing. And they did it all in one day! Totally brilliant, in fact. I couldn't have done any of this without them… And now I am babbling, because I'm so excited and it's wonderful, and did I say that it is amazing and the festival is tomorrow and…?'

'Dee.' Sean smiled and gently rested a hand on each of her shoulders. 'I spoke to Prakash. He helped, but this is your idea. Your design, your colour scheme, your concept. So I know that it is going to be wonderful.'

'Perhaps you should come back tomorrow when the exhibitors are setting up. There will be such a buzz.'

Sean looked over her shoulder into the middle distance and seemed about to say something, but changed his mind, turned back and lowered his head so that his nose was almost pressed against hers. He spoke in a jokey, firm voice.

'Dee. I want the full tour and I want it now.'

'You are so bossy!'

'I know. But that's why you like me.'

'Really? Is that the reason? I thought it was your snazzy ties and shiny shoes.'

'They only add to the allure. And you're putting off the inevitable. What is it? Why don't you want me to see your design? You know that I am going to, one way or another.'

'Yes. I know. It is your hotel. It's just that…' She sucked in a breath then exhaled on one long string of words. 'I am seriously nervous because this is the biggest thing that I have ever done on my own and I know that it's mad but my whole future depends on this being a big success.'

Then she stopped, but Sean kept looking at her with that smile on his face, as though he was waiting for her to carry on.

Then without waiting another second he stepped forward, pushed open the doors to the conference suite with both hands and stood to one side.

Then he nodded towards the space behind him, reached out and grabbed her hand. 'Come on.' He smiled. 'Show me what you have done. Show me what your imagination has created. Share it with me. Please.'

For the next ten minutes Sean walked slowly around the room as Dee explained each of the display panels in turn, starting with the history of tea production, then slowly walking from stand to stand.

She didn't need to. But he liked hearing her voice, so he let her carry on.

The whole room was decorated in co-ordinating shades of green with stencils of green tea leaves against cream, pale gold and emerald green. There were plenty of stands for the exhibitors, power points, fresh water dispensers. And a portable professional kitchen. All ready for the morning. He couldn't have been prouder.

'So this is where the magic is going to happen. I love it. Professional, elegant and attractive. It's a hit!'

'Do you really think so?' Dee screwed up her mouth.

'It looks fresh and inviting. And the colour scheme is great.'

His hands moved in gentle circles on her shoulders, up and down her arms, and slowly, slowly, the stiffness in Dee's neck relaxed and she felt her shoulders drop down from around her ears.

'You must think that I am a total idiot,' she chuckled. 'All of this work for a one-day festival of tea. The world will not end if nobody turns up to drink the tea and buy the china. And on Sunday I can go back to the tea rooms and carry on as normal. I know that; I've known that from the start. But being with you and working in the hotel here has given me so many ideas for new projects, and new ways I can sell my blended tea, I can hardly sleep at night. It is so exciting. So, whatever happens tomorrow, thank you, Sean. Thank you for helping me.'

His response was to step forward and gather her into his arms, holding her tight against his pristine shirt, not caring that he was crushing his superb suit jacket in the process. Holding her with such tenderness and warmth that she melted against him with a gentle sigh. Instantly his chin slid down and rested on the top of her hair, and his arms relaxed their grip and rested gently on her back.

It had been so long since she had felt so close to another human being. Lottie and the girls were her best friends, and she loved every one of them, but this was different, felt different; this was special.

It had been ages since her last boyfriend in the tea

house. Years of watching other girls go on the dating scene, and comforting them with tea and cake as each broken heart had healed and they'd gone out again so full of hope.

Not for her. She did not want that emotional destruction. She knew that she was too different for most men. Too quirky. Too obsessed. Too unusual.

She was not the girl that the boys in catering school introduced to their parents. She was the girl they dated until someone better came along. And it had taken her a while to realize that she was not putting up with being second best. And she never would.

Until Sean had shown her that she was a woman a man could admire and want to be with.

Sean had chosen her. Picked her out. Made her feel special. Made her feel that she was capable of running her own business and making her dream come true.

Sean. The man who was holding her in his arms at that moment.

The man who meant the world to her. But she was too afraid to tell him.

She revelled in every sensation, her eyes closed, locking each tiny moment into her memory. The heady aroma of Sean's body wash or aftershave blended with the subtle scent of laundry lavender, and a lot of Sean that only a long day in a hot office could produce. If only she could bottle that aroma, she would never be lonely again.

This was one man who had listened to what she wanted and helped her make it happen in a way which was even better than she had imagined.

She wanted this moment to last as long as possible. She wanted to remember what these little bubbles of happiness felt like.

'You are most welcome,' he replied, the sound muffled as he spoke into her hair, but the sound reverberated through her skull and came to rest in the centre of her heart. Where they exploded into a firework display of light and colour.

Exploded with such force that they made her shuffle back a little so that she could look up into Sean's face and trace the line of his jaw with her fingers. Her reward was to see his eyes flutter just a little as her fingers slid down onto his neck and throat.

This man had pressed buttons that she did not even know that she had.

'If you ever see that Frank Evans, be sure to thank him for me.' She grinned. 'Because it seems to me that I came out with a pretty good deal.'

Sean rested his hands on her hips and nodded. 'True. The Beresford Riverside is a rather more impressive venue than the Beresford Richmond Square, and you did get it for the same price. That was what you were referring to... wasn't it?'

Dee dropped her head forward onto his chest with a short laugh, only too aware that she was blushing and her neck was probably a lovely shade of scarlet.

When she did dare to lift her head, Sean was looking at her, his eyes more blue than grey in the artificial lighting above their heads, and as her eyes locked onto his the intensity of that gaze seemed to penetrate her skin.

For one fraction of a second all the need and passion of this remarkable man was revealed for her to see.

In one single look.

It took her breath away and she lifted her head higher. So high that, when his head tilted and he pressed his lips against her forehead, and then her temple, she was ready.

More than ready.

She was waiting for his kiss.

She had been waiting all day for his kiss, to see him again and to hear his voice.

And it had been totally, totally, worth the wait.

Sean took one step forward, and before Dee realized what was happening he wrapped his hand around the back of her neck, his fingers working into her hair as he pressed his mouth against hers, pushing open her full lips, moving back and forth, his breath fast and heavy on her face.

His mouth was tender, gentle but firm, as though he was holding back the floodgates of a passion which was on the verge of breaking through and overwhelming them both.

She felt that potential, she trembled at the thought of it, and at that moment she knew that she wanted it as much as he did.

Her eyes closed as she wrapped her arms around his back and leaned into the kiss, kissing him back, revelling in the sensual heat of Sean's body as it pressed against hers. Closer, closer, until his arms were taking the weight of her body, enclosing her in his loving, sweet embrace. The pure physicality of the man was almost overpowering. The scent of his muscular body pressed ever so gently against her combined with the heavenly scent that she knew now was unique to him.

It filled her senses with an intensity that she had never felt in the embrace of any other man in her life. He was totally overwhelming. Intoxicating. And totally, totally delicious.

And, just when Dee thought that there could be nothing more pleasurable in this world, his kiss deepened. It was as though he wanted to take everything that she was able to give him, and without a second of doubt she surrendered to the hot spice of the taste of his mouth and tongue.

This was the kind of kiss she had never known. The connection between them was part of it, but this went beyond friendship and common interests. This was a kiss to signal the start of something new. The kind of kiss where each of them was opening up their most intimate secrets and deepest feelings for the other person to see.

The heat, the intensity, the desire of this man, was all there, exposed for her to see ,when she eventually opened her eyes and broke the connection. Shuddering. Trembling. Grateful that he was holding her up on her wobbly legs.

Then he pulled away, the faint stubble on his chin grazing across her mouth as he lifted his face to kiss her eyes, brow and temple.

It took a second for her to catch her breath before she felt able to open her eyes, only to find Sean was still looking at her, his forehead still pressed against hers. A smile warmed his face as he moved his hand down to stroke her cheek.

He knew. He knew the effect that his kiss was having on her body. He had to. Her face burned with the heat coming from the point of contact between them. His heart was racing, just as hers was.

Dee slowly, slowly slid out of his embrace and almost slithered onto the floor. And by the time she was on her unsteady legs she was already missing the warmth of those arms and the heat of the fire on her face.

She had to do something to fight the intensity of the magnetic attraction that she felt for Sean at that moment. Logic screamed at her from the back of her mind: they were both single, unattached and they wanted one another.

She had never had a one-night stand in her life. And, if she was going to do it, this was as good a place as any, except of course it would never be casual sex. Not for her. And, she suspected, not for Sean either.

Would it be so ridiculous if they spent the night together?

Sean gently drew her back towards him so that their faces were only inches apart at the same height.

His hand moved to her cheek, pushing her hair back over her left ear, his thumb on her jaw as his eyes scanned her face, back and forth.

Her eyes opened wide and she drunk him in—all of him. The way his hair curled dark and heavy around his ears and neck; the suntanned crease lines on the sides of his mouth and eyes. And those eyes—those amazing blue eyes which burned bright as they smiled at her.

She could look at that face all day and not get tired of it. In fact, it was turning out to be her favourite occupation.

Sean was temptation personified. And all she had to do was reach out and taste just how delicious that temptation truly was.

Did he know what effect he was having on her? How much he was driving her wild?

Probably.

Panting for breath, she rested her head on his chest, listening to the sound of Sean's heart under the fine cloth, feeling the hot flood of blood in his veins and the pressure of his fists against her back. She could have stayed there all night but suddenly the silence of their private space was broken by the loud ringtone from the mobile phone inside Sean's jacket pocket.

'That can wait,' he whispered and carried on stroking her hair. 'Now, tell me about the tea. What delicious aromas can the hotel expect…?' But he never got to continue because his phone rang again, and this time is was a different ringtone.

'Oh, I don't believe it.' He sighed, stood back, tugged out the phone and checked the caller ID. 'It's my dad's personal line.' He shook his head. 'I am so sorry about this. Stay right where you are. Two minutes.'

* * *

Dee sat down at the reception table just inside the door and watched Sean stride out into the main hotel space, the phone pressed to his ear. He was pacing up and down, one hand pressed against the back of his neck in a nervous gesture that she had seen him use a couple of times.

She pressed her fingers to her mouth, which was feeling slightly numb, and covered a chuckle. He didn't even realize that he was doing it.

Dee stood up and strolled into the kitchens between the display areas. She was just about to pour some water when one of the flyers dropped to the floor in the cool breeze from one of the floor-to-ceiling sliding glass doors that was still half-open.

But, instead of closing it, Dee stepped onto the stone courtyard area outside the conference room and slowly inhaled the cool evening air.

After the heat of the past hour it felt deliciously cool on her hot skin.

In the cool February air she could see the lights of the high-tech businesses, city offices and homes which lined the opposite bank of the river Thames. The hotel was partly shaded from the riverside public footpath by landscaped grounds and trees creating a calm and open feel.

It was exactly what she wanted: no white plastic underground basements, just a well-lit and modern space which opened up to the air whenever she wanted.

There was a faint rustling from the room behind her, and Dee looked over one shoulder as Sean came to join her on the terrace. His face was in shadow but she would recognize his shape anywhere.

A soft and silky Sean-warmed suit jacket was draped over her shoulders and she snuggled into it as a cold shiver ran down her spine.

She could feel the warmth of his chest through the many layers of clothing as he pressed his body against her back and wrapped his arms around her waist so that they were both facing the river and the superb view of the city spread out in front of them.

It was as if they were the only people alive at that moment and in that space.

Instinctively she leant backwards so that the back of her head was resting on his chest. The beat of his heart was steady in her ears, then faster.

She did not need to hear it to know that it grew faster for her.

Sean was breathing faster, his pace matching her own.

'No stars tonight,' she whispered and pointed up at the clouds which had already covered the crescent moon. 'But you can still make a wish if you like. You don't need a shooting star to have your dream come true. I know that now. So tonight is your turn.'

His reply was a hoarse whisper and she felt his hands slip away from around her waist as he spoke. 'I wish I could. But I can't. In fact, I have to go and get packed straight away.'

Dee slowly turned around in the circle of his arms so that they were facing one another, and suddenly a shiver ran across her shoulders. In the light from the room she could see the new harsh lines on Sean's face. All easy chatter and smiles had been wiped away as if they had never been there.

'Packed? I don't understand. You are not due in Paris for another few days and you've only just got back. You told me that yourself. You don't need to get packed tonight.'

He licked his lips and looked at her, his gaze darting across her face. 'I thought that I had at least a week. But that telephone call changed everything.'

Sean lifted his chin as though he was preparing himself.

'I am sorry, Dee, but I am booked on a flight to Chicago. We have an emergency at the new Beresford hotel we opened at Christmas and they need me to help sort things out. I have to go. And I have to go tonight. So you see, I'll be gone by the morning.'

Dee stepped backwards and out of his arms, her fingers running down his shirt sleeves so that she was clinging on to him with only a thin layer of fine cotton.

'Tonight? Do you really have to? We have worked so hard on this together. I…I was hoping that you would be here for the festival tomorrow.'

Dee turned and stared out into the dark night. Her eyes fixed on the movement of the wind in the trees that she could just see in the light from the hotel. There was a cold, damp wind blowing up from the river and she could feel the moisture cooling her face. But it didn't help to cool the fire burning inside her head.

She felt as though she had been caught in some kind of tornado that had been spinning her round and round from the moment she'd met Sean. Spinning so fast that she had never truly had the chance to get her feet back on the ground.

She had always known that his work in London was temporary, but Paris was only a few hours away by train. They might have had a chance to stay in touch and to stay close. If they worked at it.

If they both wanted it enough.

If he wanted it as much as she did.

He was leaving.

Just as her parents had decided to leave behind the cold, grey British winters and go back to the sunshine and the life that they loved. Just as her friends from catering college had left for jobs all over the world. Just as Josh had gone back to his real girlfriend and left his stand-in, second-best girl standing on the pavement outside his apartment reeling from what the hell had just happened.

She had coped with saying goodbye and managing the shock. And she still had Lottie and Gloria and the girls in the baking club. She could cope with saying goodbye to Sean. She was going to have to; he wasn't giving her any other choice.

It wasn't meant to be this hard.

She just wanted him to stay with her so badly.

Sean snuggled up next to her in the silence, the whole left side of his body pressed against her right side. Thigh to thigh, hip to hip and arm to arm.

She wanted to rest her head on his shoulder, and her whole body yearned to lean sideways against him for support, but she fought off the temptation.

She had to.

It was almost too much to bear when his fingers meshed with hers, locking them together in the dark.

Slowly, slowly, she found the strength to look up into the most amazing blue-grey eyes. In the bar they had been like clear, blue, fresh tropical seas, alluring, tempting and begging her to dive in. But now they were dark and stormy. Dangerous.

The warmth had been replaced with an intensity and concern that she had never seen before.

It was all there in the hard lines of his handsome face. The face that she had come to love so much over the past week or so, though she did not dare admit that to herself.

The planes of his face were brought into sharp contrast by the light from the room.

She had been so wrong to imagine that the son of Tom Beresford would have an easy office job handed down by his father.

Sean worked so very hard. And she admired him for that. But why now? Why did he have to go tonight?

'What kind of emergency is it?' she asked in a voice which was quaking a lot more than she wanted. 'Not another flood, I hope.'

His lips parted and he took in a long, shuddering breath before replying in a low, hoarse voice which to her ears seemed heavy with regret and concern.

'No; worse. Food poisoning. Rob thinks that it's a norovirus, and he is already on site working with the authorities, but the hotel is closed and guests are on lockdown. And I really do not want to talk about kitchen detox at this precise moment.'

His fingers clenched around hers and Dee tried focusing on the flickering lights on the riverbank but she could sense every tiny movement of his body which made vision a little difficult.

Her eyes fluttered closed as he took a tighter hold of her fingers and stepped away and she instantly yearned to have his body next to her again. Instead he gently lifted her hand to his mouth and kissed the back of her knuckles, forcing her to look up into his face.

'I wanted to be there tomorrow. To share your triumph. Because that is what it is going to be—a triumph.'

His head tilted slightly and one side of his mouth lifted up into a half-smile. 'You are going to be amazing. I know it. And Prakash has promised me a full report with video and photos.'

'Video?' She spluttered. 'That wasn't on the list.'

His gaze was focused on her hair and he casually lifted a stray strand of her lop-sided fringe and popped it behind her ear in a gesture so tender and caring that she almost cried at the pleasure of it.

'I ticked all of the optional extras on the checklist for you. Courtesy of the hotel management.'

'Wow,' she whispered and was rewarded with a quick nod of reply and a flash of a smile.

'Sean?' she asked in a quiet voice, and she closed the tiny gap between them. 'How long are you going to be away in Chicago? A week? Two? Then you are going to be in Paris, right?'

'I don't know. Weeks, most likely. As for Paris? There is no way I can handle that now. My dad is going to take over the project and find another manager.'

Dee exhaled a long sigh of relief. 'That's great. So when are you coming back to London? I will have so much to tell you.'

His head dropped down so that his forehead was almost touching hers and she could feel the heat of his breath on her face.

So that there was nowhere for her to escape to when he formed the words that she had been dreading.

'You don't understand, Dee. Paris is cancelled. My next assignment is in Brazil for a couple of months and then back to Australia in the autumn. I'm not coming back to London.'

CHAPTER TWELVE

Tea, glorious tea. A celebration of teas from around the world.
A simple infusion of chamomile flowers can help to relax the nerves and aid in sleep by creating a general feeling of relaxation.

From *Flynn's Phantasmagoria of Tea*

'NOT COMING BACK? Then I only want to know the answer to one question—and I don't want to hear it over the phone or in an email. Don't treat me like one of your managers. Talk to me. I want to hear your answer here and now. In person. To my face.'

She pressed both hands flat against his shirt so that the racing beat of his heart flittered up through her fingertips.

He was hurting just as much as she was.

'Do you want to see me again, Sean? Because if you don't it would be better if you told me now and be done with it, so that...' She lifted her chin. 'So that we can both get on with our lives.'

'Do I want to be with you? Oh, Dee.'

His right hand came up and flicked his suit jacket onto a patio table, exposing her skin to the cold night air, and instantly she could feel her nipples pebble with alertness. His long fingers slid down the whole length of her body from her neck, down the treacherous front of her jacket to her hips and back again.

Without asking for permission or forgiveness he slipped his warm hand up inside her jacket and cupped her breast. His thumb moved over her nipple with the perfect amount of pressure to fire up every nerve in her body.

But Sean had found the perfect distraction, kissing her forehead, temple and throat with such exquisitely gentle kisses that any idea of a question was driven out her mind as her desire for him built with each touch of his lips on hers.

And, just when she thought that her legs were going to buckle, his fingers slid away until her entire breast was being cupped by his hand and her bra was redundant and getting in the way of the exquisite pleasure.

Then slowly, slowly, his hand slid lower onto the bare skin at her waist and rested there for a second before moving away.

Arms wrapped around his head, Dee hung onto Sean as he wrapped both arms around her and held her to him.

She could feel the supressed power of his answer pressing against her hip and his short, fast breaths on her neck, fighting, fighting for control.

'Oh, Sean,' she whispered through a closed throat, and she dropped her head down to the safety and warmth of his broad chest.

They must have stayed there for several minutes, but time seemed to stand still, and it was Sean who broke the silence.

'I have been down this road before, Dee. My last girl-friend was so patient and we tried so hard to make it work. But in the end we were both worn down with the constant struggle to make time for one another between going back and forwards to the airport. It was exhausting. And it killed a great friendship. I don't want that to happen to us, Dee. Not to us.'

He was stroking her hair now, running his fingers back from her forehead. 'It could be six months before I get back here, and even then it would only be for a flying visit. There will always be some crisis somewhere, like tonight, which needs me to fly out at a moment's notice. I can't plan holidays or down time. You deserve better than that. A lot better.'

Dee looked up into his face and blinked, her mouth part open. 'No. I deserve you. All of you.'

Her words stung like ice on hot skin, burning into his brain and leaving a scar.

'The last thing I want to do is hurt you, Dee. That's why it's better that we part now and remember the good times.'

She laid her cheek on his shirt and dared to finally find the words. 'Does it have to be that way, Sean? Is there truly nobody else in the company that can cover your job? What happens when you are ill or burnt out? You can't keep going like this for ever. You have to take a break some time.'

'Don't feel sorry for me, Dee,' he replied, his hand cupping the back of her head. 'My family are very close, we always have been, and I owe my father everything. This hotel chain is my life and I want to make it special.'

'It seems to me that you have paid your family dues, Sean. Paid in full.'

'What do you mean?

Dee forced herself to raise her head and slip backwards so that she could look up into his face. 'This is your decision to leave tonight. Not your father's. Or your brother's. Yours. You have recruited an amazing team of talented professionals who would be only too happy to take on some of those troubleshooting challenges if you gave them the chance. You have made these hotels your life—and I understand that. Look at me—the tea grower's daughter who wants to set up her own tea company. We are both following in the family trade. But maybe it's time to think hard about what you want to do with your life. And who you want to spend it with.'

Then she stood back and slowly slid her fingers from his, one finger at a time, breaking their connection with each movement as she spoke.

She stood on tiptoe, pressed her lips against his in one last, lingering kiss, then ran her finger along his jaw and smiled.

'Good luck, Sean. Goodbye and thank you for everything.'

Then she turned and walked away, back into the conference room and out of his life. Without looking back.

And this time he didn't follow her.

CHAPTER THIRTEEN

Tea, glorious tea. A celebration of teas from around the world.

The traditional treatment for shock in Britain is a steaming beaker of piping hot Indian tea with milk and plenty of sugar. This remedy should be repeated until the symptoms subside.

From *Flynn's Phantasmagoria of Tea*

Saturday

HER BEST FRIEND slid a plate in front of her in the early-morning light streaming in through her bedroom window.

Dee squinted over the top of her extra-strong English Breakfast at the slice of a tall extravaganza of green-and vanilla-coloured sponge layers.

It was very green. And smelt of a florist shop. And no amount of strong tea was going to be able to wash down that amount of sugar and fat.

'I am calling this my tea festival special. It's a Lady Grey flavoured opera cake with a rosewater cream filling. What do you think?'

'Think? I am too tired to think, and my taste buds are fried. Thanks, Lottie. I am sure it will be a brilliant hit.

It looks wonderful, but I just can't face it at the moment. Way too nervous.'

Lottie rubbed the back of Dee's shoulder and kissed the top of her head.

'I had a feeling that it might be a bit over the top for six a.m. Did you get any sleep at all?'

Dee shook her head. 'Maybe a couple of hours at most. Kept waking up and couldn't get back to sleep again.'

'Never fear. I have donuts, and cheese and ham croissants. The breakfast of champions. I'll be right back.'

'You're my hero,' Dee replied and smiled after Lottie as she took the stairs down to the bakery from her apartment.

Her hero.

Dee stretched out her arms on the small table, dropped her head onto her hands and closed her eyes.

She was exhausted and her day had not started yet.

This was the most important event of her career. Months of planning. Weeks of phone calls, emails, checklists and constant to-ing and fro-ing from the hotel. And it all came down to this.

One girl sitting alone in her bedroom, drinking tea in her dressing gown. Feeling as though she had just gone through twelve rounds of a professional boxing match and lost.

Every part of her body ached, her head was thumping and she could easily fall asleep sitting upright in this hard chair.

Little wonder.

Lottie thought that she had stayed awake because of nerves about what today would bring. And that was true. But it was not the real reason she had tossed and turned until her duvet was on the floor and her sheet a tangled mess, wrapped around her like a restricting cocoon.

Sean. All she could think about, every time she closed her eyes, was Sean.

How he looked, tasted, smelt and felt. Sean.

And the worst thing?

The more she thought about what he had said to her, and repeated their conversation over and over in her head, the more she knew in her heart that he had been right to walk away and end what they had.

Sean had let her go rather than prolong the agony of always expecting her to take a place in the long line of other priorities that came with his position in the company.

He had done a noble thing.

He had given her up so that she could find someone who was able to put her first.

She *did* deserve better than to feel that she was always going to take second place in his list of priorities.

She *was* worthy of having someone to be there when she needed them. Like today.

Her parents had always put work first before her. Not because they intended to hurt her; far from it. They loved what they did and had explained many times that they wanted to be happy so that she could share that happiness.

Shame that it had never made it any easier to accept.

Shame that she would have loved to have Sean with her today of all days. To share her excitement and sense of achievement. To share her joy with the man she had come to love. The man she still wanted to be with.

The first man that she wanted to be with.

This was all so new and bewildering. Oh, there had been plenty of teenage crushes before. And broken hearts galore. But the way she felt this morning was something very different.

It was if she had tasted something so wonderful that it was terrifying to think that she might never taste it again.

Dee raised her body back to a sitting position and peered glassy-eyed at the photograph of her smiling parents, and

Lottie's bizarre but no doubt totally delicious cake, and a small chuckle made her shoulders rise and fall.

Even in the daily mayhem that constituted her mad world, falling for one of heirs to the Beresford hotel dynasty was surely the craziest.

She picked up the fork, speared a small chunk of cake and closed her lips around it, savouring the different flavours. Letting her tongue and the sensitive taste buds that made her job possible do the work before chewing for a moment and swallowing it down.

'Oh, you tried the cake. Brave woman. Go on. Hit me with it.'

Lottie marched into her bedroom with a tray, sat down on the bed and bared her teeth in fear of the honest review.

Dee raised her eyebrows and licked her lips. 'You put ground black pepper in the cream to offset the rosewater. And I am tasting orange zest and a hint of cloves and cardamom in the tea-scented sponge.'

'Absolutely. I knew that you would get it. So? Lady Grey or a green tea?'

Dee took the tray out of Lottie's hands. 'Green. But a special one. This is good. This is very good. Congratulations, Miss Rosemount. You have just succeeded in creating one of the toughest tea-matching challenges I have ever come across. Please accept this hand-crafted medal.'

'This is not a medal. It's an exhibitors badge for the tea festival.'

'Well, you don't think I would face the ravenous cake-eating hordes without you there to serve it and bask in the glory, did you? And, after all, we can't have tea without the cake to go with it! Foolish girl.'

Then Dee's smile faded and she reached out and took Lottie's hand. 'Can you come with me? Just for a couple of hours. Please? Gloria and the gang will look after the tea rooms. I just… I just need a pal by my side today. It turns out that being a tea magnate is not half as much fun when you don't have someone to share the excitement with. And I didn't expect that. I didn't expect that at all.'

Sean dug into his pocket, pulled out his mobile phone and dialled the number with shaking fingers.

He had been up most of the night, talking to Rob, who was fighting health inspectors in Chicago, and his father, who was fighting to stay awake after two hours of pacing back and forth going over the business plans for the hotel chain and where Sean was going in his career. And his life.

Please still be there.

Please answer.

Please don't throw the phone out of the window when you see who is calling you. Please take this call.

The only voice in the world he wanted to hear whispered, 'Hello?'

'Dee. It's Sean. I'm standing outside the tea rooms but I won't come in unless you want me to. Please say yes.'

The fraction of a second before she replied seemed like an eternity. 'Sean? What do you mean you are outside the tea rooms? I thought that you would be in Chicago by now.'

'Long story, but I'd like to tell you about it in person instead of on the pavement in the dark at the crack of dawn.'

'Okay. Yes, Lottie will let you in.'

It took Sean three seconds to give a very startled Lottie a quick wave, then bound up the stairs two at a time and stand puffing and panting outside Dee's bedroom.

His hand stretched out towards the door handle. And then he snatched it back.

Eyes closed, he blew out a long, deep breath, his head suddenly dizzy with doubt as the blood surged in his veins.

What was he doing here? What if she said, thanks, but no thanks? This was crazy.

He loved this woman and he had been willing to let her go because he was afraid of changing his life? Mad.

For once he was going to risk their future happiness on a crazy decision to trust his heart instead of his head.

And what if she said yes? She could be committing herself to a life where he could be on the road or in a different hotel most of the year. Was that fair?

Yes. Because he was just as determined to show Dee that he was able to give her a fraction of the love she felt for him.

And he had to do it now. Or never. Perhaps that was why he felt so naked. Exposed.

Sean straightened his back and just prepared to knock, but at the very second he did so there was movement on the other side of the door, and the handle turned on its own and cracked open an inch, then wider…and Dee was standing there.

Her eyes locked onto his as she looked at him with the kind of intensity that seemed to knock the oxygen from his lungs.

Then those eyes smiled and he took in the full effect of that beautiful face. No camera in the world could have captured the look on Dee's face at this moment.

He felt as though the air would explode with the electricity in the air between them.

'Hi,' she whispered. 'Has something happened to bring you back? Are you okay?' There was so much love and concern in her voice that any doubts Sean had about what he had to do next were wiped away.

Sean stretched out his hand and stroked her cheek, his eyes never leaving hers.

'I haven't stopped thinking about what you said. And

you were right. Leaving last night was my decision. So I did something about it.'

Sean breathed in, his heart thudding so loudly that he suspected that she must be hearing it from where she was standing so quietly, dressed in her kimono. 'I know now that I will always love you, Dervla Flynn, and it doesn't matter where I am in the world.' He licked her lips. 'I want to be with you. Love you.'

Her mouth opened to reply but he pressed one finger on her lips and smiled, breaking the terror. 'You see, I'm not as brave as you are. As soon as I left you last night, I knew that I couldn't leave the woman I have fallen in love with without trying to come up with some options.'

He grinned at her and slid forward so that both of his hands were cupped around her face as tears pricked her eyes. 'I love you way too much to let you go. I need you, Dee. I need you so much. Nothing else comes close. What would you say if I told you that I would be working out of London for the next twelve months?'

Her reply was to fall into his arms and he swept her up, holding her body tight, tight, before tilting his open mouth onto hers in a hot, hot kiss.

He cupped her face with both of his hands, his thumbs wiping away tears and water from her cheeks, and then he poured into his kiss the passion and devotion, the fear and doubts, which came with giving your heart to another human being.

'I didn't expect to be saying this standing in a cake shop, but it doesn't change a thing. I am so in love with you.'

'Oh, Sean. I wasn't sure I could go through with today without you. Can you forgive me? I have been such an idiot. Of course your family need you. You love them and want to do the right thing. I know what that's like.'

'Better than you think. I have done something rash—

there's a limo on the way to the airport at this very minute to collect two very special first-class passengers from a flight from Sri Lanka. I knew that you wanted your parents with you today to see all that you have done. Are you okay with that?'

'Seriously?' she asked, stunned. 'You flew my parents to London for the festival? You did that for me?'

He nodded. 'Seriously.' His thumb was still moving across her cheek. 'It's time that I met your parents. Because I am thinking of taking a break for a couple of months and Sri Lanka is on my list of destinations. If you come with me.'

'Oh, Sean. Do you mean it? Yes? Oh, I love you so much.'

He closed his eyes and pressed his forehead to hers, his entire world contained within his arms.

They were still standing there, kissing passionately, when there was the sound of loud voices breaking into their private world. Lottie had opened up downstairs and the first customers had arrived.

'But what about your work? Chicago? Brazil?'

'I had a long conference call with my dad and Rob last night, and we have agreed to give some senior managers a chance to show us what they can do. Plus, my dad offered me a new job this week. Could be challenging.'

'Difficult?'

'Very.' He grinned. 'Apparently he needs a new manager for the Richmond Square hotel who can fit in a bit of training now and then. Within walking distance of this cake shop and the woman I've fallen in love with. And all the tea I can drink. How could I say no?'

* * * * *

The World of
MILLS & BOON®

HISTORICAL

*Awaken the romance
of the past*
6 new stories every month

MEDICAL ROMANCE

*The ultimate in romantic
medical drama*
6 new stories every month

MODERN™

*Power, passion and
irresistible temptation*
8 new stories every month

By Request

*Relive the romance with the
best of the best*
12 stories every month

WORLD_ M&B2b